BROKEN
THINGS

ANDREA BOESHAAR

D1711879

BARBOUR
PUBLISHING

BROKEN THINGS

© 2003 by Andrea Boeshaar

ISBN 1-58660-756-1

All Scripture quotations, unless otherwise noted, are taken from the King James Version of the Bible.

"Broken Things," Mac Lynch. Copyright © 1995 by The Wilds. Lyrics used by permission. All rights reserved.

This book is a work of fiction. Names, characters, places, and incidents are either products of the author's imagination or used fictitiously. Any similarity to actual people, organizations, and/or events is purely coincidental.

For more information about Andrea Boeshaar, please access the author's web site at the following Internet address:
www.andreaboeshaar.com

Acquisitions and Editorial Director: Rebecca Germany
Editorial Consultant: Susan Downs
Art Director: Robyn Martins
Layout Design: Anita Cook

Published by Barbour Publishing, Inc., P.O. Box 719, Uhrichsville, OH 44683, www.barbourbooks.com

 Member of the
Evangelical Christian
Publishers Association

Printed in the United States of America
5 4 3

PREFACE

I believe the Lord gave me the idea for this story after I watched with a broken heart as several Christians gave up on their faith. They stumbled in their walk, got lost in the darkness, and figured there was no way back to Jesus. Worse, they believed God didn't want them back because of their blemished pasts.

How wrong they were!

While it's true that our actions, and the consequences thereof, are our responsibilities, our burdens to bear, it's also true that God will take us, and our hurtful pasts, and use them all together for His good (Romans 8:28). This truth in no way gives us a license to sin; but I have seen God take the pieces of a broken life, put them back together, and create a thing of extraordinary beauty—and one that's of service to Him.

God really does use "broken things."

So if you're reading this with a wounded spirit. . .if your outlook on life is bleak, be assured that there is hope through Jesus Christ and that you are precious in His sight. Don't let your tarnished past stand between you and a shining future.

You are valuable, priceless, and you are loved.

DEDICATION

To the "lost boys."
There is a way back to Jesus.
He's waiting for you with open arms.

Special thanks to Mac Lynch
and The Wilds organization
for allowing me to use the lyrics to "Broken Things."

To Sally and Ruth—
Your comments and advice proved most valuable.

And to my husband, Daniel—
For loving me and praying me through this project.

Five broken loaves by Galilee's shore,
Broken and scattered for thousands and more.
O what compassion, what joy Jesus brings,
Watch how He uses broken things.

©Mac Lynch, The Wilds

PROLOGUE

Allie hated moving. She felt as though she'd moved a hundred times in her life, although, in reality, it was probably more like twenty-five or thirty. Nevertheless, she despised the uprooting and transplanting, all necessary evils in the course of a lifetime. But at least she'd become an expert at the sorting and packing that went with relocating. Unfortunately, she hadn't gotten the hang of throwing stuff away.

Lowering herself onto a crate, Allie surveyed the contents cluttering the attic of the two-story home she once shared with her son, Nicholas. She had purchased this house after her husband, Erich, died eleven years ago; but now with Nick married and moved out, it made no sense to keep it. Instead, Allie thought she would much prefer a condo along the Pacific

Coast. Besides, her consulting business took her away a good bit of the time—another reason to trade a high-maintenance house and yard for a carefree condominium. Since her next job, which was supposed to have taken her to Seattle, had been postponed indefinitely, Allie now had the time to sort and pack and. . .move.

She glanced around the hot, stuffy attic at the heaps and mounds still waiting to be sifted through. *Lord*, she prayed, *please give me wisdom. I want to keep it all, but I know that's impossible.* Leaning over, she picked up a warped tennis racket. *Well, I guess I don't want to keep this. . . .*

Minutes later the door below creaked open.

"Hey, Mom, you up there?" Nick's soft but masculine voice wafted up the attic stairwell.

"Yep." Standing, Allie crossed the dusty, wood-planked floor and met her son on the landing. His face and sandy-blond hair glistened with perspiration from hauling boxes into the rented truck.

"What do you want to do with this?" he asked, handing her a shoebox.

Allie opened its cardboard top and peered at the photos inside. "Where did you find this?"

"On the shelf in your bedroom closet. It was in the bigger box with my projects that you've saved through the years." He grinned and a waggish gleam entered his brown eyes. "Just for a laugh, Jennifer and I started rummaging through the pictures I made when I was a kid and we found the shoebox. You're quite the packrat, Mom."

"Oh, hush," she playfully chided him.

Allie flipped through several faded photographs, when one caused her heart to skip a beat. She lifted it and stared hard at the four people in the picture.

"Who are they?" Nick asked, looking over the top of the photo she held.

"This is me when I was nineteen," she said, pointing to the teenager with long, blond hair, parted in the middle, "and I'm standing next to. . .Jack Callahan."

"The policeman?" Nick asked, turning the picture his way.

Allie nodded and a rush of questions flew into her mind. Where was he now? What was he doing? Was he happy?

Over the course of the last three decades, Allie had severed ties and burned bridges, deciding that her life in the Midwest was better forgotten. However, she'd heard Jack had gotten married, become a father, and had been divorced, all within eighteen months' time. That was some twenty-five years ago, but Allie still recalled how shocked she felt when she heard the news.

Shocked and heartbroken.

"Is he a friend or family member?" Nick wanted to know.

"Friend. That is, he *was* a friend," Allie said, feeling the pangs of nostalgia fill her being. "He was a good friend."

"Oh, yeah?"

"Yeah."

"Who are the others?"

"Wendy Chadwyk and Blythe Severson. I don't even know where they are or what they're doing now. The three of us girls were rather troubled souls, and Jack kept us all in line. But we lost touch after I moved to California."

Allie couldn't seem to tear her gaze from the photograph, her eyes fixed on the handsome police officer whose arm was draped across her shoulders. And Wendy and Blythe. . .those two were the quintessential "flower children" of the '60s.

"Just look at us," she murmured, shaking her head and staring at the picture. "The three of us girls were so young, and we thought we knew *everything*. But the truth was, we still had so much to learn."

A swell of remorse lodged in her chest as remembrances emerged, unfettered, for the first time in dozens of years. She had certainly made her share of mistakes. At age eighteen, Allie had been a new Christian. Within a year, she'd had some Bible studies, but she couldn't focus on growing spiritually because she'd been so consumed with all the turbulence in her life. When she left Oakland Park, Illinois, she hadn't parted on a good note with anyone, be it family member or friend.

But what if she phoned Jack—and maybe looked up Wendy and Blythe while she was at it? And her stepfather and stepsisters. Were they alive and well? Would any of them want to hear from her?

Allie pondered the idea. No. On second thought, phone calls wouldn't do.

She had to go back. . . .

CHAPTER ONE

Three Months Later

Chicago. Allie hadn't been in Chicago for over thirty years. Braking at a stoplight, she glanced up and down bustling Michigan Avenue through the windshield of the rented Chevy Cavalier. Allie marveled at how the tall buildings blocked out the sunshine, creating an almost cavernous effect, and yet it shouldn't seem like such a wonder. It was the same with every big city and Allie should know. She'd seen them all.

But Chicago was different. She'd been raised here. Then, after her mother remarried, she moved to Oakland Park, a small northeastern suburb.

The light turned green, and Allie stepped on the accelerator, nearing her destination: the Sheraton Hotel. It would be home for the next few days until the extended-stay suite became available. While she clearly knew that returning to Illinois was God's will, one might question her decision. She had no family here. Her mother had died when she was a senior in high school, leaving Allie with her stepfather and stepsisters. Since she'd been so close to graduating, she convinced her natural father to allow her to finish school and stay with her stepfamily.

Regrettably, what had been a tumultuous home became a virtual battleground.

After her mother's death, Allie's emotions ran high. She missed her mother. So did her stepfather and stepsisters, but she never considered their feelings. Likewise, they didn't know how to deal with their loss, their pain. Allie began arguing with her stepfather; and over the days and weeks, the fights intensified until one night, in a fit of rage, he slapped her. Adding insult to injury, his daughters took his side. They said Allie deserved it. Later, all three apologized, but Allie refused to forgive them. She packed her bags and moved in with her friend Blythe Severson. Because of her age, however, her stepfather notified the police. She probably wouldn't have gotten caught, though, if the Seversons' neighbors hadn't summoned the cops due to the racket all the teens in the house were making. Since Allie was deemed a "runaway," she was taken into custody.

That was Allie's first brush with the law—and a young, rookie officer named Jack Callahan.

The second incident occurred months later in 1968 during the Democratic National Convention here in Chicago. Riots and protests had broken out in the streets. Allie fought the crowd in a desperate attempt to make her way home after working as a downtown waitress. Upon graduating from high school, she'd been bent on independence. Doing things her own way. Relying on herself. But that night, she'd gotten tangled in the shuffle, and her self-sufficiency hadn't done her a lick of good. In fact, it worked against her. She suddenly realized there no longer remained a dependable friend or caring family member within a fifteen-hundred-mile radius whom she could phone for help should she be accosted by a demonstrator, a police officer, or a drunk on the street. And for the first time, Allie began to feel as though she was truly alone in the world.

Then Jack pulled her from the mob.

At first, Allie had been scared to death. She saw the police brutality around her and figured she was about to get clobbered over the head with a nightstick. But as she peered up into the familiar face, etched with compassion, her fears began to ebb.

"Don't I know you?" he asked, a quizzical frown marring his dark brown brows.

"Sort of," she replied. "I used to live in Oakland Park. Now I have an apartment here in Chicago."

"You're Mr. Bracken's daughter."

"Stepdaughter. My last name is Drake. I'm Allison Drake."

"Oh, yeah, that's right." Jack took hold of her upper arm and pulled her off the street and toward his police car.

"Are you arresting me. . .again?" she had asked, alarmed.

"No, I'm giving you a ride home so you don't get hurt." He grinned. "I just got off a twelve-hour shift."

"Oh. . ." Allie regarded the young officer with something akin to guarded curiosity. Why did he want to help her? Could she trust him?

After they'd climbed into the car and Jack started the engine, her inquisitive nature got the best of her. "Aren't you a cop in Oakland Park anymore? What are you doing in downtown Chicago?"

"Several officers from surrounding suburbs were called in to help with crowd control here in the city." He gave her a cynical little grin. "And aren't we doing a fine job?"

Allie had laughed. Jack's sarcastic wit always had a way of making her laugh.

The Sheraton came into view and Allie snapped out of her reverie. Pulling into its circular drive, she paid the valet to park the rented vehicle while a bellhop transported her luggage and led her into the hotel. After checking in at the desk, she made her way up to her room on the twentieth floor. As she entered, the fragrant scent of roses greeted her.

Allie smiled at the sight of the large, red bouquet while tipping the young man who had assisted her with her suitcases. Once he'd gone, she closed the door, kicked off her blue and white high-heeled pumps, and strolled toward the roses. Lifting the card, she read:

> *Glad you arrived safely, Ms. Littenberg. Looking forward to working with you.*
>
> *Sincerely,*
> *Evan Jacobs*

Allie's smile broadened. How kind of Evan. A sharp, capable young man, he was the CEO for Lakeland Enterprises, the largest owner of long-term and interim medical care facilities in the state of Illinois. She'd have to be sure to thank him for the flowers when she saw him on Monday, except she had a hunch they would talk sometime this weekend.

When Evan had phoned in June, asking if Allie would come to Chicago to reorganize a facility his firm had acquired, she felt it was God's affirmation and His leading her back to this city. She didn't have another job lined up; and since the Seattle arrangement fell through, Allie needed the work. But, in truth, her purpose for being here was multifaceted. Ever since Nick found that box of faded photographs, Allie couldn't seem to get her mind off of Jack, her former friends, and family members. Restitution needed to be made. This seemed like a Divine opportunity. Recognizing it as such, she accepted the assignment, knowing her "work" in Chicago had more to do with mending her past than with Lakeland Enterprises.

Walking to the windows, Allie gazed eastward over the blue-green expanse of Lake Michigan. From her vantage point, she could also see Navy Pier with its high Ferris wheel, quaint carousel, busy restaurants, and shops. She grinned, deciding she'd have to make a point to get over there and do a bit of sightseeing. Turning away from the spectacular view, Allie began unpacking. Afterwards, she showered and slipped into her comfy terrycloth bathrobe. Then, unable to deny the desire any longer, she picked up the telephone book that lay on the oak desktop and flipped the pages until she found Callahan. Running her finger down the listings, she chided herself. *Goose, you're probably stirring up trouble.* However, the self-berating didn't stop her from searching for Jack's name.

Minutes passed and Allie still didn't find his number, but she thought she'd located his younger brother, Steve. Should she call him? Ask about Jack?

Kneading at her lower lip, she debated. Thirty years changed a person. They had certainly changed her. She'd once been a confused young woman, a product of a broken home, and one who'd suffered through a horrible marriage. But over the years, she'd become a strong Christian and a successful businesswoman with a grown son. The very thought of Nick brought a smile to her lips. She was so proud of him. Tall, handsome, and with a heart as big as the moon, he felt called to the ministry when he was just a freshman in high school. Recently, he'd married a young woman named Jennifer, and Allie sensed the two had a bright future together. Would Jack want to know that?

Maybe.

Maybe not.

Allie slapped the phone book closed, still pondering, still wistful. But wasn't this part of the very reason she'd come to Chicago? To see Jack? Why the hesitation now?

To this day, she could recall his warm, brown eyes that shone like liquid brown sugar when he smiled and his thick dark hair that he kept neat and uniformly short. She remembered how his quick wit left her laughing until she couldn't breathe, and she remembered his serious side, too—the side that begged her not to go.

After the night Jack rescued Allie from the downtown riot, he had frequented the restaurant where she worked and eventually shared his faith. He'd been a solid believer, the model Christian man, in her opinion; and Allie was soon persuaded that Jesus Christ was The Way, The Truth, and The Life. She became a Christian because Jack had cared for her soul. But it wasn't long before he cared for her, too, and in a much different way than his initial "brotherly love."

And that's when things got complicated.

Complicated. A shiver of derision crept up her spine. The reality of it was that at nineteen years old, she hadn't known her own mind. She couldn't comprehend settling down with a man who said he loved her—because she couldn't comprehend love. She could think only about her natural father and stepmother in California and how much she wanted to live with them by the ocean in a state where Chicago's long winter months would never envelop her in their gloom again. After admitting to him in a letter that she was tired of trying to make it on her own, Allie's father offered to pay her way through college if she worked for him at his prestigious public relations firm. Deciding her dad's offer sounded better than Jack's marriage proposal, Allie packed her belongings and told Jack good-bye.

"Don't go," he'd pleaded, tears rimming his brown eyes. The words still echoed in Allie's head. "Don't go. Don't go."

In spite of his heartfelt appeal, she left. But she wrote to him weeks later, telling him she would love him until the day she died and that she wanted—no, *needed*—to speak with him again. She begged him not to be angry with her, but Jack never replied. Allie figured that was her cue to let things go. Burn her bridges in the Midwest. Focus on her future. A couple years later, when she heard Jack had gotten married, Allie knew she'd made the right choice.

She had also decided that she'd been right about love all along. It didn't last. It was as disposable as anything else was in this wasteful world. However, her walk with Christ had changed her outlook on relationships. Over the years, Allie had observed blissful unions, although she wasn't foolish enough to believe that married couples weren't without their troubles. Still, she'd seen her friends work at it, and she'd watched in amazement as their love for one another grew.

Unfortunately, that hadn't occurred in her own marriage. . . .

Shaking herself, she reopened the phone book and mustered the courage to call Steve Callahan. The phone rang several times before a female voice answered. She sounded young, perhaps in her teens.

"May I speak with Steve Callahan, please?"

"Sure, who's calling?"

Allie cleared her voice. "A friend of his brother's."

"Uncle Jack?"

Allie smiled. She had the right Callahan family anyway. "Yes," she replied. "Your uncle Jack."

"Hang on, I'll get my dad."

Allie fidgeted with the phone cord as she waited. She quickly rehearsed what she'd say once he got on the line.

"Yeah, this is Steve Callahan. Who's this?"

Allie wanted to laugh out loud. Same old get-to-the-point Steve. "I don't know if you'll remember me," she began carefully, "but I knew you and Jack about thirty years ago, and I wondered—"

"Thirty years ago? Who is this?"

"It's Allison Drake. Allie. Do you remember me?"

A long pause.

"Steve? Are you there?"

"Allison Drake? No kidding? Man, I haven't thought about you in years!"

"More like decades," she said trying to keep her tone light.

"Allie. . . ? Sure, I remember. . .is this really you?" His voice held a note of incredulity.

"Uh-huh." She cleared her throat. "I'm here in Chicago on business, and I've been wondering how Jack is doing. Can you tell me?"

"Sure. He's. . .well, he's changed a lot. But he's still a cop here in Oakland Park."

"That's great." Allie was all smiles, remembering how handsome he looked in his uniform. But the memory dwindled. "I can imagine how much Jack's changed. Who hasn't in all this time?"

"Yeah, well. . .Jack's had it tough. Hey, why don't you come over for supper tonight?" Steve asked, changing the subject. "We can get reacquainted. I'm grilling hamburgers. You can meet my wife, Nora, and our three kids, except two of them aren't 'kids' anymore. They've become these strange creatures known as teenagers."

Allie laughed softly. She knew about teenagers. Her son, Nick, almost made her crazy during those tumultuous years! "Well, I don't want to impose on your family on a Friday evening."

"It's no imposition. Maybe we can even get Jack to come." He paused as if in thought. "Where you staying?"

"The Sheraton on North Water Street."

"Ooh, ritzy place. You must be doing all right, huh, Allie?"

"Yeah, I'm doing all right," she drawled. "God has blessed my business."

"Well, God has blessed us too, but we're just your ordinary family here. Three kids and a dog, you know?"

"Sounds refreshing," Allie replied with another smile.

A pause. "You married?"

"Widowed."

"I'm sorry. . . ."

Allie was tempted to tell Steve not to feel sorry at all—that she and Erich Littenberg had had a stormy marriage at best. His passing, as insensitive as it sounded, was a blessing for her and Nick. Erich had been a rich man, but a cruel one, and yet God saw to it that both she and her son survived those hellish thirteen years.

"Allie? You still there?"

"Yes," she said, dragging herself back to the present. She laughed lightly, feeling embarrassed. "Sorry, Steve. I'm afraid I've grown melancholy in my old age. I'll be fifty soon, you know."

"Yeah, well, I'm going to stay thirty-nine forever."

"If you're thirty-nine, then I'm the Queen of England."

Steve chuckled. "You knew me back when, so I guess I can't pull anything over on you."

"Not a chance." Allie laughed. If she remembered correctly, Steve was four years younger than she was.

"Say," he asked, a note of concern in his voice, "was it recent? Losing your husband, I mean?"

"No. He died years ago."

"Oh, well, that's good—I mean that his death wasn't recent." Steve cleared his throat. "Hey, it'll be fun to see you again. You need a lift? I can send my oldest daughter to fetch you."

"Thanks, but I've rented a car and I think I still remember the way to Oakland Park. I just need directions to your place."

Steve explained the way to his house while Allie jotted the information down on a piece of paper.

"I'm looking forward to seeing you and meeting the rest of your family," she said. "I hope Jack will be able to join us."

"We'll have to see. He works a lot."

"Well, I appreciate the invitation all the same."

"What are friends for, eh? See you soon."

Allie hung up and stared at the phone for several long moments. Regardless of the wisdom behind her deed, or lack thereof, she'd soon be reacquainted with the Callahans.

Finally, she shrugged off her misgivings. Too late to turn back now.

Standing from where she'd been sitting on the edge of the

king-size bed, Allie headed for the bathroom. She paused to consider her reflection in the mirror. The same blue eyes as always stared back at her, eyes that had seen a lot of pain and sorrow, but eyes that had also watched the miraculous hand of God at work. It'd be nice to see Jack again and tell him about it. . .about her faith, her life.

Allie fingered her cheek and the white scar that spanned the area from the corner of her right eye to her chin. It reminded her of a strand of cooked spaghetti, and she despised it. However, she'd learned to live with it ever since her fifth wedding anniversary, and she certainly couldn't deny the blessing it wrought. Besides, after two plastic surgeries, it wasn't half as unsightly as it once had been. Even so, Allie planned to apply a good dose of cosmetics. To do anything less would be like advertising one of the biggest mistakes of her life, and she intended to make a good impression tonight.

After all, thirty years was a long, long time.

CHAPTER TWO

Allie considered it a miracle that she had found her way through Oakland Park. It only vaguely resembled the city she'd left behind so many years ago. True enough, it was still ten miles from downtown Chicago; but Central Avenue, the main drag, didn't look anything like she recalled. Thirty years ago, individual buildings containing offices and miscellaneous stores bordered the cracked and buckled sidewalks, but they had since been transformed into part of an appealing shopping district—one that impressed even Allie.

At last, she located Steve's house. Pulling alongside the curb and parking the car, she wondered about her stepfamily. Were they still living in this community? Was her stepfather still alive? She'd heard bits and pieces from friends, but they, like Allie, had lost contact with the Brackenses.

"Allison Drake? Is that really you?"

Steve's deep voice beckoned her from her musings as soon as she climbed out of the car. "It's really me," she said, meeting him on the driveway. "And you haven't changed a bit." She chuckled, noting the same unruly dark waves framing chiseled features and Irish baby-blues. Yes, he looked older, but Allie thought she'd recognize Steve Callahan anywhere.

"I'm about twenty-five pounds heavier," he admitted with a frown, patting the blue T-shirt that covered his stomach.

Allie grinned. "You were always such a stick that a little weight actually looks good on you!"

Steve hooted. "You and I are going to get along just fine." He looped a brotherly arm around her shoulders. "Come into the backyard and meet my clan."

Allie accompanied her host around the white, aluminum-sided, two-story house, where a large golden retriever greeted her.

"This is Buddy," Steve informed her.

Allie patted the friendly dog's head.

"And this is my better half. . .Nora."

Taking her eyes off the pet, Allie looked up and watched as an attractively plump woman with sandy brown, chin-length hair stepped off the octagonal wooden deck.

"Nice to meet you." Nora held out her right hand in greeting. "Steve has been telling me about you."

Taking the proffered hand, Allie felt herself blush. She couldn't help speculating as to how Steve would describe the Allie Drake of thirty years ago. Adventurous? Rebellious? Bold as brass? Selfish?

"Nice to meet you, too," she finally managed to reply.

Turning, Nora pointed to the padded lawn furniture behind her. "Let's go sit on the deck and get acquainted while my darling husband barbecues our dinner."

"As you can see, Allie, I'm nothing but a slave in this household."

She chuckled at Steve's quip just as Nora opened the patio door.

"Ricky," she called into the house, "bring our guest one of those blended fruit drinks I made."

"My son is a slave, too," Steve grumbled in jest, donning a brightly striped chef's apron.

Nora rolled her blue-green eyes at her husband and smiled at Allie. Then she looked back at Steve. "Did Jack ever return your call?"

"Nope."

Watching the couple, Allie sensed undefined emotions passing between them. Anger? Disappointment? Relief? She could only guess.

"Well, maybe it's for the best," Nora remarked, sitting down in one of the patio chairs. She wore a comfortable-looking denim dress; and as she crossed her tanned legs, she smoothed the skirt over her knees.

"I got a hold of Logan, though. He said he'd stop over."

"Logan?" Allie queried, taking the chair beside Nora. She felt the wind leave her lungs.

"Jack's son."

"Yes, I thought perhaps that's who it might be. . . ."

Allie felt torn between indignation and amusement. Logan was *their* name—hers and Jack's. Once when he had been talking about marriage, she mentioned how fond she was of the name Logan. Jack promised that their firstborn son would bear the name. However, the entire discussion had scared Allie senseless. At that point in her life, commitments and children sounded like a prison sentence. Nevertheless, she'd always been partial to the name. In fact, she might have been tempted to call her own son Logan if Erich hadn't insisted upon naming him after his father.

"Do you have any children?" Nora wanted to know.

"Yes. One son. Nicholas. He's twenty-five and just got married."

"Logan is twenty-eight. He's a great kid," Steve informed her from where he stood in front of the grill.

"Logan's hardly a kid," Nora said. "He's the youth pastor at our church in Schaumburg. He's got a special girl, but no wedding date set yet."

"Imagine that," Allie replied. "My son is in the ministry, too." She felt like exclaiming at the coincidence. . .but was it? As a Christian, she didn't believe in coincidence.

An odd expression suddenly crossed Steve's countenance—one Allie wouldn't even try to discern. Then he excused himself and he disappeared into the house, saying he had to fetch the hamburgers in the fridge.

*   *   *

Agitated, Jack marched up his younger brother's driveway. Why had he called the station? Steve never called him at work—unless it was an emergency. Was it Logan? Was he hurt? In trouble? Naw, Logan wouldn't be in trouble. Rounding the corner of the house, a cloud of smoke from the grill assaulted him.

"Jack!"

Squinting through the gray haze, he spotted Steve and shook his head in irritation. "Why'd you phone the cops? You should have called the fire department instead."

Steve laughed at the barb—like he always did. "You know me, Jack. I like my burgers well done."

"Whatever. So, why did you call the station?" He placed his foot on the first step leading up to the deck and realized Steve and Nora had a guest. Jack almost retreated, except the sapphire blue eyes staring back at him gave him pause.

Those eyes had haunted his dreams—and nightmares, too—for over a quarter of a century.

"I wanted to tell you Allie's in town. Allie Drake. You remember her, don't you?"

Jack's gaze shifted back to his brother's grinning face, and suddenly he felt like popping Steve right in the nose. Did he remember Allie Drake? What a stupid question!

"Hello, Jack."

He turned as Allie stepped forward slowly, wearing a smile

that said she wasn't sure if it was good to see him again or not. She'd soon learn. . .or maybe Steve and Nora had told her already. He'd changed. And if Allie had returned to look for the guy she'd known thirty years ago, she was wasting her time. *That* Jack Callahan couldn't be found in the deepest recesses of even his own memory. Yet, despite his honed cynicism, he couldn't deny the fact that Allie looked good. Obviously, life had treated her a whole lot better than it had treated him. Her once flaxen hair was now a lovely silvery blond that she wore swept up except for a few strands hanging fashionably along the right side of her face. But her eyes were as blue as ever. Seeing her standing there, wearing a white dress gathered at the waist with a thin red belt and a red cardigan sweater draped over her shoulders, caused the ache he thought he'd long ago suppressed to return, harder and more painful than ever.

"Hi, Allie," he managed, unable to force inflection into his voice. "Nice to see you again. How've you been?"

"Great. . .just great."

She looked great, too, Jack decided in spite of himself.

"And you? How've you been doing?"

So they hadn't told her yet, eh? he thought, glancing down at the tips of his black leather shoes. A moment later, he looked over at his brother, then sister-in-law, and finally back at Allie. "Just peachy."

He saw her startled reaction to his sarcasm, but told himself he didn't care.

"Allie's in Chicago on business," Steve said.

"That right? Well, I hope you have a pleasant stay." He swung his gaze at Steve. "Sorry I can't hang around and socialize. I'm on duty."

"Right. I didn't expect you'd drop in—"

"I was driving by and figured I'd stop." Jack chanced one last look at Allie and gave her a parting nod.

She returned a perfunctory smile.

"Drop in anytime, Jack," Nora said in her typical upbeat manner that always grated on his nerves.

He didn't reply, but headed toward the squad car, parked in front of his brother's house.

*   *   *

Steve had grilled the hamburgers to perfection, and Nora created a seven-layer salad that even the Galloping Gourmet might envy; but Allie could barely choke down a bite of food. Seeing Jack again and the stony look in his eyes—eyes that had once warmed her heart—saddened her spirit and robbed her of an appetite.

She glanced around the picnic table. Steve and Nora's three children, Veronica, Ricky, and Rachel, had joined them as well as Jack's son, Logan. The fact that Logan resembled his father, or at least the way Allie had remembered his father, caused her to feel even more unsettled.

What could possibly have happened to Jack? It wasn't so much that he'd aged badly—he hadn't. His gray hair contained only peppered reminders of its once mahogany brown shade. He looked to be in good physical shape, probably because of his profession. No, the change in Jack was more an internal one—one Allie recognized all too well. She'd seen the same hardness in her husband's eyes—a hardness that reflected his stone-cold soul.

That surely wasn't the Jack Callahan she'd known so well. . . .

"What kind of business are you in, Mrs. Littenberg?" Logan asked.

She pushed her tumultuous thoughts aside. "I'm a consultant."

"Oh. . .so you sort of walk into a place and tell everybody how they could be doing things better, huh?"

She smiled. "Something like that, yes."

"I couldn't stand the consultant my company hired a few years ago," Steve said. "The guy came in the first day, acting like he owned the place."

Allie laughed. "Well, you computer techs are the hardest people to work with."

Nora good-naturedly agreed. "That's why they work with machines and not human beings."

"Gimme a break, you two," Steve replied in mock annoyance. Allie's mood lightened somewhat and she managed to take a bite of her burger. Suddenly she realized how hungry she was. Picking up her fork, she ate some of her salad.

"We'd love it if you'd join us for church on Sunday, Allie," Nora said, sipping her fruity drink. "Steve told me you're a Christian, so I thought I'd bring it up."

"That's very kind of you, but. . ." She hesitated, forming her words with care.

"Don't worry, Jack won't be there," Steve said as if divining her thoughts. "It's a shame, too. He's as far away from God as New York is from the Hawaiian Islands."

"We keep praying for him, though," Logan added, with a glance in Allie's direction.

She set down her fork. "I had hoped he'd be glad to see me again," she remarked candidly. "I was looking forward to seeing him."

Discomfort flittered around the table, with the exception of Steve's youngest daughter.

"Uncle Jack is just like that," she announced, and Allie saw her resemblance to her mother. "Can I be excused to go ride my bike?"

"Yes. But be back when the street lights come on."

"Okay."

Rachel grabbed her plastic supper dishes and headed for the house.

"I need to be excused, too," Veronica said. She looked like a mix of her parents, Steve's walnut-colored hair and lanky frame and Nora's teal eyes. "School starts on Monday, and I'm going to meet Beth and Carolyn at the mall. That is," she added, regarding her father with a hopeful expression, "if I can have the car tonight."

"Yeah, go ahead."

Allie smiled at the exchange.

"And what are you two doing tonight?" Steve wanted to know, gazing first at his son and then at his nephew.

"We're going to hang out and watch ESPN," Ricky replied. He was a little bear of a guy whose stocky frame had the look and potential of growing another foot in the next four years. "Right, Logan?"

"Uh-huh."

Steve leaned forward. "Hey, great. . .is there a football game on?"

"Wonderful," Nora groused. "Allie and I just lost our male companionship for the evening."

"You don't like football, Nora?"

Slowly, the woman tipped her head. "Don't tell me you do," she said, wearing a look of incredulity.

"Maybe it's an acquired taste—acquired from raising a son who participated in every sport imaginable." She laughed.

"In that case, I suppose we might as well join 'em."

"But I'd be delighted to help you with the dishes first," Allie offered.

"It's a deal."

Supper ended almost abruptly, and Allie helped Nora carry dishes and leftover food into the house. Entering the kitchen, Allie noticed its walls were papered with tiny red apples on green vines. A border of the same design, only larger, detailed the circumference of the room, near the ceiling.

"You've got a lovely home," Allie remarked, setting down her armload on the marble counter.

"Thanks. I love working on each room of our house, trying to make it special. What does your place look like in California?"

"I recently moved into a condo in Long Beach, but I can't give it as much attention as I'd like."

"It sounds terrific, though. Wouldn't I love to live by the ocean!" She shrugged. "Oh, well, we've got Lake Michigan."

"Not the same. I assure you."

"Guess I'll have to take your word for it."

They shared a chuckle as Nora opened the door to the dishwasher.

"Nora," Allie hedged, "about Jack. . .I don't mean to pry, but I can't get over the change in him. I'm concerned. . .can you tell me. . .what happened?"

She considered the request. "Yeah, I guess I can. I mean, Steve said you and Jack were fairly serious about each other at one point. I'm sure you're curious about him. I know I would be."

Allie replied with a little nod.

"He's had a tough life," Nora began, "although it was pretty much his own doing as far as I'm concerned. But everyone makes mistakes. . .it's just that, for whatever reason, Jack can't get past his." Nora began packing plates into the dishwasher. "I think his downward spiral began after he met his ex-wife, Roxi. From what I've pieced together over the years—" Nora quickly scanned the room for little ears. Seeing her children weren't around, she continued. "—His ex-wife seduced him, although it's Jack's fault as much as it is hers.

"Anyway, Roxi ended up pregnant. Jack was warned not to marry her, but he kept insisting he had to 'do the right thing.' Six months later, Logan was born and about eight months after that his wife took off, leaving Jack with an infant to take care of."

"I–I'm sorry to hear that," Allie stammered.

While her heart filled with empathy for Jack, she couldn't help feeling a twinge of guilt and remorse also. How had he ever gotten himself in such a predicament? The Jack Callahan she'd known was a morally upstanding man concerned about his Christian testimony. Had her departure really wounded him so deeply?

No, she decided, she wouldn't blame herself. If he had wanted to, Jack could have contacted her. He knew her address and phone number.

"After the divorce," Nora said, drawing Allie from her reverie, "Jack got custody, but his parents primarily raised Logan until he was about five years old and Mom Callahan was diagnosed with cancer."

Allie grimaced. She'd always been fond of both Mr. and Mrs. Callahan. "Is she dead?"

"Yes. Mom went quickly. Dad had a stroke and died a few years later. But we can rejoice that they're both with the Lord."

Allie replied with a rueful grin. She remembered the older couple as being warm, caring people, devoted to Christ.

"By that time, Steve and I were married, so we took Logan in when Jack worked weird shifts. Sometimes I feel like Logan's one of my own because it wasn't until years later that Roni was born."

"It's a blessing that Jack had so much help from his family."

"We were glad to do it. Logan was one of those sweet, lovable kids, easy to have around. But I will say this: As much as Jack worked, he did manage to attend all of Logan's birthday parties and sports functions all the way through high school. The one thing he wouldn't do, though, would be to watch Logan perform in various programs at church. Then after Logan chose to attend a Christian college, Jack refused to help him with tuition." Nora gave Allie a pointed look. "*That* made me angry. Still does. The guy has money. He could have paid Logan's way through school if he wanted to."

"Aunt Nora, Dad's not a Christian and therein lies the problem."

Allie whirled around to see Logan, leaning against the doorjamb with his arms folded in front of him. It gave her something of a start to see him there, for he looked so much like Jack did thirty years ago, same dark eyes and courageous grin.

"The passage of Scripture comes to mind that says the things of God are foolishness to unbelievers," Logan said. "Everything we do to honor the Lord is foolishness to Dad—like my job, for instance. Dad is forever telling me to 'get a real job.' "

Allie shook her head, ready to protest. "Your father is a believer, Logan."

"A lot of people can talk the talk, Mrs. Littenberg. I see it happen in my youth group all the time."

"No. When I knew your father, he was serious about his faith. I wouldn't know the Lord today if your father hadn't shared his beliefs with me."

Logan's brown eyes narrowed suspiciously, so Allie recounted the story. . . .

CHAPTER THREE

Jack remembered. Clearly. Too clearly.

Lying on his back in bed in the darkness of his bedroom, he rested his forearm across his eyes. After work tonight, he'd consumed several beers, hoping to dull his senses and perhaps he'd succeeded in that respect; however, he hadn't been able to stem the memories. They washed over him in waves.

Allie. He never thought he'd see her again. Against his will, Jack recalled the last time their paths had crossed—it had been the day she told him good-bye and walked out of his life. November 5, 1969.

"Don't go, Allie." He'd just come off a double shift only to arrive home and find her in the front yard, ready to spring for the airport.

She flicked strands of her long blond hair over one, slender shoulder. "I have to go, don't you see?"

"No, I don't see." He placed his hands on her upper arms and pulled her close. "Allie, I love you. Marry me. I'll make you happy. I promise. We'll have a great life together."

She stepped backwards, out of his grasp. "I can't."

"Why?" His heart knotted painfully.

"Because. . ." Taking a deep breath, Allie looked upward before bringing her gaze back to his. "I don't have a high opinion of marriage, Jack. Look at my parents and stepparents. . . what did marriage do for them? It didn't last, and now my mom's dead—"

"Marriage didn't kill her," Jack said, trying to understand the comparison. The woman had died of a ruptured brain aneurysm. Allie had told him her mother complained of a terrible headache that morning. When she returned home from school, Allie learned her mother was gone.

"Maybe marriage did kill her," Allie replied on a sour note. "All the arguing she and my stepfather did would kill anybody."

Jack shook his head, trying to clear the confusion. "Hold it. Didn't you once say your mother and her husband loved each other?"

"Sure, but who needs their kind of love? Love that hurts. . . that maims."

Jack softened. "It's different with believers, Allie."

"Maybe, but I'm not ready to commit my whole life to somebody. I've got to find out who I am first. I've got to get my head together. Taking this job with my dad in California—"

"Don't kid yourself. You can get your head together and still be my wife. Everything you need is in God's Word, not California."

With a wag of her head, Allie let him know she wouldn't be persuaded.

Jack clenched his jaw against the mounting disappointment. "I thought you loved me." The comment was but a whisper on the late autumn breeze.

"Oh, Jack. . ." Allie closed her eyes in apparent remorse.

"Were you lying to me all this time?"

"No," she said, her sapphire eyes now snapping to attention. "Not lying. I just. . ."

"Just what?"

"Please understand."

"I can't!"

"Well, I can't, either. And I can't explain it. All I know is I've got to go. I've got to get out of here."

"Then you don't love me."

She swallowed hard. "I'll write to you."

"Don't bother," he ground out.

"You don't mean that, Jack. I know you too well." Her gaze hardened to blue ice. "But suit yourself."

With that, she'd turned and walked away, down the sidewalk, across the brown lawn, and into the waiting taxi. His pride wouldn't allow him to do anything but watch the vehicle pull away.

Time after time, days and months later, he thought about contacting Allie in California. However, he wasn't the one who had the problem with marriage. It was Allie. He prayed fervently, begging the Lord to work in her heart, change her mind; and Jack looked forward to the day when Allie would return, tell him she was sorry, that she wanted him back. But the day never came. The truth was, she didn't love him. And the acknowledgment hurt, more than the gunshot wound he'd once sustained in the line of duty. The assailant's bullet had torn the bone and flesh, but Allie's rejection had lacerated his very soul.

Enough reminiscing!

Jack peeled back the sheets and shot up out of bed, heading for the kitchen.

"Dad, you okay?"

He grabbed a glass out of the cupboard and, standing at the marbled island in which the sink had been installed, he flipped on the faucet. "Just needed a drink of water." He gulped down several swallows. "What are you doing awake at this hour?"

"Thinking."

"Don't hurt yourself."

Logan threw him a dubious glance, and Jack chuckled.

"Hey, I need to talk to you about something that happened tonight."

With a sigh, Jack considered his adult son reclining on the plaid sofa in the adjacent living room. He knew he hadn't been a good father to him, even though he'd tried. But sometimes things just don't work out, despite a man's best intentions. So three months ago when Logan asked to share his condo because he was thinking of getting married and wanted to save a few bucks, Jack consented. He figured he owed Logan that much—even though he'd expected the worst. After all, Logan had every right to be angry—just as angry as when he was a teenager. But he wasn't. Of course, he had a point to prove. . . .

"What's up?" Jack asked.

Logan stood and strolled to the half-wall dividing the rooms. He reminded Jack so much of himself—the way he once was—that it hurt at times to even look at him.

Like now.

Lowering his gaze, Jack stared into his water goblet. "What's on your mind, Son?"

"That woman at Uncle Steve's tonight. . .Mrs. Littenberg—"

"Littenberg?" Jack brought his head up sharply. "Is that her last name now? Littenberg?" He produced a curt laugh that sounded spiteful to his own ears. *Littenberg. . .so that's the name of the guy she fell in love with. The guy who was better than me. . .*

"Dad?"

Jack refocused on his son. "What?"

"Mrs. Littenberg told me how she became a Christian. She said you led her to the Lord." Logan tipped his head and his brown eyes narrowed suspiciously. "Is that true?"

"Hard to believe, isn't it?"

Logan brought his chin back, incredulously. "It's true?"

"Yep."

"But—"

"But I don't act like a believer? Is that what you're going to say? Well, that's true, too."

"Why?"

"Why. . .what?" Jack frowned.

"Why. . .why didn't you tell me? All this time. . ." Logan shook his head. "Dad, I don't get it."

"Look, I stepped out of the circle of Christianity a long time ago after I realized prayer doesn't work and faith isn't all it's cracked up to be."

Logan shook his head. "Aw, Dad. . .you're so wrong."

"Yeah, well, before you pass judgment, walk a mile in my shoes, okay?"

"I'm not passing judgment. I want to help you."

"Don't waste your time." Jack held up a forestalling hand. "Besides, this topic's not open for discussion. There are just some things better left alone and this is one of them. As for Mrs. Littenberg," he fairly sneered, "she had better mind her own business from now on."

"Dad, talk to me. I want to understand."

"Drop it, Logan."

The warning hung between them until finally the younger man backed down.

"Fine. Whatever you say." Logan paused. "I'll change the subject." He paused in thought, pursing his lips. "Uncle Steve told me that you and Mrs. Littenberg were a pretty hot item once upon a time. He said you two were—to use his words—'in love.' "

Jack felt the muscle in his jaw tighten, the way it did whenever he was stressed. "Your uncle Steve's wrong. *We* were never in love." He turned on his heel. "And this topic is not open for discussion, either. Good night."

Jack moved away from the sink and started toward his bedroom. He'd told the truth. He and Allie never loved *each other*—it was only him. He'd loved her more than anything, the sun, the moon, the stars, the earth, his family, his job. . .his very being! But she hadn't shared his feelings. Instead, she'd left him for a lousy job in California and married some guy named *Littenberg!*

* * *

Marilee Domotor stood in the choir loft as the rest of the members filed into place. To her right, she could see bald-headed Mr. Tearly behind the organ and his slim wife, Sandra, at the grand piano stationed next to him. Strains of "A Mighty Fortress Is Our God" filled the large, modern sanctuary and its balcony. Marilee couldn't help scanning the congregation in hopes of seeing Logan. She hadn't seen him since school let out Friday afternoon; and though she tried not to think that way, she surreptitiously wondered if he'd lost interest in her—in them. Logan Callahan was a hard man to read. Sometimes he seemed so brave and confident of God's will; and at others, he was reticent, almost fearful of taking those next steps of faith. Like an engagement. Marriage. To a certain degree, Marilee understood his hesitancy since Logan had told her about his former fiancée. Even so, it was hard to be patient.

Marilee squared her shoulders and pushed aside her troubled thoughts as the music director took his place just in front of the podium. He lifted his arms, and the members of Parkway Community Church opened their music binders, then opened their hearts and mouths in song to the Lord.

When they reached the chorus, joy and hope filled Marilee's soul as it always did when she sang this song. To think the Lord could use her—or any of His children—never failed to humble her.

Broken things.
Broken things.
Our God still chooses to use broken things.
"Break Thou myself," oh, make my heart sing,
For God can use this broken thing. . .

They finished the piece, harmonizing on the last few notes, and tingles flittered down Marilee's spine. Perfect. *May You be glorified, Lord*, she prayed.

With the number completed, the music director led the congregation in a hymn, while the choir members gracefully exited the loft and headed for the practice room, where they deposited their music. Next, they made their way through the lobby and into the sanctuary.

Setting out to find a seat of her own, Marilee spotted Logan at long last. Wearing khaki dress pants, a French-blue shirt, and coordinating tie, he stood near the doorway with two rough-looking teenagers. When he saw her, he smiled and waved her over.

"I want you to meet a couple of people," he said as she approached. As usual, his dark brown hair was slightly mussed. "This is Eddie Russo," he announced, indicating a young man with four tiny hoops pierced through each earlobe and a tiny, diamond nose ring. "He's sixteen, and this is his first time here. The two of us met yesterday at the basketball hoop in the park and I invited him to church."

"It's nice to meet you," Marilee replied, smiling genuinely and extending her right hand.

Eddie took it, and she noticed his loose, uninterested grip.

"And this is Kate Thompson," Logan added, nodding toward a young lady with dyed black hair, dark eye makeup, and a pasty complexion.

"Hi, Kate. I'm Marilee. Good to meet you, too." They shook hands, and Marilee sensed some enthusiasm from the girl. "Do you guys need seats? If so, you're welcome to sit with me."

Kate glanced at Eddie, who shrugged again.

"They just came from this morning's Bible study and they're debating whether to stay for the service," Logan informed Marilee.

"I see. . ." She grinned politely at both kids, then looked into Logan's eyes. They were smiling back at her in a way that made her knees weak. "Maybe we could sit together. . . ."

"I'll look for you once these two decide what they're going to do," Logan promised. "Oh, and by the way. . ." He took Marilee's elbow and guided her a few steps away. "Steve and Nora invited us to lunch. They've got an old friend with them this morning—someone who knew my dad, and. . .get this: My dad led this woman to Christ when she was a teenager!"

Marilee's brows sprang up in surprise. "Your dad?" She knew something about Sergeant Callahan's background and couldn't begin to fathom why Logan had elected to move in with him. His father behaved about as antagonistically toward the gospel as Saul had toward the early church. How was it possible that he led someone to Christ?

"It's true," Logan said. His expression seemed a blend of elation and disappointment. "I confronted Dad and he verified it. But what bothers me is that I sense he's hurt or angry or bitter. . . maybe all three, and he refuses to talk to me about it. My guess is that he's never talked to anyone about it."

"And it's eating him up inside."

"Something like that." Logan glanced over his shoulder at the teens. "I guess we'd better finish this discussion later. Right now I've got some convincing to do."

Marilee took the hint. "I'll be praying."

"Thanks." Logan's brown-eyed gaze caressed her face before he turned his attention back to Eddie and Kate.

With her heart soaring, Marilee entered the sanctuary.

*   *   *

Allie smiled a thank-you as the waitress placed the chicken salad-stuffed croissant in front of her. She watched as the rest of the table was served: Steve, Nora, their three children, Logan, and his girlfriend, Marilee.

Allie's smile broadened as her gaze rested on the young lady. If ever a name fit a personality, it was Marilee—as in "merrily." She seemed friendly, outgoing, quick to smile and laugh, eager to please, although she also had a very academic look about her. Her straight, nut brown hair had been gathered back in a plastic, tortoise-shell clip; and she wore fashionable, dark-rimmed glasses. Allie soon learned her speculations were correct; Marilee taught third grade at the Christian day school affiliated with the church Logan helped pastor. It appeared to Allie that Logan Callahan had found a gem in Marilee.

The object of Allie's scrutiny suddenly met her gaze. The young woman flashed a grin that caused Allie to notice Marilee's twin dimples.

"That was a beautiful number the choir sang this morning," Allie said.

"Amen. I'm glad you thought so. That piece is one of my favorites."

The young lady scanned the table, and seeing the waitress still in the process of serving, she looked back at Allie. "Are you staying in the area, Mrs. Littenberg?"

Allie nodded. "At the Sheraton. . .downtown. But I'll soon be moving to an extended-stay hotel."

"Downtown Chicago? Oh. . .the traffic alone can be so intimidating."

"Not for me. I'm accustomed to large cities."

"That's good."

"Besides, Allie grew up here," Steve interjected. He smiled before adding, "Let's pray, shall we? Logan, how 'bout you do the honors, huh?"

"Sure."

Heads bowed reverently while Logan asked the blessing. Then, as the eating commenced, Steve continued in his previous vein.

"Allie used to be a waitress in Chicago. . .in the days of hippies, protests, and riots."

"That was a lifetime ago," Allie replied, laughing in spite of herself.

Steve chuckled as well.

"How did you meet my father?" Logan asked.

"He arrested me."

"No way!" Logan looked amused.

Allie nodded. "My stepfather had the police pick me up because I ran away from home. Later, I met your dad again during one of those riots your uncle just mentioned. He recognized me as being from Oakland Park and pulled me out of harm's way." Allie smiled sadly, glancing at her plate. "He certainly was something of a hero back then."

"Still is," Logan said. "Dad's gotten awards for his bravery in the line of duty."

"I don't doubt it."

"I think he could have really climbed the ladder of success inside the OPPD, except he hates desk jobs. He's always got to be out and working with the public, so his options for advancement are limited."

"Well, that," Steve added, "and the fact he got injured."

Allie tipped her head, curious. "How did he get hurt?"

"Gunshot wound. . .in his left thigh," Logan said. "If he's tired, he limps; but Dad tries not to let anybody see." The young man stuck a French fry into his mouth. "Except somebody saw. One of his higher-ups, and now he's being forced into early retirement—because he's too stubborn to take an administrative position."

Nora shook her head, looking remorseful. "I didn't know this, Logan. Your father will die if he can't work."

"Will he?" Logan countered, his dark eyes shining earnestly. "Or will he finally have to deal with some issues from his past—namely my mother, whoever and wherever she is."

Fork in hand, Allie picked at her sandwich. A wave of empathy washed over her; and she couldn't help wondering if, like her own son, Logan Callahan had managed to emerge from his parents' messes unscathed. She considered him from across the table. At twenty-eight years old, Logan had likely dealt with his own set of. . .*issues*.

"Maybe Jack will pick up a hobby," Steve said. "Like woodworking or something. Maybe I'll even get to finally teach him how to use a computer!"

Chuckles flittered around the table.

"Maybe Uncle Jack'll have time to come to my school again and talk about being a policeman," Rachel Callahan piped up with hope filling her voice.

"Maybe," Nora replied, before adding, "Maybe he'll have time for a lot of things he never used to be able to do because he was working all the time."

"That's an awful lot of maybes," Marilee pointed out.

Allie silently agreed.

"Yes, but God can do anything," Logan said, biting into his broiled steak sandwich.

This time Allie voiced her concurrence. She knew firsthand how God could take an impossible situation and work it all for good. After all, she'd lived through Romans 8:28 dozens of times during the course of her ill-fated marriage. "And we know that all things work together for good to them that love God, to them who are the called according to his purpose."

Allie sighed inwardly. If she'd only been a strong believer when she met Erich, she would have known better than to marry him, a man who thought God and the Bible were useless sentiments. But the delicate threads of her faith had deteriorated after moving to California, and Erich had been so utterly charming. . .at first.

"Mrs. Littenberg?"

At the sound of her name, Allie snapped from her musings. She saw Logan gazing at her questioningly. "Yes?"

"I said I'd like to throw my dad a retirement party. Would you be willing to come?"

"Well, um, I don't know. . . ."

"He's really not an ogre."

"What are you talking about?" Steve said, laughingly. "Jack wasn't an ogre Friday night when he stopped by. He was in one of his polite moods."

Allie raised a brow in question while Nora chuckled softly.

"And don't let my aunt and uncle bully you into staying away from Dad's party, either," Logan said, giving the couple a quelling glance before looking back at Allie.

"Don't worry, I'm not scared off that easily. But I will have to check my schedule. What's the date?"

"Haven't decided yet. Depends on when the police force gets Dad to retire."

"Better make it the Twelfth of Never then," Steve muttered sarcastically, causing Allie to grin.

A few more remarks were made in jest before the topic changed, and the remainder of the meal progressed pleasantly. After they'd finished, Allie and the Callahan family sauntered toward the front door of the restaurant. While Steve paused at the cash register to pay the bill, everyone else stepped outside onto the sidewalk. Allie lifted her face to the sunshine, realizing that this coming week marked the last days of August.

"Mrs. Littenberg?"

Lowering her chin, she found Logan gazing at her. He wore a heavy expression.

"Mrs. Littenberg," he began again, "I don't know how close you once were to my dad, but I've sensed this weekend that you used to be very important to him. He hasn't slept well since Friday night, and he's been grumpier than ever." Logan paused as if he were unsure how to continue. "I've been praying for him for a long time. I'm burdened for him."

"I know. I can tell."

"Every so often, I see glimmers of the real Jack Callahan— the one buried beneath that rock-hard facade of his." The young man forced a smile. "Well, I just wanted you to know that

I think there's hope for him."

"There's always hope, Logan."

"Right, but I'm thinking maybe you are that hope."

"No, not me. God."

"But the Lord delights in using His people, and I think He might use you."

Allie exhaled audibly and cast her gaze off in the distance, across the busy street to where some children were playing basketball on a fenced-in, asphalt playground. Was she? Was she that strand of hope God would use to reel Jack back into His fold? True, she had felt a purpose in accepting this job and coming to Chicago. True, she'd been almost preoccupied with thoughts of Jack Callahan for the past couple of months; however, she wasn't sure if she had the strength to deal with another volatile man.

Turning back to Logan, she noticed Marilee had come to stand beside him, her arm looped around his left elbow.

"We never know how God will use a believer to accomplish His will," Allie said, looking from one to the other. "But I've tried assuming God's thoughts before, and my good intentions backfired. Now, you could be right, Logan. The Lord might use me to bring your dad back around. But be assured: I will not step out on my own."

He grinned broadly. "I wouldn't want you to. I just wondered how open you'd be to stepping out at all."

Marilee smiled and cast an adoring glance up at Logan, who just stood there grinning sheepishly. Allie couldn't suppress a laugh.

"Listen, Pastor Callahan," she retorted, "save your antics for your youth group."

"Yes, Ma'am," he replied, except he failed to wipe the amusement off his face.

Steve stepped out of the restaurant, and they all began walking toward the parking lot and their respective vehicles. After thanking Steve for lunch, Allie climbed behind the wheel of the rented Cavalier and stuck the key into its ignition. She felt oddly doomed. If she hadn't already signed a contract with Lakeland Enterprises, she'd be tempted to buy a one-way ticket back to California ASAP!

Lord, You're going to have to put Jack into my path so that I trip over him if You want me to help. Help? What could I possibly do?

She maneuvered the car into the street and headed for the hotel. She thought of Erich. . . .

No, there's not a single thing I can do, Lord. Not a single thing. You're going to have to do it all!

CHAPTER FOUR

Logan stared out over Lake Michigan from the balcony of Marilee's parents' high-rise apartment. The vast body of blue-green water stretched as far as the eye could see, meeting the dusky evening sky at the horizon in an inspiring display. A sense of peace washed over him as he gazed upon God's magnificent creation. The panorama surpassed any implied portrayal of eternity he'd seen in books or hanging on art gallery walls.

"I really love water, ocean, lake, or river," he murmured. "There's just something about it."

"I agree," Marilee said, standing beside him. "I sometimes wish my parents had lived here while I was growing up instead of in Lake Forest."

Lifting his glass, Logan took a long drink of his lemonade. "Maybe I should plan a waterskiing activity for the youth group before it gets cold."

"You've got about a month."

"Yeah." He swirled the ice cubes around in his glass. "Wish

I had thought of waterskiing earlier."

"Oh, Logan, those teens have done everything but water-ski," Marilee contended. "We've taken them rafting, camping, swimming, horseback riding. . .not to mention the amusement park we went to last weekend." She grinned. "Your youth staff has kept those kids busy and out of trouble this summer. And you've kept *us* busy!"

Logan felt himself smirk at Marilee's subtle sarcasm. But at least she was honest enough to speak her mind. In fact, she was the first Christian woman he'd dated who didn't practice passive resistance, a tactic that grated on his nerves. He much preferred a candid reply to concealed disagreement and feigned acquiescence.

"Logan?"

He turned and gazed down into Marilee's questioning, chocolate brown eyes.

"You've been a million miles away today. And I didn't hear from you all weekend. I hope there doesn't have to be a youth activity in order for us to see each other."

Logan chuckled. "No, there doesn't have to be a youth activity."

"I thought maybe you had second thoughts. . . ."

"No, Marilee. I'm not having second thoughts about our relationship. Not a single one." He sighed. "It's just that with Mrs. Littenberg arriving in town on Friday, my conversation with my dad that night, then mounds of paperwork to sort through and phone messages to return yesterday, I just got busy. But I guess I could have found a few minutes to give you a call. I apologize."

Marilee shook her head before she lowered her chin. "Maybe I expect too much."

Logan smiled, his heart swelling with affection. He longed to pull her into his arms, hold her close, and soothe her insecurities. However, he embraced a strong, personal conviction regarding limited physical contact between men and women during their dating season, and he occasionally shared these views with his youth group. Sure, his ideas sounded old-fashioned and even backwards to a modern society, but Logan knew from experience that promises between couples didn't always materialize at the altar. Therefore, he figured it was better to err on the conservative side than give into feelings that only muddied the waters later. Besides, the teens at church were watching him, and Logan had vowed early on to practice what he preached.

But it sure made things hard on a guy. If he and Marilee didn't get married soon, he'd likely go crazy despite his senior pastor Noah Warren's assurance that this process was developing Logan's "character."

Even so, if he didn't get married soon, he just might be out of a job.

Two years ago, when he was offered the position of youth pastor at Parkway Community Church, Logan had been engaged. He and Sarah Malloy began dating while Logan was completing his Master's degree. Sarah was an undergrad in her senior year at the same college. Over the Christmas break, they'd met each other's friends and family. Everyone approved. Everything seemed wonderful.

After graduation, Logan asked her to marry him, and Sarah said yes. Unfortunately, they were separated during the following summer months. Sarah kept busy, planning their wedding; however, as the day grew closer, Logan became more and more unsure. While he couldn't put his finger on anything specific, he couldn't seem to shake the feeling that Sarah Malloy wasn't the woman for him. When he phoned her at her parents' place in Michigan and expressed his concerns, Sarah turned quiet, refusing to discuss the matter.

She was hurt, Logan knew. But he needed reassurance, although he never received it. Two days later, Sarah called off the wedding, leaving Logan with his own wounds. He wondered how she could give up on their relationship so easily. She had professed to love him—enough to agree to marry him. But obviously, her "love" hadn't been strong enough to weather his gale of insecurity, and Logan realized his inner promptings had been correct: Sarah wasn't the one for him.

Thus, he became Parkway Community Church's first single youth pastor, much to the dismay of its congregation. The majority of its fifteen hundred-plus members hated the fact that he didn't have a wife, children, and the experiences that came with having his own family. Although Pastor Warren acted as his frequent defender, Logan felt an intense pressure to marry. . .or to leave the ministry, something that would tear his heart apart.

Nevertheless, he refused to rush things. It had to be right. Perfect. The woman he married had to be God's choice for his wife. And Marilee seemed the primary candidate. She challenged Logan spiritually; and since they'd begun seriously dating, Logan believed his walk with Christ had grown closer, his faith stronger. Of course, it had taken him the better part of a year to ask her out. He'd been that petrified of repeating his mistake with Sarah. Or worse, he didn't want to end up like his dad, divorced, bitter, and alone. Logan knew the story. His father had been forced to marry his mother. . . .

"Earth to Logan."

Marilee's sweet voice penetrated his reverie, and he discovered he had gazed off in the direction of Lake Michigan again. Looking back at Marilee, he grinned. "Sorry."

She smiled. "It's okay. I just wish I could help with whatever is troubling you."

"By just being yourself, you're helping. Although, for the record, I'm not really 'troubled' about anything in particular."

Marilee nodded slightly while a pensive frown furrowed her dark brown brows. "You know Logan. . .well, I'm probably speaking out of turn. . . ."

He laughed. *So what else is new?* "Go ahead. I'm listening."

She hesitated, seeming to weigh her words with care. "Logan,

I'm not Sarah; and our relationship is different than the one you had with her, isn't it?"

"Definitely," Logan replied. He had confided in Marilee about the situation, wanting her to hear it from him and not someone else in their congregation. "And if I have somehow been comparing you to Sarah, I'm really sorry. It hasn't been intentional."

"I don't know if you have or not. It's just a guess."

He pursed his lips in thought, uncertain as to how to reply. It was true that his past experience caused him to be leery of jumping into another engagement without being absolutely sure of God's will. But he didn't think he went so far as to match one woman to the other.

"Logan," Marilee said softly, "I want to get married. I'm twenty-six years old, and I'm not getting any younger. I want to have children someday. Don't you think you and I have arrived at a point in our relationship where we could take the next step toward marriage. . .soon?"

"Don't beat around the bush, Marilee. Just come right out and say what's on your mind."

She gave him an indignant roll of her eyes, and Logan laughed.

"Okay, maybe you're right," he relented. "Maybe it's time for that 'next step.' But I don't want to feel coerced into proposing, not by you and not by the well-intentioned parents of the kids in my youth group. And I'm not just thinking of myself, but of you, too."

"I know." She sighed. "I don't mean to force you into a decision. I only meant to. . .prompt you a little."

Logan noted the twinkle in her eyes and grinned.

She gave an exaggerated shrug. "Okay, so I'll be forty when I give birth to our first child. So what?"

"Maybe you should give up on me and find another guy," Logan said, half-teasing. He figured his heart would break if that happened, but he wanted Marilee to be happy. "A dozen deserving bachelors at church would consider it a miracle if you'd date them."

"And it would be a miracle, Logan Callahan," Marilee retorted, folding her arms in front of her. He had to chuckle at the wry grin tugging at the corners of her nicely shaped mouth. "My heart is set on you, and I'll stick it out for as long as it takes."

"You might be sorry," Logan warned her, smiling all the while. In truth, he felt like popping the question right now and eloping tomorrow afternoon. But, again, giving into an urge, a feeling, might produce mistakes they'd both come to regret.

"I won't be sorry," Marilee promised. "Unless God shows me otherwise or shows you otherwise, I'm committed to our relationship."

Logan gave her an affectionate wink, then glanced toward the lake again. Thoughts of his biological mother, a woman he'd never known, surfaced from out of the blue; and Logan wondered if she had ever felt "committed" to either him or his father.

"What are you thinking about?" Marilee asked, stepping closer. "Tell me. Please?"

After a moment's hesitation, Logan saw no reason to harbor his musings. "Ever since I was old enough to understand, I've wondered what would make a mother leave her eight-month-old son the way my mother left me. My speculations have increased since Mrs. Littenberg came to town." He sighed, and an undefined longing filled his being. "Mothers aren't supposed to desert their kids. My aunt Nora would throw herself in front of an oncoming locomotive if she thought it'd make a difference in any of her children's lives. I'm sure she'd do it for me, too. And most mothers I deal with would probably do the same for their teens. But not my mother. She abandoned me. Dad said I'd probably been by myself for a couple of hours that afternoon until he came home from work."

"I don't mean to sound cruel, Logan, but the woman obviously had some psychological problems. I can't imagine abandoning my baby. . .or anyone else I love."

"Maybe my mother didn't love me. Maybe she was forced into marrying Dad and giving birth to me and she despised her circumstances."

"Maybe." As Marilee considered Logan's profile, the subtle downward slant of his eye, his perfectly shaped, straight nose, and strong jaw line with its hint of stubble, she gleaned an insight into his heart. *He's afraid I'll leave him, too*, she realized. *His mother left, and for all intents and purposes, Sarah abandoned him.* Marilee wondered how she could prove herself different from those women who had hurt him so much. *Help me, Jesus. Help me to show Logan Your grace and love. . . .*

"I'm thinking of searching for my biological mother," Logan blurted.

Marilee was taken aback. "Why do you want to find her? Don't you think the past is better left alone?"

"No. Not in my case." He turned to her again. "I want to look my mother in the face and ask her how she could leave her infant son—how she could leave me."

"What if the answers aren't what you want to hear?"

"Couldn't be worse than the ones I've imagined all these years."

Marilee's heart ached for him. "What about asking your father. I'm sure he knows."

"He refuses to talk about my mother, although I've managed to extricate bits and pieces out of him over the years." Logan exhaled audibly. "It's just not enough." He paused, pursing his lips in thought. "I'd look into hiring a detective, but I don't think I could afford it. Even if I could, I often wonder what it'd do to Dad if I found my mother."

Marilee marveled at how sensitive Logan was to his father's feelings. But then she reminded herself that Logan's compassion for others was the very quality that drew her to him in the first place.

"I'm just praying that if God intends for me to meet her, He'll orchestrate the whole thing—either that or He'll drop the means right into my lap. That way I won't have to worry about hurting my father for my own selfish purposes, and the Lord will get all the glory."

Marilee smiled. Logan Callahan was one terrific guy—one definitely worth waiting for!

*   *   *

Cynthia Matlock lay in the uncomfortable hospital bed, listening to the voices just outside her room. The door stood wide open. Did they think she was deaf? The two female attendants spoke about her as though she were already dead. "Pain-in-the-neck patient," they both called her. Well, the two of them were the lousiest excuses for caregivers she'd ever seen!

"Water!" Cynthia croaked. "I need water!"

A good minute passed and she cried out again. Finally, one of the women stepped back into her room.

"What part of 'no' don't you understand, Mrs. Matlock?" the dark-headed attendant asked with a bite in her voice. Her sharp, blue eyes sparked with one thing and one thing only—irritation.

"I'm thirsty. Don't you get it?"

The woman huffed. "You've got a G-tube, which means everything that goes in, comes out. No water. Only ice chips."

"I'm dying," Cynthia lamented. "How can you deny a dying person water?"

"Doctor's orders," she stated callously before exiting the room.

Alone once more, the story of her life, Cynthia cursed her two daughters for admitting her to this atrocious place!

CHAPTER FIVE

After a tour of Arbor Springs Healthcare Center, one of Lakewood Enterprises' facilities, Allie seated herself in the dining room across from Evan Jacobs, the company's CEO.

"Can I get you a cup of coffee?" he asked, "and maybe a sweet roll or something?"

"No, thanks. I'm fine," Allie fibbed. In truth, she wasn't "fine" at all. She felt depressed after seeing scores of elderly patients tied into wheelchairs and lined up in corridors on the second floor. Alzheimer's patients wandered the hallways on third, and cancer patients moaned in agony on the fourth. The wards were dark and dreary, and Allie had noticed that most patients wore miserable expressions as though they had been handed a life sentence and Arbor Springs was where they'd fulfill it. Allie found herself secretly hoping and praying that she'd never end up in one of these places.

You're going to have to help me through this, Lord Jesus. . . .

"Do you have any questions?"

Giving herself a mental shake, Allie looked across the table at the young man with reddish brown hair and bright hazel eyes. Smartly dressed in a suit and tie and an easy smile, Evan appeared just as chipper now as when they'd entered Arbor Springs. Obviously, he'd gotten used to the sights and sounds of this facility. But Allie wondered if she'd ever grow accustomed to them.

"I don't have any questions at the moment," she said at last, "but I'm sure that'll change once I get my bearings."

He chuckled. "Probably." Pulling several pieces of paper from his attaché case, he slid them across the table to Allie. "Let me give you some particulars."

"All right." She scrutinized the documents in front of her.

"First, you should know that we have about a hundred and ten patients in this facility. There are three distinct classifications of patients—elderly, subacute, and long-term. Many of our long-term patients are terminally ill; and unfortunately, most don't have family members who can take care of them or the income to hire someone, and that's why they're here."

"Why aren't they in hospitals or hospices?" Allie had to ask.

"Too expensive. That's the number one reason, but health insurance coverage might be an issue for them as well."

"I see. . . ."

"Now if you'll look at that next piece of paper I gave you," Evan continued, "you'll see a copy of the state's inspection. Officials came through several months ago; and as you'll notice, Arbor Springs got cited for some violations. Some of them have been corrected, but some haven't. That's why you're here, Mrs. Littenberg."

"Allie," she said, disliking the formality. "Please call me Allie."

"Okay, Allie it is."

He smiled, and Allie returned it.

Then she glanced over the report, noting the citations. They ranged from insufficient staffing to dietary and housekeeping concerns.

"The entire place has been spruced up since the inspection," Evan informed her. "It's been painted, wallpapered, carpeted in the visiting areas, and new flooring has been installed on each unit."

Allie nodded. She didn't have a problem with the facility's décor, per se, although she would prefer light-filtering blinds over the windows rather than the heavy draperies now covering them.

"I think what's needed here," Evan stated at last, "is some major reorganization. Once we've got that in place, our goal is to use Arbor Springs as a model for our other healthcare facilities. The most important thing is to avoid more citations and any fines." Evan cocked his head to one side. "Think this is something you'd like to tackle?"

"Yes, I think it is." Allie suddenly felt the familiar spring of determination well up from somewhere within her while a sense of purpose enveloped her. She could reorganize Arbor Springs. No problem. She specialized in reorganization. She'd had plenty of experience in other healthcare facilities, although she previously targeted billing and administrative offices. But this wasn't so different. And if she gave this job her all, she might even contribute to the happiness of Arbor Springs's residents.

*   *   *

Hours later, Allie acclimated herself with what would become her office for the next few months. Located on the first floor, it was down the hallway with the other administrative offices and physical therapy rooms and directly adjacent to the lobby. She had a window and a nice view of the small courtyard behind the facility. The environment was conducive to her success; and if all went well with this job—as she sensed it would—Allie figured she'd be home in California by Christmas. Perhaps Nick and Jennifer would be expecting a baby by that time.

A baby. . .

A new generation. . .and one whose beginnings would be

founded on God's Word, unlike my own. Unlike Nick's. . .

Allie couldn't help a wistful smile as she sifted through her desk, making a mental list of the supplies she'd need. Evan had told her to purchase any necessary items and turn in an expense report.

Glancing at her watch, she decided to duck out early. It might be her only day to do so. Starting tomorrow, Allie knew her hours would be consumed with interviewing each supervisor and his or her employees—and this facility ran three shifts, twenty-four hours a day, seven days a week.

Gathering her computer and handbag, she left Arbor Springs for the sunny, summer day. Climbing into the rental car, Allie tried to remember where she'd seen a discount office supply place.

And then she realized it: Arbor Springs Healthcare Center was halfway between the city of Chicago and Oakland Park.

No, I couldn't, she thought as an idea formed, and yet she wondered why not. There was still plenty of time before nightfall. What harm could there be in just cruising through the old neighborhood? Gorgeous day for a drive. . .

Allie started the engine and grinned. She hadn't had much chance to see Oakland Park the night she went to Steve and Nora's for dinner, and the opportunity didn't present itself to ask questions about her family members. Perhaps she'd find some answers today.

Lord, she prayed as she pulled onto the street, *I just want a few answers. I promise not to pry open any doors that You want to stay closed. But if there's restitution to be made, I'd like a chance at it. . . .*

The drive took her longer than she anticipated. She'd gotten caught in the late afternoon traffic and then wound up taking a wrong turn. It was nearly six o'clock when she finally entered the quiet neighborhood in which she had lived thirty years ago. Located about five miles away from the area in which

Steve and Nora resided, Allie was amazed at how much the same everything appeared. Oh, perhaps, the trees were taller and the houses sported a different color of paint than what she'd remembered. But overall, it seemed like the same old place.

Nostalgia filled her being as Allie parked the Cavalier and climbed out. She strolled to the edge of the front lawn, staring ahead at the two-story, brown stucco house in which she'd lived with her mother, stepfather, and stepsisters. She recalled vividly how each spring her mother used to plant marigolds in front of the hedges. In another flowerbed alongside the house, she'd plant an assortment of annuals, usually whatever she'd find on sale.

Funny, Allie thought, *how after thirty years and being almost a grandmother myself, I still miss my mom.*

Children's laughter wafted on the warm wind; and for a moment, Allie thought she'd imagined it—until a group of kids rounded the house, chasing each other. She smiled, watching their antics. She thought about her own son, Nick, and remembered when he was a boy. She had tried to shelter him from his father's unpredictable wrath as best she could, even sending him to boarding school during his elementary years. Consequently, she missed some very important times in her son's life. But Nick said he could live with it. He wasn't holding onto any baggage from his boyhood. Amazing how alike Logan Callahan and Nick were. . .

Allie heard car doors slam shut behind her. Startled from her reverie, she turned and saw none other than two of Oakland Park's finest coming her way.

One of the officers was Jack Callahan.

He narrowed his eyes. "I had a feeling I'd find you here. As soon as we got the call and I heard the address, I just had a feeling. . . ." He turned and muttered something to his partner, who ambled up the front porch steps and rang the doorbell.

Allie was confused. "What's going on?"

"The woman who lives in this house says you've been watching her kids for half an hour. She was afraid you were some weirdo, getting ready to nab them."

"Oh, that's ridic—"

Allie cut herself off short. Why wouldn't the woman think such a thing? In this day and age, a mother couldn't be too careful with her precious children.

Allie shook her head, glancing at her high-heeled feet and then bringing her gaze back to Jack. "I should have introduced myself and explained that I used to live here. . . ."

"Your family's long gone, Allie, and so are your friends," Jack said tersely. "You've got no business back in Oakland Park, and you know it."

The remark stung. So much so, it brought tears to her eyes. But, blinking back her emotion, she knew Jack spoke the truth.

"You're right. I guess I shouldn't have allowed myself the luxury of reminiscing."

"Sign of old age," Jack said, flipping his palm-size notebook open.

Allie smiled and took a few steps toward him. "I'm not afraid of growing old. Are you?"

He didn't reply, but kept writing in that little book of his.

"I hope to be a grandmother soon."

Finally pocketing the spiral-bound pad, he looked at her. "Bully for you. Now, you'd best be on your way."

"Sure," Allie said. With a parting glance at her former home, she headed toward the rented auto. Reaching the door, she turned back and, finding Jack's eyes on her, she decided to ask one more question.

Again, she walked in his direction. "Jack, do you have any idea what happened to my stepfather and stepsisters? Any idea where I might find them?"

Allie watched while he seemed to wrestle with something threatening to explode within him. She knew that look and took a step backward.

At last, Jack swallowed hard and said, "Your stepdad's most

likely dead. I heard he had cancer. . .that was about fifteen years ago. Brenda married someone she met in college, and Colleen married Royce Strobel. Remember him? Royce? He lived right up the block."

"Royce. . ." Allie searched her memory. "Oh, of course! The Strobels lived right over there," she said, pointing at a white, wood-framed home.

"Still live there. Mr. and Mrs. Strobel are in their eighties now."

Allie smiled. "So Colleen married the boy next door. . .well, almost next door. Three doors away." Suddenly she took note of Jack's scowl and her smile faded. "What's wrong?"

"You're what's wrong. Did it ever occur to you that you're about twenty-five years too late in coming back here? It's long past the time for happy reunions, Allie. Everyone's got his or her own life, and you're not part of them. But that was your decision. Remember?"

"Yes. . .I remember." Allie's heart twisted painfully. "And perhaps I am too late on some accounts. Maybe even on most accounts. But I refuse to believe that at least a few of the bridges I burned can't be rebuilt."

"Oh, I get it," he muttered. "You're trying to appease a guilty conscience. Well, did you ever consider the cost of that, Allie, or are you still thinking of only yourself? Everyone you once knew has gotten along perfectly fine without you for decades. Your dredging up the past isn't going to rebuild bridges. It's going to blow up in your face—and everyone else's, too. More hurt. Is that what you want? You want to cause more hurt?"

"Of course not." Folding her arms and feeling somewhat obstinate, Allie sensed Jack was speaking for himself more than he was protecting her former friends and family members. "I never hurt my stepfamily. I never hurt my friends. I couldn't deal with my circumstances thirty years ago, and I didn't even know how to try and begin. So I ran away. It's as simple as that." Letting her arms fall to her side, she faced Jack once more. "I was very young, Jack." She paused, praying that somehow her words would begin to mend his heart. "I'm sorry I hurt you. More sorry than you'll ever know." Allie wanted to add that he'd hurt her, too, but decided now wasn't the time. She'd start with an apology and go from there.

Jack stared at her hard, and Allie saw the steely glint in his dark eyes. "Kind of a trite little speech there, Mrs. *Littenberg*."

She brought her chin back at the sharp reply, shocked and disappointed in that Jack refused to forgive her.

"Hey, Sarg, everything's cool with Mrs. Patterson," Jack's partner told him, coming to stand at his side. He was a young man who looked as eager to please as a puppy.

"Great, then let's get something to eat. I'm starved." Jack gave Allie a rigid glare. "Go back to California or wherever you came from. There's nothing for you here. In fact," he added, opening the door to the squad car, "there probably never was."

Moments later, Allie watched the vehicle pull away from the curb and drive off down the peaceful, suburban street. She felt discouraged. More than discouraged. She felt downright dismayed. What if Jack was right? Had she made a mistake in returning to Illinois?

The summer breeze suddenly held a chill, and Allie shivered. Pivoting, she walked back to her car; but as she opened the door and prepared to slide in behind the wheel, she heard a light, but decidedly female voice hailing her from off in a distance. Glancing to her right, she saw an elderly woman waving at her.

Allie smiled. "Mrs. Strobel," she said under her breath, although she wouldn't have recognized the woman under any other circumstances. But since she'd obviously emerged from the home in which the Strobels had lived ever since Allie could remember, it had to be her.

Closing the car door, Allie headed toward the old woman.

"Allison Drake. What a surprise," she stated when Allie

reached her. "And then when I saw you talking to our very own Officer Callahan. . .why it took me back a whole generation!"

Allie laughed in spite of herself. "I'm sure it did."

The old lady held out blue-lined, arthritic hands, and Allie took them in hers.

"It's good to see you again, Mrs. Strobel."

"It's good to see you, too, Dear." A little sigh escaped her. "My, but it's been so very long, hasn't it?"

"Yes."

"Will you come in for awhile and tell us what you've been doing with yourself? Where do you live now?"

"California. . .and, sure, I'll come in and visit awhile."

Together, they strolled up to the front door.

"I understand Colleen married Royce," Allie said.

"Oh, yes, and they're very happy. They've had their share of ups and downs, of course. Haven't we all? But, truly, they're doing fine. Three children, two girls and a boy. . .all in college now."

"Is that right?" Allie paused beside the woman just inside the door. "Say, Mrs. Strobel. . .do you think Colleen would. . . well, do you think she'd want to see me again? I'd like to see her, but I don't want to. . .to dredge up any bad memories," she said, borrowing Jack's verbiage.

"I'd love to see you, Allie."

Turning sharply, Allie suddenly came face-to-face with her stepsister.

CHAPTER SIX

Colleen Strobel gave Allie such an exuberant hug that it brought tears to her eyes. She knew she didn't deserve the welcome, but she was thankful for the bit of encouragement. Perhaps she hadn't made a mistake coming back here after all.

"Let's all sit down, shall we?" the older woman suggested, leading Allie and Colleen away from the front hall. "Philip's asleep on the sofa and I don't want to wake him," she said, referring to her husband. "A cup of tea sounds good, doesn't it? I'll set the kettle to boiling."

Entering the kitchen, wallpapered in gray plaid accented with bright red cherries, Allie seated herself at the table, across from Colleen. She noticed the kitchen set was fashioned after the old 1950s dinettes, right down to the chrome and red vinyl chairs.

"This is a charming room," Allie remarked, glancing around the spacious room. "So quaint."

"We redid it last year," Colleen said.

"But it probably doesn't look like it, because Colleen likes old-fashioned stuff, and she's rubbing off on me. For instance, I never would have thought I'd buy one of these kitchen sets," Mrs. Strobel said with a laugh. "My mother had a table and chairs much like these in her kitchen." She shook her gray head. "And now they're back in style. Who would have ever thought?"

Allie smiled and glanced at her stepsister. Time had filled out the once skinny teenager who liked cheerleading and gymnastics. "Catch me up, Colleen," Allie said. "Tell me about yourself and your family."

"Well, let's see. . ." The brunette, whose hair was graying at the temples, grew pensive. "Where should I start?"

"What happened after I left?"

"Nothing right away, I guess. Brenda and I finished high school and went to college. Dad remarried."

"Is he still alive?" Allie asked.

Colleen shook her head. "He died of cancer."

"I'm so sorry."

"It was a long time ago. My kids were still in grade school. But I'm glad they got to know their grandfather for a little while."

Allie nodded, saddened by the fact that she would never be able to make amends with her stepfather. That opportunity had escaped her.

"After college, I got married first," Colleen said. "Then Brenda. We both sent you invitations."

"You did?" Allie shook her head. "I never got them."

"I called your dad in California and got your married name and address. When we didn't hear from you on both occasions, Brenda and I just figured you weren't interested in coming."

"Oh, Colleen, I don't know if I would have come or not, but I honestly didn't receive the invitations. I suspect my husband intercepted them and didn't pass them on to me. That was rather typical."

"Are you still married, Allie?" Colleen wanted to know.

She shook her head. "Widowed."

Mrs. Strobel gasped. "At such a young age? How sad."

Allie shrugged and picked at an imaginary piece of lint on her black linen skirt. She didn't want to sound heartless and say that Erich's death had set her free. But it was the truth.

"Hey, Jack's available." Colleen laughed, and Allie looked up in time to see a spark of mischief in her stepsister's hazel eyes.

"Jack can't stand me. He told me to go back where I came from."

"He said that? Oh, man!" Colleen wagged her head from side to side as if she couldn't believe what she'd heard. "Well, I like Jack. He and Royce play on the same baseball team. But Jack's got issues. You probably don't want to get involved with him anyhow, Allie."

"He's a different man today, that's for sure."

"Yeah, he is."

"I'm determined not to feel guilty, but sometimes I think it's my fault."

"Allie, you have no control over the actions of others. I mean, maybe you did hurt Jack. Everyone knows he was crazy about you. But I think a lot of Jack's problem happened when he got married. I heard his wife ran off with another guy while he was working and she left their baby at home alone. That would devastate anybody—and it had lasting effects. Jack was stuck with a kid to raise."

"How did he ever get involved with a woman like his ex in the first place?" Allie asked. "Do you know?"

"Same way he got involved with you," Colleen quipped. "He felt sorry for her and wanted to save her soul."

Allie had to laugh—it was either that or sob. Thirty years ago, Jack had loved people. To him, they were precious souls. He volunteered regularly at a rescue mission for alcoholics and drug addicts in downtown Chicago. He led scores of men to Christ. He reached out to her, Blythe, and Wendy, and, obviously, to his ex-wife. Allie had no trouble envisioning the scenario.

"And you should see Jack's son," Colleen said as Mrs. Strobel set a steaming, porcelain teapot on the table. "He's a chip off the old block."

Allie smiled. "Yes, I know. I've met Logan. Steve and Nora invited me over for a barbecue the first night I arrived in town."

"It never fails," the older woman stated, settling into a chair. "Whenever I see Jack's boy, I always call him by his father's name. Can't seem to help it."

"Logan's a fine young man," Allie said.

"A minister, isn't he?" Colleen asked.

She nodded.

"I hope he's got more sense around women than his dad."

"Thanks a heap, Sis," Allie retorted, wearing a little grin.

"Oh, I didn't mean you, Silly. I meant Roxi. His ex-wife."

Allie frowned. "Did we know her? Did she go to the same high school?"

"I didn't know her. I don't think she was from around here. Someone told me she was a floozy and that Jack met her when the cops raided a tavern that used to be on the edge of town."

"Lovely." Allie couldn't help the sarcasm as she gratefully accepted the cup of tea Mrs. Strobel had poured.

"Now, girls," the older woman said as if Allie and Colleen were teenagers instead of pushing fifty, "he must have seen some redeeming quality in his ex-wife. Jack was an upstanding man. . .still is, in my book. Who doesn't make mistakes?"

"You're right, Mrs. Strobel," Allie said, feeling properly chastened. "You're absolutely right. Who doesn't make mistakes?"

*   *   *

The pain had once more become unbearable.

"Help me! Help me!" Cynthia Matlock cried, hoping some-one would hear her. She felt as though she'd been calling out for hours. But no one came. "Help me! Help me!"

At last, the door of her room opened and a male attendant walked in. He stood at least six feet in height with broad shoulders and a straight back. His eyes were a lively bluish green, and Cynthia guessed his hair would be a nice shade of light brown if he hadn't shaved his head completely bald. "What are you hollering about?" he asked briskly.

Wasn't there a compassionate heart anywhere in this place? She wondered. Well, that would be her daughters' doing. They had made sure she wound up in the worst place possible, and Cynthia figured they would be pleased to know her dying days were filled with pain and suffering.

"What do you want?"

"Some pain medication," Cynthia rasped. "And water. I need water."

"No water. You've been told that before."

The man turned to go.

"Wait! Help me! Help me!"

Ignoring her pleas, he left.

At that moment, Cynthia hated the whole world and everyone in it. She couldn't wait to die.

But minutes later, the attendant returned and, to her surprise and relief, he held a syringe in one of his gloved hands. Good. He'd brought the pain medication. However, he inserted the needle into her flesh with such force that Cynthia screamed, feeling the tube in the back of her throat reverberate.

"Shut up, old lady."

With that, the nurse departed, leaving Cynthia in tears.

She'd heard it said that before people die, their lives sometimes flash before their eyes. Cynthia's life wasn't exactly "flashing," but segments played over in her head like reruns on TV—reruns she was unable to turn off with a switch.

In her mind's eye, she envisioned the small town in Iowa in which she'd grown up. Her parents, John and Esther Taylor, were farmers and had great aspirations for their oldest daughter. According to their plans, she would be the first in their family to attend college. But Cynthia had her own ideas. She wanted excitement. Adventure. College could wait.

Then one night, she ran off with Tom Addison, the local "troublemaker," according to the church-going folks in town. The year was 1965, and Tom was dodging the draft, saying there was no way he'd go to 'Nam. To Cynthia's fifteen-year-old way of thinking, defying the United States government sounded like a grand escapade, so she decided to dodge the draft with him.

But they'd gotten caught at the Canadian border, and Cynthia was sent back home. Alas, the ordeal caused quite a stir in town and brought shame to her parents—a fact they never let her forget for years to come.

Finally, at age nineteen, Cynthia left home for good. Not for college, but for the bright lights and excitement of Chicago. She changed her name and found work in a tavern, serving food and drinks. Sometimes she even sang with the jukebox and entertained the patrons. That's what she'd wanted—a stage career; however, it never came to pass the way she'd envisioned.

Eventually she found her way into an escort service where Cynthia made more money than she knew what to do with. Young, pretty, and sought after, she quickly learned how to please a man. As a result, she kept her customers coming back for more.

Ah, yes, those were the days, Cynthia thought as the narcotic worked its magic on her failing body. At that point in her life she had money. She had power.

Now all she had was pain.

*   *   *

Walking down the hallway, Logan spotted Marilee leading her class outside for recess. When she saw him, she waved a greeting.

"Forsooth, fair maiden, your presence here at the castle warms this knight's heart," he said in a Shakespearean accent. He topped off his theatrics with a gallant bow.

"This isn't a castle," one little girl in pigtails was quick to point out. "This is just a plain ol' school."

Shouts of agreement went up from the munchkin mob.

Marilee now wore a pretty blush and her dimples winked at Logan. "Oh, never mind Pastor Callahan, boys and girls. He likes to joke around a lot. That's why he's the youth pastor."

He frowned, unsure of whether he'd just been insulted.

"I can't wait till I'm in the youth group," one of the boys said, pushing up his glasses. Logan tousled the kid's dark hair, but the childish expression of adoration didn't go unnoticed. "My sister says you're the best youth pastor ever!"

"I'm glad she thinks so. I have Jesus to thank for that."

Despite his upbeat reply, Logan cast a troubled glance at Marilee. The teenage girls in the youth group were becoming a problem. But she merely smiled back. "He is the best youth pastor ever, Michael," she said. "Now get back in line or there'll be no recess this afternoon."

Logan saluted and clicked his heels together, and the children giggled and hooted. Then, once he felt like he'd caused Marilee enough havoc, he went on his way.

Chuckling to himself, he had to confess that he enjoyed pestering Marilee whenever they ran into each other in the hallways. It was his personal challenge to get her to blush; and once the mission was accomplished, he felt a special little joy in his heart that words couldn't describe.

He returned to the church office suites, where five teenage girls were cutting out postcards for an upcoming outreach, which consisted of volleyball on the beach and a bonfire afterwards. He planned to have a few of the teens give their salvation testimonies; and afterward, one of the senior high guys could preach a short message. Of course, there would be plenty of food—he couldn't entertain teenagers without it!

"All done?" he asked the girls. They were sitting around a table in the conference room across from his office. "Nice of you ladies to use your study hall to help me out."

"Hey, this beats boring textbooks any day; and to answer

your question, yes, we're all done," Kim Bernette said, swinging strands of her blond hair over her shoulder. Then she looked up at Logan, and he didn't miss the dreamy spark in her blue eyes. "Anything else you'd like done?"

"Ah. . .no. Nothing. Thanks." *Oh, good grief,* Logan thought. *Here we go.*

He'd been informed that several of the youth group girls had "crushes" on him, but Logan hadn't wanted to believe it. However, he believed it now. . .ever since they started flocking into his office during their seventh-hour study hall, asking if they could "help" with anything. "I think that's it for today. I appreciate your assistance. You gals can go back to the library for the remainder of your study hall."

"Don't you need some filing done?" Heidi Lutz asked. A petite, somewhat pudgy young lady, she stood and looked up at him with hopeful brown eyes.

"Um. . ."

"Your desk is kind of messy," redheaded and freckle-faced Sabina Lewis pointed out. "I could stay and straighten it for you."

"Kind of you to offer, but that's not really a mess you see in there," he said, looking over his shoulder.

"It isn't? What do you call it?" Kim wanted to know.

"It's a collection of organized piles. I know exactly what's in each one, too. So if you clean it up, I'll be lost."

The girls burst into giggles.

"Okay," Logan said, smiling in spite of himself, "back to study hall with you. Scoot. Go on." He held the door of the church office suites open for them.

The girls complied, albeit grudgingly. But he breathed a sigh of relief once they were gone.

"Looks like you've got some groupies on your hands, Pastor."

Logan paused in the threshold of his office in time to see Mrs. McMillan, the church secretary, leaning over her desk and grinning at him.

"Yeah, it appears that way, doesn't it?"

"Well, not to worry. I'm going to start collecting work for them. I spend a couple hours each day at the copy machine, copying and collating various documents. It's a perfect job for those girls, don't you think? It'll sure free me up."

"That's a marvelous idea. You're a genius."

The older woman laughed. "No, I just have a daughter in the youth group. . .and she's a groupie, too."

Logan groaned.

"But I've forbidden her to come in here and make a nuisance of herself. She really needs her study hall to. . .well, study."

"Imagine that. I didn't think anyone studied during study hall." Logan chuckled.

"Pastor, if you don't mind me saying so," Mrs. McMillan said, wearing a suddenly solemn expression, "a wife would really deter these girls."

Logan let out a weary sigh. "I'm working on it," he said, entering his office. "I'm working on it."

CHAPTER SEVEN

Allie looked around the extended-stay suite she'd moved into over the Labor Day weekend. Almost within walking distance to the healthcare facility in which she now worked, the room was complete with a small sitting area, sofa, armchair, small round table and two wooden chairs, a partitioned-off bedroom, kitchenette, and bathroom. As she began to tidy up, she tried to decide if she should accept Nora's picnic invitation. There was a chance Jack would show up, and Allie really wanted to stay out of the guy's way.

On the other hand, Nora said he rarely showed, even though he was invited year after year.

Deciding to brave the picnic, figuring it beat sitting in her hotel room alone on this gorgeous, sunny day, Allie headed for the shower. Afterwards, she dressed in a denim skirt and a blue-and-white-striped, short-sleeved sweater. She brushed out her hair and applied her cosmetics, adding concealing cream to her unsightly scar. With that completed, she slipped her feet into comfortable, navy leather flats, grabbed her purse, and left the hotel.

As she drove to Oakland Park, Allie reflected on this past week at Arbor Springs. After conducting several interviews, it didn't take her long to discover she was in over her head. She met opposition at every turn, largely because the nursing staff resented her for not having a medical background. Every one of the nurses and nurses' aides stated that he or she was "overworked and underpaid" and that the upper echelons in administration didn't care as long as the Medicare and Medicaid funds kept rolling in. To a point, Allie understood their frustrations. But she felt powerless to help them because the majority of the staff had poor attitudes and was unwilling to cooperate with the reorganization process.

Now, what do I do, Heavenly Father? Allie prayed. After several long moments, she finally relaxed. God would show her; He always did.

*   *   *

Jack grumbled as he pulled on his blue jeans and wondered how he'd let Logan talk him into showing up at Steve and Nora's picnic today. Well, that's not exactly true; he knew how Logan had gotten to him.

"Aw, c'mon, Dad. It'll be fun. Besides, I want you to get better acquainted with Marilee. I want to pop the question soon, and—"

"I met her," Jack countered. "She's a nice girl. What more do you want me to say? It's your life."

Logan had turned pensive. "I just don't want to make a mistake," he said at last.

Like you did.

Those three unspoken words hung between father and son until Jack felt the bile rise up into his throat.

"You're a smart guy, Logan. Just listen to. . .well, you know. . .God. Listen to God. You're in the ministry, after all."

"I trust the Lord each step of the way, but I'd still appreciate your input. Can't you just show up for an hour or so? You're not working today. When's the last time you had a holiday off and enjoyed it with your family?"

"All right! All right!" Jack held up his hands to forestall further argument. "I'll come."

Logan had grinned from ear to ear. "Great. I'll see you there." On that note, he'd left the condo.

But that was nearly two hours ago, and Jack supposed it was high time he got himself in gear and made his promised appearance.

"Man, that Logan is one persistent kid," Jack groused, pulling a red cotton crewneck sweater over his head.

Kind of like his old man.

Jack straightened and stared hard into the mirror. Just as quickly, he looked away, afraid he might see a trace of the man he once used to be.

The past is dead and gone. Can't change it. Just got to go on. He'd been giving himself those lines for three decades, and one of these days they were bound to sink in.

Sitting on the edge of his bed, Jack put on his athletic shoes and tied the laces. Between Logan living here and talking about the Lord all the time and Allie coming to town last week, stirring up all kinds of trouble, Jack felt like he was losing his grip on his tightly reined-in emotions.

Those two are going to make me crazy.

With a sigh, he stood, slid his wallet off the top of the polished bureau, and pocketed it. Lifting his car keys, he headed for the side door, leading into the attached garage. He had a sneaking suspicion that Allie would be at the picnic this afternoon, which made him dread the outing all the more. That woman had a lot of nerve, showing up after all these years.

And she said she was sorry. . .

Jack inhaled a contemptuous snort as he climbed into his

black Ford Explorer. Sorry didn't even begin to cut it, and he viewed Allie's act of contrition to that of a rapist apologizing to his victim years later. No, there were just some things in life that a person couldn't take back—and didn't he know that firsthand?

Nevertheless, he'd show up at this picnic today—Allie or no Allie. Jack had given his word to Logan. He'd make an appearance, just as he said.

*   *   *

The sunshine warmed Marilee's face, neck, and arms as she sat beside Allie at the picnic table. Off in the distant part of the backyard, Logan set up a volleyball net for the kids.

"I hope he doesn't want me to play," Marilee muttered. "I'm exhausted." She turned from watching Logan to face Allie. "After the first week of school, my third graders succeeded in tuckering me right out."

"You're just out of practice," Allie replied with a smile. "You'll soon be back into the swing of things."

"Thanks for the vote of confidence, Mrs. Littenberg."

"Call me Allie. Mrs. Littenberg has always been my mother-in-law."

Marilee smiled. "Okay. . .but don't you like sharing your mother-in-law's name?"

"Oh, well. . . ," Allie hedged, "I wasn't ever close to my mother-in-law, but she's a terrific grandmother to my son, Nick. Spoils him rotten."

"Is she a Christian?"

"No, but amazingly enough, she and my father-in-law financially support Nick's ministry."

"Your son's in the ministry?"

Allie nodded. "Yes, and I'm so very proud of him, as you probably can tell." She laughed. "Except, Nick's talking about becoming a missionary to Germany—that's where his father and grandparents are from. I would really hate to see him and his darling wife go."

"I can understand that." Marilee tipped her head and regarded the other woman whose eyes were such a vibrant blue that they rivaled the cloudless sky above. "Does your daughter-in-law like to be called Mrs. Littenberg?"

"Probably not." Allie laughed. "Although, she and I have a special relationship—and she and my son are in love and very happily married. I guess therein lies the difference."

Marilee opened her mouth to ask another question; but before a single word could escape, a large man in a pink and green Hawaiian shirt descended upon them.

"I'm Paul Baer," he said. "I'm Steve and Nora's next-door neighbor."

"Nice to meet you," Allie replied with a polite and dignified air. "I'm Allie Littenberg and this is Marilee. . ."

"Domotor," Marilee quickly put in. "A pleasure to meet you, Mr. Baer."

"Well, thanks, ladies," he said with a jovial grin as he pulled up a lawn chair.

It creaked beneath his enormous weight, and Marilee feared the netting would burst. However, Mr. Baer didn't seem the least bit worried as he raked beefy fingers through his jet black hair.

"My wife passed a few months ago," he announced, his smile fading to a frown, "and so when Steve invited me over this afternoon, I decided to take him up on his offer. It's been real hard on me, having my wife gone, you know? I mean after being married for twenty-nine years, I'm suddenly a bachelor again."

Marilee gave the man a sympathetic grin, then looked over at Allie, whose features were etched with compassion.

"I'm very sorry for your loss, Mr. Baer," Allie said.

"Oh, you can call me Paul." His grin returned. "And, thanks. . . I mean for being sorry and all. It's real hard."

"I can imagine. My husband died about eleven years ago."

"Really? So you know what I'm going through."

Allie nodded.

"I didn't realize you're a widow, Mrs. Lit— I mean, Allie," Marilee said.

She replied with a tiny smile and another nod of her blond head.

"How'd he die?" Paul Baer asked, leaning forward.

Marilee felt a twinge of embarrassment for Allie, who'd just been put on the spot.

But she replied very matter-of-factly, "He was in a yachting accident in South America."

"Goodness!" Marilee gasped.

"My husband was an art dealer, and. . .well, he dealt in other things, too. Things that weren't legal. His lifestyle caught up to him."

"Wow," Paul said, "sounds like a double-O-seven flick." Slapping the knee of his huge khaki pants, he hooted.

Allie laughed as well. "Hardly double-O-seven."

"Were you there?" Marilee couldn't help asking. "When it happened, were you there?" After a pause, she quickly amended. "If I'm out of line asking such a thing—"

"It's quite all right," Allie said, touching the top of Marilee's hand. "No, I wasn't there when it happened. I never accompanied my husband on his business trips. But I was forced to help the authorities after his death. They searched our home and everything in it looking for evidence. For a time, they even thought I was part of Erich's illegal operation, and I had FBI agents following me everywhere. But Erich never told me anything, and I was as shocked as everyone else to learn what he'd gotten involved in. I guess you might say that, in my case, ignorance was truly bliss."

"Still, that had to be a very trying time," Marilee declared.

"Actually, no. I knew I had nothing to hide and that God would protect me. . .and He did. It was more a gross inconvenience than anything else."

"Steve and Nora talked to my wife about God before she

died," Paul said. "It was a real comfort to her, I know."

Marilee smiled at the man, then glanced out over the back-yard to where Logan was assembling a small group for volleyball. At that moment, their gazes met and Marilee felt her insides turn to mush the way they always did when Logan looked at her.

"Marilee," he called, "c'mon over. Game's about to start."

Tired as she felt, Marilee couldn't find it in her heart to refuse the request. She loved Logan so much that she'd play volleyball until she dropped if it meant she could spend time with him.

"I guess volleyball's in my future after all," she said to Allie while standing from the picnic bench.

"Have fun."

"Thanks."

As Marilee walked away, she heard Paul Baer begin to speak about his deceased wife again. She died of cancer. She'd been sick for a long while. He'd been doing all the laundry for the past six months, but he still didn't know how to cook very well. . . .

Allie's a better woman than I am, Marilee thought. After all, it took someone special to sit and patiently listen while a guy like Paul unloaded his burdens. In that moment, Allie Littenberg had won Marilee's utmost respect.

*   *   *

"Who's the dude following Allie around like a puppy?" Jack couldn't help asking his brother before taking another bite of his grilled bratwurst.

"Oh, that's Paul Baer, our next-door neighbor. His wife died not too long ago, and he's really lonely."

"He's been making a pest out of himself with Allie for the past hour," Nora said from where she sat on the other side of the picnic table next to Steve. "But Allie's being a good sport about it."

"The guy talks nonstop," Steve added. "But he's all right."

"Hmm. . ." Jack allowed his gaze to roam the backyard. Near a volleyball net, he spotted Logan and his girlfriend sitting on the grass, eating their picnic lunch. Steve and Nora's three kids surrounded them. Allie sat off in a lawn chair with her newfound friend practically fastened to her side.

Allie's keeping her distance. Good. Jack forked some potato salad into his mouth.

After he'd parked his SUV in front of Steve's house, he'd noticed Allie's car, so he knew she'd come to the picnic today. . . just as he presumed. But she'd managed to stay out of his way, helping Nora in the kitchen and keeping that blubbering neighbor occupied.

"Steve, call those two over here to socialize with us," Nora said. "I feel sorry for Allie. Paul isn't her responsibility."

"Allie's a big girl," Jack replied. "She can hold her own."

"She's trying to be polite," Nora argued.

"Hey, Paul and Allie," Steve bellowed, causing Jack to scowl, "why don't you two join us? And Logan and Marilee," he added, swinging around on the bench. "Hey, kids! We're requesting your presence over here."

As the group assembled, Jack was forced to move over and make room for his seventeen-year-old niece, Veronica, and his nephew, Ricky, who insisted he be called "Rick" now that he was thirteen. Jack's youngest niece, Rachel, plastered herself against his back and wrapped her arms around his neck.

"Rachel, your uncle is trying to eat," Nora reprimanded.

"She's okay," Jack muttered.

"Yeah, Uncle Jack doesn't mind if I try to choke him while he's eating," the girl quipped before giggling into his neck.

Jack grinned before glancing over his shoulder where, just inches away, Rachel's pointy, little chin was digging into his back.

But she was right; he didn't mind. For whatever reason, Rachel adored him. Even as an infant, she would always want "uppy" from her uncle Jack; and then she'd snuggle into his arms when he granted her request. As she grew, she developed a plucky little personality that Jack found amusing; and he had to admit, he adored Rachel right back.

"When are you coming to my school to talk about being a policeman?"

"I already came to your school," Jack said, finishing his bratwurst.

"But my class forgot what you said."

"They did?" Turning his head, Jack eyed his young niece. "I'm wounded."

Rachel rolled her blue-green eyes. "Not me, Uncle Jack. My class."

"Oh, well, that's different." He looked over at Steve and grinned. Next, he reached over his shoulder and lovingly tweaked Rachel's nose. "Okay, tell you what. . .have your teacher call the station and ask for me, and I'll see what I can work out."

"Yes!" she cried triumphantly as her anaconda-hold around Jack's neck tightened.

"Well, don't come to my school," Veronica said facetiously. "I wish my friends didn't know that my uncle is a cop."

"Oh? Got something to hide?"

"No." Roni flicked several strands of her long, nut brown hair over her slender shoulder. "It's just that everywhere I go it seems like the Oakland Park cops are watching me. I can't even have fun at a football game without one of the officers coming up to me and saying, 'Hey, aren't you Sergeant Callahan's niece?' And then there's the fact that my cousin is my youth pastor. I can't even go to church in peace." The young lady exhaled an indignant sigh. "I'm sick of it."

"Well, what's your idea of fun and peace?" Jack had to ask.

A tsk came from Veronica's tongue. "Nothing illegal or immoral, if that's what you're implying. I'm a Christian and so are my friends."

"So? Just because you're a Christian doesn't mean anything."

Veronica rewarded Jack with a look of disgust.

"You know, I always felt kind of important when I was in

high school," Logan said, making himself comfy in a nearby lawn chair. His girlfriend sat in the chair beside him. "All the cops knew who I was, and it had its perks." He grinned. "I used to get rides home in a squad car after football games and the other kids had to walk."

"Big deal," Veronica replied, looking unimpressed. "I think it's. . .well, an invasion of our privacy to have the cops watching my friends and me just because I'm your niece," she said with a pointed stare at Jack.

He gave her a wink. "I feel real sorry for you."

"Sure you do," Veronica grumbled.

"Hey, I'll have you know I pay a lot of taxes to have the cops keep an eye on you," Steve told his daughter.

After another exasperated sigh, Veronica got up and left the picnic table. Entering the house, she slammed the back door behind her.

"She's gone crazy," Steve said in an apologetic tone as he looked at Jack.

"Don't worry, Logan was just as crazy when he was seventeen." Jack glanced at his son. "We used to argue all the time."

Logan groaned and shook his head. "We sure did. Guess I wasn't the model teenager."

Suddenly those years flashed before his eyes. "Aw, you were a pretty good kid, considering the fact I wasn't around much and, well, there was a lot going on."

"True enough," Logan replied.

Jack picked at the pears in his red Jell-O, aware that Allie was now sitting close by and listening to him interact with his family members. Talk about an "invasion of privacy"!

"My wife and I never had kids," Paul said. "She couldn't conceive for whatever reason. We talked about adopting children, but nothing ever came of it. After awhile, Jeannie was content with just taking care of me." He chuckled. "Guess I'm a big kid."

His back to the large man, Jack rolled his eyes just as Rachel reached over and helped herself to several of his potato chips. She crunched on them in his ear and earned a look of reproof from her mother.

"Say, Allie," Paul said, "do you think you'd go out with me? I haven't had a date in thirty years, but I think I still remember what to do."

"Oh, well, um. . ."

Oh, brother! Jack thought, grimacing; and in that moment, he didn't know which of the two he pitied the most. But after a moment's deliberation, questions came to mind. How could she go out with him? Wasn't Allie married?

"I'll have to check my schedule," he heard her reply.

Guess she's not. Jack's curiosity was now piqued, but he tamped it down. Allie wasn't any concern of his.

"Paul, Allie's here on business," Steve said, obviously trying to dissuade the guy, "so she's really, really busy."

"I understand," the neighbor replied, although Steve's remark didn't put him off in the least. "What about tomorrow night, Allie? Do you like bowling? Square dancing? We could go square dancing on Friday night."

Jack let go of a hearty laugh at the thought of the whale of a man square dancing. And if he remembered correctly, Allie had little to no coordination in that area. The idea of the two together on a dance floor was hilarious!

Peeling Rachel's arms from around his neck, he turned on the bench and set the girl down beside him. "Hey, Allie, when's the last time you went square dancing?"

She seemed to search her memory for the answer. "I don't know," she said at last. "Gym class my senior year in high school?" She chuckled under her breath. "I think I flunked."

Jack laughed once more. "I think you did, too."

Allie's blue eyes expressed her surprise, and Jack lowered his gaze, feeling chagrined. Those words had flown right out of his mouth. The worse part was, he knew Logan sat nearby taking in the entire scene. No doubt, it would fuel his son's curiosity.

Jack cursed inwardly, rubbing his jaw. He wished Allie would go back to California and stay there.

"Oh, I love to square dance," Paul said, oblivious to the sudden undercurrent. "Course, I haven't done it in years. But Jeannie and I used to go every other Friday night, and we were members of the American Square Dancing Association. I headed up the local chapter here in Illinois for awhile."

"Well, isn't that something." Jack did his best to recover and sound interested. Then he looked over at Allie again in spite of himself.

*　　*　　*

Trying to imagine Paul square dancing, she had to smile. The man reminded her of the former comedian, John Candy, and there was something very lovable about him. Perhaps it was the fact that he seemed like such a helpless creature since his wife died. Even so, Allie knew she couldn't go out with him. She'd made a promise to herself—and God—shortly after Erich died that she would never date for dating's sake. She would only accept a man's invitation to dinner, the theater, and so forth if she felt a nudge in her spirit from the Lord.

Although no meaningful relationships had come of it, other blessings had. Allie always figured a woman couldn't ever have too many friends.

Ironically enough, that had once been Jack's philosophy, too. He hadn't believed in casual dating. To this day, she could recall him sitting at the counter in that rundown café in downtown Chicago, telling her all about the Lord. . . .

Allie lifted her gaze and came face-to-face with the very object of her thoughts. She wondered what he was thinking as he regarded her. Did he even suspect that his remark about her gym class had thrown her? Well, it had; but it also gave her a semblance of hope that Jack Callahan wasn't as coldhearted as he'd like her to believe.

Doubt suddenly filled Allie. She'd thought the same of Erich, too, before they were married. . . .

"So tell me about this American Square Dancing Society," Jack said, returning his attention to Paul. He leaned forward, elbows resting on his knees. "I never knew such an organization existed."

"The SDS? Oh, sure. It's been around forever. Well, not really forever. Since 1936. . ."

As Paul began to recite the story of the club's inception, Allie smoothed her denim skirt over her knees. A heartbeat later, she saw Nora out of the corner of her eye and glanced in her direction. The brunette pointed toward the house and beckoned Allie to follow her.

Standing, Allie tried to be discreet in her exit. When she deemed her move a success, she quickened her pace.

Nora held the patio door open for her. "You poor thing."

Allie frowned. "Who, me?"

"Yes, you—putting up with both Jack and Paul. I wouldn't be surprised if you never speak to me again."

"Don't be silly. Everything's fine."

Chapter Eight

Cynthia screamed as the male attendant lifted her by the hair into a sitting position. She swore at him, and he swore right back, calling her every name imaginable. Then, he whacked her across the face with the urine-saturated pad that he had been summoned to change.

With shaking fingers, she wiped the sickening moisture from her cheek. "I'm filing a complaint!" she yelled into the dark-skinned face looming above her. "I'm not afraid of you or anybody else." She inhaled, an act that took great effort. "Someone is going to hear about this!"

"You wanna complain?" the man said, "Sure, go ahead, and you can jest stay the way you are until tomorrow morning when administration gets in. How's that?"

With a jolt of her hair, he pushed her back into the bed, sending knife-piercing pain through Cynthia's neck and down her spine. "You can't leave me like this, you moron!"

The words, however, were lost on the attendant, who stalked

out of the room. But he left the door wide open, and Cynthia could hear strains of a familiar television show. She heard laughter, no doubt from the nurses, who idled their shift away. They hated to be bothered; she had learned that much.

More laughter from beyond her dank room, and Cynthia overheard her assailant telling his coworkers how he was going to "tame that crazy old lady in room eight."

She fought back a tear. Wasn't there a single, compassionate soul in this entire unit?

Lying in the open air, cold and exposed, Cynthia wondered why she wasn't dead yet. The doctors had said she "didn't have long," and her health had deteriorated to a point where her daughters couldn't—no, make that wouldn't—care for her anymore.

"Curse them, those wretched girls," Cynthia said aloud, gritting her teeth and staring at the water-stained ceiling. "Curse them! Curse them! Curse them!"

*   *   *

Allie finished cutting up a fat, juicy watermelon and set its pieces onto a large plastic platter.

"Oh, that's great, Allie," Nora said. "I'll take the melon outside along with this pan of brownies."

"Well, save some for me. I'll be out as soon as I wash my hands."

Nora laughed. "You got it."

Walking the short distance to the sink, Allie turned on the water, pumped a squirt of soap into her palms, and made quick work of the task. She grabbed the apple-printed hand towel, dried off, and hung it back up. As she stepped around the corner, she met Jack on his way in.

"Beware, Paul's still out there," he said, opening the fridge and blocking her path.

"Oh, Paul doesn't bother me. He's harmless."

"Not if he takes you out on the dance floor." Laughing, Jack shut the refrigerator door, a cola in his hand.

He popped the tab on the can, while Allie shook her head at him. His humor hadn't changed much, except for its biting edge.

"How'd you get that scar on your cheek?" he asked after taking a swig.

Allie froze, trying not to let on how much the question stunned her. She resisted the urge to bring her hand up and hide the mar. Truth to tell, she'd expected someone to ask about it. It was inevitable. When people began to get acquainted, they became curious. Even so, Allie had assumed it would be Nora to inquire, not Jack.

Lifting her chin, she chose to be as direct as he. "My husband filleted my cheek."

Now it was his turn at surprise. His brown eyes widened, and he held the cola in his mouth before swallowing it down with a gulp. "Nice guy," he said at last. "Did you divorce him?"

"No."

"No?" Brows raised, he regarded her with interest.

Allie felt dizzy, realizing that at this very moment, God was answering one of her most heartfelt prayers. This is what she had come here for! *Oh, Lord, please keep everyone out of the kitchen so I can tell Jack what You've done for me. . . .*

"No, I didn't divorce him. I couldn't. He threatened to take my son away from me if I did. But God used this incident," she said, fingering her scar, "to protect me over the years that followed. I think it frightened Erich to know he was capable of such a violent act, and he never touched me again. Meanwhile," Allie said with a smile, "the Lord got a hold of my heart and I began to attend church, read my Bible, and grow as a Christian."

Jack narrowed his gaze, as if deciphering the information.

"When I left here, I wasn't a solid believer and I was an emotional mess. But I finished college and got a good job. I met and married Erich because he was charming and his family had a lot of money. Money meant security to me. I never even thought to ask about Erich's religious background. By then, I had put God in a box like. . ." She searched her mind for the right analogy. ". . .like you might pack away textbooks you never thought you'd use again. It was only when the physical abuse started that—"

"Hey, Allie, you coming out?"

Hearing Nora's voice, she glanced toward the patio doors. "Coming right now." She looked back at Jack, reached out, and gave his wrist an affectionate squeeze. "I'm so glad I had the chance to tell you all this," she said with a smile.

Turning on her heel, she walked out of the kitchen and followed Nora onto the deck.

*   *   *

Jack stood in the middle of the kitchen, holding his can of cola and feeling like he'd just been in a fistfight—and lost.

So Allie didn't have it so good, either, he mused. He would have never guessed. She seemed so perfect, her life so together. Up until this very moment, he'd hated her for it.

He forced himself to inhale and exhale in regular intervals, realizing he'd been holding his breath. Allie at the hand of an abusive spouse? Jack shook the vision out of his head. He'd seen enough domestic violence in his career to know the particulars that accompanied it. They weren't pretty.

Staring at his cola, he took a swig. His brief conversation with Allie made him want to know more. Where was this dude she'd married? Didn't sound like she loved him. Why was that comforting?

Maybe because he'd never loved his ex-wife, either. But he had tried.

Jack squeezed his eyes shut against the ocean of memories flooding his being.

Lord knows he'd tried. . . .

*   *   *

Hours later, with his hands on the steering wheel of his Mercury Sable, Logan turned onto Waukegan Road and headed for

Schaumburg. The drive took about thirty-five minutes from Oakland Park to the townhouse that Marilee and two other teachers shared. The night was dark, illuminated only by the streetlights, and a cool autumn breeze blew in off the lake. But as the car picked up speed, both he and Marilee closed their windows.

"I had a nice time today," she said from the passenger seat.

"Yeah, me, too." He smiled, but didn't take his eyes off the road.

"I had the chance to speak with your dad this evening. I. . ." She hesitated. "I like him. I don't feel so intimidated by him anymore."

"Good. I had prayed something like that would come out of this afternoon's picnic." He glanced her way and grinned. "I'll confess that I was surprised at Dad's sociable mood, especially since I coerced him into going. He didn't want to. But that's what God can do—change a man's heart."

"Yes. . ."

Marilee's voice trailed off, and Logan sensed she had more to say. "What is it?" he finally prompted.

She took an audible breath. "I hope I'm not out of line in saying this, Logan, but I think you should drop the idea of finding your biological mother. Your dad is warming up. But if you consume yourself with searching for your mother—"

"Consume myself?" he asked, making a right onto Lake Cook Road.

"Logan, I know you. Once you get an idea in your brain, you've got a one-track mind. It's all you think about."

He laughed. It was true. Marilee knew him well. Moreover, she was right about another thing: He didn't want to hurt his dad. He desired a close relationship with him and had been working on cultivating it. Logan sensed, even more strongly after today, that beneath the rocky resolve of his father's beat an extremely tender heart—one that, Logan guessed, had been wounded far too many times. Did he dare challenge him with the past and add to it?

Logan's thoughts plagued him until they reached Marilee's townhouse. Located in a lively neighborhood, it was within walking distance to the church and school. Pulling up to the curb, he parked, climbed from the car, and walked around to the other side, where he opened the door for Marilee.

She smiled. "It always amazes me what a gentleman you are," she said as he helped her out. "You're the first guy who ever insisted I stay seated until he opens the door for me."

"Good training," he quipped.

Her smile broadened.

Together they walked to the front door.

"Will I see you tomorrow?" she asked, fishing her keys from her purse.

"Sure. I'll be around all day."

Beneath the porch light, Marilee bobbed her brunette head and stuck the key into the door. Turning back to him, she said, "I had a lovely afternoon. Thanks."

He nodded, feeling a tad uncomfortable. *This would be the part where the guy kisses the gal good night,* he thought. And he had to admit, he wanted to kiss her. But he knew if he succumbed to his feelings right now, he'd betray himself and everything he wanted to stand for. Besides, he would be a hypocrite in every sense of the word. He would know it in his heart, and there was at least one young lady that he knew of who lived on this block and attended the youth group. What if she saw? She would think all pastors were phonies who imposed rules on others but didn't follow them themselves. It would destroy her faith.

He shifted from one foot to the other and stuffed his hands into his pants pockets. Then he let out a long, slow breath and looked across the tiny porch. "Sometimes it's no fun being a youth pastor, you know that?"

Looking back at Marilee, he saw a mischievous spark in her

chocolate brown eyes. "I wouldn't let you kiss me," she whispered, "even if you tried. So there."

Logan laughed, and suddenly the tension evaporated. "You're good for me. You keep me on track."

"I'm glad you finally noticed."

Marilee's delicate laughter wafted on the autumn breeze, and Logan felt his face warm with embarrassment. But he figured he deserved it; he was the one dragging his feet in this relationship.

"G'night. See you tomorrow."

" 'Night, Marilee," he said with a parting smile.

She entered the house and closed the door behind her. Hearing the lock turn, Logan strode back to his car.

*   *   *

"Listen, ol' lady, this is what I want you to say. I want you to say that I'm the best CNA that ever took care of you."

"What's a CNA?" Cynthia asked weakly as she eyed the man who had made her last nine hours a waking nightmare. Her requests for pain medication went unanswered. She'd defecated and needed her underthings changed, but he refused. Worse, he wouldn't allow another nurse to care for her, and he had slapped her twice when she'd screamed for help. Now the flesh around her left eye felt bruised and swollen.

"CNA—certified nursing assistant. That'd be me. Now when my supervisor comes in this morning, that's what I want you to say. Got it?"

Cynthia clamped her mouth shut. She would do no such thing.

"Can you go all day with no pain meds?" the man with slick, black hair sneered. "I'm real good at changin' doctor's orders."

"All right, I'll do it. I'll say anything you want," Cynthia lied, feeling the perspiration trickle off her brow. The pain slicing through her bones felt so intense, she could barely breathe. Even so, she refused to say a single good word about this. . .this CNA or anyone else in this rotten place. When someone, anyone but the nursing staff, came by, Cynthia planned to holler for all she was worth. But for now, she'd hold her tongue.

The attendant smiled. "See, I knew I'd whip you into shape. You ain't gunna give us no problems no more." He wrinkled his nose at the pungent odor filling the room. "Now I'll jest get that lazy Katrina in here to clean you up. . . ."

* * *

Allie figured her biological clock had sprung a spring when she'd awakened at three in the morning and couldn't fall back to sleep. For some odd reason, she felt anxious to get to work today. Even so, she made a miniature pot of coffee and lingered over her daily Bible reading and made breakfast before readying herself for the day.

Scanning her wardrobe, she decided on comfort, so she chose a knit navy dress with a red, white, and yellow paisley print. To complete the outfit, she pulled on a red blazer in case she'd require a more professional image.

As she headed for her office at Arbor Springs, she couldn't believe that the clock in the rented Chevy Cavalier read 6:00. She yawned. It was going to be a long day. But on the plus side, this could work out for the best. She might be able to leave early and run some errands. Besides, she thought, pulling into a parking place at the healthcare facility, she hadn't introduced herself to the third-shift employees. Maybe now would be a good time.

Allie let herself into the facility via the building's side door, making sure it slammed shut and locked once she was inside. She walked to her office; but before unlocking its door, she glanced around the lobby and noted the security guard was nowhere in sight.

Maybe he's on break, she mused, wanting to be fair and give the guy the benefit of the doubt. But suddenly she was thankful she'd come in so early. . .and unexpected.

After locking her purse in a filing cabinet, Allie closed her office door and headed for the elevators. Looking at the numbers on the panel inside the car, she selected 4, thinking she might as well begin with the top floor and move down. But when the doors opened and she stepped out, a foul odor assailed her; and Allie thought she'd be sick. Her gut instinct was to retreat into the elevator and escape to her office. But she tamped it down.

However, as she made her way into the ward, the sight that greeted her was almost as sickening as the smell.

Half a dozen employees congregated at the nursing station, a square unit in the center of the ward. There they watched television while potato chip bags, bottles of soda, plastic cups, and an empty pan of what Allie assumed were once brownies littered the counters around the station. That wouldn't have been entirely so bad, except for the moans and shouts for help that went ignored

"Ma'am, how'd you get up here?" a heavyset woman said, ambling toward Allie. "Visitor hours aren't till nine o'clock."

"And a good thing, too," she quipped.

The woman paused. Blond, with a short, spiky haircut, she wore blue pants and a matching top, called "scrubs," Allie had recently learned.

"I'm the new consultant here." She held out her right hand. "Allison Littenberg. And you are?"

"Um. . ." The woman glanced over her shoulder at the station before looking back at Allie. She appeared about as guilty as a bank robber caught in the vault. "I'm, um, Jessie."

"Jessie?"

A resigned expression crossed her wide face. "Jessie Nardin. I'm the RN up here on night shift."

"I see."

"We were just having a little Labor Day party since we had to work the holiday."

"I don't have any problem with that, except you might want to clean up the mess now."

"We were just about to do that."

Allie nodded. "Good. Now would you mind explaining why it smells so awful up here?"

"Um. . .we have a lot of incontinent patients up here."

A man suddenly emerged from the room to Allie's left. Cupping his hands over his mouth, he bellowed across the entire ward, "Hey, Kat, get your carcass in here and change this ol' bag's diapers. She's learned her lesson. I think she sat in it long enough."

"She's not my responsibility," a female shouted back. "Change her yourself!"

The attendant swore.

By now, Allie was sure her eyes were as wide as dessert plates. And here she'd thought Nurse Ratchet only existed in *One Flew Over the Cuckoo's Nest*.

"This is unacceptable!"

The man's dark head spun in her direction.

"Kenny, this is Ms. Littenberg," Jessie began on a tentative note. "She's that new consultant we got the memo about."

The man's expression crumbled, and Allie admitted to feeling a semblance of gratification. "Looks like we need to work on our customer service skills," she said with a cynical grin, "among other things."

"Yes, Ma'am," he said, suddenly transforming into a polite young man.

"Now why don't you tell me what's going on?" Allie said. "Why did you say this patient has 'learned her lesson?' "

"Oh, she's jest crazy. She always be cussin' and swearin' at us."

"Help me! Help me!" the woman began to scream in a hoarse, broken voice.

Allie felt tingles of apprehension climb her spine. She knew something was wrong—very wrong. "Why is she on this floor if that's the case?"

"Psych ward was full, I guess," Kenny said.

"Don't listen to him!" the woman rasped. "That's a lie. I'm

dying, that's why I'm here. I'm dying. . . ." A pause. "Wish I were dead. . ."

Allie stepped forward, but Kenny held out his palms to forestall her. "She just wants to be changed, and we're gunna see to that right now."

"Good."

"No, no, please don't leave! That man's not fit to take care of a goldfish, let alone a human being. None of these people are. Please, please, help me!"

Kenny chuckled. "Poor thing. She's outta her very mind."

Allie nibbled her lower lip in indecision. On one hand, she could well believe the distraught individual was "out of her mind." But at the same time, Kenny's behavior didn't warrant Allie's trust. . .or her respect.

"I want this patient cleaned up immediately."

"That's jest what I was 'bout to do."

Allie took another step toward the woman's doorway.

"Now you be careful," Kenny warned. "She's violent."

"I couldn't hurt a flea, you idiot! Otherwise you'd be dead for all the things you did to me!"

Imagining what sort of "things" caused Allie's egg and toast to creep up her esophagus. Narrowing her gaze at Kenny, she said, "Get this patient cleaned and changed—and do it as though your job depends on it. Because it does."

"All right, all right." He walked away at a snail's pace. "Ever'one's in a hurry these days."

Casting a glance at Jessie, Allie saw contrition pooled in the nurse's eyes, so she held back another reprimand.

"Miss, don't leave me. Please. Please. . . ." the woman began to sob. "Please, for the love of God, don't. . .leave. . .me. . . ."

At that moment, Allie knew she couldn't abandon the woman, crazy or not. She would, however, take special care in case the patient was, indeed, violent or suffered with something contagious.

Standing to one side, she half-peered into the repugnant-smelling room. She cringed, wondering how these employees could stand working in such stench. Worse, how awful to be a patient and left to lie in it!

Squinting into the darkness, Allie could barely make out the ghostly figure in the bed. She almost laughed. The patient had been right: In her feeble state, she couldn't hurt a fly, let alone a strapping young man like Kenny. "I won't leave, Ma'am. I'll make sure you're cared for. When you're cleaned up, I'll come in and talk to you. All right?"

Allie had to pull back out of the room to breathe again.

"Don't leave, don't leave. . . ." the woman whimpered. "Pleeeeeeese!"

"I won't leave," Allie promised again. Looking hard at Jessie, she added, "I'm going to stay right here and make sure everything is in order before the first shift arrives."

CHAPTER NINE

With each passing minute, Allie grew more appalled by the sights around her. The patient in Room 8 wasn't the only one suffering from neglect. The man in Room 3 appeared to be in similar shape, although he wasn't conscious as far as Allie could tell. Out of the twenty patients residing on this floor, Allie discovered four who required immediate attention; and three of them, including the woman in Room 8, were calling out for help—or had been until Allie arrived. Many others were heavily sedated.

"Where would I find an incident report?" Allie asked, stepping into the nurse's station.

A slender, short-haired African-American woman yanked open a bottom drawer from the filing cabinet to the right of where she sat near the computer. Pulling a printed form from a hanging file, she said, "This would be what you need."

"Thanks." Allie held out her right hand. "I'm Allison Littenberg, the new consultant here."

"I'm Sherelle Barnes, the unit secretary."

"Nice to meet you."

They clasped hands in a mutually polite shake, and the young woman nodded before resuming her work on the computer.

Form in hand, Allie made her way into Room 8. "Ma'am? Can I come in?"

"Yes," the woman rasped.

The heavy draperies were closed, so Allie walked to the windows and pulled them open. The sky was bright, but the sun still hadn't made its way past the surrounding high-rises.

"Looks like it'll be a nice da—"

Allie's sentence died on her lips as she turned and viewed the mere specter of a woman, lying in the bed. She looked like a skeleton with fragile rice paper pressed over her bones. Allie guessed her age to be at least ninety, and she was amazed at the patient's feistiness, given her present condition.

"My name is Allison. . .Allie Littenberg." The woman's head lolled in her direction and rheumy blue eyes stared at her. "I was hired almost two weeks ago as the consultant here at Arbor Springs. We're in the process of making improvements."

"Plenty of room for improvement around here."

"Yes, so I see." Allie narrowed her gaze and took a step closer. "Is that a bruise around your left eye?"

"Probably. That imbecile CNA hit me. Then he wanted me to say he was the best nursing assistant I ever had." The patient let out a guffaw. "He can go straight to he—"

"I get the picture," Allie put in quickly as she pulled up a chair. "But let's you and I agree to something right now. I'll talk like a lady to you and you do the same. No profanity, okay? It's not necessary."

The patient eyed her skeptically before nodding. "Okay."

"Good." Allie smiled. "Now, why don't we start at the beginning? With your permission, I'm going to fill out an incident report."

"Go for it."

"Last name?"

"Matlock."

"First?"

"Cynthia."

"Middle initial?"

"R."

"Home address?"

"None."

Allie glanced up from her form. "None?"

"Well, this place, I guess. I'm essentially homeless." The woman exhaled a wheezy sound.

"No family members whose address—?"

"I said I'm homeless," Cynthia barked.

Saying nothing, Allie wrote "N/A" in the address line.

"Sorry," the woman said grudgingly. "I'm in a lot of pain. I didn't get a shot all night." Tears slipped from the woman's eyes, now closed. Her head wagged back and forth on the pillow. "I hurt so much. . . ."

"Let me see what I can do. I'll be right back."

Exiting the room, Allie hailed Jessie to the nurses' station. "The patient in Room 8 wants some pain medication."

"She just had some."

"Who gave it to her?"

"Um. . ." Jessie frowned, looking confused.

"Since you're the only RN on the floor during third shift, and since the rest of the staff are CNAs, I'm assuming it would have to be you who dispersed the medication. Correct?"

"Yes, but I thought. . ." Jessie's gaze swept the surrounding area before coming back to Allie. "Um, let me check the chart and talk to Kenny. I'll get back to you."

"Thanks."

Returning to Mrs. Matlock's room, Allie added disorganization and insufficient nursing skills to the growing list of problems.

She thought back to the day she'd first toured this floor. Things had seemed to run smoothly. Was the problem solely with the night shift crew?

Allie hoped so—prayed so.

"The nurse is going to come in soon."

"I won't hold my breath," Cynthia rasped. "That's what they say all the time."

Allie grimaced and picked up the form. "Okay, where were we? Oh, yes, no address. . ."

"If you must know, my two daughters dropped me off here one day and left. I had no idea they'd planned to stick me in a nursing home. I would have slit my wrists if I had known. Before here, I lived with them in a rented duplex. I've since tried to call, so has the doctor, but the phone's disconnected. I think they moved. It'd be just like them."

"I'm. . .I'm sorry."

Dying with no family, no loved ones close at hand? Allie was moved with pity for the woman. . .until the thought crossed her mind that she could be making the whole thing up. Perhaps she was delirious. Maybe she had been given narcotics just before Allie arrived on the floor.

At that moment, Jessie came in, holding a syringe. She gave Allie a guilty look. "I was under the impression that Mrs. Matlock didn't have orders from her physician for any more pain medication. But I was. . .um. . .misinformed."

"That's because that—" Cynthia seemed to remember their bargain as she looked at Allie. "That jerk," she said pointedly, "said he was good at changing doctor's orders. He said he wouldn't give me any pain medication unless I did everything he told me."

Watching the injection being administered, Allie had to ask. "What did he want you to do?"

"Shut up."

"Excuse me?"

"Oh, not you. That's what that jerk wanted. He wanted me to shut up, but I wouldn't. I needed to be changed. I needed medication. . . ."

The woman's voice trailed off just as Jessie pulled the needle from her arm.

"You'll feel better soon, Mrs. Matlock."

"Yeah, no thanks to you. Where were you all night? Where were you when that attendant pulled my hair and hit me?"

Jessie's face reddened. "I don't know anything about that," she said, looking at Allie.

"Course not," Cynthia crooned on. "You were too busy watching TV."

Allie raised an inquiring brow.

"I'm not saying anything until my supervisor comes in this morning."

"What time is that?"

"Eight."

"Fine. I'll be here."

Allie watched the nurse leave before returning her gaze to Mrs. Matlock. "Why don't we continue?"

"Sure. But you'd better hurry. I'll be out soon. With any luck, I'll die in my sleep."

Allie wanted to rebuke the woman for such a remark, but realized she would most likely feel the same way, given the circumstances. Of course, Allie knew heaven awaited her. . .did Mrs. Matlock have that same peace?

"Date of birth," Allie asked.

"Twelve, thirty-one, forty-six."

Allie's pen lingered above the numbers as she did the math. That made this woman only four years older than she. Looking over at Cynthia, she asked, "You're fifty-three years old?"

"Yep. And I was born on New Year's Eve. That's why I like to party. Party hearty. . .or, I used to. Until I got cancer."

Allie swallowed the rest of her surprise, wondering if Mrs.

Matlock's lifestyle had aged her beyond her years more so than her terminal illness.

"Will you please tell me in detail what happened last night and this morning?"

"My pleasure. . ."

* * *

"We're not calling the police, Allie."

With arms folded, she regarded Evan Jacobs from the far end of her office. It was nearly noon, and they'd been discussing the situation for the better part of the morning. "It's the right thing to do," she replied. "A crime has been committed."

"No, allegations have been made. There is a difference."

"Perhaps. But after taking Mrs. Matlock's report and having heard two other patients' complaints of neglect this morning, I have reason to believe there is more wrong with the care here at Arbor Springs than mere allegations suggest. In any event, Evan, it's up to the police to make that decision, not us."

"Look, you said yourself the woman doesn't have any family—"

"Yes, but the other two patients have family members who visit on a regular basis. They're going to find out. You can't bury this incident."

"Who's trying to bury it?" Evan stepped closer. "Lakeland Enterprises is fully prepared to make restitution where restitution is due. . .and quit shaking your head at me like that."

"Not good enough."

"Allie, you don't understand. If we call the police, the media is going to find out about this and then Lakeland Enterprises will be smeared across the front page of the *Tribune*. We can't afford that kind of PR."

"I'm well aware of the ramifications," Allie replied in a tight voice. "But I think Lakeland will fare far better with the press if its executives come forward about the. . .the allegations instead of handling them internally."

Suddenly an idea struck and Allie snapped her fingers. "Evan, you should hold a press conference this afternoon."

"What?" He shook his head. "That's out of the question."

"Listen, Evan, it's a great idea." Allie paused in thought, working her lower lip between her teeth. "You can say something like Lakeland is playing a proactive role in all this, and getting the police involved is only the first step. You can announce that you've hired a consultant to reorganize Arbor Springs's internal affairs and that you intend to do everything within your power to see that justice is brought to the assailants of these mistreated patients."

"Except we're not sure that they were really mistreated. Besides, publicly admitting something of that nature opens us up to lawsuits." Evan gave a derisive snort. "Mrs. Matlock would suddenly have relatives coming out of the woodwork. Mark my words."

"Hm. . ." Again, Allie thought it over and decided he was probably correct on that account. "All right then. Just say that Lakeland plans to do everything in its power to aid in the investigation."

"That sounds a little better." Evan sighed audibly. "This is my worst nightmare."

"It's all a matter of perspective. You could turn this thing around, you know?"

"I'll have to phone the other board members. . . ."

"Fine. But in the meantime, if you don't call the police, I will. There's a dying woman upstairs who, I believe, was brutalized last night and something must be done."

Evan gave her a hard stare, and Allie knew he wasn't pleased with the ultimatum. But she would stand her ground—to the point of releasing Lakeland Enterprises from its contract if need be. She refused to work for a healthcare corporation if it had so little regard for human life.

Besides, Allie felt she'd attained her primary goal in coming back to Chicago. She had been able to see Jack again, as disappointing as it was, and she'd been given the chance to tell him what Jehovah God had done in her own life. She had seen her stepsister Colleen and planned to see Brenda this weekend.

All in all, her trip had been a success. She didn't need this job or the aggravation that would follow once the police were notified.

"Very well," Evan said at last. "Call the cops. But I've got some phone calls of my own to make, so if you'll excuse me. . ."

Allie nodded. "By all means."

She watched Evan leave her office before lifting the telephone's receiver to her ear. She pressed the three keys for Directory Assistance and felt grateful that Arbor Springs Healthcare Facility wasn't in Oakland Park. If it were, she might have Jack and Evan both to contend with, and wouldn't that be just—to borrow Jack's word—peachy!

*   *   *

Logan yawned as he turned the key and entered the bi-level condominium he shared with his father. Once inside, he closed the door behind him and walked up the beige-carpeted stairs, where he could hear the television.

"Hello, hello?" he called before depositing his briefcase and notebook computer on the oak side table in the hallway. "Anyone home?"

"In here."

Logan made his way through the foyer and into the adjacent living room. "What are you watching?"

"Quiet."

Somewhat taken back by the brusque reply, Logan regarded his father, noting he still wore his uniform. Then he glanced at the television set.

"Breaking news or what?"

"Sort of. Steve called to say Allie was on TV, so I thought I'd tune in and find out what kind of trouble she got herself into this time."

Relieved that it wasn't something more serious, Logan collapsed into the plaid sofa beside his dad. Out of curiosity, he "tuned in" as well.

"We at Lakeland Enterprises are committed to excellence," a man with reddish brown hair said. "We will assist the police department in its investigation any way we can."

"You assigned to this case, Dad?"

"Nope. Not our jurisdiction."

Returning his gaze to the TV, Logan saw Allie standing off to the left and behind the speaker. On the right stood three impeccably dressed businessmen.

"What's going on?"

"Some patients were allegedly assaulted at a local nursing home, and this is a replay of the press conference earlier this afternoon. I'm not really sure how Allie's involved, though."

"Hm. . ."

The man finished his tidy speech and left the microphones. Allie followed him, and the other businessman walked off camera after her.

"She's a rose among the thorns," Logan said. "The corporate game is still played by men's rules."

"Ha!" Jack retorted. "If she's in business with those guys, they have their hands full."

Logan grinned. "On second thought, I might agree with you there. Allie said she's a consultant, so I imagine she's uncovering all kinds of dark secrets at that place."

"Could be," Jack replied, his gazed fixed on the television.

The anchorman in the studio wrapped up the story and promised to keep his viewing audience informed.

"She's a consultant, huh?"

"Yeah. That's what she said that first night I met her at Uncle Steve's."

Jack stood and turned off the TV. "Whatever happened to Mr. Littenberg?"

"Who?" Logan asked with a frown.

"Allie's husband."

"Oh, um, Aunt Nora said she's a widow."

Jack made some unintelligible sound as he absorbed the information.

"You interested, Dad?" Logan teased, unable to help himself.

Jack shot a quelling glance.

"I'll bet she'd go out with you if you asked really nice."

"Don't you have something to do?"

"Nope." He grinned and crossed his leg, ankle to knee, and observed his father pulling several ingredients out of the fridge.

"It's nine-thirty at night," Jack said. "All good youth pastors are supposed to be sleeping."

Logan chuckled. "Yeah, sure they are. Hey, are you making sandwiches?"

"Yeah. Want one?"

"I'd love one. Make that two."

His father sent him a quizzical look. "No supper tonight?"

"No, I stayed at church and surfed the Net."

"Sounds like an oxymoron—the church and the Internet."

"You've got a point there," Logan agreed. "But the Internet's a great resource."

His dad said nothing as he smeared mayo and mustard on four large bagels.

"I've been, um, doing some online research. I think I'd like to locate my biological mother," Logan blurted, deciding there was no way to soften the blow. He stood and walked slowly toward his father. "I'm going at it wholeheartedly, but I believe it's something I need to do."

Amazingly, Jack didn't miss a beat. "Why? No, wait. Let me guess. This was Mrs. Littenberg's idea, right?"

"What?" Logan brought his chin back. "This has nothing to do with her." He tipped his head. "Why did you think it would?"

"Oh, because Allie has these fairytale fantasies about happy reunions." Jack slapped on slices of American cheese while he spoke.

"Got any tomatoes?"

Jack looked up at his son. "What does this look like? A deli?"

"Lettuce?" Logan persisted.

Muttering under his breath, his father turned back to the fridge and pulled out half an onion, pickles, lettuce, and tomatoes.

Logan chuckled. "All right! Now we're talkin' sandwiches!"

Jack grinned in spite of himself.

"In answer to your question," Logan said, pulling out a knife and slicing the onion, "I want to find my birth mother because I seem to have some kind of. . .oh, I don't know. . .some phobia, I guess, when it comes to relationships."

"Baloney."

"Yeah, that sounds good," he replied, nodding toward the refrigerator.

Jack laughed. "I didn't mean that kind of baloney, you knucklehead. I'm referring to that pseudo-psychological nonsense about relationships. You're a well-adjusted male. It's just that, like every guy, you're nervous about getting married."

"Were you?"

"Heck, yeah!"

"Will you tell me about it. . .and about my mother?"

"Must I?"

Logan met his father's unwavering gaze with a firm one of his own. "I'd hate to do anything to hurt you, Dad, but at the same time, I need to know."

"And Allie didn't put you up to this?"

"Nope. The topic never came up."

After regarding him a moment longer, Jack shrugged. "I guess I always knew this time would come. I suppose I'm fortunate to have held out this long." He sighed, sounding exasperated. "So what exactly do you want to know?"

"Did you love her?"

"Who?"

"My mother!" Logan laughed. "Dad, get Mrs. Littenberg out of your head for right now, okay?"

"She's not in my head. . .*okay?*"

Logan bit back a retort. Since his father was suddenly willing to broach a subject that he never before agreed to discuss, Logan decided it might be in his best interest to refrain from teasing him any further.

"Did you love my mother?"

"No." Jack tossed him the tomato. "Slice that up, will you?"

"Sure." Two slices later, he asked, "Why did you marry her if you didn't love her?"

"Because I got her pregnant."

Logan knew this already. He'd heard how his father had met his mother and that she'd been expecting at the time they were married.

"And don't ask me how it happened, either. At your age, you ought to have some idea—even if you are a pastor."

"How it happened is irrelevant at this point."

"Maybe so. But I will say this much; it was a one-time mistake that cost me a lifetime of consequences."

"Yep, that sounds just like sin. Wrecking lives. Destroying people's faith." Logan pursed his lips thoughtfully while several passages of Scripture ran through his mind.

"Don't preach to me," his father warned. "I've heard it all before."

"Well, if you heard it all before," Logan asked, hoping he sounded as earnest as he felt, "why haven't you done something about it? God is ready and waiting to forgive you if you'd only ask."

"Who says I haven't asked, and since when do you speak for God?"

"I speak from—"

"Don't go there, Logan."

Faced with the choice of challenging his father about his

spiritual condition or pursuing the topic of his birth mother, Logan decided he'd make more progress with the latter. . . for now.

"Dad, why did you marry her? I mean, surely there were other alternatives."

"There weren't. Trust me."

"But—"

"Your mother wanted an abortion. But I didn't want to add murder to the mess I made—and, yes, it's my opinion that abortion is murder. Was then and still is. . ."

At his father's pause, Logan looked up from the now-sliced tomato.

"So I promised your mother everything I could think of in order to get her to marry me and have the baby—you."

Logan thought he detected the edge of remorse in his dad's tone. "Were you ever sorry you didn't let her go through with it?"

"Nope, never was." Jack looked him square in the eye. "Let's settle one thing here and now. I'm not sorry you were born. Got it? And if it ever seemed that way, well. . .I'm sorry."

Logan almost fell over from shock. His dad? Apologizing? This was a rare moment, indeed—and an answer to a decade-long prayer.

"I hated myself for my mistake," Jack continued. "I never hated you. Ever. You're my son. My flesh and blood. I. . .I've always loved you."

Setting the tomato slices on the sandwiches, Logan wrestled with his sudden onset of emotion. He wanted to bawl like a little boy—except his father had told him he loved him before. Logan never really doubted that while growing up.

"I love you, too," he said at last.

"Good," he replied in his usual gruff tone. "Let's eat."

CHAPTER TEN

For several long minutes, the two men munched on their food in silence while Logan gathered enough steam to press on with his impromptu interrogation.

"So my mother agreed to marry you and give birth to me. . . and then what happened? Did you guys have a bad marriage from day one or what?"

Jack shrugged and chewed his mouthful and swallowed. "I wanted it to work and I think she did, too. . .initially. Your grandma used to stop in every day and try to encourage Roxie—your mother. I don't know if you remember, but your grandmother loved being a homemaker. She had it down to a science. Martha Stewart could have taken lessons from her. But Roxie couldn't adjust. She was bored and she started to resent me because I was used to Mom, who enjoyed her domestic role."

Logan watched as his father seemed to wrestle with the remainder of his reply. He sensed how difficult revisiting the past must be; however, Logan had to know about it. And suddenly it occurred to him that all these questions, like leprosy, had been eating at him since he was old enough to know to ask. This conversation should have taken place a long time ago.

"I assume that after I was born, my mother's boredom and resentment escalated until she. . .just left?"

"Pretty much, yeah."

"Well, therein lies the basis of my problem!" Logan declared after swallowing a bite of his bagel. "What kind of mother abandons her child?" He shook his head. "None that I can think of. I mean, even in the abuse cases I've read about—"

"Logan, use your brain. What's my profession?"

"A police officer. So?"

"So what do you suppose a guy like me would do to an irresponsible woman who took off with my son?"

Logan blinked as the reality of it set in.

"You got it. I would have gone after her, number one. I would have pressed kidnapping charges against her, number two. . . ."

"I get the picture." Logan couldn't suppress a smile at the ferocity of his father's feelings. Sure, he'd guessed they were there all the time—somewhere. But hearing it made every difference in the world. "Why didn't you tell me this when I was a teenager and wanted to know? Don't you remember how angry I was and how I blamed you for everything that went wrong in my life?"

"Yeah, including your team losing the football game on Friday night," Jack retorted. "Sure, I remember. And maybe I was selfish to hold out on you, but I figured I would just look worse in your eyes, not better. Your mother clearly left me, Logan, not you. But I did warn her that I would get custody if she divorced me."

"Why were you so confident of that?"

"Just was."

"Dad, don't clam up on me now."

"Oh, fine," Jack muttered. "If you must know, your mother

went behind my back and got a job as a stripper at a nightclub in downtown Chicago. Given her occupation, past and present, and the fact that she'd left you unattended for hours—"

"I get it. Oh, man. . ." Logan shook his head. "You could have told me this sooner—like when I was in high school. Things are making more sense to me now that I know the truth."

Jack exhaled a long, weary-sounding breath. "I could have told you, yes; but if you recall, we went through a period where you habitually accused me of lying. Why would you believe anything I said? I figured you'd just think I was trying to make myself look good."

With a grimace, Logan set down his sandwich. His dad was right. "I was a rebel who took on any cause back then. What can I say? I hope you've forgiven me."

"You were a kid trying to find your place in the world. Nothing to forgive." His father stood. "Want something to drink?"

"Yeah. Thanks."

Logan mulled over what he'd just heard. It shed a whole light on some things, but it cast long shadows on others.

"So you got awarded custody just as you predicted. Did my mother ever request visitation rights?" Logan asked as Jack handed him a cola. For himself, his father had chosen two cans of beer. "Dad, you don't need that—the alcohol."

"Who says I don't?" He flipped open the tab and took a long swallow. "And, no, she never requested visitation rights."

Logan threw his hands in the air. "See, this is what I mean. What mother doesn't want to see her own son?"

"A mother who's in trouble with the law," Jack replied, taking another drink of beer. "And one whose ex-husband is a cop." Giving Logan a wry grin, he added, "Bad combination."

"What sort of trouble was she in?"

Jack shook his head. "Let's not go there."

"Dad, I want to know."

"Prostitution."

Logan winced.

"Satisfied?"

Logan sat back in his chair, deciding that satisfied didn't describe how he felt at the moment. Overwhelmed. Unsettled. Disgusted. Those words came close.

Jack finished eating the rest of his meal and brushed several breadcrumbs into his palm. He walked to the sink and Logan heard him dump the remainder of his beer down the drain. Then his dad returned the second can to the fridge.

After Jack left the room, Logan stuffed the remainder of his sandwich into his mouth and stood. Tossing his napkin into the garbage on the way out, he pursued his father. He wasn't about to let this subject die now.

"Dad?" He found him in his room, unbuttoning his shirt. "Dad, let me ask one more thing and I'll stop pestering you." When no reply was forthcoming, he continued, "Why you do act like my mother's actions hurt you if you didn't love her, and why didn't you remarry and bring some normalcy to your life. . .and to mine? Would that have violated some personal belief of yours?"

"That's three questions," Jack pointed out. "But I'll give them my best shot. After that, this discussion is over—forever. If you want to find your mother, that's your business. But keep me out of it. Got it?"

"Got it."

Jack nodded at the agreement, then seemed to search his mind for the right words. "Why do I seem hurt? Guess I am— well, not really so much anymore. But I was. Your mother's betrayal hurt me. Her disregard for our marriage in general hurt. Why didn't I remarry? That's simple. I have terrible luck with women!"

Logan tried to suppress a grin. "Does that include Mrs. Littenberg?"

"Yeah, if you must know, it does. And now you've asked four questions too many."

Jack paused and gave Logan one of his steely police officer glares that, as a kid, caused him to stand up a little straighter. Now, however, it just made him smile because he knew his dad was a regular marshmallow underneath that stony façade.

Lord, break it, Logan prayed. *Break him. . . .*

"Look, Logan," Jack said at last, "I don't have much respect for the institution of marriage. It, like Christianity, doesn't work. I found that out the hard way."

He shook his head. "You're so wrong."

"Prove it. Marry that nice girl and raise a family. Be happy. That's all I ever wanted for you. Happiness."

Before Logan could reply, his dad closed the bedroom door.

*   *   *

Every afternoon for the following four days, Allie went up to visit Cynthia Matlock before she went home. Evan said he didn't care as long as they didn't discuss the allegations or the police investigation. Finding his request most reasonable, Allie gave her word. And even though she could think of a hundred different things she'd rather do, she couldn't seem to stay away from Mrs. Matlock's room. The thought of her—or anyone, for that matter—dying a painful, lonely death broke Allie's heart. But the idea that Mrs. Matlock might leave this world without hearing about Jesus was more than she could bear, and Allie prayed for an opportunity to share her faith.

However, introducing the subject of eternity hadn't been easy—or welcomed. Instead of discussing any sort of future, the frail woman preferred to linger in the past, in a time when she was young, pretty, and financially secure. Allie could hardly fault her for it. Who wouldn't relish those memories? But at the same time, it was hard to listen to her ramblings because they brought back emotional remains that Allie had thought she'd long since laid to rest.

"Do you remember that song, 'Angel of the Morning'?" Cynthia asked that sunny Friday afternoon. "Not the one that came out several years ago, but the one that came out in '68. I remember the year because I just turned twenty-two when I first heard that song. Everyone said I sounded just like the singer."

"I remember." Sitting on the edge of Cynthia's bed, Allie smiled ruefully into the dying woman's sleepy gaze. It was difficult to imagine this woman at twenty-two. But it was even tougher for Allie to remember herself in 1968.

Her mother had just died.

Allie ran away from home.

She met Jack Callahan.

She turned eighteen, graduated from high school, and vowed never to speak to her stepfather and stepsisters again.

"Well, that's what you are."

"What am I?" Allie asked, thinking the name would be none too flattering.

"You're my angel of the morning," Cynthia replied groggily.

Allie laughed under her breath. "No, I'm not an angel."

"Oh, but you are."

Looking to take advantage of the spiritual turn in their conversation, Allie said, "I suppose you could say that I'm a messenger of God because I like to share the news about God's gift of salvation—that gift is Jesus Christ."

Cynthia opened her eyes with great effort.

"I'm a born-again Christian." Allie surveyed the pale woman's face. "That's just my way of saying I've asked Jesus to forgive my sins and I'm committed to living my life for Him."

Cynthia's eyes fluttered closed and opened again. "My first ex-husband was one of those."

Her first?

"Do you mind my asking how many times you were married?" Allie queried, unable to quell her curiosity.

"Four times."

"Mmm. . ."

"And I can honestly tell you Mr. Right doesn't exist."

Allie couldn't help a little grin. "Well, none of us is perfect. We're all sinners. . .only some of us have been forgiven." She paused, sending up an arrow of a prayer before continuing. "What about you, Mrs. Matlock?"

"Call me Cynthia. Me and my angel gotta be on a first name basis."

Allie laughed. "I'm not an angel. I'm far from it. I'm a sinner. . .a sinner saved by grace. That's it. What about you?"

"What do you mean. . .saved by grace? How does grace save somebody?"

"Good question. Now let's see if I can answer it." The silvery-haired angel pursed her lips in thought. "We're speaking of God's grace here. Grace and mercy are two of those words that we seldom use today, but they are important in understanding just how much God loves us. I once heard someone define them like this: Grace is the granting of a gift we don't deserve, while mercy is the withholding of the punishment we do deserve. You see, salvation isn't something we sinners deserve. It's the gift of God. . .His grace."

"Well, I don't know if I understand all that, but I'll admit to being a sinner. Except, I learned a long time ago that sinners have a lot more fun than saints."

"That's all a matter of perspective. Christians have fun."

"Not all of them." Cynthia's words came slowly. "My first ex-husband was the most miserable guy I ever met. He was mean, too. He wanted a June Cleaver clone for a wife—you know, the kind who wears her dress and pearls to vacuum the living room? The kind who hands her husband his lunchbox and kisses him good-bye at the front door when he leaves for work?" She drew in a wheezy breath. "But I couldn't be that kind of a woman, and I didn't want to be, either. Besides, he didn't love me. All I ever wanted in my life was to be loved. So I decided to. . .to dance and sing. I had a really good voice, too," the woman rasped. "People said I sounded like the gal who sang 'Angel of the Morning.' "

"Shh. . ." Allie patted Cynthia's hand, sensing that she'd only go on repeating herself at this point. "Sleep now."

"Okay, Angel," she said as the tension on her ashen face began to ebb. "Okay, I'll sleep."

*　　*　　*

I'm going to do it, Logan thought, sitting on the end of his bed, staring at the phone in his palm. *Now is the time.* He had been praying about it for months, and at last, he felt in his soul that it was the right thing to do. However, he couldn't deny the fact that his father's words had spurred him on. "Prove it," he'd said. "Marry that nice girl and raise a family. Be happy."

Well, Logan would prove it. This was his chance. Besides, he didn't know of a better way to overcome a phobia than to face it, wrestle with it, and conquer it. That's what he was fond of telling his youth group. Now it was his turn to act.

Pressing the ON button of the cordless phone, he punched in the Domotors' number. He knew it by heart, having called it three times this evening only to disconnect before anyone answered.

But this time, he wouldn't hang up.

"Hello?"

"Mr. Domotor," he began, doing his best to quell the anxious pounding of his heart, "this is Logan Callahan."

"Well, Pastor Logan, how nice to hear from you. What's up?"

"Is this a convenient time for you, Sir? I'm not interrupting your dinner or anything, am I?"

"No, I'm free to talk." A pause. "Is something wrong?"

"No. . .I, um, well. . ." Logan swallowed hard, hoping he didn't sound as nervous as he felt. He took a deep breath. "I would like to ask Marilee to marry me. . .if it's okay with you."

Stan Domotor chuckled. "You had me worried there for a minute. Sure. . .you have my blessing. You're a fine young man, and I know how my daughter feels about you."

"Did you want to pray about it first?" Logan held his breath.

"Naw, I've been praying all along."

"Glad to hear it." Logan started to relax.

"When do you think you'll pop the question?"

"I was thinking tomorrow, seeing that it's Saturday and we don't have an activity planned with the youth group." Rubbing the back of his neck, Logan still didn't know how that happened. He thought he'd filled every weekend through the end of the year. "Maybe I'll take Marilee out to dinner, and—"

"Let me put her mother on."

Logan waited as the phone was passed, but not before Mr. Domotor informed his wife of the news.

"How exciting, Logan!" Eileen Domotor squealed. "Now, about the engagement ring. . ."

Oh, right, he'd need one of those. How could he have forgotten that little detail?

"There's a store in the mall called Precious Gems, and Marilee has absolutely fallen in love with a wedding set there. Of course, it won't be sized by tomorrow. But you could give it to her and she could get it sized."

Logan found a pen in his desk drawer and jotted down particulars. "She won't be disappointed if the ring doesn't fit right away? I mean, I could wait a week or two before asking her—"

"Oh, no, no, no. Don't wait."

Logan tamped down his mild disappointment. But in the next moment, he realized he didn't want to put off the inevitable any longer.

"I'm so delighted about this," Mrs. Domotor shrilled. "Now, let me tell you about the ring Marilee wants. It's a gold and silver band with a solitary diamond. . . ."

Logan made his notes, hoping he'd find the right one. Glancing at his watch, he figured he still had a couple of hours to get over to the mall before it closed.

"Now, about tomorrow night. . .why don't you plan to come to our apartment first?" Mrs. Domotor said. "I'll get Marilee over here by making up a little fib." The woman laughed. "Once you get here, my husband and I will slip out of the living room and you can propose. What was that, Dear? Oh, wonderful. . .Logan, my husband said he'll buy a dozen roses for the occasion and have them in the living room. Marilee will be so surprised."

Logan had to chuckle just imagining Marilee's expression. He'd barely seen her all week because he'd been so busy. When he "popped the question" tomorrow, she would likely pass out from the shock.

"Five o'clock, Logan. Does that sound all right?"

"In the morning?" he said, grinning. "Sounds great."

Silence met him at the other end of the phone.

"I'm kidding." He laughed and his tumultuous case of the nerves dissipated. "Guess I'm just a little excited myself."

CHAPTER ELEVEN

Jack couldn't believe he was braving the mall with Logan on a Friday night—and for an engagement ring, of all things!

"How did you manage to talk me into this?"

Logan chuckled from the passenger seat in his dad's SUV. "Call it answered prayer. God knew I needed the moral support."

"Look, you don't *have* to buy a ring tonight, you know," Jack advised. "You could shop around awhile and make sure you're getting a deal."

"Sure, I could. . .but don't I need something to give Marilee tomorrow when I propose?"

"Don't ask me. This is out of my league. When I got married, I bought a couple of wedding bands from a guy I knew who used to run a pawn shop."

"How romantic," Logan quipped.

Jack grinned. "Better watch it, Kid. My sarcasm is rubbing off on you."

"Hm. . .good thing you pointed that out."

Pulling into the mall's busy parking lot, Jack chuckled. He had to confess that the more time he spent with his son, the more he actually *liked* him. It's as though their relationship had reached the father/son boundary and now teetered on friendship.

"You're all right, Logan, know that?" Jack said as they strode to the doors of the mall.

His son let out a long sigh. "Let's hope Marilee agrees."

Jack smiled. "She will. Anyone can see she's nuts about you."

"You can tell, huh?"

"Of course I can tell. Can't you?"

"Yeah. . .but I've got half a dozen girls in the youth group who are 'nuts' about me, too. I don't intend to marry any one of them." Logan slowed his pace. "I just wish I knew for certain that—"

"Well, you can't. There's nothing 'certain' about life. Just read the Book of Job. God might decide to make an example out of you, too, and rip everything near and dear right out from under you."

"Dad. . ."

"Don't get me started."

Logan didn't say another word as they eyed the marquee just inside the mall's entrance. Locating the store, they ambled off in search of it.

Jack had not been in a mall for years for anything other than a shoplifting call. Passing him in either direction were young people of various ages and stages of dress—or rather undress. He noticed, and not for the first time, either, that both males and females wore earrings in parts of their bodies that Jack, in his wildest imaginings, would never dream of piercing. He had to admit to an apprehensive pang when he thought of these kids as the next police chiefs, doctors, lawyers, and legislators.

"Heaven help us," he muttered.

"What?" Logan said, turning his way. "Kinda noisy in here."

"Look around you. You've got your work cut out for you, Mr. Youth Pastor."

"I'll say!" A slow grin curved his mouth. "We'll actually be recruiting here in the mall for our hayride and bonfire activity pretty soon."

Jack just nodded. He knew a lot of these teens and young adults probably needed a sense of purpose. He had spent enough years counseling in juvenile hall, especially early on in his career. But how could he advocate what Logan peddled as "the Way, the Truth, and the Life"? At one time, he believed it; but Jesus Christ had turned His back on him when Jack needed Him most.

"Here's the jewelry store."

Jack gave himself a mental shake and entered the shop right behind Logan. He eyed the sparkling diamonds inside glass cases while his son approached the salesman behind the counter. In Jack's summation, the trinkets were far too pricey.

"Dad." Logan waved him over. "This guy says he knows just the ring I described."

"How much is it?"

"I haven't gotten that far yet."

"That should have been your first question."

The blond salesman, who looked no older than twenty, gave Jack a condescending grin. Then he set a black velvet-lined tray of rings in front of Logan.

"All our wedding sets have names and are as unique as the artists who design them," the salesman said.

Jack rolled his eyes, unimpressed.

"The set you described is called 'Here's My Heart.' It's four-teen karat gold with a sterling ribbon inlay." He handed Logan a small magnifying glass. "The diamond is almost half a carat, and as you can see, it's heart-shaped. Notice, also, that the wedding band fits exquisitely around the engagement ring."

"That's pretty nice," Logan said, after inspecting the ring. He looked over at Jack.

"How much?"

Logan gave the salesman a quizzical stare, and the man flipped the price tag around.

Seeing his son blanch, Jack laughed. "That much, eh?"

"Too much. *Way* too much."

Jack laughed all the harder.

"I'm a poor youth pastor," Logan told the clerk. "I can't afford this on my salary. Do you have anything comparable?"

"No, nothing. Sorry." The clerk put the ring back into its velvet crib.

"Logan, this isn't the only jewelry store on earth," Jack said. "We can look around."

With a resigned sigh, he nodded. "Hey, what about your friend at the pawn shop?"

Jack grinned. "Last I heard he was doing twenty years."

"Great."

After another round of chuckles, Jack looked at the clerk. "Don't you have any sales going on right now?"

"Well. . .I suppose I could give you fifteen percent off. That's our VIP discount, which we give to only our best customers."

Jack came around and stood beside Logan. Lifting the magnifying glass, he inspected the ring, glanced at the price, and whistled. "This costs as much as the down payment on my first house."

"Times they are a changin'," the clerk crooned.

Jack gave him a quelling look and set the ring down. Rapping Logan in the upper arm, he said, "Let's go."

"Okay." Nodding politely at the salesman, he thanked him for his time.

Jack led the way out of the store and into the mall. From there he and Logan visited two other jewelers, but found nothing to Logan's satisfaction. They ended up in the food court with colas and slices of pizza so their trip wouldn't be a total waste of time.

"How much money did you want to spend on a ring?" Jack asked.

Logan wiped his mouth with his paper napkin. "A thousand. I think that's about how much I paid for. . .for Sarah's ring."

"Don't tell me you still have feelings for that girl."

"Sarah?" Logan shook his head. "No. It's just that it was awkward having to ask for the ring back. I ended up selling it back to the jewelers and took a big loss. And then there was all the emotional junk that went along with the broken engagement. I just don't ever want to go through something like that again."

"I never did like her, you know."

Logan's eyes widened. "No, I didn't know."

Jack nodded. "I thought she was stuck-up. . .snooty."

"I hope you like Marilee."

Having just taken a large bite of pizza, Jack could only nod. "That's encouraging."

"She seems down to earth, honest. . . ."

"Yeah, she is." Logan fiddled with the straw on his covered cup. "So what should I do about a ring? I doubt I'll find just the right one for the price I want to pay."

Jack set his pizza down and wiped his hands. "Let's go back and buy that first ring. You put a grand toward it and I'll pay the rest."

Logan raised his dark brows in surprise. "Are you serious?"

"Yeah, I'm serious. This idea has been floating around my head since we left that shop—in spite of its smart-aleck clerk." Jack narrowed his gaze and regarded his son, noting his troubled expression. "Look, you might as well make Marilee happy right from the start."

"I don't know. You'd have to fork out an awful lot of money."

"Consider it an early wedding present."

Logan took a long drink of his cola. "I don't want Marilee to think I've got plenty of cash. That would be like. . .false advertising or something."

Jack grinned. "She's smarter than that. Besides, I don't think Marilee cares. In fact, I'd go so far as to bet she wouldn't mind if her engagement ring came from a Cracker Jack box. She's that crazy about you."

"Yeah? You think?" Logan wore an ear-to-ear grin.

Jack nodded. "I'm a good judge of character."

"I'd have to agree with you there."

Glancing at his watch, Jack realized they only had half an hour before the mall closed. "Come on," he said, standing and tossing his empty paper plate and cup onto the red plastic tray. "We've got a diamond ring to buy."

*　　*　　*

Bone tired after a grueling week, Allie slept in on Saturday. When she finally roused herself, she made a light breakfast and phoned Nicholas. The two of them chatted away the rest of the morning as they caught up on each other's busy lives.

"Just be careful, Mom," Nick said. "Sounds like you're getting pulled into some muddied waters, and I don't want to see you get in over your head."

"I'm a big girl, Nick," she said with a grin.

"I'm just trying to be a good son and look out for you," he countered.

"Well, all right. . ."

Allie chuckled and took a sip of her coffee.

"So you're seeing your stepsisters tonight?"

"Yes, and for some weird reason I'm nervous."

"Understandable."

"Colleen seems very sweet, and we had no problems getting reacquainted; but Brenda and I never really got along. I'm hoping things will be different now."

"Jen and I will be praying for you."

"That's a comfort to me in and of itself. Thanks. Now tell me, what's happening at church?"

"Nothing really new since I last e-mailed you."

Nick gave her a few more particulars, none of which were all that exciting, although Allie had to admit to a sense of homesickness. She missed her friends and church family in California. But it wouldn't be long and she'd be back home.

After finishing her call, Allie set down the phone, showered, and dressed. She spent the better part of the afternoon running errands, first to the dry cleaners, next to the Laundromat, and finally a stop at the grocery store. She returned to her hotel suite in time to ready herself for her dinner date with Colleen and Brenda.

Dressing for the event, she pulled on an A-line navy skirt and a deep pink cotton sweater, ornamented with crocheted flowers of deep blue and white. Next, she brushed out her hair. As she applied her cosmetics, Allie tried to remember the last time she'd seen Brenda. It had to have been the night her step-father slapped her, because Allie had packed her things and left at a time when she knew no one would be at home.

"You deserved it," she recalled Brenda sneering while Allie sobbed in her bedroom after the assault. As a teenager, Brenda had been built more like a man than a budding female, with her broad shoulders and slim hips. "You think you're such a princess, but you're a stuck-up, spoiled brat! We all hate you!"

The following day, Allie's stepfather apologized and forced his daughters to do the same. While Colleen expressed sincer-ity, Brenda had not, although she had muttered the word "Sorry." Even so, it was too late in Allie's opinion. Her mind was made up. She planned to run away from home. . . .

And that's exactly what she did.

With her makeup on, Allie slipped small gold hoops into her ears and slid a thick multicolored bangle onto her wrist. She inspected her reflection once more, then walked to the edge of her bed and got down on her knees.

"Heavenly Father," she prayed, "please bless this coming evening. Please soften Brenda's heart if she still harbors any ani-mosity toward me. Give me a chance to tell her—no, show her that I've changed. Allow her to see that I no longer resemble that confused, selfish, rebellious older sister, but that I'm now a God-fearing woman."

Allie lingered over her short prayer before standing. Taking a deep breath, she grabbed her purse and keys and left the hotel suite.

*　　*　　*

"What gorgeous roses!" After inhaling their fragrant scent, a horrible thought shot through Marilee. She whirled around and faced her parents. "Did I forget your anniversary?" She searched her memory.

"No, Silly. Dad and I were married in March."

Marilee sighed with relief and her mother laughed.

"I just bought those. . .oh, just because," her father said with a strange grin.

All afternoon, her parents had been displaying rather bizarre behavior. Her mother invited her to dinner and, instead of a simple fare, she'd prepared a Thanksgiving-like feast. In addition, Mom and Dad, both, had dressed in their Sunday best, and they fussed over minor details as though they expected the president of the United States to make an appearance. And now her dad brought out a dozen long-stemmed red roses in a crystal vase and set them on the end of the baby grand piano in their living room.

"You two haven't set me up with a blind date or something, have you?" Marilee asked suspiciously.

"Now why would we do that?" her father said, his brown eyes twinkling. "We know you're serious about a certain youth pastor."

The reference to Logan caused Marilee to feel a mite discouraged. She hadn't seen him all week, except for the midweek worship service when she helped with the youth group. But even then, she and Logan barely said five words to each other. How could they, with all those girls vying for his attention? To his credit, though, Logan handled things with his usual finesse. His challenge to all the teens that evening had been to obey

God's Word and do things to His glory, rather than trying to be a "man pleaser" and impress others—namely their handsome youth pastor. Marilee could only pray the girls had taken his message to heart.

"All right, what's going on here?" Marilee asked.

"You'll find out soon enough," her mother replied, pushing several brunette tendrils off her forehead.

"Ah-ha! So you did plan something!"

"Sort of," her dad said, his balding head perspiring slightly from his efforts at readying their condo to nothing short of perfection. "Let's just say we're in on the planning. This was someone else's idea."

"Whose?"

"Stop asking so many questions, Marilee," her mother said, turning on her heel and reentering the kitchen.

The phone rang, and her father laughed. "Saved by the bell."

Marilee rolled her eyes at the remark. In resignation, she plopped herself on the floral-upholstered sofa and grabbed a magazine off the coffee table. She eyed her faded denim skirt that had seen better days and suddenly felt underdressed. "You should have told me to wear something nicer if the queen of England is coming to dinner," she called to her mother.

No reply.

"Marilee?"

She looked at her father, who extended the telephone toward her. "It's Logan. He wants to speak with you."

"Logan?" Eileen Domotor fairly raced from the kitchen, wiping her hands on the red-and-white-checked apron she wore over her dress. "Why is he calling? He should be—"

"Never mind, Dear. Something's come up. I'll tell you about it in a moment."

Accepting the phone from her dad, Marilee watched as he ushered her mother back into the kitchen.

What is with these two? she wondered, raising the portable phone to her ear. "Hello?"

"Hi, it's me."

"Me who?"

"Logan."

"Logan who?" she teased him.

"Very funny. . .although I suppose I deserve it."

Marilee grinned. At least he could admit it. "How did you know where to find me?"

"Um. . .lucky guess. Hey, listen," he said, all traces of humor disappearing from his tone, "I need your help. Susan Rushford was hit by a car this afternoon while riding her bike."

Marilee gasped and sat up straighter on the couch. "Is she okay?"

"For the most part. She's got a few broken bones. I'm at the hospital with her parents and I wondered if you'd come down."

"Of course. Which hospital?"

"St. Anthony's."

"I'll be right there."

"Thanks. I knew I could count on you."

The comment warmed Marilee's heart and somehow made up for this past week's neglect. Pressing the OFF button, she unceremoniously tossed the phone onto the couch. "I gotta go," she called to her parents.

Stan and Eileen appeared side-by-side at the doorway. Their expressions seemed a mixture of dread and disappointment.

"Sorry about running out on you like this."

"Don't worry about it," her father said. "Logan explained everything."

"We'll be praying for Susan," her mother added.

After a nod, Marilee picked up her purse and draped its strap over her shoulder. Then she left her folks' apartment.

CHAPTER TWELVE

Allie arrived at Brenda's house on Pine Street in Oakland Park. Located in the center of the block in an older part of the community, the home was a typical Midwest duplex, complete with a wide front porch. Stepping up to the door, Allie ignored the fact that the wood siding and trim needed paint, as did the porch. She pressed on the bell, which set a couple of dogs to barking. Moments later, a rotund man in a white undershirt appeared. Through the rusty screen door, Allie could see that his brown hair was disheveled and his trousers rumpled. He looked as though he'd just awakened from an afternoon snooze on the sofa.

"Sorry to disturb you," Allie began, "but I'm looking for Brenda."

The man nodded. "She'll be right out."

He turned and hollered at the dogs to be quiet before walking away and leaving Allie to wait on the porch. She couldn't say she really minded. The late afternoon sun felt warm in spite of a cool breeze. While it wasn't officially fall yet, autumn was definitely in the air.

Standing there waiting, Allie glanced around the neighborhood. Tall elm trees lined the sidewalk and formed a leafy canopy over the quiet street. A car suddenly turned the corner, pulled alongside the curb, and parked. Allie smiled, seeing Colleen climb out from behind the wheel.

"What are you doing on the porch?" she asked, stepping up to the house. She wore a blue-and-white-striped T-shirt dress with a white sweater draped over her shoulders. "Isn't anyone home?"

"Yes, someone's home. The man who answered the door said Brenda would be right out."

Colleen rolled her eyes. "Oh, that's Dave. He's such a goof." She pressed on the bell. "Dave, it's Colleen. You've got company. Let us in."

Again, the dogs began to bark until Dave hushed them and came back to the doorway. "Brenda will be right out."

"Let me in, will you?"

Dave unhooked the screen door and Colleen opened it. Two cocker spaniels bounded out of the house, their tails wagging. Allie petted the friendly animals while Colleen spoke in undertones with Dave, who Allie assumed was Brenda's husband.

"Oh, fine," she said at last. "We'll wait out here. But tell her to hurry. I'm hungry."

The dogs were called back into the house, and Colleen explained the situation.

"Brenda doesn't want you to see her house because she had to work overtime today and didn't get a chance to clean."

"I totally understand. Been there myself."

"Kind of hard to imagine—you with a messy house, I mean. You were always such a neat-freak."

"Well, you're right," Allie confessed, "about the neat-freak business. But I do understand because I have a son and, in his younger days, he was messy."

"Now multiply that by three, because Brenda's got two boys in high school. . .and she's got Dave. Biggest kid of all."

"I heard that, Colleen," he called from the living room.

She laughed, unrepentant.

Allie just smiled, trying to get a sense of what her stepsisters' lives were like now.

"At least it's not raining," Colleen muttered as she folded her arms and made impatient little taps with her foot.

Dave came to the door. "Brenda's changing clothes 'cause she found out you both are wearing dresses."

"For pity sakes!" Colleen exclaimed. "Who cares?"

Her husband shrugged. "Don't ask me."

"Dave, I'm Allie Littenberg. I take it you're Brenda's husband."

"Yeah. Nice to meet you."

"Oh, where are my manners," Colleen said with an apologetic glance at Allie. "I should have introduced you two. I'm sorry."

"No problem," Allie said.

Without a word, Dave walked away again.

As if sensing Allie's wonderment over Dave's peculiar behavior, Colleen steered her off the porch and toward the street.

"Brenda's divorcing Dave," she whispered, "so things are pretty tense between them right now."

"I'm sorry to hear that."

Colleen shrugged. "I just try to act natural around them and pretend I don't know what's going on."

"Any chance of reconciliation?"

"Not unless you believe in miracles."

Allie smiled. "I do."

"No, Allie, I'm talking a real act of God."

"He moved mountains and parted seas in Moses' time, and He's the same God today."

Colleen shook her head. "We're talking Brenda and Dave here. Not the movie *The Ten Commandments.*"

Allie laughed, knowing her stepsister didn't understand. But she did. And she could pray. . .

The screen door opened, and both Allie and Colleen looked back to see Brenda emerge from the house. She still had the same stocky build as Allie recalled, but she offset it by a shoulder-length, feminine hairstyle.

"I thought you were changing," Colleen said.

"I own one dress and I have no idea where it is at the moment," Brenda retorted.

"You look fine," Allie said, taking in the other woman's black slacks and white blouse. Her black and white beaded necklace complemented the outfit. "It's nice to see you again, Brenda."

"Notice that she's a redhead now," Colleen teased.

After throwing her sister a dubious glance, she looked at Allie. "Well, well, if it's not the princess in all her glory standing on my front walk."

Allie's heart plummeted into the pit of her stomach. Brenda's resentment is what she had feared would spoil this evening.

"Oh, come on," Colleen said with a little laugh. "That was eons ago, Brenda. You weren't perfect back then, either, you know?"

The woman's stiff glare appeared to soften.

"Brenda, you're right," Allie said, hoping to bridge the gap by admitting her fault. "I was a spoiled little brat who always wanted my own way. But can we put that all behind us?"

"Guess we'll see what happens."

"Fair enough," Allie said, smiling.

Brenda's frown seemed to intensify.

"Allie, we decided on the Mexican restaurant on Central Avenue," Colleen said.

"Lovely," she replied, disguising the fact she disliked Mexican food. However, she wasn't about to voice her opinion and have Brenda accuse her of being "the princess" again.

"Should we take my car, or would you prefer to follow Brenda and me?"

Allie deliberated the options and decided on taking her own vehicle. "I'll follow you. That way I can drive back to the hotel from the restaurant."

"Okay, we'll see you there." Colleen looked at her sister. "Come on."

"I'm coming," she all but growled.

Once inside the rented Cavalier, Allie began to pray. This evening wasn't starting out the way she had hoped, although Colleen was proving to be a wonderful mediator.

Reaching Central Avenue, Allie found an empty parking space a few cars away from her stepsisters. Getting out of the vehicle, she searched her purse for some loose change. Finding it, she put several coins into the parking meter before proceeding up the sidewalk to meet Colleen and Brenda—

Only to see them conversing with Jack.

Oh, great, she thought on a facetious note. Although Allie reminded herself that on Labor Day, Jack was almost cordial to her. Almost.

"Hey, Jack, did you see who's in town?" Brenda said, thumbing to Allie from over her broad shoulder. "A blast from the past."

He glanced at Allie, then nodded at Brenda. "Yeah, I know." As she neared him, he looked at her again. "Hi, Allie."

"Hi." Allie smiled, relieved that Jack seemed to be in an amiable mood.

"Saw you on TV the other night," he said, placing a parking ticket on the windshield of a car.

Allie frowned in confusion. "The other night?"

"On the news. You were standing behind some red-haired guy during a press conference."

"Oh, of course. . ."

"A press conference on TV?" Brenda muttered in a sarcastic vein. "Whoo-hoo, how impressive."

Jack raised his brows and gave Brenda a curious glance. However, he didn't comment on her remark. Allie, on the other hand, wondered if her stepsister was trying to be funny or purposely insulting.

"So, Jack, want to join us?" Brenda asked. "We're going to La Fiesta, where I plan to have several margaritas."

"Don't let me catch you driving home," he replied in his standard dry manner.

"Not to worry. Colleen is my DD."

Allie glanced down at the tips of her navy pumps and wished she were anywhere else right now. She dreaded the rest of the evening and could only imagine how ugly things might get if Brenda became intoxicated.

"Come on, Jack," her stepsister persisted.

"You're more than welcome to join us," Colleen said, "but you're probably on duty all night, right?"

"Right."

"Well, even cops have to eat," Brenda said.

At his hesitation, Allie felt obligated to concur. She looked at Jack. "If you get a dinner break, join us."

He glanced at each of the three women and grinned. "I'll think about it, okay? Now, go eat before your meters run out and I have to give you all tickets."

Brenda put her hands on her straight hips. "Don't Oakland Park cops have something better to do on Saturday night than give out parking tickets?"

"Guess not," Jack replied with an edge in his voice.

"I think we've harassed this poor man enough," Allie said, hearing what she deemed was annoyance in his tone. "Let's go eat and. . .Jack," she added, "our offer stands if you change your mind." With that, she began walking toward the restaurant. Footsteps behind her said Colleen and Brenda followed.

Once inside the colorfully decorated restaurant, they waited nearly ten minutes to be seated. Finally escorted to their table, they slid into its semicircular padded bench, and the greeter handed them menus. True to her word, Brenda, sitting in the middle, ordered a margarita while Colleen requested a diet cola and Allie an iced tea.

Studying the menu, Allie searched for something that suited her tastes.

"I know what I'm having," Brenda said, slapping her menu down on the table.

"Yeah," Colleen answered. "I think I know what I want, too. . . . Oh, look! Here comes Jack!"

Allie had only enough time to look up at Colleen before Jack slid onto the bench beside her.

She scooted over, nearer to Brenda.

"I decided to live dangerously," he said, lifting the discarded menu. The small radio he wore on his shoulder crackled with sounds of a dispatch. Jack listened, but seemed unimpressed with the call.

He opened the menu and nudged Allie. "Hey, I remember when you couldn't stand Mexican food."

She tried to cover her surprise at his remark—and her surprise that he remembered. "Well, you know how it goes," she replied with purposed ambiguity, careful to keep her eyes on the menu.

"This is my favorite restaurant," Brenda told him. "I come here all the time. So when Colleen said Allie was in town and wanted to go out for dinner, I suggested it."

"Hmm. . ."

Allie felt like dissolving into a fit of laughter. The tension warranted it, and she knew Jack had just guessed that her dislike for Mexican food hadn't changed in thirty years. With her thumb and forefinger on either side of her mouth, she pursed her lips together to keep from smiling and hoped she looked as though she were deep in thought.

But then she made the mistake of glancing at Jack. Meeting his knowing glance, she laughed aloud.

"What's so funny?" Colleen asked as the waitress set down their drinks.

"Nothing," Allie said, shaking her head at her own silly behavior.

"Some things never change," Jack muttered, looking over the menu. "Like square dancing."

Allie laughed again, relieved to see her stepsisters weren't paying her much attention as they gave the tall, willowy waitress their orders.

"They have good steaks here," Jack murmured.

"Whew, that's a relief," Allie said, still chuckling.

Jack actually grinned at her reply.

When the waitress looked her way, Allie ordered. The New York strip, medium-well, and a tossed salad with onions, tomatoes, and green and red peppers.

Jack ordered the restaurant's "Saturday Night Special," a variety of Mexican samplings, and a large cola.

Gathering the menus, the waitress left.

"How's Royce?" Jack asked Colleen.

"Oh, he's fine. He's going bowling tonight with some guys from work."

"I understand your baseball team stunk this past year," Brenda said with a hooded glance at Jack.

He shrugged. "You win some, you lose some."

"Some? You guys didn't even win *one*."

"We'll do better next year," Jack said, reclining in his portion of the booth.

"Are you and Colleen and Brenda's husbands all on the same baseball team?" Allie inquired, looking at Jack.

"No, just Royce and me—although Dave could play if he wanted to. It's a little community team and we go up against the neighboring suburbs."

"My husband only watches baseball on TV from the couch," Brenda said. "He's a regular sofa spud."

No one replied, and Allie felt the tension mounting once again.

"I'm getting a divorce, Jack. Did you hear?"

"No, I didn't." He didn't ask why, but Brenda explained anyway.

"I don't love him anymore. In fact, he repulses me as much as his dirty socks. The thrill is definitely gone!"

Brenda finished her margarita and hailed the waitress for another. Allie occupied herself with the lemon floating in her glass of iced tea, thinking of the generational consequences sure to follow Brenda's decision. It was for that very reason that Allie chose to stay with Erich.

Jack sniffed loudly. "Let's hear it for 'for better or worse.'"

Allie gave him a curious glance before looking at Brenda.

"Oh, shut up. Who invited you anyway?" She laughed at her own sarcastic quip.

The waitress brought the second margarita and Jack's cola.

"So, Allie," Colleen said, changing the subject, "how long will you be in town?"

"Probably until the end of November."

"That long, huh?" Brenda quipped.

Allie gave her a curious stare and marveled over her stepsister's blatant rudeness.

"And you're a consultant, right?" Colleen continued. "What exactly does that involve, and where are you working?"

"I'm at a long-term healthcare facility," Allie replied, focusing on Colleen and her questions, "and I'm assisting Lakeland Enterprises, its parent company, in a reorganizational project."

"From what I saw on the news," Jack said, "you've got your work cut out for you."

"Yes, I do," she admitted.

"I work at Steelcast on an assembly line," Brenda said in a biting tone. "I've got a college degree, but I'm in a factory. Go figure."

"What did you major in?" Allie asked.

"English."

Allie thought it over and came up with a half-dozen occupations suitable for someone with an English degree.

"And don't start spouting off a list of all the things I could be doing, either. I don't need anybody telling me my business. Some of us had to make tough choices. We didn't get everything handed to us on a silver platter."

Allie watched Brenda take a long drink of her margarita and understood that the latter had been directed at her. And while she wished she could talk about her own life's trials, she said nothing, sensing it wouldn't do any good at this particular time.

"So, Jack, now that I'm going to be single again, how 'bout the two of us getting together? You and me?"

Allie raised her brow, incredulous, while Colleen nearly choked on a sip of her cola. Brenda gave her sister a couple of whacks between the shoulder blades, and Colleen's coughing abated.

"Better now?"

Colleen nodded.

"Brenda," Jack began, sounding amused, "I wouldn't date you if you were the last woman on earth. It'd be like dating a kid sister or something. I've known you since you were ten years old."

"See, Allie, it's all your fault," Brenda lamented, but once more Allie had to wonder if it was in jest. "You ruined my chances with Jack."

"I didn't even move to Oakland Park until you were fifteen," Allie reminded her. "That means you ruined your own chances with Jack."

"I love it when women fight over me," he muttered with his usual sarcastic flare.

Colleen laughed and Allie rolled her eyes.

"It's still your fault, Allie," Brenda maintained.

"Oh, fine," she said in resignation. "I guess we all need someone to blame for our troubles."

The waitress arrived with their food, and Allie prayed for a new topic of conversation.

"So who do you blame for your troubles, Allie?" Jack asked.

She was just about to bow her head and quietly ask God's blessing on her food when the question struck. She knew Jack liked her about as little as Brenda did, and she chafed under what she felt were the beginnings of another affront.

"I don't blame anyone," she said. Then she couldn't help delivering a sarcastic quip of her own. "I'm the princess, remember? I've had everything handed to me on a silver platter."

Jack had the nerve to chuckle.

"See? She even admits it," Brenda said.

Jack sat back, his food untouched for the moment, and Allie felt her chest constrict with unshed emotion. This was a mistake. This whole dinner was a sham! She wasn't helping anyone. She wasn't bringing glory to the Lord.

Out of the corner of her eye, she saw Jack lift his napkin and spread it across his lap. Out of a sense of propriety, she did the same.

"Look, Brenda," he said, "I happen to know Allie hasn't had it so great, either. So lay off, okay?"

"Good of you to defend her after what she did to you," Brenda shot right back.

"Brenda!" Colleen exclaimed, wearing a shocked expression.

"Look, Brenda," Allie said in a constrained voice, "it's true we didn't get along as teenagers. But we're adults now. Can't things be different?"

"No, they can't. Not as long as you sit there without a hair out of place, with your manicured nails, in your designer sweater—"

"I purchased this sweater at Goodwill!" Allie contended.

"—And your important job that gets you on TV," Brenda went on, talking right over Allie's explanation. "You're living the perfect life now, and you came back to Oakland Park to wave your success in our faces!"

"That's not true!"

"Yeah? Then why didn't you come back years ago?"

Allie opened her mouth to reply, but couldn't find a single excuse.

"That's what I thought." Brenda tossed her napkin onto her plate and muttered something to her sister, who stood up and allowed her out of the booth.

Colleen gave Allie an apologetic look. "She wants to go. I'm. . .I'm sorry."

"Don't worry about it."

"I'll call you and we'll get together before you leave, okay?" Allie nodded. "I'd like that."

Colleen bobbed her head in affirmation. "Bye, Jack."

"Bye, Kiddo."

With that, she strode away from the table to find her sister.

Sitting forward, Allie placed her elbows on either side of her plate, her fingers entwined, and resting under her chin. Several awkward moments lapsed, the only sounds coming from the other patrons and Jack's ever-squawking radio.

"Go ahead and say it," Allie said at long last. "Say, 'I told you so,' because my attempt to make amends with Brenda just blew up in my face."

"I told you so."

Tears sprang into her eyes. She felt emotionally battered, and to think that Jack probably relished the fact hurt her even more.

He forked a bite of food into his mouth. A moment later, he said, "Allie, you couldn't have been so ignorant to think that everyone would be happy to see you again."

"No," she said, sitting back in the seat and dabbing her misty eyes with her napkin, "but I thought they'd give me a second chance."

"Not everyone believes in second chances."

"I guess not."

Jack continued to eat his dinner. "I don't think you know how you appear to others," he said at last, in between mouthfuls. "It's like Brenda said. You look like you're living the perfect life and you've come back to gloat."

"That's not true."

He took a drink of his cola. "It's a sin to waste that steak, Allie."

She shrugged. "Seems I'm not very hungry."

"Well, in that case, you'll have to pardon me for eating in front of you. But this is the only supper break I get."

Allie nodded. "Please, go ahead and eat." She drank some of her iced tea and then picked at her salad, hoping her appetite would return.

"I kinda felt like Brenda does," Jack said, "until Labor Day, when you told me how you got that scar on your cheek."

Allie gave him a curious glance. But instead of expounding on his remark, he devoured another forkful of Mexican food.

She wrinkled her nose. "I don't know how you can eat that stuff."

He chuckled. "Tastes great. I love this place."

"You and Brenda have more in common than you know."

"Don't start, Allie," Jack said, giving her a severe look. "I might think you're jealous or something."

Allie laughed. "Oh, cut it out. You never did scare me."

He had the good grace to smile at her quip.

Cutting into her broiled meat, Allie decided she felt a little hungry after all. "So am I correct in assuming that you don't hate me anymore?"

"No, I don't hate you."

"Can we be friends?"

"Friends?" Jack hurled the word back at her and it stung.

Allie set down her utensils and wiped her mouth with her napkin. She tried to tamp down the hurt she felt, reminding herself that it was entirely her own fault that she was here and in this difficult situation. But if her Heavenly Father needed her to endure this for her own spiritual growth, she would. She'd lived through worse.

"Don't push your luck, Allie."

Gazing out over the restaurant, she blinked back errant

tears. Steadying her emotions, she took a deep breath and forced herself to concentrate on her dinner. "Okay. . ."

Several moments of strained silence lapsed in which Allie chose to give up eating and take home the remainder of her meal.

"Let me ask you something," Jack said at last.

Allie gave him an expectant look.

"You were never the kind of female who would tolerate a guy smacking her around. Why did you stay with your husband if he was abusive?"

"It's like I told you on Labor Day. Erich said he'd take my son away if I divorced him, and I knew he had the money and the means to do it. Then, after. . . ," she inadvertently touched her cheek, ". . .after he cut my cheek—"

"Were you arguing?" Jack interrupted.

"Sort of. I had a tendency to, um, talk back to my husband. I know you find that hard to believe, Jack—"

He grinned.

"—but it's true, and it really irritated him. At the time of the. . .accident, I was cooking dinner for our fifth anniversary when he told me to do something and I sassed him. Erich picked up the knife I had just set down and swung. I correctly refer to it as an 'accident,' because I believe he intended to slit my throat, but I ducked. He got my cheek."

"And you stayed with the guy? What's wrong with you?"

Allie didn't even flinch; the question had been thrown at her many times before. "As I said, God got a hold of my heart after that, and I strongly believed He wanted me to live out First Peter, chapter three, verse one. I obeyed, and the Lord protected me through the years until Erich's death." She sipped her tea and set down the glass. "Of course I don't go around advising women with abusive spouses to do as I did. That's simply what God wanted me to do." There was an intermittent pause, so she added, "God blessed my obedience. He kept Erich away—overseas. I rarely saw him after the. . .accident."

Jack tossed his napkin onto his now-empty plate. Sitting back, he stretched an arm over the top of the booth's seat. "When did he die?"

"About eleven years ago."

"Long time to be widow. How come you never remarried?"

She shrugged, unsure of whether she wanted to share that part of her past. While there had been two men she'd seriously considered marrying over the years, things hadn't worked out.

"What about you? You've been divorced longer than I've been widowed. Why didn't you remarry? Personal conviction?"

"Hardly."

Jack gave her a hard stare, and Allie thought he might tell her to mind her business. Then, again, he wasn't exactly minding his.

"I found out marriage isn't so great an institution after all."

"If you'll recall, I told you so," Allie quipped.

"Very funny."

She smiled, although she really hadn't intended to be "funny."

As the waitress passed, Allie waved her over and requested a box for the rest of her meal. Nodding, the young woman took Jack's plate away.

Silence ensued until the waitress returned. She handed Allie a Styrofoam box and set down the check, thanking them for their business.

Allie reached for the bill, but Jack snatched it up first.

"My male ego won't let you pick up the tab," he said in a matter-of-fact tone.

"Fine." Allie began to empty her plate into the box. "My female sensibilities are more than happy to let you pay."

Wearing a wry grin, Jack crawled out of the booth and for the first time, Allie saw him limp when he took a few steps forward. She remembered what Logan said about the gunshot wound and how Jack tried not to let anyone see. . .except his higher-ups had seen and now they were trying to force him into retirement.

Retirement or checking parking meters, perhaps.

Once Allie was ready, Jack politely helped her out of the booth with a hand at her elbow. Next, he motioned for her to go on ahead of him, which she did; and while he paid for their meals, she stepped outside. Darkness had descended and the wind had turned cold. *A fitting ending for a dismal evening,* Allie thought, disliking the cynicism in her heart. Hadn't she prayed over this dinner? Yes. Then she had to believe its results were the Lord's will. She couldn't fathom any good coming of it, but God's ways were higher than her ways.

Jack walked out of the restaurant. "I've got to get back to work."

Allie nodded. "Thanks for. . .picking up the tab."

"Sure."

After a parting smile, she turned and strode up the block to her car.

CHAPTER THIRTEEN

A northwest wind whipped around Logan as he sat in the hospital parking lot on the trunk of his maroon Mercury Sable. One foot on the bumper and leaning on his blue jean-encased knee, he thought the brisk air felt good after a night in the much-too-warm emergency room. But one glance at Marilee, standing beside his car, let him know she was freezing.

He shrugged out of his jacket and tucked it around her shoulders. "Better?"

Beneath the white beam of the streetlight, Logan saw her dimpled smile. "Much better. Thanks."

He studied her face for a long moment, thinking she was the prettiest woman he knew.

"You were a real blessing to the Rushfords tonight," she said.

"I couldn't have done it without you." He meant every word, too.

Her smile broadened. "We make a great team."

"Yeah?" He grinned. "So what's your point?"

After a cluck of her tongue, she gave him a playful sock in the arm.

He laughed, glancing around the sparsely populated lot. If she only knew what he'd planned tonight. . . .

The truth was, Logan ached to propose, but he wanted the perfect setting in which to ask Marilee to be his wife. A hospital's parking lot just wouldn't do.

"Want to grab something to eat?"

Marilee shook her head. "I'm still full from that cheeseburger I ate earlier."

"Yeah. . ."

Logan wasn't hungry, either. His stomach had been somersaulting all week from a good case of the nerves as he anticipated this very night. If he waited any longer, he'd probably have an ulcer.

"Want to go for a walk?"

"No, I'm tired. It's almost eleven o'clock, Logan."

"Mmm. . ."

"Aren't you tired?"

"No. I sort of have. . .um, unfinished business. I probably won't sleep until it's taken care of, either. If you haven't noticed, I'm one of those obsessive-compulsive people."

"I'll agree with the obsessive part."

Logan chuckled.

Marilee snuggled deeper into his jacket. "Is it about finding your birth mother?"

He shook his head. "No. . .no, it's not about her."

"Oh? Then what?"

Logan looked her way and explained. "My dad and I had a couple of heavy conversations this week. He answered every question I threw at him."

"I'm so glad to hear that. It's time the two of you talked."

Logan shrugged. "Yeah, but what's sad is that my mother heard the gospel and rejected it. She could have had a husband who probably would have grown to love her—and vice versa—had she given their marriage a chance. But she rejected that, too. My father told me why she never tried to contact me—she was in trouble with the law and was afraid of him, since he's a cop. But I still think she could have at least sent me a lousy birthday card each year."

"Oh, Logan, I'm sorry. But don't you see? That's all the more reason to leave that part of your past alone. Your biological mother's love is not love worth finding." She moved closer. "But mine is."

Logan smirked. "Is that right? Well, maybe you've got a point. Maybe I need to put my energies into something else. Something more constructive."

"Such as the youth group?"

"Mmm, no. Something much more important and time consuming."

"Oh." Marilee fell silent. "Like what?

He swiveled so he could face her, wishing he could forestall this moment until they weren't in a parking lot and yet dying to pop the question. "See, I want to. . .well, it's. . . Oh, man, I don't know how to say this. . . ."

Marilee's expression fell as she tipped her head and scrutinized his every feature. "What don't you know how to say, Logan? Is it about us?"

"It sure is."

She stood there, gaping at him, and her eyes filled. "You don't want to see me anymore? Is there someone else you're interested in?"

Logan set his hands on her shoulders, feeling bad for teasing her. "No, no, nothing like that. Marilee, didn't you hear what I said before? You were a great help to me tonight. I don't know what I would have done without you."

The wounded frown slowly disappeared from her face. Pushing himself off the end of the car, Logan walked around to the passenger side. He couldn't put it off any longer. Digging out the keys from his pocket, he unlocked the door and then the glove compartment. He located the ring box and stuffed it in the sleeve of his sweatshirt. That done, he closed the car and strode back around to where Marilee stood beneath the lamppost.

"Okay, this isn't the way I had it planned, but I've got an idea. We'll dissociate a little. Close your eyes."

"Huh?"

"Close your eyes."

She did as he bid her.

"All right, now imagine that we're in your parents' upscale apartment. The sun is streaming through the patio doors and—"

She inhaled sharply. "Are there red roses on the piano by any chance?" she asked suspiciously, peeking at him through one opened eye.

Logan grinned. "Yeah, as a matter of fact there are."

She stared at him wide-eyed. "Logan, what's going on?"

"Shh. . .close your eyes."

After a sweet little pout, she complied.

"Okay, now imagine that there's soft, romantic music playing on your dad's stereo system."

"Is it Bach or Chopin. . .Mozart?"

"Whatever."

Marilee laughed softly.

Logan took a step closer and gazed down into her face. Even in the dark and with her eyes closed, he could make out Marilee's every feature. In that moment, she reminded him of Sleeping Beauty and he was hard pressed to squelch his desire to kiss her.

Just then, she opened her eyes and appeared startled. She laughed. "You were so quiet that I thought maybe you ran off and left me here looking like an idiot with my eyes closed."

"No. . .no youth group pranks tonight." Logan swallowed hard. He'd had a nice, little speech all worked out, but suddenly he couldn't recall any of it. He tried to think of how to begin.

Marilee put her hand around his. Her fingers felt ice-cold. *The poor woman is freezing to death and I'm tongue-tied.*

"Logan, why don't you just speak from your heart," she suggested. "Just say whatever's on your mind and we'll go from there."

"Okay. . ." He took a deep breath and exhaled slowly. "Marilee, I want you to be my wife. Will you marry me?"

Marilee stared at him, uncertain that she'd heard him correctly. "Marry you?"

"Yes, marry me. I had this all planned and your parents were in on it. Tonight's the night I decided to propose. Unfortunately, Susan had her accident and. . .well, you know the rest." Like a magician's act, Logan pulled out something from inside his sleeve. "Here," he said, lifting her hand and placing a velvety ring box in her palm.

Accepting the gift, Marilee stood back into the light so she could have a better look. She opened the box and, seeing the engagement ring of her dreams, felt tears spring into her eyes.

"I don't believe this. . . ."

"I hope you'll forgive the less-than-romantic setting," Logan said, stepping forward and taking the box. He removed the ring. "But having made up my mind, I just couldn't seem to let the night go without 'popping the question' as your dad referred to it."

Marilee lifted her left hand and Logan slipped the ring onto her finger.

"Looks like it's kinda big," he said. "You'll have to get it sized."

She nodded, still dumbfounded. She truly hadn't expected a marriage proposal since last time they talked Logan had some soul-searching to do.

"Well?"

"It's gorgeous. It's the most beautiful ring I've ever seen." She looked back at him. "Did my mother tell you about it?"

Logan nodded. "And our Heavenly Father provided for it through a means that I still can't quite get over. I'll tell you the whole story another time."

"Okay. . ."

"Once I got it in my head to ask you to marry me, God affirmed it three times this week." He expelled an audible breath. "And, man alive, was I nervous!"

Marilee smiled at his boyishness.

"Now, I'm wondering why I got myself so worked up."

She shrugged.

"Except. . .you haven't answered me. Will you marry me or not?"

"Yes. A thousand times yes!"

Caught up in the moment, Marilee threw her arms around Logan's neck. With her cheek pressed against his, Marilee decided she'd never been happier. The man she loved had just asked her to be his wife!

But then she remembered his personal conviction and her promise to abide by it.

"Oh, Logan, I'm so sorry," she said, stepping back as his jacket slipped from her shoulders. She caught it before it hit the ground. "I forgot."

"It's okay," he said, looking chagrined. "It's kind of a special occasion, and it was only a hug."

She gave him a grateful smile. "What about a wedding date?"

"What are you doing next weekend?"

Marilee rolled her eyes. "You are so silly."

"Silly? I'm serious!"

"Weddings take at least a year to plan," she informed him. "Sometimes longer."

"What?" Logan brought his chin back. "I'm not waiting a year to marry you."

"Logan—"

"No way. Look what just happened—and that was only a hug. Can you even imagine the temptations we'll face being engaged for a year?" Logan shook his head. "Uh-uh."

Marilee swallowed any forthcoming argument. She knew her mother would have a fit trying to plan a wedding any sooner than a year. Perhaps, together, they could reason with Logan. As for the temptation aspect. . .well, as with any other, they would just have to pray up and be on guard.

"I'll give you three months," Logan said, sitting down on the trunk of his car again. "I think you can plan a beautiful wedding in three months."

Marilee refused to voice her disagreement and ruin this wonderful moment.

Logan suddenly leaned forward, took hold of her sleeve, and pulled her closer to him. Cupping her chin, he forced her gaze to meet his.

"Are you in love with me or in love with the idea of getting married? It's me you're going to have to live with."

"Of course I'm in love with you, Logan," she told him in all sincerity. Reaching up, she removed his hand from her chin and gave it a quick squeeze. "I feel bad that you even asked me such a question."

"I was trying to make a point, that's all."

With her back against the proverbial wall, Marilee acquiesced. "All right. I've got the man of my dreams, the engagement ring of my dreams—"

"I bought the complete wedding set."

"You did? Oh, wow!" In the shadowed light, she saw Logan's pleased grin. "Well, then, under the circumstances," she drawled playfully, "I suppose I can compromise on the wedding plans."

He chuckled. "That's my girl."

Marilee smiled and looked at the diamond on her finger, sparkling under the florescent glow of the streetlamp. Logan's girl. Now she was really Logan's girl!

*　　*　　*

Cynthia had to admit that service had gotten a little better around here since her angel arrived on the scene. The only thing that had freaked her out were the two cops who entered her room, asking all sorts of questions about the night the CNA hit her. While the policemen had been polite enough, cops in general made Cynthia uneasy. They reminded her too much of her first ex-husband.

It was at that moment another portion of her life flashed before her, and Cynthia tried in vain to will away the image of a brown-eyed infant whose pudgy arms reached out for her as he sat in his crib.

"Nurse! Nurse!" she cried, thrashing at the memory. "Nurse!"

"What is it?" a man asked, opening her door.

"Medicine. I need more medicine."

*   *   *

Jack couldn't sleep. His leg ached like crazy, but that was the least of his problems. There were issues at work, namely the new police chief who seemed bent on driving him off the force. The rumor flying around the department was that Chief Anderson wanted a new breed of officers whom he could "mold and shape" into Oakland Park's finest. Word coming down through the chain of command was that there wasn't room for "set in their ways" veterans—even dedicated ones, like Jack. Two of his buddies had been reduced to trivial administrative tasks, and now Jack was checking parking meters.

Well, he wouldn't put up with it. He'd opt for retirement, although it galled him to give Anderson his way.

And then there was Allie. Was she a tough little lady or just another martyr? He wondered. He wondered, too, why the fact that she didn't remarry pestered him like an annoying horsefly. An intelligent, pretty woman like Allie—she was a good catch for any guy looking to tie the knot. But maybe since she moved around a lot on her consulting job, she never had the time to form lasting relationships. On second thought, that didn't make sense, considering her remark: "If you recall, I told you so."

Yeah, you told me so. The memory of Allie's leaving that day back in '69 replayed through his mind for the umpteenth time.

Finally, he'd had enough of strolling down memory lane. With an irritable groan, he threw off his covers and climbed out of bed. When his leg bothered him, everything else in the world did, too. He made his way into the kitchen, deciding on some warm milk and a couple of ibuprofen tablets. He found Logan sitting at the table working on his notebook computer.

"What are you doing awake?" Jack asked, reaching for a mug.

"Finishing up my Bible study lesson for tomorrow. . .er, make that today." He grinned. "By the way, Marilee said she'd marry me."

"I'm not surprised. Congratulations."

"Thanks. So what are you doing awake at two A.M.?"

"Thinking. I should know better by now. Thinking can be a dangerous thing." Opening the fridge, Jack lifted out the container of milk and poured some into the cup.

"I know it's none of my business, but, you know me. I can't help asking anyway. . .what are you thinking about so hard that you can't sleep?"

"Work, mostly. I'm taking a couple of vacation days. . .right after I put in for my retirement first thing Monday morning. My decision's made."

"Things have gotten that bad, eh?"

"Yep."

"Sorry to hear that. I know your career means everything to you."

Jack stuck his milk into the microwave and watched the numbers count down from forty-five. In those passing seconds, Logan's remark began to fester. "I know your career means everything. . . ."

Beeee-ep.

Jack removed his warm milk. "Listen, I was a lousy excuse for a father and I'm sorry, okay? Life hasn't exactly been all peaches and cream for me, you know."

Logan gave him a puzzled look. "Where's that coming from?"

"You. You insinuated that I've always put my career before you, and you're right. I did. I knew I was a good cop, but I wasn't a good father, so I threw myself into what I did best." He paused, his heart heavy. Now he wasn't even a good cop.

"Dad, we've been over this. I'm not angry with you. Not anymore."

"Well, you should be."

"Why?"

"Because all the wrongs I did can never be undone." Jack sipped his warm milk and grimaced. "Why am I drinking this? I hate this stuff!" He poured the remainder down the sink's drain.

"Dad, I forgive you for any mistakes you made in raising me. But I think I turned out okay regardless." Logan stood and walked over to where Jack was rinsing out his cup. "Now it's time to forgive yourself. Let's move on." He grinned. "I'm getting married in a few months!"

Jack turned off the faucet. "A few months? Why the rush?"

"Why wait?" Logan countered. "If I had my way, we'd elope this week."

Jack grinned and opened the cupboard containing the ibuprofen bottle. Like Logan, once he made up his mind to do something, it was as good as done. "You really are a chip off the ol' block, aren't you?"

"That's what the old ladies in the grocery store tell me."

Chuckling, Jack shook out a few pills and popped them into his mouth. He washed them down with a gulp of water. "Just don't mess up like your old man, got it?"

Logan gave him a confident smile. "Got it."

CHAPTER FOURTEEN

Just as Evan predicted, the media had a field day reporting on what it dubbed "nursing home abuse." Arbor Springs, among other facilities, was fair game; and Monday morning brought dozens of phone calls into Allie's office. She did her best to handle each one according to the script she and the board members of Lakeland Enterprises created.

The accused employee had been suspended without pay, pending police investigation.

An internal evaluation of all staff and a reorganization of each department were in process to ensure the safety of all patients.

While most people with loved ones in Arbor Springs seemed satisfied with the explanation, several opted for transfers to other facilities. Allie had no choice but to let those patients go, knowing all the while that their leaving meant less revenue and peeved board members.

At noon, Allie forwarded her phone to a voice messaging system and took her lunch in the dining room. She sat with the supervisor of the billing department, Gordy Henderson. A jovial African-American man, Gordy exuded optimism and welcomed Allie's presence at Arbor Springs to the point of offering his assistance. Moreover, Allie discovered he was a Christian and a devoted husband and father—traits she respected. In short, he was fast becoming an ally.

"I can't believe this place actually serves a tasty meal," Allie said. "I would have expected the food to be something akin to pabulum."

Gordy laughed and it echoed through the dining area. "That's one thing Arbor Springs does right—its cooking." He laughed again. "And its billing, of course."

"We'll see," Allie said with a wry grin.

His cocoa brown eyes widened at the comeback, but he didn't appear worried in the least, only surprised. Then he chuckled, and the rest of their lunch break passed in amicable banter.

Later, as Allie returned to her office, the security guard at the front reception desk hailed her.

"There are two women out here wanting to speak with you," he said.

She thanked the blond-haired, bright-eyed young man before taking note of his attire for the second time that day. Faded blue jeans, a wrinkled white shirt, and yellow smiley-face tie. She reminded herself to ask Evan about uniforms for security personnel. They showed up in various outfits, some less than professional, but all within the vague dress code guidelines. However, no one in the security department seemed terribly authoritative, and Allie thought imposing a new dress code standard might initiate a change. There was just something about a uniform that commanded a certain level of respect, not to mention professionalism.

"They're over by the TV," the guard told her.

Allie nodded. Glancing in that direction, she spotted the two young ladies. She walked over to them and introduced herself.

"I understand you want to speak with me."

They both stood.

"Our mother is a patient here," the female on Allie's right stated, "and we were told to make sure she's being taken care of."

"Because of what's been on the news," the young lady on the left added.

Both women had long, dark hair, brown eyes, and tanned skin. Each wore a tangled collection of gold necklaces, multiple earrings in each lobe, and several bracelets on their wrists. They were dressed in shorts and halters, and Allie guessed the young ladies to be in their twenties. They had a Hispanic look about them, and she thought she detected a slight Spanish inflection in their voices as they spoke.

"We want to talk to somebody who can tell us about our mother," the gal on the right said.

"You're welcome to visit your mother and check on her yourself," Allie told them.

They looked at each other before simultaneously shaking their heads. Their earrings jangled.

"We don't want to see her," the one on the right said. "We just need to know she's okay."

"What's your mother's name?"

"Cynthia Matlock."

Allie hid her surprise. So these are the daughters whom Cynthia claimed had "dumped her off" and refused to visit her. Very interesting. . .

"Who advised you to check on her?" Allie couldn't keep from asking.

The woman on the left squared her shoulders. "My boy-friend's father is a lawyer, and he is advising me and my sister."

"I see. Well, if you'll kindly step into my office, I'll take your names. We can call up to the floor and get the latest report on your mother. . .that is, if you're sure you don't want to visit her and see for yourself how she's doing."

"Your office is fine," the woman on the right replied.

Allie nodded, her curiosity mounting. "Then if you'll both come this way. . ."

Leading them down the hallway, Allie showed them into her office. The women sat down in the two hardback chairs in front of her desk. Taking her own seat, Allie found a sheet of paper and picked up an ink pen.

"Your names?"

"I'm Patrice Rodriquez," said the one whose boyfriend had a lawyer-father.

"And I'm Kelly Acevedo," the other replied.

"You're Mrs. Matlock's daughters?"

They bobbed their heads in unison.

"Your addresses and phone numbers?"

"What do you want that for?" Patrice demanded.

"Well, in case—"

"In case, nothing," Kelly said. "Look, we don't want to be contacted. We just want to know our mother is all right. After that, we're leaving."

"And if she's not all right," Allie proceeded cautiously, "who should we call?"

Patrice slipped her hand into her shorts pocket and produced a business card. "You can call my boyfriend's dad at his law firm. Here's his address and phone number. You can reach us through him, too."

Allie accepted the card and then phoned the fourth floor. Once she had the nurse on the line, she handed the receiver to Patrice.

"You need to hear the update on your mother for yourself," Allie said, deciding she dare not play the go-between, lest these two accuse her of lying.

"Hi. . .yeah, my mother is Cynthia Matlock and I want to know if she's one of the patients who's been abused in this place," Patrice said. After a few minutes of listening, she tossed the phone at Allie. "I don't care about Mom's 'vital signs,' and that's all the stupid nurse would give me."

"Well, the alternative is to go upstairs and check for yourself," Allie said.

On one hand, she prayed they wouldn't accept the offer because Cynthia still sported an ugly bruise around her left eye. But on the other, Allie wished the young ladies would make amends with their dying mother.

The girls whispered something to each other before Kelly answered for both of them. "Maybe we'll come back another time. And maybe we'll bring my boyfriend's dad."

"That's entirely your choice." Allie stood. "Visiting hours are between 8 A.M. and 8 P.M."

"Yeah, we know," Patrice muttered.

Watching them exit her office, Allie felt remorseful and a tad guilty that she hadn't been more honest with Cynthia's daughters. However, her loyalty was to Lakeland Enterprises. After a few more minutes of deliberation, she lifted the phone and called Evan. Allie thought this situation might be moving beyond her expertise. Perhaps these phone calls and family members should be referred to a corporate attorney.

"Allie, I saw this coming," Evan said.

"I know, I know. I never said it would be easy, but we did the right thing."

"Glad you think so."

His tone sounded cynical, but she refused to feel intimidated. Sitting back in her padded desk chair, Allie prayed that God would prove her right to Evan and other board members. The ethical way of conducting business was always the right way. Allie sensed that Evan believed that, too, even though he obviously disliked the present consequences.

They talked awhile longer, and Allie introduced the subject of uniforms for the security guards. Evan liked the idea and encouraged her to bring up the matter at the next board meeting.

Allie promised she would.

After wrapping up the call on a positive note, she finished printing the productivity logs she'd created. Last week, she had informed all the supervisors the logs were coming, and the news wasn't well received. But the documents were a necessary evil if Allie was to get the feel of the workflow at Arbor Springs.

Papers in hand, Allie began the distribution process. She went from the first floor up, speaking with supervisors and familiarizing them with the forms.

Riding the elevator to the top floor, Allie glanced at her wristwatch. Ten minutes of five. The doors opened and, stepping out of the car, she immediately recognized Cynthia's cries for water. She saw the disturbed expressions on visitors' faces and felt frustrated that nothing was being done to quiet the poor woman. However, when she entered Cynthia's room, Allie witnessed the patient's misconduct. Up until now, she had only heard about it from the nurses and their assistants.

"Mrs. Matlock," the male nurse at her bedside said, "you can't have any water because of the stomach tube—"

Cynthia cursed a blue streak. Next, and much to Allie's horror, she yanked the plastic tube from her nose. She coughed and sputtered, and Allie nearly gagged when she glimpsed the sticky, yellowish coating at the end of the tubing. She concluded, and not for the first time, that nursing was definitely not her calling.

"Nice going," the RN said calmly, while shaking his sandy-blond head. "You just pulled out your G-tube."

"I'm thirsty! Can't you understand that?"

"Oh, I understand. But now you're going to the ER to get that G-tube replaced."

Cynthia let loose with another string of obscenities.

"Stop it!" Allie demanded in a cool tone.

Silence filled the room as both patient and caregiver glanced her way.

"Angel," Cynthia murmured.

"Don't 'Angel' me. I'm appalled by your bad behavior. This man is trying to help you."

"Thank you," the nurse replied. His hazel-eyed gaze narrowed as he considered Allie for a long moment. "Hey, you're the new consultant, aren't you?"

"That's right. Allison Littenberg."

"I'm Nate Ryden. Nice to meet you."

"Same here."

"Angel," Cynthia gasped, moving her head from side to side, "he's not helping. He's adding to my misery. I need water."

"Can't have it," Nate said. "Doctor's orders."

Tired as she felt, Allie searched her brain for some compromise. "Can you call her doctor and ask him if she really needs that tube?"

Cynthia continued to thrash about.

Nate shrugged. "I suppose I can. But there's a reason he ordered it in the first place."

"Because he wants me to suffer," Cynthia rasped. "You all want me to suffer."

"That's not true," Allie said softly, coming closer to the bed. Her intention was to console Cynthia, but the agitated woman succeeded in pulling out her IV. She flung it haphazardly, and the needle stuck Allie in the forearm.

Allie pulled it from her skin, fighting the instant panic. She looked wide-eyed at Nate. He motioned her toward the door.

"I'm sorry, Angel. I didn't mean to hurt you!" Cynthia cried. "Don't go. . .don't go. . . ."

Cynthia started sobbing, but Nate closed the door on her. Her muted cries followed Allie like a shadow; however, any compassion she once felt for the dying lady had been replaced by sheer fright.

"Please tell me that woman is not HIV positive," Allie said to Nate when they reached the nurses' station.

"She's not."

Allie closed her eyes in relief and praised God.

"And the only reason I know for sure," Nate continued, handing her a prepackaged alcohol swab, "is because she bit me last week and we had to run labs on her."

Opening the wipe, Allie cleaned the tiny puncture wound on her arm. "Can you tell me what exactly she does have?"

"Nothing contagious if that's what you're worried about. Metastatic lung cancer."

"Need another incident report?" Sherelle Barnes, the daytime unit secretary, asked. She glanced from Nate to Allie.

Allie hesitated.

"Might as well fill one out," Nate said. "Especially with the media's hype about how we all abuse patients. Besides, Room 8's chart is full of 'em."

"Incident reports?"

"You got it."

Allie sighed and accepted the form from Sherelle.

"So how come Mrs. Matlock calls you 'Angel'?" Nate wanted to know as he reclined against the counter. "Wait. I know. It's because of your heavenly presence."

"Oh, brother," Sherelle muttered, rising from her chair. She walked to the other side of the station.

Allie grinned in her wake before answering Nate's question. "I've sort of befriended 'Room 8.'"

"You're the only one."

"I've gathered as much."

She glanced at Nate from out of the corner of her eye. He was cute; and by his stance, she could tell he knew it. Allie also guessed he was about half her age.

"I understand you're here to whip us all into shape."

Completing her form, she met his gaze. "That's an understatement."

A slow smile spread across Nate's face. "Oh, yeah?" He obviously liked a challenge.

However, Allie wasn't interested in bantering. When Sherelle returned, she handed over the incident report. "Now what happens?"

"Marcy Crandon, the day supervisor, will review it. She'll probably order some lab work. You'll have to give us some blood."

"Fine. Is Marcy still here?"

"Yep. In her office."

"Great. I'll hand the incident report to her myself."

"Hey, before you go," Nate began.

Allie paused.

"A few of us are going out for drinks after work. Want to join us?"

Allie forced a smile. "Thanks, but no." Incident form and productivity logs in hand, she excused herself and walked around a grinning Nate.

"Well, okay. There's always next time. . .Angel."

"Don't hold your breath."

He chuckled as she moved away from the counter. Passing Room 8, Allie heard Cynthia's muffled wails and decided this day couldn't get much worse.

*　　*　　*

Sitting on the couch in her parents' apartment, Marilee watched her mother pace the plush, off-white carpeting. A late afternoon breeze sailed in through the patio doors, carrying with it a warm reminder that summer wasn't over just yet.

"Three months is not enough time to plan a wedding," Eileen said. "What is Logan thinking?"

"He doesn't understand, Mom. That's all."

"It'll take that long to order your gown and have the appropriate alterations made. And the invitations will have to be printed and then mailed. We'll need to rent a hall for the reception. . . ." She gave an exasperated sigh. "Nothing, and I mean nothing will be available in the Chicago area at Christmastime!"

"I know. I know. . . ."

Marilee felt despair rearing its ugly head. While yesterday had been so perfect, the announcement of their engagement at church followed by an impromptu luncheon celebration with her parents at Steve and Nora Callahan's home, today was a sorry contrast as reality set in. Her mother was right: Three months was not enough time to plan a wedding.

"I thought that maybe you and I could. . .well, explain things to Logan. There's a chance he'll change his mind."

"You think so?" Her mother sat down beside her and tapped her forefinger against her lips. The silver bracelets on her wrist jingled. "Hm. . ."

"I'd really like to get married in May—after school lets out."

"Of course. That's only reasonable. And if we could set the date eighteen months from now, that would be ideal."

Marilee thought so, too, but she doubted Logan would agree to wait that long. Seven months, perhaps. A year and a half, no way.

"Logan is a reasonable man. I think we can talk some sense into him." Marilee grinned. "He's probably still at church."

Eileen Domotor's eyes widened with possibilities. "What are we waiting for? I'll get my purse."

"We could hit a bridal shop on the way home, too."

"Marvelous idea."

Marilee had to laugh as she trailed her mother out the door and down the hallway to the elevators. She could barely keep up with her!

*   *   *

Cynthia awoke to see her angel standing beside her bed. "You came back," she said, realizing she could speak much clearer without that nasty tube in her throat.

"Yes, I came back." She hiked up the shoulder strap of her purse. "I wanted to make sure you're okay before I left for the day."

"I'm sorry about before. . .you know. . ."

"Yes, I know. But from now on," her angel said with a

warning glint in her blue eyes, "I want to hear good reports from the nurses. No more biting, scratching, and swearing at them. You hear?"

"I hear, Angel."

She smiled. "That's not my name."

"But that's who you are to me." Through worn and medicated eyes, Cynthia thought her angel's silvery-blond hair had every appearance of a shiny halo. And her outfit. . .was that a white robe she wore?

"I'm just a regular person."

Cynthia didn't reply. She'd watched that TV show about angels who touched people's lives and helped them through difficulties enough to know that angels didn't readily admit who they were.

"Your daughters were here this afternoon. Patrice and Kelly."

"Oh, what did they want? Money? That's all they ever want."

"They wanted to check on you."

Cynthia cursed. "I. . .I don't believe it. They must have had an ulterior motive for coming." She struggled to take a breath. "Patty and Kelly don't care if I live or die."

Her angel didn't reply, and several strained moments passed.

"I see Nate brought you a Coca-Cola," she finally said.

Cynthia glanced at the retractable tray on the other side of her bed. "Yeah, the doctor said I don't have to have the tube or the IV." She looked back at her angel. "We talked on the phone and he said I'll die quicker without them, but that's fine by me. I want to die."

Her angel frowned and sat down on the edge of the mattress. "Mrs. Matlock, what do you think will happen when you die?"

"Call me Cynthia."

"All right." She smiled and sat down on the edge of the bed. "Cynthia, what do you think will happen?"

"When I die I'll finally have peace."

"How do you know?"

"Because. . .I don't know. It's what I feel, I guess."

"I thought about death in a similar way, until my mother died," Angel said. "But after her unexpected passing, I began wondering what really happens to a person when he or she dies."

"Were you close to your mother?"

"Very close."

Remorse filled Cynthia. She'd never been close to either of her parents.

"Mom was my best friend all through grade school. We moved around a lot. But then she remarried when I was a teenager, and suddenly I had to share her affection with a step-father and two stepsisters."

"Bet you hated that."

"I did. I became very rebellious and stubborn, refusing to obey my mom and stepdad. I started getting into a lot of trouble around town."

"You?" Cynthia wanted to laugh except it hurt too much. "Hard to imagine you like that. You seem so. . .perfect."

"Hardly," her angel replied with a smile. "And any good you see in me is because of Jesus Christ. The glory goes to Him alone."

"Figured you'd say that, being an angel and all."

"I'm not an angel, but I am a born-again Christian."

Cynthia nodded. She'd heard Angel say that before and she had to admit other Christians had gone out of their way for her in the past. Her first husband was one of those born-again people, and he'd seemed like a knight in shining armor. . .at first. Being married to him was a whole other story. Then there was his mother. . .Cynthia recalled the times the older woman would read to her from the Bible. The passages sounded like some boring Sunday school lesson, and Cynthia rarely paid attention. However, she could remember one verse to this day. Her mother-in-law repeated over and over, "For God so loved the world that he gave his only begotten Son. . ." There was more, Cynthia knew, but at the moment, the words escaped her.

"I tend to avoid Christians," Cynthia finally stated at last. "Seems like they all have hidden agendas."

"Like what?"

"Like. . .they want you to join their church, be one of them."

"Well, I suppose to some extent that's true," her angel said. "I, for instance, would like nothing more than to know that you've asked Jesus into your heart before you die. Have you ever done that? Prayed and asked Jesus into your heart?"

"No. . ."

"Do you know what I mean when I say that. . .ask Jesus into your heart?"

Cynthia frowned, but then admitted, "Not really, and I really don't care." Her angel's expression conveyed disappointment, which in turn caused Cynthia a good measure of guilt. This woman didn't have to be here. She wasn't obligated to keep her company—especially after what occurred this afternoon. It was a miracle that Angel even came back.

"Oh, all right," Cynthia relented. "Go ahead and tell me."

After a moment's pause, Angel said, "Well, from my own experience, I can tell you that I didn't know what inner peace really was until I dedicated myself to Christ. And let's face it: In this life, we dedicate ourselves to all sorts of things. Our jobs, our dreams, our relationships with others. Sadly enough, most of what we've given ourselves to can vanish in a heartbeat. It won't last."

"I know that's true. Look at me. I have nothing. Not even my daughters, those two little witches."

Angel gave her an empathic look, and Cynthia sensed she could relate.

"Friends and family members might desert us, but Jesus never will."

Cynthia shrugged for lack of a better reply.

"Jesus was and is God. The Son of God."

That verse her mother-in-law liked to quote flittered through Cynthia's head. *"For God so loved the world that he gave his only begotten Son. . ."*

"Jesus died for your sins and mine. He died and rose again on the third day and He sits at the right hand of God the Father in a place called heaven. Those who ask Jesus to forgive their sins and ask Him to save them—ask Him into their hearts— will live with Him forever."

Angel picked up Cynthia's bony hand and held it between both of hers. Warmth spread around Cynthia's fingers while a knot of emotion caught in her throat. When was the last time someone cared enough about her to hold her hand?

"Where you spend eternity is the choice you have to make here on earth," Angel said as her blue eyes darkened with intensity. She smiled. "I hope to see you in heaven."

Cynthia nodded, feeling as mesmerized as she was amazed by such a display of emotion. "No one has ever cared about me. . . except you."

"Oh, I'm sure that's not true," Angel said, patting her hand before gently setting it back on the thin hospital blanket.

"It's true, all right. Everyone I've ever loved wanted something from me. They never wanted just me."

"Well, Jesus wants you because He loves you." Standing, Angel fished a piece of paper from her purse. "I'm going to leave this with you. It's a Bible tract. Will you promise to read it?"

How could she refuse? This woman had been so kind to her. "Okay, I'll read it, Angel."

She laughed. "Will you stop calling me that? I told you before my name is Allie."

Another jolt of familiarity. How weird that she equated the name with her mother-in-law and that verse from the Bible. "Do I know you?" she asked. "Have we met before?"

Allie squinted, obviously giving the matter some thought. "I don't believe so. I'm not from around here. I live in California.

I'm a consultant and I'm here temporarily."

"Yeah, I think you told me that before."

Exhaustion settled down around Cynthia like a heavy, black blanket. "You go now, Angel. I have to sleep."

"All right, but please think about what I've said."

"About heaven?"

"Yes, about heaven."

"For God so loved the world. . ."

With those words dancing across her mind, Cynthia closed her eyes and drifted off into a peaceful slumber.

CHAPTER FIFTEEN

Jack put in his request for retirement and had what he felt was a productive chat with the police chief. It wouldn't change anything, but Jack decided that getting a load off his chest felt great.

With the rest of the day to kill, he went over to a buddy's house and sat with him in the yard. He listened as his friend rambled on about the benefits of retirement; however, when Jack left, he didn't feel anymore convinced that he'd enjoy it. After all, the last thirty years of his life had been consumed with what he was—an Oakland Park police officer. Now he was just plain old Jack Callahan; and for whatever reason, that guy scared him.

Maybe because he didn't know who Jack Callahan was. And maybe he didn't want to find out, either.

Out of sheer boredom, he stopped by his brother's house. Steve wasn't home from work yet, but Nora insisted he come in. She seated him at the kitchen table, served him a glass of iced tea. . .and didn't stop talking for the next hour. The only reprieve Jack had was when the kids periodically came in and interrupted her.

Finally, Steve arrived and Nora began dinner preparations. They invited him to stay, but Jack didn't feel up to it. In truth, he didn't know what he felt like doing, but dinner alone in front of a Monday night football game seemed like the obvious plan. He supposed there were worse alternatives.

Driving home, Jack did a mental inventory of what he had in the refrigerator and cupboards. He didn't really want to stop at the grocery store, but there wasn't much in stock at his condo. As he stopped at the light near the La Fiesta restaurant, he considered getting a carryout order. He'd enjoyed his dinner Saturday night.

The food, anyway.

The light turned green, and Jack abandoned the La Fiesta idea and continued on his way home. He had to admit that his conscience bugged him the past couple of days. Perhaps he'd been a little too harsh with Allie on Saturday night. She'd been smarting over the failed reunion with Brenda, and he'd all but poured salt in her wound. Well, he'd tried to warn her. . .the same way she had tried to warn him about marriage thirty years ago.

If you recall, I told you so. . . .

And that was the other thing that bugged him—bugged him more than his conscience—the fact that she remembered!

Jack pulled into the condominium complex and parked his SUV. He'd sold his house on Side Circle Drive the same year Logan went to college. Earning a tidy sum in the deal, he purchased this place, newly built with all the modern conveniences included. He hadn't been sorry, either. No lawns to mow, bushes to trim, and no siding to paint. It was a bachelor's dream come true.

But it was also lonely, although Jack rarely gave into that sentiment. He worked extra shifts instead and then fell into bed, exhausted, not giving any room to thinking or feeling. Truth was, he'd shut off his emotions like a faucet years ago. However, Allie's return to Oakland Park had started a slow leak; and now that he wouldn't have his career to fall back on, Jack was faced with the fact he might have to deal with some issues.

Namely his past, present, and future.

What a lousy situation to be in at fifty-five years old, he groused, lifting an array of envelopes from the mailbox. He walked to his front door and, turning the key, let himself into the condo. He busied himself; but after twenty minutes, Jack realized he'd putzed long enough. He went and stood at the fridge, door open, and gazed in at its sparse contents. Then he thought of Mexican food. . .and Allie.

Great. I'm going to end up in the nut house before long.

Closing the refrigerator, he looked at the phone and considered his options. What if he asked Nora where Allie was staying? He could offer to take her to dinner as recompense for Saturday night. He could agree to bury the hatchet, as it were, and he'd have something to eat. Besides, it didn't look like Allie was going away too soon. So, like every other misfortune that came his way, Jack would just have to buck up and accept it.

Picking up the phone, Jack dialed his brother's number.

*   *   *

Allie entered the cozy lobby of the extended-stay hotel. The place, it seemed, was never in want of patrons. Fireplaces were located at each of the far walls, opposite each other, and scattered around them were several brightly upholstered sofas and small, round wooden tables and chairs. Twin television sets were positioned at inverse corners, ever running some popular movie, and a small bar and restaurant conducted a thriving business just beyond the center doorway.

Walking to the front desk, Allie asked for her mail and messages. A lanky young man with short auburn hair handed them over and announced that Allie had a visitor. He inclined his head to the right, and Allie turned to find Jack seated comfortably on a couch, reading a portion of the newspaper.

Seeing his dark hair with its frosty highlights bent over a

section of *USA Today*, she wanted to sob. If she didn't think her day could get any worse, it just had.

Thanking the clerk, she headed in Jack's direction. As if sensing her approach, he glanced up and set the paper aside.

"Jack, what are you doing here?" she asked, forcing a smile.

He stood. "I thought I'd take you to dinner."

Suspicion filled her being, and she narrowed her gaze. "What for?"

He brought his chin back, acting surprised. "Now, Allie, you said you wanted to be friends, right? So, friends go to dinner once in awhile."

I'm too tired for this, she thought. "I. . .I appreciate the offer, but I've had a bad day. I don't want to spar with you. I just want to take my shoes off, make a bag of microwave popcorn, and watch a couple of mindless TV shows."

She turned to go, but he caught her elbow. "No sparring tonight. You have my word. In fact, that's why I wanted to take you out—to sort of make up for the, um, sparring on Saturday night."

"That wasn't your fault. That was between Brenda and me."

"Well, I feel like I contributed. . .and stop shaking your head like that. You're not the only one with a conscience, you know!"

Allie found the admission interesting, but she was hardly persuaded. "Let's make it another time, okay?" She tried to ignore the glimmer of disappointment in his brown eyes.

She headed for the elevators; however, his next reply halted her steps.

"I put in for my retirement today. . . ."

Surprised, she swung back around. The man whose career meant so much to him was giving it up without even a skirmish? Why?

As if he'd read her thoughts, he said, "Can't fight city hall, and all that."

"Yes, you can," she said, hiking up the shoulder strap of her maroon, leather attaché case.

"Not at my age."

The quintessential bleeding heart, Allie felt her will dissolving by the second.

Jack glanced at his watch. "I could probably have you back by nine. Lots of mindless TV shows on then—including the local news."

Allie laughed before giving up altogether. "Oh, all right. Let me take my stuff up to my suite and change clothes. Give me, um—" She paused to think about it. "Give me fifteen minutes."

"You got it." Sitting down on the sofa once more, Jack slid the newspaper back onto his lap.

Riding the elevator to her floor, Allie was a little amazed at the preceding event. Now that was the Jack she remembered! Persistent. Wouldn't take no for an answer. But she still wasn't sure why he sought out her company tonight. Because his conscience bothered him? Allie supposed that marked some progress. Perhaps he was sorry for hurting her so long ago and maybe, just maybe, he would even forgive her for hurting him. Maybe he'd give his life back to the Lord.

That's an awful lot of maybes. . . .

The words echoed back to her from that first Sunday in town when she'd had lunch with Logan, Marilee, Steve and Nora, and their kids. Nevertheless, Allie remained warily hopeful.

Once inside her suite, she deposited her mail and attaché case on the bed. She kicked off her heels and shrugged out of her brown and cream checked blazer. Next, she removed the suit's matching skirt and unbuttoned her off-white blouse. After hanging up the garments, she selected a casual, blue, collared T-shirt dress from the closet. She deemed it appropriate since Jack had on faded blue jeans and a white short-sleeved polo.

Walking into the bathroom, Allie washed, touched up her makeup, dressed, and then slipped a pair of multicolored-strapped flats onto her feet. Grabbing her purse and a light jacket, she made her way back down to the lobby.

Jack glanced at his watch. "Twelve minutes. Pretty good."

Allie rolled her eyes, but she felt oddly flattered. Of course, she reminded herself, it wasn't as though he'd complimented her on her appearance.

Jack said he would drive, so they walked to his black Ford Explorer. He politely opened the door for her, and Allie climbed up into the passenger seat. She had just finished fastening the seatbelt by the time he walked around the vehicle and crawled behind the wheel.

"Mexican food all right?"

"Very funny, Jack."

He smirked as he backed the SUV out of the parking slip.

Pulling onto the interstate, he headed for downtown Chicago.

"So when will you be officially retired?" Allie asked.

"End of this month. I figured I wouldn't wait until the end of the year. Why put off the inevitable?"

Allie grinned, thinking that was another trait just like the Jack she used to know. Once he made up his mind to do something, he did it quickly.

"What are you going to do with your time? Enjoy it, I hope. There are a lot of people in the world who aren't healthy enough to enjoy their retirement."

"True. But. . ." He paused, changing lanes. "But to answer your question, I don't have any plans at the moment."

"What about starting up your own business? Got any hobbies you could turn into money-makers?"

"Not really. The police force has pretty much been my life for the past thirty-two years. And since I'm not interested in administrative work, which is what the police chief has in mind for me, I'd rather quit."

Allie turned pensive, reflecting on Jack's words and thinking about the past when the two of them had been the best of friends. He had always been the all-or-nothing kind of man. It was his way or the highway, and that caused a good amount of friction between them years ago. But back then, Allie assumed Jack just didn't understand her, couldn't relate to her feelings, her needs. Now, however, she saw the cold hard truth: He was just plain stubborn!

Jack exited the interstate and drove to a hole-in-the-wall place called Zippo's, which was located in a deteriorating part of Chicago. Allie felt a little uneasy, walking down the alley with its cracked pavement and the crumbling brick buildings on either side. But Jack assured her that cops liked to eat at this place, so they were probably safer here than most places in Oakland Park.

"I'll take your word for it," Allie murmured as he held the door open for her.

She stepped in and surveyed her surroundings. Framed pictures of policemen throughout history decorated the white-washed stucco walls, and Allie understood why cops liked this place: It touted their profession in a positive way. On the downside, this establishment had a tavern's atmosphere about it, and she didn't have any trouble imagining patrons bellying up to the bar and drinking their troubles away.

"Hey, Jack!" the bartender called, waving from beneath the clear glasses that hung upside down in a rack above the bar. A nice-looking man, he appeared smaller in stature and wore a white dress shirt, minus a tie. "Good to see ya again. Need a table for two, eh?"

"Yep."

"Follow me."

The man with a shock of ebony curls on his head tucked menus under his arm and led them into the next room. He seated them at a booth against the wall. Allie sat down on one side of the table and Jack the other.

"Want a drink?"

Jack shook his head. "Not tonight, Zip. Thanks. Bring me a cup of coffee."

The man looked at Allie. "How 'bout you?"

"A glass of seltzer with a twist of lime, please."

"Sure. Coming right up." Zip handed them each a menu, then swatted Jack on the arm. "The dame's got class, eh? Nice goin'."

"Get outta here," Jack said, looking thoroughly embarrassed.

Laughing, Zip walked away.

Allie opened her menu, feeling uncomfortable. She much preferred the family-style restaurants, and Zip's reference to her as a "dame" was irksome.

"Allie, don't mind him," Jack said as if divining her thoughts for a second time tonight. "Zip owns the place, as you might have guessed, and he's forever trying to set me up with some-one—usually one of his fabled homely sisters. But he teases all the single cops who come in here. It's a long-standing joke. So now that I've actually brought a date—"

"Date?" Allie asked, glancing at him from over the menu. "We haven't even gotten past friends yet."

Jack gave her a wry grin. "Touché, Mrs. Littenberg."

Allie couldn't help smiling as she glanced back down at the menu.

"All kidding aside, if you want to leave we will," he said. "But I promise you Zip makes the best Italian food you've ever eaten."

"I guess this is all right," she acquiesced, too tired to protest.

Zip returned with their beverages and took their orders, lasagna for Allie and veal Marsala for Jack. Once he left, Jack took a drink of his coffee and then began drumming his thumb on the table to the soft beat of the sultry saxophone music play-ing in the background. Sipping her seltzer, Allie watched him and noted the muscle working in his jaw. *Odd how some things never change*, she thought.

"What's bothering you?"

"Hmm?" Jack lifted his brows in question.

"You're clenching your jaw. What's bothering you?"

Jack gave her a peculiar stare, but in the next moment, he seemed to give up the pretense. "You said something on Saturday night that has been eating at me the past two days."

"What's that?"

"We were talking about marriage and I told you I found out it's not so great. You said, 'If you recall, I told you so.' "

Allie brought that particular conversation back to mind and nodded. "Yes, what about it?"

"Well," he hedged, "I guess I've been wondering if you remember the day you told me so."

She did. Of course, she did. Meeting his brown-eyed gaze, Allie nodded. "It was the day I left Oakland Park." She tipped her head, still considering him. "Do you remember?"

"Every day for thirty years."

"Give me a break." She laughed, assuming the remark was another of his sarcastic quips; however, Jack didn't seem amused in the least. The smile dying on her lips, she shook her head in wonder. "Jack, how can you hold a grudge for thirty years? Especially since I apologized."

He didn't reply, but looked somewhere out over her left shoulder.

Allie felt her defenses rise. "You know, if you really loved me so much, you could have called—or answered my dumb letter! You've always been the unrelenting sort. Even in my wildest dreams, I never imagined that I wouldn't see or hear from you again. But when you didn't reply, I figured it was really over between us. When I heard you had gotten married, that pretty much cinched it."

Jack gaped at her. "What are you talking about. . .a letter?"

"Oh, you remember everything else except the four pages on which I poured out my heart. Great," she drawled facetiously. "You know, Jack, if either of us has a cause to be bitter, it's me. I didn't get married first, you did."

"Whoa, Allie," Jack said, palms up. "Put on the brakes!"

Lifting her glass of seltzer, she sat back against the bench. She had to admit that it felt rather good to unburden herself like that. Had she really been carrying around that hurt and animosity all this time? Amazing.

"Back up, okay? What letter are you talking about? I never got a letter from you."

"Yes, you did. I sent it a couple of months after I arrived in California."

"I never got it."

"You don't remember."

"I never got it!" Jack insisted with an edge to his voice.

Allie regarded him suspiciously; however, she couldn't think of why he would lie. Which meant that if he was telling the truth. . .

She closed her eyes and exhaled.

"Maybe you forgot to mail it."

"No." She shook her head. "I mailed it." She pictured herself handing it to the postal worker that day so very long ago.

"What did it say?"

She couldn't recall every word she'd written, but one promise had remained ingrained in her memory.

Long moments passed as Allie toyed with the decision to divulge the letter's theme or simply answer with a vague reply. The truth might encourage Jack in an impossible way, for it wasn't as though they could just pick up where they left off thirty years ago. He was a very different man, one who wasn't walking with Christ. She was a very different woman, one whose faith meant everything. On the other hand, perhaps the truth would set Jack free of his anger and bitterness once and for all.

Maybe it would free her, too.

"In my letter," she began, choosing painful honesty, "I wrote about how sorry I was that we had argued the day I left, and I said that. . .that I'd love you until the day I died."

Jack flinched as her words hit him, and then he appeared to struggle with something inner and undefined.

"That letter would have changed my life, Allie," he said hoarsely.

"Your reply would have changed mine."

Again, he drew back as if she'd struck him. But once more, he pressed on. "Why didn't you write another one? Why didn't you call me? You knew my phone number."

Allie shook her head. "In the letter, I gave you an ultimatum. I gave you a choice. Don't you see, Jack? Everything hinged on your reply. When you didn't. . ." She gave him a helpless shrug.

He narrowed his gaze, and Allie saw the warning glint in his eyes. "You swear you're telling the truth, or are you just making this up so I feel guilty?"

"What do you think?"

"I think. . ." Jack paused and stared off in the distance for several moments before looking back at her. "I think that if you're telling the truth, our lives are shaping up like some Shakespearean tragedy."

"I would almost agree with you there, Jack. But this is where God's sovereignty comes into play. I believe He controls all things. He obviously lost that letter on purpose."

"And why would He do that?" Jack asked, looking back at her.

Staring into her seltzer, Allie searched for a reply. Suddenly Nicholas came to mind. Returning her gaze to Jack, she thought of Logan.

She smiled. "Maybe God knew we would be of more use to Him apart than together. Today there are two young men in full-time service, preaching the truth of the Bible and furthering God's kingdom. Neither would exist if you and I had gotten married."

He inhaled slowly and, seeing his eyes grow misty, Allie's heart crumbled.

Lord, please, Allie prayed, *please use this moment for Your will and glory. Use me, Lord. . . .*

Jack blinked and grunted out a cynical laugh, an obvious cover for his raw emotions. Lifting his stoneware mug, he took another drink of his coffee. "I can't find God anywhere in this situation. Do you know how many times I prayed that you'd come back, Allie—that you'd come back, tell me how sorry you were for leaving me, and that you'd say you still loved me? A billion times, that's how many." He narrowed his gaze. "What are you grinning at?"

"You." Allie shook her head, unable to believe the obvious. "Jack, God answered your prayers. Don't you see?"

He raised a brow.

"Here I am!"

CHAPTER SIXTEEN

Jack felt the air leave his lungs as though he'd been dealt a powerful blow. *Is she serious?* On one hand, he longed to believe she meant every word. On the other, he knew it just couldn't be true.

His reason returned, along with his initial hunch that Allie had come back seeking the man he'd been three decades ago. He almost laughed. So now that her life was all peachy, she thought she'd visit an old flame and see if she could stir something up. Well, she was certainly doing that—stirring things up, namely trouble.

"Look, Allie, the guy you think you loved doesn't exist anymore."

"I know."

Her simple admission hit him again, and Jack couldn't believe how bruised he felt. He wanted to strike back.

"And I'm not interested in resuming our relationship, okay?"

"Okay."

"I don't even want to be your friend, got it?" After finishing his coffee, Jack glanced at her and awaited her reply. He figured he'd see some tears and then she'd have a few choice words for him. He was an ornery guy, and women didn't like mean men. *Go ahead, Allie, say it. Tell me you hate me. Wouldn't be the first time a woman said that to me.*

"You are such a liar, Jack," she stated at long last. But instead of tears, there was a hint of amusement in her blue eyes. "You went out of your way to take me out to dinner tonight. You said your conscience bothered you because you weren't very nice on Saturday night. I think you want to be friends—maybe even more than friends, but you're too stubborn and proud to admit it."

"It's a free country. You can think whatever you want."

Allie didn't say anything more; and several minutes later, Zip brought their food.

"More coffee, Jack?"

"No. Bring me a beer."

"Sure." Zip looked at Allie. "Anything else for you?"

"Yes. You can call me a cab. I'll be finished eating by the time it arrives."

"Um. . .yeah, sure."

Jack hid his surprise at Allie's request. But as it sank in, he considered the consequences. Zip, no doubt, would razz him about his "date" walking out on him for months to come. Worse, he'd tell all the guys and Jack would never live this one down.

"Forget the beer, Zip," he ground out, hating the fact that he had to relent. "I don't want the lady to think I drink and drive—I don't."

"I know you don't, Jack," Zip said. "One beer won't hurt."

"Naw, bring me a cola. And, Allie, I'll drive you home whenever you want."

Zip glanced at her and bent slightly forward. "Is that acceptable to you?"

To Jack's relief, she nodded, albeit reluctantly.

Zip left, and Jack watched Allie pray over her food. Simultaneously, they lifted their utensils and began eating in silence, which proved a sort of torture because it left too much room for his thoughts.

"How's the lasagna?" he asked, deciding it would serve him right if she threw the plate at him. That'd really give Zip something to talk about.

Instead, Allie tossed him a polite smile. "It's good. How's your veal?"

"Great. Just great." Hearing Allie set down her fork, Jack gave her an expectant glance.

"You know what? Misery is a choice. Just like happiness. Everyone has hard times in life, and—"

"Put a lid on it, Allie." He took a bite of pasta and sauce, wondering if he should have let her take the cab and braved his buddies' teasing.

Zip brought the cola. "Everything okay now?" He looked from Jack to Allie, and they both nodded for lack of a better reply.

Once he left, she said, "Jack, there are a lot of people who want to love you and be close to you—including the Savior. Why don't you let them?"

He gave her a quelling look, refusing to reply; and she wisely clammed up through the rest of their meal.

Once they finished eating, Jack tossed a few bucks on the table, paid the cashier, and waved a good-bye to Zip. Wordlessly, he and Allie walked out to his SUV.

On the way home, she didn't speak and Jack didn't bother trying to make polite conversation. Instead, he occupied his mind by concentrating on driving Allie back to her hotel. After that, he decided to go home alone and watch *Monday Night Football*.

He reached the hotel and pulled into a parking space near the front entrance. When Allie didn't move, he silently cursed.

Opening his door, he climbed out and walked around the vehicle to play the proper gentleman. He pulled open her door and she held out her hand. He took it in order to help her from the SUV's front seat. But he suddenly became aware of how soft and delicate her long fingers felt in his palm. Regret filled his soul. He shouldn't have lashed out at her. She didn't deserve his animosity. She had suffered over the years, too.

"Sorry about tonight," he muttered. "I'm a coldhearted guy, aren't I?"

"Is that what you want me to think?"

Yes, he realized, that's exactly what he wanted. He had taken Allie out tonight seeking answers, and he'd gotten them. But instead of closing off the trickling of his emotions, as he'd hoped, they'd brought on a steady stream. But if she hated him, that would dam up his feelings for good. He could deal with hatred; and yet, in his heart of hearts, he had to admit that he yearned for quite the opposite.

He looked down at her hand, still in his. He rubbed his thumb across her fingers. Night had fallen, but the SUV's cab light threw off a warm glow that matched the balmy September breeze.

"Oh, Allie, why'd you come back here? Don't you know how much it hurts to see you again?"

"I didn't want it to hurt, Jack. Please believe me. The whole point in coming back to Oakland Park was so I could tell you what God did in my life. You're the one who led me to a saving knowledge of Christ. I thought you'd want to know. . . ."

He lifted his gaze, peered into her upturned face, and saw the moisture glistening in her eyes.

"I thought you'd be glad to see me," she said.

An errant tear slipped down her cheek, and his calloused constitution all but dissolved. Pulling her forward, he gathered her into his arms and marveled at the power of that one lonesome tear. He was accustomed to seeing women cry. In the line of duty, he'd answered calls ranging from domestic violence to an old woman's cat stuck in a treetop. But Allie's solitary tear seemed so much different.

Holding her in his arms, he realized that, in spite of her sturdy disposition, she felt as fragile as fine porcelain. He hated the thought of her husband physically hurting her. It made him sick when he imagined the ugly scene in which the guy had cut her cheek.

"You should have called me, Allie. I should have called you."

"No regrets, okay?" she replied, and Jack felt her give him a little hug.

"Regrets? That pretty much sums up my life."

"No—"

"Yes! And as long as I'm confessing," he murmured, his cheek against her temple, "you're right. I lied earlier tonight. But I don't know about being your friend, Allie. . .or anything more than your friend. Except that's all I've been thinking about. Maybe I'm a nut case as well as a liar."

He heard her sniff, then felt her kiss his cheek before she stepped back, out of the embrace. "Maybe you're just human."

He shrugged, wondering if that really excused his dithering behavior of late.

"May I suggest that we both let go of the past, Jack? We can't change any of it. My prayer for you is that you'll look to Christ again and that we'll both trust Him with our futures." She smiled up at him. "Like my son Nick always says, 'The Christian life is an adventure.'"

Jack said nothing, but he recalled a time when he thought that same way.

A few awkward moments went by.

"I should go in," Allie said at last.

He nodded.

"Thanks for dinner."

"Sure."

Jack watched her walk to the hotel, where she disappeared into its well-lit lobby. Closing the door of the SUV, he made his way around to the other side and crawled back in behind the wheel. Starting the engine, he began his journey home.

*   *   *

Cynthia awakened with a start only to discover that she'd been dreaming again. While most times her dreams were a welcomed diversion from her pain, this one left her feeling troubled. In it, she was young again. That part didn't disturb her. Not in the least. What bothered her was the man who had entered her dream.

There she sat on a summer afternoon, on the front porch steps of a quaint little home, bouncing an infant on her knee. He smiled and cooed. Putting a chubby finger in his mouth, he drooled all over her bare legs. She wiped the slobber away with the clean cotton diaper that she habitually kept over her shoulder in case more than spittle came out of his mouth. It was known to happen.

Then suddenly her first ex-husband was standing in front of her. He wore his uniform, and she smiled because he looked so tall and handsome. But he didn't smile back. Instead, he snatched the baby off her lap.

"Wait!" she cried. "Don't take him."

"He's mine," he said, turning his back on her. "You didn't want him, remember?"

"But I do now."

"Just look at you. You're filthy."

Glancing down, she realized what he said was true. She tried to brush off the dirt and grime that seemed to cover her from head to foot. She didn't know where it had come from, but she sensed it was her fault.

"You're an unfit mother."

"Wait. Just give me another chance." The words echoed in her head. *Another chance! Give me another chance!*

That's when she woke up. Her hair, what was left of it after the chemotherapy she'd undergone two months ago, was wet with perspiration. Her skin felt clammy. But worse, she felt that maternal wrenching of her soul—

Just like when she had to give up her baby.

*   *   *

Logan entered the condo and found his dad sitting on the couch staring at the television set. The only problem was, the TV wasn't on.

"Yoo-hoo. . ." Logan waved his hand in front of his father's face. "Anybody home?"

Jack glanced at him with an unnerved expression. "Where have you been all night?"

"I have been the victim of a sneak attack." He grinned at his dad's concerned frown. "Marilee and her mother," he explained. "The two of them ganged up on me tonight and I never even saw 'em coming."

Uncrossing his leg, Jack put his feet up on the coffee table. "Yeah, I can relate to those kinds of sneak attacks."

"So they both start telling me why it's impossible to plan a wedding in three months," Logan ranted on, in a good-natured way. He'd lost fair and square, and he determined not to be a sore loser. "I held my own until. . ." He sighed. ". . .until Marilee gave me one of those puppy-in-the-window looks. Then I knew it was all over."

Jack chuckled. "When's the wedding?"

Logan expelled a disappointed puff of breath and collapsed into the couch beside his dad. "End of May. Next year."

"No Christmas wedding, eh? Your aunt Nora will be disappointed. That's all she could talk about this afternoon."

"Nobody could be more disappointed than I am. Once I make up my mind about something, I don't want to wait for it to happen."

Jack chuckled.

Smiling, Logan looked at his father. "When did you see Aunt Nora?"

"I stopped by earlier."

"Guess I'd better call her tomorrow and tell her the bad news." One thought led to another, and Logan added, "And I guess I'd better develop some backbone if I'm going to be the head of my household. I can't let Marilee sweet talk me around every issue."

"Good luck, Kid."

Sitting forward, Logan cocked his head. "What's that s'pose to mean?"

"You've got a Bible. Read Genesis. Ever since Eve talked Adam into taking a bite of that apple, we men are downright vulnerable when it comes to that age-old female persuasion."

"Bummer."

"But, on the other hand, it does have its advantages. Sometimes it's kind of fun being persuaded."

"Maybe we'd better continue this conversation a little closer to my wedding date," Logan said, thinking the topic might lead them into dangerous waters. "I've got almost a year to wait."

"Stay busy. It'll go fast." Jack dropped his head back against the couch. "All of a sudden you'll be my age and you'll wonder where all the time went."

Logan studied his hands, dangling over his knees, before looking back at his dad. "Is that what you've been sitting here thinking about? Where all the time went?"

"Not exactly."

Jack gave him a speculative glance, and Logan wondered if his father was debating whether to say more.

Finally, he did. "I had dinner with Allie tonight, and I learned that she sent me a letter, years ago, shortly after she left Oakland Park. She wanted to get back together, but I never got the letter." Jack closed his eyes. "Allie thinks God lost it on purpose, and all for good. But, to me, it seems like a cruel joke on

God's part. I loved her so much. . . ."

Mulling over what he'd just heard, remorse tweaked Logan's soul, and anger gripped his heart. In so many words, his dad had just wished away his very existence.

"You know, I hate to say it, but I'm going to anyhow." Logan clasped his hands. "You're sounding like a selfish man. I mean, think of that classic old movie, *It's a Wonderful Life,* and consider for a moment how many people wouldn't be here today—or would be in hell right now—if you were God."

Jack scowled at him. "Get down from your high horse for a sec, Logan, and try to imagine how I feel."

"You're pining over a past that never was," he shot back. "You're feeling sorry for yourself. What's to imagine?"

Logan stormed from the den, struggling to keep his resentment in check. Reaching his bedroom, he stepped inside, turned on the light, and closed the door behind him, fighting the urge to give it a good slam.

Lord, I feel like I'm an angry teenager again, he prayed. *I feel like going back into the other room and starting a major argument with my dad.* Logan squeezed his eyes shut and grit his teeth, tamping down the desire to rail on his dad. *Keep me from doing that, Heavenly Father. It'll ruin everything I set out to accomplish by moving into this condo with him. Help me turn the other cheek and show him Christ-like love.*

The moments ticked by; and suddenly, Logan felt a calm settle over him—a calm mingled with contrition. Was he really so insecure that he'd overreacted to his dad's admission? So he'd been in love with Mrs. Littenberg. Big deal. That wasn't much of a surprise. Logan had suspected it from the first night she came to town. But, perhaps, his aggravation—and his hurt—stemmed from the fact that he was a product of the past his father condemned. Logan wished it wasn't true, but it was. And he wished he could accept it, but he couldn't.

So many wishes. . .

Walking to the window, he pulled open the blinds and peered out at the star-strewn sky. *Lord, You can turn the hearts of kings. Surely, You can turn my dad's.* After a moment's pause, he added, *And mine too.*

CHAPTER SEVENTEEN

Allie walked out of a two-hour meeting with the supervisors on each floor of Arbor Springs feeling a sense of satisfaction. They had accomplished more than she'd hoped this afternoon. Heading to her office, she glanced at her watch and realized it was almost time to wrap up the day. As she pulled out her briefcase and began packing up paperwork that she intended to work on tonight, the phone rang. She wondered if it was Jack calling. She hadn't heard from him in a couple of days, and she was curious if anything had come out of their dinner "date" Monday night.

She lifted the receiver. "This is Allison Littenberg."

"Hi, Allie. It's Colleen."

Hearing her sister's voice, she smiled. "Well, hi. I'm glad you called. I've been feeling a little bad about what happened on Saturday night."

"Yeah, I know. Me, too. What's more, Brenda wants to apologize. You wouldn't believe what happened. I had to call you right away and tell you."

Allie frowned and sat down behind her desk. "I hope it's nothing serious."

"Oh, no." Colleen laughed. "In a way, it's sort of funny. Jack pulled her over while she was on her way home from work a couple of hours ago. Lights and sirens—the whole bit. Brenda forgot to turn her blinker on when she made a left turn. Jack gave her a citation and then proceeded to chew her out for being so rude on Saturday night."

Allie grimaced. "Oh dear. . ."

"Well, she deserved it. I lectured her on the way home, but coming from Jack, I guess it really hit home. She called to tell me I should invite you to dinner. Brenda said she'll come, too; and we can put last Saturday behind us and start all over."

"A wonderful idea!" Allie said, her heart soaring. *Thank You, Lord, for answering my prayers!*

"I told Brenda that's what you'd say, but she was so broken up over Jack's tongue-lashing that she was afraid you'd give her another one."

"Listen, I'm rejoicing at this turn of events." Leaning forward, Allie dug through her briefcase and found her planner. "When would you like to get together?"

"How 'bout Friday night? Can you come about six o'clock?"

Allie didn't have any plans. "Sure." She penciled in the time.

"Hey, um. . .should I invite Jack, too?"

Allie laughed at the conspiratorial tone in Colleen's voice. "Sure, go ahead and ask him."

"Are you two—"

"Friends?" Allie put in quickly. "We're working on it."

Smiling, she picked up an ink pen and doodled as the memory of being in Jack's arms flitted across her mind. She hoped they were friends. She wanted to be friends.

"Hm. . .okay. Well, we'll see you Friday night."

"Sounds good. Thanks for calling, Colleen."

Hanging up the receiver, Allie allowed herself a moment to reflect on the conversation. Then she glanced at her wristwatch. Almost six o'clock. She wanted to go up and see Mrs. Matlock before she left. Yesterday, the poor woman had been confused, and she rambled on about all sorts of nonsense. But maybe today she'd be more coherent.

Leaving her belongings on the desk, Allie walked out of her office. She locked the door behind her and headed for the elevator, praying for another chance to share Christ with a dying soul.

*   *   *

Logan stood in the back of what was fondly referred to as "Youth Group Hall." He and the kids and the four volunteers had just finished praying for Susan, the young lady who had been struck by a car, and now it was time for tonight's skit. It always amazed Logan what the teenagers came up with. Sometimes the short dramas were serious, other times they were comical acts, but the messages were always poignant and a source of help for those kids struggling with various issues.

Tonight the skit began on the humorous side—at least it was supposed to be. The kids up on the makeshift stage were doing their impression of Logan proposing to Marilee. It was interesting to see how the teens' imagined that night. According to their reenactment, he'd taken Marilee out to a classy restaurant for dinner, but instead of pouring out a proposal, he spilled his glass of grape soda in her lap.

Oh, brother! Logan thought, shaking his head. Next, the actor portraying him cut into his New York strip. While doing so, he knocked his salad onto the floor. Finally, when he got down on his knee to pop the question, he had steak sauce on his hands and got it all over the actress playing Marilee, who was wearing a pale yellow dress.

Grinning, he rolled his eyes before scanning the room for his real-life fiancée, but she still hadn't shown up. Unusual for her. Marilee was always in attendance when the "Teen Scene" began each Wednesday night. Upstairs in the auditorium, the rest of the congregation listened to Pastor Warren's midweek message, which would be followed up with a time of prayer. Logan could only assume that something happened with one of Marilee's students. What else could have detained her?

The kids wrapped up their skit. The on-stage Logan got a shaving cream pie in the face after the waiter tripped. Then, with their clothes soiled and the white tablecloth discolored from spills, the couple exclaimed that God had a perfect plan for everyone's life and that it included a soul mate. No need to worry about the future; God had everything under control. The drama ended after the actor playing Logan said, "It took a really long time. I'm pretty old. But God worked it all out and now I'm finally getting married."

The couple on stage gave each other feigned looks of adoration, and the skit ended.

Old, my foot! Logan thought as the teenage audience clapped with enthusiasm. Even his niece, Veronica, was smiling. So to humor them, he did his best old man interpretation. Hunching his back, he shuffled up to the front.

"All right now, boys and girls," he said, his lips covering his teeth to infer the "old man" had none, "it's time for our nap."

Giggles and groans emanated from the group.

Smiling, Logan straightened to his full height. "Okay, fun's over. Time to get serious."

"So how did you really propose?" a freckled-faced, red-haired girl asked. Logan didn't recognize her as one of his youth group's regulars. But her question sparked the others to ask and, in moments, there was a veritable uproar.

"All right, all right. Settle down." Logan waited for the kids to quiet before he continued. He hated to confess that he'd asked Marilee to be his wife in a lousy parking lot while she was half-freezing to death.

"I believe I saw roses on my parents' baby grand," a delicate voice said as it wafted through the hall.

Looking toward the doorway, Logan grinned, seeing Marilee standing there, arms folded as she leaned against the metal frame.

"It was quite the romantic setting," she continued. "I couldn't have imagined anything better."

Logan's smile grew. "Imagined" was right! He did a sweeping glance of his youth group. "Everyone satisfied?"

"Did you say yes right away?" Debbie Kilgers asked Marilee. "Or did you make him squirm a little?"

"I accepted immediately."

Marilee gave him an adoring look, and Logan knew it wasn't just for show. He suddenly thought he knew the meaning of "warm and fuzzy" because that's what his insides felt like.

"You should have made him squirm, Miss Domotor," another girl said.

More giggles and a lot more groans broke out, the loudest emanating from his cousin Ricky.

"You shoulda said no, Miss Domotor," the stocky lad called, his hands on either side of his mouth. "You don't know what you're getting into."

Logan narrowed his gaze and pointed at Ricky. "I'll take care of you later."

The kid laughed.

Logan grinned, imagining all kinds of things he'd like to do to his little cousin. Cayenne pepper in his next glass of cola. . . hmm, that idea had possibilities. . . .

"Miss Domotor couldn't string him along," Veronica said, standing. "She didn't want him to change his mind!" When the noise settled, she looked right at Logan, adding, "Took him long enough to ask!"

"I love you, too, Roni," Logan quipped, thinking that she was more like a baby sister to him than a cousin.

She replied with an uninterested little shrug and sat back down.

A lively debate broke out between the guys and the girls— to make him squirm or not to make him squirm—until Logan put his forefinger and thumb in his mouth and let out a piercing whistle that hushed the teens in seconds.

"Simmer down, you guys." He paused, waiting for the command to set in. "Okay," he said at last, "I'll tell you what. Since you're all so interested in marriage, let's see what God's Word has to say about it. Take your Bibles and turn to Ephesians chapter five." The rustling sound of pages being turned filled the room. "I've studied this subject in great detail, and it's my opinion that the Lord gave men some tall orders. That's why it's important not to run headlong into marriage. You've got to think it through. Pray about it. And, not just the guys, but the girls, too."

Logan read verses twenty-two through twenty-five, emphasizing the word "sacrifice." He went on to explain how God's idea differed from the world's "what's in it for me" view of marriage. Then he wrapped it up by challenging the teens to prepare for their future roles as husbands and wives, should the Lord desire them to be married, by putting others first in their lives now. And to those who might remain single, he added that such a fate was not worse than death—especially if it's God's perfect will.

"Think about it. Singleness has its blessings. There are a lot of ministries a person can't be involved in if he or she has a spouse and family."

Feeling like he might be talking himself into some trouble, Logan glanced at Marilee and sent her a sheepish smile. "Except this ministry. It's been pointed out to me numerous times that I need a helpmeet." He cleared his throat, glad to see she laughed along with some of the kids.

"But whether you end up single or married," he continued, "our faith demands our time, talents. . .our lives. So next time, instead of doing what you want," Logan suggested, "try doing what your parents and teachers ask. Instead of insisting on having your way, let your friend have his or her way. And, most importantly, let God have His way in your lives. You might think you're giving up your rights, but you're not. You're opening yourself up to blessings." He closed his Bible. "Let's pray. . . ."

* * *

Marilee bowed her head and prayed along with Logan. She still felt as though she were walking on rainbows, her head in the clouds. The man she loved had finally asked her to marry him. They were engaged, and he'd given her the diamond ring of her dreams. Marilee could hardly wait until she got it back from the jeweler. What's more, Logan had agreed to give her some time to plan the sort of wedding that she and her mother used to fantasize about when Marilee was a young girl. She and her mom had always been close, while her sister Joy had been the ultimate "daddy's girl." Even so, Joy's wedding had been gorgeous, and Marilee wanted nothing less.

When Logan finished praying, the kids were dismissed. Several girls crowded Marilee and interrogated her about the wedding plans. Marilee divulged the few decisions she'd made in only four short days since Logan proposed. She'd selected two of her colors—teal and ivory—and she bought her wedding dress, all satin, pearls, and lace. She had actually purchased it years ago while shopping in New York with her mother, but she didn't tell the girls that. She didn't even want Logan to know that she'd had the gown and all she'd needed was the guy. But the truth of the matter was, when she first met Logan Callahan, she knew in a heartbeat that he was the one for her.

The girls chattered on like magpies until another of Logan's infamous shrills put an end to their conversation.

"If you ladies don't have anything to do," he said, "we could use some help cleaning up."

"I gotta go," one gal said. "My parents are waiting."

Several more agreed and left. Only two girls stayed with Marilee and volunteered to help.

Youth Group Hall began to empty, and Marilee watched with disappointment as Veronica Callahan slipped quietly out the door. They would be family soon, and Marilee wanted to be close to Logan's cousin.

I should ask her to stand up in the wedding, Marilee thought. *That would make six bridesmaids. . . .*

"I hope he's not going to whistle for you like that after you're married," Joan Oliver said, her hazel eyes twinkling with amusement.

"What?" Marilee snapped from her musings.

"I can see it now," the girl said. "Pastor Callahan will be like the captain in *The Sound of Music* just after Maria arrives on the scene. He had certain whistles for each of his kids—and for her, too."

Marilee had to laugh, recalling that part of the story. "Like Maria, I'll have to put an end to all of Pastor Callahan's bad habits."

Logan frowned. "I don't have any bad habits."

"That you know of," Melissa Chandler quipped. "My brother and my dad don't think they have bad habits, either, but they do. They don't put the cap back on the toothpaste, and they leave their smelly shoes in the middle of the living room."

"My dad sleeps on the couch all the time," Mark Pershing, a rail-thin freshman, divulged. "My mom gets really mad cuz he rumples everything up and makes the couch sag."

Logan chuckled. "Hey, now, a man's home is his castle and he can sleep wherever he wants and he can leave his shoes wherever he wants."

"That's what my dad says, too," Joan replied as she and Marilee began folding up chairs and stacking them against the wall, opposite the doorway. "But my mother says she's like Queen Esther and she can sweet talk 'the king' into anything."

Marilee laughed and looked at Logan. He stood on the platform wearing black pants and blue shirt. His tie was askew from moving furniture and his chestnut brown hair was slightly mussed. Placing his hands on his waist, he pursed his lips, furrowed his brows, and after a wink in her direction, Marilee anticipated a smart aleck remark.

He didn't disappoint her. "Queen Esther, huh? So that's what it's all about. Marilee, I think I'm finally beginning to understand the male/female thing. And it took a bunch of teens to help me figure it out."

"He's just figuring it out now?" Melissa inquired with wide, sarcastic eyes.

"Anything else you need help with, Pastor, just ask," Jason Edwards said, wearing a mischievous grin. A stocky young man with thick glasses, it was apparent that he adored Logan and would try to lasso the moon for him. Being raised by a single mom, Jason appeared to need the role model Logan provided.

"I was kidding, okay?" Logan gave the teenager a playful shove. "Wise guy."

Jason hiked up his glasses while his shoulders shook with laughter.

Marilee shook her head, smiling at the scene; and she had to admit, the clowning around made the cleaning up rather enjoyable. Next, she wondered if Jason should stand up in their wedding. Wouldn't that encourage the young man? Or perhaps he could be the ring bearer.

Once the room was sufficiently tidy, Logan jumped off the platform and walked towards Marilee. Her heart quickened its pace.

"Want to get something to eat?"

She'd already had dinner, but she wasn't going to pass up the chance to have Logan's undivided attention. "Sure."

"Good."

She couldn't resist the urge to straighten his tie. "I'm crazy about you, Logan," she said softly.

"Yeah, that's what I hear." He smiled, searching her face. "How come you were so late tonight?"

"Oh, I had to take my wedding gown to the seamstress; and while Mom and I were there, we started looking through patterns for the bridesmaids' dresses." Marilee grinned. "I think we found one, too!"

"Couldn't that have waited until tomorrow?" Logan asked, and Marilee didn't miss his hint at a frown.

"No, Mrs. Avery, that's the seamstress, is going out of town and won't be back for two weeks. Mom and I wanted to hurry and get over to her shop because Mrs. Avery said her schedule is full until Christmas and filling rapidly for next year already."

Logan sighed, then shrugged. He obviously wasn't pleased with her explanation.

"Look," she said in her own defense, praying he'd understand, "I don't usually plan things for Wednesdays. My responsibilities here come first. But this couldn't be helped."

"Okay, not a problem." Logan grinned and Marilee sensed, much to her relief and satisfaction, that the discussion was over.

Slipping his arm around her shoulders, Logan turned to the remaining four kids who were horsing around on the platform. "Hey, everyone. Time to go," he said, guiding Marilee toward the doorway. "Thanks for your help tonight."

The kids walked out with them. Stepping inside the elevator, they all rode up to the main floor. When they reached the lobby, the teens scattered and Marilee and Logan made their way to the front doors.

Logan waved to his aunt and uncle, who were conversing with Mrs. Littenberg. *Allie*, Marilee reminded herself. *She wants me to call her Allie.*

"I'm worried about my cousin," Logan said as they walked through the parking lot. "She seems kind of down about everything. Pessimistic. Cynical."

"She's having a difficult time with things right now. From what she told me on Labor Day, she's struggling at her public high school. She and her friends have been open about their faith so they get snubbed and ridiculed by the other kids sometimes."

"I wish my uncle Steve would have put her in our academy."

"Kind of late now," Marilee said. "Roni's a senior and she wants to graduate with her friends. And just remember, kids can be mean even in a private school. You know how it is with some of the teens in our youth group and the situations that arise."

"Good point," Logan said on a note of chagrin.

Marilee smiled as they reached her car. It was on the tip of her tongue to ask Logan about including Veronica in their wedding party, but she decided to wait until they were seated at the restaurant. "Where do you want to eat?"

"How 'bout that family restaurant just up the street? Seems convenient for both of us."

Fishing her keys out of her purse, Marilee nodded. The establishment was just blocks from the townhouse she rented and close to the interstate, which Logan took back to Oakland Park.

"I'll meet you there," he said.

"Sounds good."

Getting into her car, Marilee closed the door and fastened her seatbelt. Slipping the key into the ignition, she started her vehicle's engine and the tape in her cassette deck played a lovely wedding waltz. Excitement enveloped her once more. Planning her own wedding was the most fun she'd ever had!

Chapter Eighteen

Sunshine streamed into Cynthia's room, and she wondered who had opened her draperies. With her head swimming from medication, she glanced around, but didn't see her angel. Only Angel would have allowed the light in. Whenever Angel was in her room, it seemed brighter—even with the curtains drawn.

I'm not an angel. My name is Allie.

The words echoed in Cynthia's mind, along with everything else she'd said. Had it been yesterday? The day before?

"For God so loved the world. . ."

Cynthia ferreted her memory for the connection between the name and the passage of Scripture. In her mind's eye, she saw herself rummaging through a man's black wallet that contained the picture of a woman with long blond hair, parted in the middle and hanging straight down, past her shoulders. It was a professional snapshot—a high school senior, wallet-sized portrait, and seeing it caused a jolt of jealousy to shoot right through Cynthia. But who was she? One of her daughters' friends? Whose wallet? One of her ex-husbands'?

Thinking of men's wallets caused her to think of the men she'd married, each time hoping she had hit the jackpot—in more ways than one. But each marriage proved more disastrous than the one before. Out of her four husbands, two were Hispanic and lived in the Southwest—and Cynthia had lived there, too, until she met and married Bill Matlock. Patti was in high school and Kelly in junior high when he and Cynthia tied the knot. Ironically, Bill was from Chicago, just like her first husband. She only wished that she hadn't allowed him to talk her into coming back here. Things might have been different had they stayed in Oklahoma. Bill might not have lost his job, started drinking, and molested Patti and Kelly. Her daughters might not hate her for "letting it happen," as they claim.

Stupid girls, Cynthia thought bitterly. *I didn't let it happen.* "And I divorced the jerk right after I found out. My lawyer saw to it that he got jail time. Wasn't that enough?"

Someone touched her arm, and Cynthia realized she was thrashing about. She opened her eyes and blinked, focusing on the male nurse standing at her bedside. It was the one named Nate.

"Do you need more pain medicine? Another Coke?"

"Why are you being so nice all of a sudden?"

"I was always nice, Mrs. M—even though you tried to take a bite out of my arm."

"Sorry," she muttered, just in case her angel stood nearby.

"Apology accepted, especially since your lab work came back okay. That means you're tamer than a rattlesnake. Now, what's it going to be?"

"Can you give me something. . .something to stop the. . .the dreams?" Cynthia rasped.

"Not legally." Nate chuckled. "I can get you some more pain medicine."

"Can you get my angel?"

Nate chuckled again. "Nope. Your angel is busy handing out

pink slips. Now, do you need something or not?"

Cynthia closed her eyes. "I wish I had some company."

"Can't help you there. Your angel's got us filling out productivity reports." She felt Nate slide the call button into her palm. "But if you need something—something reasonable—you know what to do."

"Yeah, I know what to do," she repeated, growing sleepy. "I know what to do."

*　　*　　*

As was his habit whenever life became too complicated, too painful, Jack busied himself at work, picking up extra shifts in addition to his own. He'd learned long ago that his thoughts couldn't plague him if he was too tired to think. Unfortunately, when he was tired, his leg bothered him and it obviously disturbed the police chief, too. Consequently, the axe fell first thing Thursday morning.

"The department has a new policy about paying out vacation time to retiring officers," the chief said. "It's all a part of the city's attempt at cutbacks." The younger man, who, in Jack's eyes, resembled a new recruit straight out of boot camp, flipped open a file. "According to the report out of payroll, you've got six weeks coming, Callahan. You either take 'em or lose 'em. Those are your options."

Options, yeah, right, Jack thought, recalling those words as he pulled his SUV into the garage attached to his condo. He knew the chief just wanted him gone, and the sooner the better. Well, he'd opted for taking his vacation, but he wasn't happy about it and he let all the higher-ups know it. Little good that did.

Muttering, Jack climbed out of his vehicle and walked to the side door. After pushing the button to close the garage, he unlocked the door and stepped inside. He found Logan at the kitchen table, sipping coffee and reading the morning paper.

"Hi," he said, after a glance in Jack's direction.

Jack murmured a greeting.

"Tough night?"

"You might say that."

Logan set down the newspaper. "Want to talk about it?"

"No, I don't want to talk about it! Why does everything have to be discussed and analyzed?"

"Hey, forget I asked, okay?"

* * *

Logan watched his father leave the kitchen and noted the limp. He was aware of the long hours his dad had worked the last couple of days. Suddenly Logan wished he'd come up with a more spiritual reply.

"A soft answer turneth away wrath: but grievous words stir up anger."

Logan closed his eyes. *Lord, please forgive me. It doesn't seem like I can do anything right when it comes to my dad. Is it pointless for me to keep trying? Maybe I should move out. . . .*

Hearing the refrigerator open, Logan ceased his prayer and looked across the room where his father now stood in only a T-shirt and boxers. He pulled out a beer, looked at it, and then threw it, along with what remained of the twelve-pack, into the trash. Logan took it as a good sign, although he wasn't sure what it meant. Could be his dad just didn't like that brand of beer.

"Listen, I'm sorry for biting your head off."

An apology from his dad? Second time this month! Logan decided it was another good sign.

"I got canned today. . .well, not exactly canned. Same difference, though. I'm being forced to take my vacation time before I retire. So, to sum it up, my career as a police officer has come to a screeching halt."

"That rots," Logan said, trying to imagine how he'd feel if he were ousted from the ministry. Hurt. Angry. Disappointed. Scared.

"Yeah, well, that's why I'm in such a foul mood."

"I appreciate you sharing that with me."

Jack opened one cupboard after another. "Why don't we have any food around here?"

Logan grinned. "We're two bachelors who work all the time, that's why. Hey, I've got an idea. How 'bout if you take up cooking, now that you're retired, so we don't starve to death?"

His father sent him one of his "you've got to be kidding" glares, and Logan laughed.

"How 'bout you just hurry up and get married and I'll conveniently show up at mealtime?"

"Works for me," Logan replied. His smile faded as he remembered the message lying by the phone. "Someone named Colleen called for you. She left a message on the answering machine, asking if you wanted to come over for dinner tomorrow night."

Jack walked to the phone and read the message.

"She said she invited Mrs. Littenberg."

"So I see," Jack replied. "Thanks."

"Are you going?"

"I don't know. I'm too tired to think about going out tomorrow night."

"At least you'll get fed."

Jack grinned in spite of himself.

"Dad, I'm curious. . .are you thinking about a relationship with Mrs. Littenberg?"

Jack closed his eyes as if steeling himself, and Logan realized the question had shaken him.

"Sorry I asked. It's none of my business."

"I don't know how to answer you, Logan. I'm a divorced guy who doesn't have a relationship with Christ, and Allie's a devoted Christian. How much hope do you think there is for the two of us?"

"According to Mrs. Littenberg, you used to have a relationship with Christ. What happened?"

"I got involved with your mother, that's what happened!"

"David got involved with Bathsheba, but he's still considered a man after God's own heart."

"Logan, I'm too tired to have this discussion."

"Right. You told me that. I apologize," he said sincerely. He hadn't meant to poke and prod. He merely wanted to help. Lifting the newspaper, Logan reread the headlines.

"Oh, I give up," his dad said at last. "Forget breakfast. I'm going to bed. See you later."

"Sure."

Peering over the paper, he watched his father head for his bedroom. Logan had to admit that he felt somewhat encouraged. He sensed God was at work in his dad's heart.

Standing, he crossed the room and hoisted the garbage bag out of its plastic bin. He tied it up and took it out to the dumpster at the far end of the parking lot. As he walked back to the condo, he realized what a perfect day it was, mild temperature, no clouds in the sky, a light breeze blowing. Inhaling the fresh, fall air, he decided it was a great day to be alive.

*   *   *

Jack wished he were dead. His leg throbbed, his life lay in a shambles, and his career had been snatched out from under him. In short, he had nothing to live for.

Turning onto his side, he endeavored to ignore his mounting frustration. He tried to switch off his thoughts and sleep, hoping he'd wake up and discover this past month had all been a bad dream. But his attempts failed. Instead, he recalled Allie sitting across the table from him at Zip's place, saying, "If either of us has a cause to be bitter, it's me. I didn't get married first, you did."

Oh, God, what did I do? How could I have let the love of my life go? How could I have fallen into sin with a woman I didn't even like?

Next Jack clearly remembered the disappointed expression on Pastor Barlow's face when he confessed to being intimate with Roxi. He hadn't yet known she was carrying his child. The act alone had pierced his conscience. Jack said he was sorry. More sorry than any man could ever be. He vowed it wouldn't happen again. But instead of forgiveness, Jack got a tongue-lashing—which he deserved. He violated God's laws, after all. But when Pastor Barlow requested he leave the church and never return, that had been a blow Jack hadn't expected. He never thought Pastor Barlow, one of the godliest men he knew, would cast him out of the church he loved—and in a time when he needed the comfort and support of fellow Christians the most!

Leaving that day, Jack had left his faith, too. He realized seventy-times-seven was a concept preached from the pulpit, but it obviously had little bearing in the real world. He had begged for forgiveness, but was turned away.

Then he learned Roxi was pregnant. He figured that was God's final judgment. A life sentence. He would forever live with the consequences of his sin. . .and he had.

However, what Logan said earlier was true. Jack remembered that much from the Bible. King David had committed a similar transgression: adultery and murder. Funny, but Jack hadn't ever thought of his situation in the light of King David's. All Jack knew was that God banished him from His presence.

So why him and not David?

Tossing aside his covers, Jack got up and left his bedroom in search of Logan. He almost collided with him near the kitchen.

"Got a question for you, Mr. Youth Pastor."

"Shoot."

"You mentioned David earlier and how he sinned with Bathsheba. Well, I guess I don't understand why David was forgiven and I'm not."

A deep frown furrowed Logan's brow. "What do you mean?"

"I mean. . ." Jack hesitated. But in the end, he managed to swallow his pride and tell his son about the incident with Pastor Barlow. Something in his soul just needed to know the truth.

He figured Logan, with all his years at a Christian college and seminary, could shed some light on the subject.

When he finished relaying the story, Logan shook his head. An expression of remorse crossed his face. "Dad, I'd venture to say that pastor reacted in the flesh and not under the influence of the Holy Spirit. You said you were his protégé?"

"Something like that."

Father and son walked into the living room, where Jack collapsed into the armchair and Logan sat down on the couch.

"He was training me to head up what he called a 'layman's ministry,'" Jack continued, the memories coming forth but this time unfettered. "Our job as laymen was to win souls to Christ and build up the church."

"That's all well and good, but it's my opinion that the pastor still didn't have the right to absolve or condemn you—especially when you came to him with a confession and a repentant heart." Logan grinned. "You actually had one up on David; he tried to cover up his sin with Bathsheba. God had to send Nathan to point it out."

Jack paused. "I don't know. Seems like God agreed with Pastor Barlow."

"Hmm. . ." Sitting forward, Logan looked at him askance. "How well do you know the Bible?"

Jack shrugged. "I don't know it like you do, after four years of Bible college and a Master's degree. But there was a time when I memorized Scripture on a regular basis."

"Do you remember 1 John 1:9? 'If we confess our sins, he is faithful and just to forgive us our sins, and to cleanse us from all unrighteousness.'"

"I. . .I guess I don't remember that one," Jack stammered, probing the recesses of his memory.

"What about Proverbs 24:16?" Logan asked. "Are you familiar with that verse? 'For a just man falleth seven times, and riseth up again.'"

Had he known that passage of Scripture? Jack couldn't be sure. "If God forgave me, why haven't I ever felt forgiven?"

"Remember 1 John 3:20? 'For if our heart condemn us, God is greater than our heart, and knoweth all things.' Just because you feel something, doesn't mean it's true. Weren't there days when you woke up and didn't feel like a father or a police officer? But you were, in spite of what you felt."

Jack mulled everything over.

"Dad, are you sure you're on your way to heaven?" Logan asked after a time. "The Bible says we can know for sure that we'll have eternal life. Again, I'll quote from 1 John. 'These things have I written unto you that believe on the name of the Son of God; that ye may know that ye have eternal life.'"

"Yes," Jack replied, feeling an odd lump begin to form in his throat. "I accepted the Lord when I was seven years old. But—"

"No 'buts.' You're either a believer or you're not. If you are a believer, one who asked Christ into your heart at some point in your life, then you're one of God's children. 'If we confess our sins, he is faithful and just to forgive. . .'"

"You don't understand, Logan. I sinned big time. I violated God's laws. And all these years I've been lukewarm. In Revelation God says He will spit lukewarm Christians out of His mouth." Jack paused, his heart fairly wrenching within his chest. "I think God spit me out a long time ago."

"Maybe, but that doesn't mean you can't renew your relationship with Him. 'If we confess our sins'—"

"Logan, I confessed. A hundred times I confessed!"

"All right, now you've got to believe that God will do what He promised. You're forgiven."

Jack didn't know what to say. If Logan was right and God's Word was true, then he'd lived with the pain of a gross misunderstanding for thirty miserable years, a greater misunderstanding than the one that had kept him and Allie apart.

But why? Why did God allow it to happen?

As if divining his thoughts, Logan said, "Dad, I believe there are two truths in this world, God's sovereignty and man's responsibility. In a book I once read, the author wrote, 'It's a sovereign God who holds man responsible,' and I agree. We're responsible for our thoughts and feelings, our decisions—and our mistakes. But a sovereign God has promised to work it all together for good for those who love Him." Logan grinned. "What a blessing!"

Yeah, what a blessing, Jack thought wryly as he stood. He didn't think he could abide much more of this conversation. "Guess I'd better get some sleep," he muttered.

He crossed the room, but when he reached the hallway, Allie's words whirred in his head. *Today there are two young men in full-time service, preaching the truth of the Bible, and furthering God's kingdom. Neither would exist if you and I had gotten married.*

Yes, Jack had to admit, Logan was a blessing. He'd been the one bright spot in Jack's bleak world.

Contrition and remorse filled his being. If only he'd been a better father. . .

Pivoting, he swallowed hard and faced his son. "I appreciate your taking time to answer my questions this morning. I. . .I'm sure you had better things to do."

"You're welcome, and I didn't have a single thing going."

Jack forced a little smile, born of discomfort. It had been a long time since he'd shared his heart with anyone, let alone his own son. "Logan," he began, "if God had any good come out of my past and out of all my mistakes, it's. . .it's you."

Logan pursed his lips and narrowed his gaze, looking as if he hadn't heard correctly; and Jack's regret turned to utter sorrow.

"I guess I should have told you that long before today. I probably should have said a lot of things that I didn't."

"Yeah, you probably should have. But better late than never. I really needed to hear those words from you." Logan smiled and sat back on the couch. "Thanks."

After a single, conciliatory nod, Jack turned and walked down the carpeted hallway. He entered his bedroom, closed the door, and strode to his bed, fighting his feelings all the way. Lying on his back, he stared at the white ceiling. It began to swim in a strange way, and Jack realized that tears had pooled in his eyes. The tears of a man who never allowed emotions to sway him, not even his own.

Until now.

"Oh, God," he whispered, pressing his eyes closed, "if You haven't already, I beg that You'll forgive me and. . ." A verse from the Psalms miraculously entered his head. To the best of his ability, Jack recited it in silence. "Create in me a clean heart, O God; and renew a right spirit within me. Cast me not away from thy presence; and take not thy holy spirit from me. Restore unto me the joy of thy salvation; and uphold me with thy. . .thy. . ."

Jack couldn't recall the rest and it really started to bug him. Climbing out of bed again, he walked to his closet and opened one of the two sliding doors. He pulled down several boxes from the top shelf and peered inside each one, hoping to find his Bible. Finally, he located it, nestled away with a few other things, which he had no desire to rummage through right now. Sitting on the edge of his bed, he opened The Book and flipped through its delicate pages. He paused here and there to read what he'd written in the margins decades ago.

At last, he reached the Book of Psalms. Had he known before that it came right after the Book of Job? The realization seemed like a sign of hope from above.

And then he found it. Psalm 51. Jack read the preceding information. "To the chief Musician, A Psalm of David, when Nathan the prophet came unto him, after he had gone in to Bathsheba."

Jack closed his eyes. Another sign of hope.

He read the entire chapter and it became his own prayer. "For I acknowledge my transgressions: and my sin is ever before me. . ."

Jack nearly choked on the words as he read on with misty eyes. "Make me to hear joy and gladness; that the bones which thou hast broken may rejoice. . . .

"Create in me a clean heart, O God. . .restore unto me the joy of thy salvation; and uphold me with thy free spirit.

"Thy free spirit. . ."

Jack exhaled slowly. He felt like. . .no, wait. . .he believed God had heard his prayer.

Lord, I'm going to believe You have forgiven me because I asked and because You promised. I'm going to believe You planned this morning's conversation between Logan and me, and I'm going to believe You reminded me of this particular psalm for this particular reason. . .so I would believe.

With that, Jack closed his Bible and stretched out on his bed. He tucked God's Word into the crook of his elbow and slept as hard as the ocean ran deep.

CHAPTER NINETEEN

I t was a very different Jack Callahan who sat beside Allie on Friday night at Colleen's dinner table. Allie noticed the change in him almost immediately. The hard, cynical angles in his face seemed to have diminished, and his voice had lost its biting edge.

Unfortunately, she couldn't say the same for Brenda, still the taunting disparager. Allie concluded she wouldn't get more than the apology her stepsister offered her earlier tonight.

"So, Allie," Brenda began, "I hear you're a widow."

"Yes, that's right."

"Some women get all the luck."

Colleen gasped. "Brenda!" After shooting her sister a pointed stare, she forked a bite of broccoli coleslaw into her mouth.

At the other end of the table, Colleen's husband, Royce, didn't say a word but continued eating a piece of chicken he'd barbecued out on the grill. He looked quite the same as Allie remembered, tall, lanky, reddish-brown curly hair. The only change was that Royce's face looked fuller and his hairline had receded, leaving a shining bald patch that went all the way back to the center of his head.

"So, Allie, tell me your secret," Brenda said. "How'd you kill off your husband without landing in jail?"

"Oh, I didn't kill him; Erich managed that on his own," she replied on an easy note. Allie sensed the question was somehow another attempt to denigrate her character; however, the more Brenda tried, the worse she made herself look, and Allie pitied her.

"Allie, I don't mean to be nosey, but how did your husband die?" Colleen asked with a sincere light in her eyes. "I hope he wasn't ill."

"In a sense he was. You see, unbeknownst to me, he was in the drug-laundering business. The entire time I thought he was buying, selling, and shipping antiques."

Jack sat back in his chair, and Allie felt the weight of his regard. "I didn't know that."

Feeling somewhat uncomfortable, she looked at him and shrugged. Then she glanced at everyone around the table. "Please don't feel sorry for me. God used Erich's tragic death to make me who I am today, and for that I'm grateful."

"Well, like they say," Royce began, "every cloud has a silver lining, huh?"

"Oh, I don't believe it. How could you not know your husband was dealing drugs?" Brenda asked with an incredulous glare.

"Erich and I lived very separate lives. I was ignorant of his business ventures," Allie said emphatically.

Brenda's expression said she didn't buy the explanation.

"You know," Jack said, resting his elbow on the back of Allie's chair, "it's pretty typical for wives to be in the dark when it comes to their spouses' shady activities. You couldn't even begin to imagine the stories I could tell. One time we raided a house and there was a virtual arsenal in the basement. The guy had been robbing his wealthy neighbors' homes for years and his wife didn't have a clue."

"Hey, I remember reading about that years ago," Royce said.

Jack nodded. "And another time, my partner and I answered a call where the bank had foreclosed on a woman's house, but she refused to get out. She denied up and down that her house had been foreclosed on, but then it came out that her husband lied to her month after month about paying the mortgage and instead he gambled away all their money."

"What a shame," Colleen said.

"See, Brenda," Royce told his sister-in-law, "things could be worse."

"Oh, shut up," she quipped.

"Brenda, I know you're going through a hard time in your marriage," Allie began as gently as she could, "and I'm sorry to hear it. But divorce isn't the answer."

"Don't start, Allie," she replied before slamming down her fork and napkin. Next, she glanced around the table. "You all condemn me. I see it in your faces. But did you ever think about how I might feel?"

"Brenda, I've been there," Allie said. "I know."

"We've all been there, Brenda," Colleen added. "Royce and I have had our ups and downs, too."

"This isn't an up or down. It's a done deal."

"You just want a divorce," Royce said. "An easy way out. But did you ever stop to think things might get worse if you actually go through with it?"

"I've considered my consequences, yes."

Royce shrugged. "I think Dave's a nice guy. He goes to work every day and brings home his paycheck. He's faithful—"

"Big deal."

"Hey, in this day and age, that is a big deal!" Royce exclaimed.

"Dave is boring. He's got no ambition, no goals in life. But

I do. I want a better job, a vacation in Florida in February."

"So? What's stopping you?" Jack asked.

"Dave! I drag him around like a ball and chain."

"Maybe he just needs some encouragement," Allie suggested. Colleen agreed.

"Why are you all on his side?" Brenda said as tears filled her eyes.

Allie empathized with her stepsister and wished she could say something that would soften Brenda's heart. *Lord, could You find a way for me to share my testimony?*

Jack nudged her with his elbow. "Maybe you should share your story. . .you know, about your cheek. That is, if it's not too personal."

"It's not too personal at all,' " she replied, smiling. "I was praying for the very opportunity."

She glanced around the table. Everyone was listening.

"God has done so many wonderful things in my life. I love to tell people about them." Looking at Brenda, she brushed back the hair from her cheek. "See this ugly scar? Well, there's a story behind it. I'd love to share it with you."

Colleen inhaled sharply. "I hadn't even noticed the scar, Allie."

"I hide it well." She looked back at Brenda, awaiting a reply. When the woman didn't protest, Allie began. "It happened on our fifth anniversary, and I was making dinner. . . ."

*   *   *

Logan glanced around the restaurant. Crystal chandeliers hung above each table—and each table was draped with a long white linen cloth. Soft, classical music streamed through built-in speakers, and the servers were dressed in the standard black and white garb as they walked with professional sophistication across the plush Oriental-styled carpeting.

"Pretty ritzy place," Logan said.

"Wait until you see the banquet room," Eileen Domotor added. "It's exquisite." She laughed softly and hugged Marilee.

"Only the best for my baby girl's wedding."

"Oh, thanks, Mom. . ."

While the women locked themselves in an embrace, Stan put his hands in his pants' pockets. "We'll see how the food is tonight before making the final decision. If it's satisfactory, I'll write a check for the down payment."

"I'm sure we'll enjoy it, Stan," his wife said. "This restaurant is known all over the country. One of Chicago's most elite dining experiences."

"Sounds expensive," Logan muttered.

Stan chuckled and Eileen waved a hand at him and laughed. But he really wasn't joking. Renting the banquet hall here would cost a pretty penny, and to think of Marilee's folks dishing out that kind of dough made Logan feel a tad guilty. Surely they had better things on which to spend their money.

"We could always have a simple cake and punch reception at the church."

"Don't be silly," Eileen scolded him. "This isn't some potluck for the youth group we're planning. It's your wedding day!"

Logan chafed beneath the reprimand, but didn't reply. Marilee threaded her arm around his elbow.

"It'll all work out," she whispered. "You'll see."

Moments later, the maitre d' appeared, greeting them in French, and escorted them to a table. In English, he listed the "du jour" dishes, then turned on his heel and strode back to the foyer area.

"The Shrimp Quenelles sound divine," Eileen said.

"I have to plead ignorance here," Logan replied. "I mean, I know what shrimp are, but—"

"Quenelles are like fish balls or dumplings."

"Hm. . .I see."

Marilee laughed. "Not interested, eh?"

"Mai, non," he replied, using the little French he knew.

"Hey, that was pretty good, Pastor."

"Merci." Logan was on a roll now.

Stan chuckled. "I'm thinking of roasted shallot and mustard-coated rabbit. Haven't had that since I was in New Orleans on business."

Logan tried not to wrinkle his nose at the idea of eating rabbit. Although, when he was in college and vacationing in Miami with some friends, he was dared to eat deep-fried alligator strips—and he did. "Tastes like chicken" was the joke among all the guys the rest of that holiday.

"What are you grinning at?" Marilee wanted to know.

After Logan relayed the story, she and her parents had a good chuckle.

"You are the perfect youth pastor," Eileen said with a smile.

"I suppose someday you'll want to pastor your own church, though," Stan added.

"Yes, someday. That's the plan."

"You know, it's really a miracle that you're in the ministry, given your upbringing."

"You mean because of my dad?"

Stan nodded. "But no insults were intended, Logan. It's an observation. That's all."

"I understand completely, and I'm not insulted. You're right. If it weren't for my grandparents and my aunt and uncle, I might not be a Christian today, let alone in the ministry. They were godly examples to me."

"I never knew your grandparents, but Steve and Nora are wonderful people."

Logan couldn't agree more. "The good news is my dad has renewed his relationship with the Lord. He told me about it. It's really a miracle."

"Isn't that great?" Marilee put in. "It's answered prayer."

"I'll say," Stan replied. "Just proves to me again that God has really got his hand on you, Logan."

He smiled, pleased by the remark.

"I only hope that when God gives you and Marilee a church, He doesn't take you too far away from us," Eileen put in casually, but Logan took note of her slightly puckered brow.

"Never know," he answered in all honesty. He wasn't sure where the Lord might call him. But he knew he would obey.

The waiter showed up to take their orders. There were no menus, but the aproned, dark-haired young man proved knowledgeable about every dish the establishment served.

At last, they each decided on something, Logan selecting the beef burgundy fondue. Marilee chose Sole Meuniere, while Stan and Eileen stuck with their original choices, the rabbit and fish dumplings.

While they waited for their food, they discussed various topics; and Logan learned that the Domotors named their two daughters "Joy" and "Marilee" because they had been so happy their babies were whole and healthy.

"I never knew that," Logan said, grinning. "I never put the two names together like that, either."

"Well, after all the miscarriages I had and after our son emerged from my womb lifeless, I all but gave up on having children." Eileen's rueful expression turned suddenly cheery. "And then the Lord blessed me with Joy and Marilee! They were answers to my prayers."

"Mine, too," Stan said.

"Yes, Dear, yours, too."

The older couple shared affectionate smiles, and Logan grinned. It did his heart good to see that, after all the years and all the trials, the Domotors still loved each other.

He glanced at Marilee, and she rewarded him with one of her adoring looks—the kind that always made him feel about ten feet tall. It was like another affirmation from God. He'd done the right thing in asking Marilee to be his wife.

* * *

Allie could barely believe that Brenda had sat quietly through her entire testimony, beginning with Jack leading her to Christ and ending with Erich's death eleven years ago. Even Royce and Colleen appeared captivated by the story.

"I think you'll be blessed if you commit yourself to making your marriage work, Brenda," Allie told her. "But realize that you'll never have the peace and happiness you're seeking until you ask Jesus into your heart."

Brenda's gaze came to rest on Jack, and she regarded him with a curious light in her eyes.

"Don't look at me if you want to see an example of a Christian," he said, as if divining her thoughts. He gave Allie a quick and contrite glance before returning his attention to Brenda. "I haven't acted like much of a Christian."

"Oh, Jack, you've always been a perfect gentleman," Colleen said. "A little rough around the edges, but a gentleman."

Royce and Jack looked at each other, then down at their plates.

"No, not always a gentleman," Jack confessed. "Especially on the baseball field."

Royce chuckled. "You had the worst mouth on the team, Callahan."

"Yeah, I know."

Allie noticed that while Royce grinned over the fact, Jack didn't.

"So have you turned over a new leaf now?" Royce asked.

Jack hesitated, and Allie suddenly realized she was holding her breath. Forcing herself to relax, she sat back in her chair.

"A new leaf? Yeah, you could say so. What I did is get right with God."

"Because of Allie?" Brenda said in a snide tone.

Jack shook his head. "No. Actually, it was Logan who. . .who straightened me out. My own son." Again, he wagged his head. "Kind of embarrassing."

"I think it's terrific," Allie said, smiling. "That's actually the most encouraging news I've heard all day."

"Pity you," Brenda replied as she rose from her place. She grabbed her plate and walked into the kitchen.

Looking in Colleen's direction, Allie forced a polite smile in an effort to conceal her disappointment over tonight's results. She had hoped to be friends with Brenda, but obviously, nothing had changed between them. "Thanks so much for inviting me to dinner. The food was delicious."

"I believe you," Royce said with a small laugh. "You ate everything on your plate."

"Well, except for the chicken bones," Allie countered.

Chuckles went around the table.

Royce stood, as did Colleen, and they both began clearing the table. They insisted they didn't need any help, so Allie and Jack moved into the living room.

Looking around, Allie admired her stepsister's decorating ability, as the entire house had a cozy, welcoming feel to it. In essence, it was a reflection of Colleen; and Allie would have thoroughly enjoyed herself tonight if Brenda had not brought about such strife and tension.

"I think I'm going to leave," Allie told Jack, pivoting so she faced him.

"Going straight to your hotel?"

"Well, yes. . ." On some outlandish impulse, she added, "Unless you've got a better offer." She laughed at Jack's somewhat taken aback expression; however, he recovered quickly.

Narrowing his gaze, he said, "You're as sassy as when you were seventeen."

Smiling, she turned and gazed up at the framed print, hanging above the fireplace. It was a nostalgic scene, an old-fashioned wooden bridge spanning a stony brook. "Oh, not really," she said in answer to his remark. "I'm not really sassy at all. I think you're just a bad influence on me." She glanced over her shoulder to gauge his reaction.

He could barely contain his grin. "Yeah, right. You're

going to have to come up with something better than that, Mrs. Littenberg."

"Hmm. . ."

She pretended to be thinking up her next excuse, but then Royce entered the room.

"It's kind of a warm night for coffee, but Colleen said she'll make a pot if you two want some."

"Not for me," Jack said.

"Me, either. Thanks."

"Sure."

"I think we're going to take off," Jack announced, and Allie didn't miss the word "we." Neither did she miss the smirk on Royce's face.

"Hey, um, you two thinking of getting back together again?" he inquired, wagging a finger between them. "A little romance in your autumn years."

"Aw, knock it off, Strobel," Jack replied, waving a hand at him. He appeared unaffected by the jest.

But Allie felt uncomfortable. Was that what she wanted—to fall in love with Jack again? It wouldn't be difficult. The physical attraction was there, and perhaps the spiritual draw wouldn't be long in coming since it seemed he'd gotten back on the proverbial "straight and narrow." But they seemed worlds apart. He had just retired, and she was still on the go, traveling all over the country. Allie wasn't about to give up her career now. She had a few good years left in which to work.

Like déjà vu, Allie remembered telling Jack good-bye that one November day. She had broken his heart—and hers, too.

Oh, Lord Jesus, I can't let that happen again. . . .

"Allie, you okay? You look worried."

Snapping from her musings, she glanced at Jack. "Do I?"

Royce chuckled. "Is it the romance part or the autumn years that's troubling you?"

"Neither," she fibbed, lifting her chin. "I'm fine."

Jack gave her a skeptical glance before returning his attention to Royce. "Thanks for dinner."

The two men clasped hands. "We'll have to have you two over again before Allie goes back to California."

She surreptitiously cast a curious glance at Jack, but his expression remained unchanged.

"Sure. That'd be great."

Allie collected her purse and the light jacket she wouldn't need on this balmy late-summer night and followed Jack and Royce to the front door. "I should really thank Colleen," she began.

"I'll relay the message. She's in the kitchen right now and Brenda's crying her eyes out."

"Oh, no. . ." Allie felt sorry for her stepsister.

Royce sighed. "She'll be okay."

"I'll keep her in my prayers." Allie forced an encouraging smile, and Royce gave her a parting hug.

"Good seeing you again." Looking out the door, he called, "See ya, Jack."

He was already descending the cement steps of the porch. "Yep. Thanks again."

Allie walked to the stairs and Jack offered up his hand. "Careful, it's kind of steep."

She accepted his help, noticing that his grip felt strong and sure. She also noticed Jack didn't release her hand as they walked to the street.

Something was brewing between them, and Allie wasn't certain God was leading her in this direction. She felt anxious and eager at the same time. Who didn't want a love to last forever? Furthermore, she might be tempted to wager that Jack was as lonely as she was in those quiet hours where all a person had for company was his or her own mind and there was nothing else to do but think.

They reached her car, and Allie still didn't know what to do.

She wasn't about to go to his place, and she definitely wouldn't invite him to hers; neither, in her opinion, were appropriate options for two single Christians who felt attracted to each other. A restaurant wasn't an alternative since they'd already eaten. What was left?

"Allie, I think you're a little tense," Jack said, dropping her hand.

She realized what he said was true and tried to relax her limbs and shoulders, her neck. She'd been holding herself as stiff as a board.

"I think Royce's comment hit a nerve."

"You're right," she confessed. "It did."

"It kind of did with me, too." He looked over her head and down the quiet, tree-lined avenue. "To be perfectly honest, I'd sort of like some romance in my autumn years."

As she regarded him, standing there under the dim street lamp, Allie felt her heart melt. Jack looked so tall and brave. He had once been her hero as well as her very best friend.

"Me, too, but. . ."

"But what?" He returned his gaze to her, and Allie didn't miss the hint of a challenge in his tone.

"Okay," she relented, "I'll be perfectly honest also. I don't want either one of us to get hurt again."

"I don't want that, either, but I suppose that's a risk we'll have to take. I'm game. Are you?"

"I don't know," she hedged. But then, again, she decided to be direct. "Look, Jack, one of the things I'm uncomfortable with is the fact that you're a divorced man. That was one of the first ground rules I laid after my husband died—I'd never get involved with a divorced guy."

"I can appreciate that," he conceded. "But as far as I'm concerned, Roxi's dead. I mean, she walked out on me and I haven't seen or heard from her in twenty-five years."

Allie understood his rationale, but she still didn't feel a

measure of peace. After all, Jack's being divorced was only one of her concerns. The other was his spiritual condition. If he did, indeed, "get right with God," as he said at dinner tonight, it meant he needed to grow as a Christian by faithfully attending church and reading his Bible. After Erich died, Allie promised herself that she'd never remarry unless her prospective mate's walk with Christ matched or exceeded her own. It wasn't as though she were being a snob; she'd just lived with an unbeliever for far too long to desire anything less than God's best. Of course, she couldn't tell this to Jack. He either might not understand or he might develop a faith just to please her, and that would be tragic.

On the other hand, Allie couldn't deny her feelings for him. She meant what she said last Monday night. She really would always love him. She didn't have peace about walking out of his life, either.

"You're awfully quiet, Allie."

"I. . .I guess I'm at a loss for words at the moment," she stammered.

"Well, I know there's a chance you're not interested in pursuing a serious relationship with me. I can respect that—and even accept it. But if that's the truth, I wish you'd say so. We can put an end to things right now and walk away as friends. And that's what you wanted, right? You wanted to be friends. I'm offering you a choice."

"Good grief, Jack! Don't I get a chance to pray about it?"

"You should have been praying about it since Monday night."

"Monday night?" With a huff of indignation, Allie folded her arms and leaned against her rented automobile. "I don't appreciate rigid stipulations, especially when it comes to relationships."

"And I don't want to be a nice little distraction for you while you're in town on business."

Allie brought her hands up and covered her face with her palms. She couldn't think, she couldn't pray. . .but she suddenly remembered. Clearly.

"Jack," she said, lowering her arms, "do you realize that this is exactly what drove us apart in the first place—your unyielding demands? I do not intend to use you as a. . .a distraction, but I need some space. I can't think when I'm pressured. I feel trapped. Why can't we just take things one step at a time, praying about our relationship as we go?"

A moment of silence passed between them.

"Is that your answer?" Jack asked at last.

Frustrated, Allie gritted her teeth. But it was as though her Heavenly Father spoke right to her soul. *Let him go.* Heeding the warning, peace enveloped her. So in reply to Jack's question, she nodded.

"Okay, then. . ."

Turning on his heel, Jack pulled out his keys and strode across the street to his SUV.

CHAPTER TWENTY

Cynthia lay in her dark, silent room, trying to remember all the fun she'd had in her life. She wanted to die thinking about something good, something positive. Unfortunately, the only memories that surfaced were those she had hoped to blot out of her mind forever.

Like remembrances of her first ex-husband. . .why couldn't she stop thinking about him? That marriage had been doomed before it even began. But he'd been so insistent, and she'd been a sucker for a guy in uniform. Strange, but at her present stage in life—or stage in death—her first ex-husband seemed like a fine catch. Maybe she should have hung onto him. He had definitely been a far sight better than Bill, and he had never cheated on her the way Ramon had, nor was he a cocaine addict like Luis.

Cynthia gave up on the fight and allowed the memories to sweep her into the past. Suddenly she was twenty-four again and married to a handsome police officer named Jack Callahan.

"You're going to have to put on something more modest," he said.

She had just come downstairs on a summer afternoon wearing a pair of thigh-high shorts, which accentuated her long legs, and a skimpy top that laced up in the front. With platform sandals on her feet, she'd thought she looked good. . .sexy.

"Hey, I just had a kid six months ago, and I got my shape back. I think I deserve to show it off."

"Yeah, but show it off to only me!" Holding their infant son, Jack traded the baby from one arm to the other. "We're going to a picnic with a bunch of guys I work with. I don't want them gawking at my wife."

"It's my business if I want to get 'gawked' at," she argued. "You should feel proud to be seen with a woman like me."

"You look cheap. Go change."

The remark stung. But by that time, she was growing used to his criticism. She had overheard talk about the girl whom Jack once loved; and it was obvious to Cynthia, as early on as her wedding day, that she wouldn't ever measure up. But she convinced herself that she could make Jack love her. How wrong she was! Nevertheless, on this particular afternoon, she did as he told her. She changed her clothes. She selected what she thought was the ugliest outfit she owned, a plain red skirt and baggy red-and-white-striped T-shirt. When she presented herself a second time, Jack didn't say another word. He let her go off to the picnic looking like some frumpy old maid.

And that, she presumed, was what he wanted in a wife.

But that's not what Cynthia wanted to be.

Months went by and things between her and Jack didn't improve. By spring the following year, they barely spoke to each other. He expected certain things from her like cooked meals and clean laundry; and to spite him, she refused. He got angry and she, more rebellious. But what she really wanted was his love and attention. She wished Jack would tell her the same words he often told their son. "I love you." Each afternoon when he left for his shift, he'd kiss Logan good-bye, but tossed her a contemptuous glare.

Cooped up all day with only a baby to care for and afternoon soap operas for company, Cynthia grew restless and depressed. She felt as though she were wasting the best years of her life on a man who didn't love or appreciate her. What 's more, her meddling mother-in-law frequently stopped over to straighten up the house, cook, and wash clothes. Mother Callahan liked to open her Bible and preach, which only aggravated Cynthia all the more.

So she began doing errands—anything, just to get out of the house. Known as "Roxi" back then, a shorter version of her middle name, Roxanne—and the stage name she had selected upon leaving home—Cynthia dreamed up a list of tasks that took hours to accomplish. One of those tasks took her into downtown Chicago, where she ran into her former boss. He was looking for dancers to perform at his nightclub. She jumped at the chance, although she knew Jack, with his old-fashioned, overbearing ideas, wouldn't allow it. For that reason, she lied to his mother, saying she'd joined a ladies' club that participated in all kinds of charitable deeds—and would she baby-sit three nights a week while Jack worked?

Mother Callahan agreed, and Jack didn't seem to care if she belonged to a "ladies' club." He said it might even be good for her to do something nice for other people for a change. Cynthia had chafed beneath his snide remark, and it only fueled her desire to get back into dancing.

For the next few months, life was fun and exciting. Performing in front of men who enjoyed her curvy figure was a sure cure for her depression. It increased her self-confidence, her self-worth. She made good money and began to fantasize about packing up her baby and escaping from her domineering husband.

Then one night a ritzy-looking gentleman told her that he was visiting Chicago and he was lonely. He offered to pay her for a "private" dance performance; and when he waved five hundred dollars under her nose, Cynthia accepted. Little did she know the gent was an undercover cop. Shortly thereafter, she was arrested for prostitution.

Her boss posted bail, and Cynthia went home. The very next day she worked on renting an apartment in Chicago. Her plan was to leave Jack and file for divorce before he discovered her secret occupation and the trouble she'd gotten into. She wouldn't risk facing his wrath. However, he was quicker to find out than she was to move. The best she could figure was that someone in the Chicago precinct recognized her last name or her address and informed Jack. But, oddly enough, he didn't scream and yell. He didn't curse her out. He didn't harm her physically. Instead, he listened to her confession with a surprisingly tolerant ear.

At long last, he said, "You want a divorce? Go for it. But you can't have Logan. And if you try to take him, I'll have every cop in this state hunting you down; and you'll spend the 'best part of your life,' as you described it, in jail. I will personally make sure of it. Understand?"

She did. She also knew it wasn't an idle threat. Jack had enough connections with lawyers, district attorneys, and judges to destroy her life if she defied him. But how could she leave her baby son?

Cynthia tried to stay for Logan's sake, but Jack was a silent ogre who threw menacing glances at her whenever their paths crossed. And each time she left the house, even to take her baby for a stroll, she felt as though she were being watched. After hearing a *click-click* when she'd placed a call to her boss, she decided the phone line was being tapped. Her paranoia increased, and soon she imagined that Jack wanted to kill her. He was just biding his time. Waiting to make his move—just like the dude on the afternoon daytime drama she watched. Every thump and creak in the house became terrifying and

Cynthia never felt so helpless and alone in all her life.

Finally, she couldn't stand it any more; and one hot summer afternoon, she put Logan down for his nap and packed her belongings, including the money she had earned from her dancing. She hated the thought of leaving her baby, but knew if she didn't, she would lose her very mind. Before she made her escape, however, she had crept into Logan's bedroom. She ran her fingers down the back of his head, enjoying the feel of his silky dark brown hair for what would be the last time.

"I'll come back for you," she'd whispered to her baby's sleeping form. "I'll only be gone a little while."

Tearing herself away from the crib, she fled the house that hadn't ever felt like a home. She figured Logan wouldn't be alone for more than a few minutes, not with Jack's watchdogs lurking about. She took the car and stopped at the bank, withdrawing every nickel from their joint savings and checking accounts.

Weird, she thought now as she shifted on her bed's hard, uncomfortable mattress, but Jack never squabbled in court about the funds she'd taken. All he'd fought for was their baby.

And he'd won.

The judge awarded Jack sole custody and pronounced Cynthia an unfit mother because of her prostitution conviction and for what he termed was "child abandonment." When the gavel came down, it splintered her heart. She hadn't even been given a chance to explain.

And she never got a chance to tell her baby good-bye.

"Nurse!" she called. "Nurse! Nurse!"

The silence was deafening as she waited. Finally, the door opened, revealing one of the snippy female CNAs that worked the night shift. "What do you need, Mrs. Matlock?"

"Pain medication," she panted. "I. . .I need something to. . .to stop the pain!"

*   *   *

"Logan, I'm so happy I could burst!" Marilee's exclamation was rewarded with a pleased smile. "Thank you so much for agreeing to wait a few extra months so I can have the wedding I really want."

"Well, you know if I had my way—"

"Yes, I know," Marilee cut in with a laugh. "But you gave me my way," she added on a sincere note, "and I love you all the more for it."

"I could tell it meant a lot to you."

She smiled. "So what did you think of the restaurant? Won't our reception be awesome in that banquet hall?"

"Sure will. I can't believe your father actually put down twenty-five hundred bucks to rent the place. That's an awful lot of money."

"Not really. Not if you consider what's included."

Logan chuckled as he rounded a curve on the interstate. "I'll leave the details to you. Just tell me when and where I have to show up."

"Oh, Logan!"

He laughed all the harder. "I think I'm going to start calling you 'Princess,' but the bad news is you're about to marry a pauper."

"Money isn't an issue."

"It might be down the road. I mean, I'm not going to be able to afford the lifestyle you're used to."

"God will provide," she said. "Besides, all I need and want is to be your wife."

"Honey, that's great for now, but what happens when the scales fall from your eyes and all you see is my dirty laundry?"

"I'll love your dirty laundry, too." Marilee didn't miss the endearment. He'd called her "Honey"!

"I wish I had a tape recording of this. I'd play it back to you in the years to come."

Marilee shook her head, feeling sure that her love for Logan would only be deeper by then.

"Think about it, Marilee. I've told you how much I make a

year. It's probably the same amount your folks are going to spend on our wedding. One day versus a year of my paychecks."

"It's not the same. Mom and Dad have planned and saved for this day."

"There's a good chance we won't be able to do the same for our kids, should God bless us with children."

"That might be true, but I'll still want the best wedding for my daughter—the best that we can give her."

Logan didn't reply, and Marilee sensed he was absorbing everything she'd just said.

"I just don't want you to ever be unhappy," he said at last. "I think that would destroy me inside."

"Oh, Logan, that will never happen. I promise." Sensing his insecurities resurfacing, Marilee determined to squelch them. "Don't you know I lost my heart to you the very first time we met? As far as I'm concerned, my options are either marry you or stay single the rest of my life. There's nobody else in this world for me. I'm convinced of it." She paused, calculating his reaction. Beneath the moonlight and swiftly passing street lamps, she saw him smile. "Remember when Pastor Warren first introduced us?"

"Mm-hum. We walked into your classroom and you were at your desk correcting papers or something. School was out for the day."

"What did you first think of me, Logan?" she couldn't help asking.

He sighed audibly. "I'm embarrassed to even say."

"What?" she persisted.

"It was sinful—or at least I thought it was at the time."

"What do you mean? Tell me."

Logan laughed. "I kept looking at your pink lips and thoughts went through my head that a youth pastor shouldn't have."

"You wanted to kiss me?"

"Yeah, I did."

Marilee laughed. "That's normal, don't you think?"

"No. Not when I was under the impression that you were married."

She inhaled sharply. "No way! Really?"

"Really. When we were on our way to your classroom, Pastor made mention of a newly married teacher; and because I wasn't paying attention, I assumed it was you. For days afterward, I didn't want to even glance in your direction because I felt so ashamed to be attracted to another guy's wife."

Marilee dissolved into girlish giggles. "And here I thought you didn't like me because you avoided me—and after I went out of my way so you'd notice me!"

"I noticed, all right," he readily admitted, "and I thought it was kind of odd that we *coincidentally* kept running into each other. Finally, I asked somebody and found out you weren't married." Logan chuckled. "Man, was I relieved."

Again, Marilee laughed. "Why didn't you tell me this before?"

"Because this is stuff a guy only tells God. . .and maybe his fiancée if she pushes him hard enough."

"Oh, I see," she drawled. But she suddenly felt very flattered and special.

Too soon, they arrived in front of the townhouse Marilee rented, and Logan walked her to the door. He didn't dally, though, much to her disappointment. Her roommates were home, and Marilee had hoped to invite him in so they could talk awhile longer.

"I'll see you tomorrow up at church," he said, backing down the walkway. "Wear your comfy shoes. I want to spend most of the day recruiting for the bonfire event."

"Okay." Turning the lock, Marilee opened the door. "Bye, Logan. I love you."

He smiled. "I love you, too." Then he blew her a kiss and walked to his car.

He said it! He actually said he loved her! Marilee felt like her knees were about to give way, but at the same time her heart soared above the clouds. Stepping inside the small entryway, she closed the door and leaned her back against it. Her roommates, Charmayne and Jill, stopped what they were doing and stared at her.

"I'm engaged to the most handsome, wonderful man in the world!"

"Oh, brother." Tall, athletic, and always the pragmatic voice, Jill rolled her brown eyes. However, Charmayne shared Marilee's enthusiasm.

"Let's make some chocolate chip cookies," Char said, her hazel eyes sparkling, "and you can tell me all about it."

"Sounds perfect," Marilee replied. "In fact, if I don't tell someone, I'll probably explode from sheer joy."

"Good grief," Jill said, flopping onto the couch with a stack of her high school students' papers in her hands. "You're hopeless."

"No, she's not." Dressed in a fuzzy beige bathrobe with pink slippers on her feet, Char put her hands on her hips. "She's in love and planning her wedding day. You're just not a romantic."

"True, true, so spare me the gory details, okay?"

Marilee and Charmayne agreed as they strode to the kitchen. Before long, the aroma of melting butter and chocolate filled the house—and Char was asking if Logan had a friend.

CHAPTER TWENTY-ONE

Sunday dawned hot and muggy. Allie turned on the air-conditioning in her rented auto as she drove to the little church in a neighboring suburb. Lisa Canton, a physical therapist at Arbor Springs, had learned Allie was a Christian one day last week as they conversed before a meeting; and the following day, Lisa invited Allie to attend a worship service with her and her family. Allie decided to take her new friend up on the offer. She enjoyed visiting different churches—and Nick took pleasure in hearing about what she liked and disliked, agreed with and disagreed with in various services. It made for lively conversations.

Smiling as she thought about her son, Allie drove onto the interstate, following the directions Lisa had given her. She hoped Jack would feel a tug in his heart this morning and attend church services with Logan. *Lord, he needs to get back into Your Word so desperately. Please, Lord, remind Jack of the fervency he once had for You. . . .*

Locating the church, Allie pulled into its parking lot and found a space. She got out of the car and walked up to the quaint-looking chapel. Inside stood a greeter, an older woman with white, coiffured hair.

She handed Allie a bulletin. "I'm Mrs. Meyers, and you're new to us, aren't you?"

Smiling, Allie nodded. "Lisa Canton invited me."

"Oh, wonderful. Come with me. I'll show you where the Cantons are seated."

Allie followed Mrs. Meyers into the sanctuary. Lisa was all smiles when she saw their approach. Scooting over, she made room for Allie next to her and a girl who appeared about eight years old.

"Let me introduce you to my family," Lisa said. "This is my husband, Mike; that's my daughter, Leah, to your left; and on the other side of her is my son, Tim."

"Nice to meet you all," Allie replied with genuine enthusiasm.

Within moments, the pastor stood at the pulpit and the service began.

*   *   *

Logan stood in the hallway, knotting his tie. "So, Dad, you coming to church this morning?" He grinned, expecting a wisecrack—just like every Sunday.

"Yeah, I thought maybe I would."

Logan froze, wide-eyed and wondering if he'd heard correctly. "You're coming?"

"Yeah." Jack peered out the doorway of his bedroom. "I just hope the roof doesn't fall in on me or something."

"Not a chance," Logan said, recovering. "God's angels are rejoicing right now."

"I'll take your word for it."

Logan could barely believe what was happening. He'd prayed

long and hard for this moment—ever since he'd gotten his heart right with the Lord during his senior year of high school.

Whispering praises and thanksgiving, Logan returned to his room and finished getting dressed. Minutes later, he met his dad in the kitchen.

"I'm so used to seeing you in your uniform, but you look good in a suit," Logan said with a scrutinizing eye. "Nice tie. Can I borrow it sometime?"

"Sure," Jack replied, sipping his coffee. "You just can't spill on it."

"You'll never let me live that one down, will you?" Logan said, shaking his head at the memory and chuckling. "I was sixteen years old the last time I spilled on one of your ties."

Jack grinned. Finishing his coffee, he set his cup in the sink. "Doesn't seem to make sense to take two vehicles to church," he said. "So whose car are we taking, yours or mine?"

"Good question." Logan lifted the coffeepot and poured a fair amount of the steaming brew into a travel mug. "We can take yours if you'll come to lunch with Uncle Steve, Aunt Nora, and Marilee and me. But just to warn you, the Domotors will most likely come along because they'll want to meet you."

"Yeah, I suppose it's high-time I meet your fiancée's parents, isn't it?" Jack muttered.

"Better late than never," Logan said.

"You're the ultimate optimist, aren't you?"

Logan shrugged.

The conversation continued about whose car they should take. At last, it was decided that they would drive their own vehicles since Jack wasn't sure of his afternoon plans. He did, however, agree to lunch.

On the way to church, Logan couldn't help calling Marilee from his cell phone.

"You'll never believe it. My dad's coming to church. He's following me right now in his Explorer."

"Oh, Logan, that's awesome!" Marilee said. "God's answered our prayers."

"Most definitely." He chuckled. "Aunt Nora's going to pass out when she sees him—that is, if Ronnie doesn't go down first."

With laughter in her tone, Marilee asked, "Do you think we could talk your dad into going out for lunch after the service? I want my parents to meet him."

"He's already agreed to it. He wants to meet your parents, too."

"I—I. . .oh, my goodness!"

Logan chuckled at her loss for words; however, he knew exactly how she felt. "Why is it that we expect great things from God, but when He does them, we're shocked?"

"Maybe because we lack faith. I'm humbled, Logan."

Her soft voice and honest reply warmed his heart. "Me, too. But I think I have a new challenge for the teens this week. I just love it when the Lord allows me to experience firsthand the things I preach on."

Marilee laughed. "You go, Logan!"

*   *   *

Jack walked into the large church building and forced on his best smile as Logan introduced him to just about everyone they passed. It wasn't easy to be personable with his stomach in a knot, but Jack made the effort. It had been so long since he'd stepped foot into a church with the intent to worship the Lord that he felt nervous. He kept envisioning his former pastor rounding the corner and banishing him again. But he reminded himself that Pastor Barlow was dead, gone some eight years already. Jack hadn't even gone to the man's funeral.

Logan showed him to a seat and then excused himself, stating he needed to fulfill some pre-service duties. Jack sat down and made himself comfortable. In the past, he'd walked into countless situations and hadn't ever been afraid to face the unknown, but somehow he felt anxious and a tad self-conscious as he waited for things to begin. Even so, he sensed the Lord wanted him here today, and Jack wasn't about to ignore the prompting. In the past few days, Jesus had made Himself real again to him, and Jack mourned the decades he had gone without hearing the Savior's voice.

Jack decided to take his mind off his discomforting feelings. Glancing around and taking in his surroundings, he noticed that no pews lined the aisles, but instead the congregation sat in padded seats, similar to those found in theaters. Down in front, tubs of flowers graced the space surrounding the pulpit. Behind the colorful floral arrangements, the choir was quickly filling up their designated area, and Jack spotted Marilee among the members. Narrowing his gaze, he watched her for several moments. She was a pretty gal with a sweet disposition and a desire to honor Christ. Jack had no doubt that she would make Logan happy.

And they'll make me a grandpa. Jack winced. He hadn't thought about that. He didn't feel old enough to be a grandfather!

"Jack! I don't believe it. Logan said you were here, but I thought he was kidding."

Looking up at his younger brother, who stood in the aisle to his left, Jack grinned. He figured his return to church would mean that he'd have to swallow that proverbial "humble pie" around his family members. But he also figured they'd find it in their hearts to forgive him and welcome him back into the fold.

He glanced at Nora, who had tears in her eyes. "I don't believe it." She shook her head. "Jack, it's so wonderful to see you here. Steve and I pray for you every night."

"Looks like it paid off," Jack said as he stood. He lifted his hand, indicating to the seats beside his. "Plenty of room. Want to join me?"

"Of course we do!" Nora exclaimed.

Jack moved out of the way, and she went in first, followed by Veronica, who gave her uncle a tight grin. Ricky scooted in next, then Rachel and finally Steve.

"So. . ."

Jack glanced at his brother.

He sighed. "Man, I'm so flabbergasted, I don't even know what to say!"

"I know. I'm a little flabbergasted myself." Jack looked straight ahead when he spoke.

"Jack. . .what happened? I mean. . ." Steve sighed. "You're probably going to say it's none of my business, and you'd be right. But I can't help it. I've got a ton of questions."

"Maybe I can answer those questions later. . .after church."

"I feel like I've finally got my brother back," Steve said with misty eyes.

Jack turned away, feeling misty himself. "Knock it off, will ya?"

Nora sat forward. "Jack, will you join us for lunch? I put a roast in the oven before we left."

As he regarded his sister-in-law, he saw the caring light in her hazel eyes. He marveled at all the offers she made over the years. Christmas dinners, Easter, Thanksgiving. . .Jack always declined and, instead, volunteered to work. It just seemed easier to patrol the streets of Oakland Park than to allow himself some measure of happiness with his family. In hindsight, Jack realized he'd been serving a self-imposed sentence, instead of accepting God's grace and forgiveness. But as far as family was concerned, it was a wonder Nora even spoke to him, let alone continued to invite him over.

"Sure, I'll come for lunch," he replied. "Thanks for asking."

"I always ask."

He chuckled. "I know. But I have to warn you, Logan wants Marilee and her parents to join us."

"The more the merrier. Is Allie here?"

"Haven't seen her." Jack sat back and gazed at the pulpit. Moments later, he realized he was clenching his jaw. He forced himself to relax. He looked back at Nora and decided to come clean. "As of Friday night, Allie and I are. . .just friends. Nothing more."

"Doesn't sound like that was a mutual decision," Steve said.

"It wasn't." Jack crossed his leg as music began to play. "But we'll discuss that later, too, okay?"

"Okay."

Murmurs from the congregation subsided till all was quiet. The music director raised his hands and the choir began to sing.

*   *   *

After the service, Allie insisted upon treating the Cantons to lunch at a restaurant of their choice. They were a sweet family who made Allie feel like she fit right in. Leah talked her ear off about the books she'd read, and Tim impressed her by listing his accomplishments in both academics and music. It seemed apparent to Allie that Lisa and Mike were doing a fine job raising their children.

After lunch, Allie said her good-byes to the Cantons and made her way back to the hotel. But then, as she drove by the turnoff for Arbor Springs, she decided to stop and visit Cynthia. Spending the remainder of the afternoon encouraging a dying woman appealed to Allie more than idling the hours away alone in the solitude of her suite.

Besides, she hadn't seen Cynthia since Thursday evening. *Oh, Lord, she didn't die over the weekend, did she? I hope I'm not too late.*

She parked and, entering the facility, Allie found the security guard lounging in the lobby watching a football game. He was so engrossed with the TV that he didn't notice when she walked by. Feeling troubled, Allie thought of several hypothetical situations. Any crazy person could walk in and jeopardize patients' and employees' safety. Something had to be done.

As she pushed the elevator button, Allie thought of Jack and wondered if he would consider putting together some sort of training seminar for Arbor Springs's security personnel. He knew the laws and safety techniques, but would he be interested? And would she want to work with Jack in that capacity? His presence at Arbor Springs would mean their paths would cross often—and, at the moment, Allie wasn't even sure if they were on speaking terms.

Oh, Lord, I don't know, she prayed, stepping into the elevator. *You're going to have to lead the way here.*

The elevator doors opened to the fourth floor; and Allie decided that, in some respects, Jack reminded her too much of Erich. Or had it been Erich who reminded her of Jack in the first place? Odd, but up until this very moment, she'd never seen the resemblance in the two men.

Allie shook off her musings as she entered Room 8. Cynthia lay in her bed, her eyes closed. But she was breathing, and relief flooded Allie. Standing at her bedside, she touched Cynthia's frail hand. It was several moments before the other woman's eyes fluttered open.

"Angel. . ."

"Hello," Allie said, acting cheerful. "How are you feeling today?"

She stared at her for some time, as if trying to focus her eyes. "I. . .I've been remembering," Cynthia rasped, "and I. . .I know who you are."

"Well, of course you do. I've been coming to see you for a good part of a month." Allie wondered if Cynthia was delirious again. It had happened before.

"Do you know who. . .who I am?" The words were spoken with great effort.

"Yes. You're Cynthia Matlock."

"Wh–when I was a girl. . ." She struggled to inhale. ". . .folks called me Cindy."

"Do you want me to call you Cindy?"

"No. . .I mean. . .it doesn't matter." She paused to suck in a breath. "Wh–when I left home, I. . .I changed my name. I. . .I wanted to be a singer."

Oh, not this again, Allie thought. Reaching out a hand, she smoothed back Cynthia's thin, scraggly bark brown hair. "Shh. . . just rest now. Don't talk."

"You. . .you don't know who I am, do you?"

Retracting her hand, Allie sighed, wondering how to reply.

"I. . .I remember you. I saw. . .saw your picture. Allie. . .I remember you."

"Yes, I'm Allie." *What picture is she talking about? Was it here at Arbor Springs? Did she see me on the news weeks ago?*

"You're the one. . .the one Jack couldn't get over."

Allie's jaw dropped, and she saw a hint of a smile curve the dying woman's lips.

"Y–you don't know me, do you?" She fought for her next breath. "I. . .I can tell."

Allie felt tingles of apprehension climb her spine. "Are you talking about Jack Callahan?"

"Uh-huh. . .he was my. . .my first husband."

Allie froze, and for a moment, the world whirled around. She struggled for her bearings. *No, Lord, no!* She peered down at the woman in disbelief. This? This hollowed-out shell of a woman was Jack's ex-wife? How could that be?

"If Jack didn't. . .didn't send you, then you. . .you must really be sent from God."

"Jack didn't send me," Allie murmured, still trying to fend off her shock.

"I can tell by the look. . .the look on your face."

Managing her astonishment, Allie became increasingly concerned by Cynthia's inability to breathe properly. "I'm going to get your nurse," she said, thinking that she, herself, could use a stiff cup of coffee. Allie had the feeling it was going to be a very long afternoon.

CHAPTER TWENTY-TWO

Jack hadn't ever been the sort of man to unburden himself to others. There were only a select few people in his life that he trusted enough with his personal business. But today, Steve and Nora joined the ranks as confidants. They'd been granted some time alone since Logan and his future wife and in-laws left to do some shopping. Jack never saw two women so excited about planning a wedding, and he was proud of Logan for being such a good sport. Stan Domotor, Marilee's father, seemed like a pretty tolerant guy, too, and that impressed Jack. Any man who could put up with female sensibilities won his instant respect. That was something Jack needed to learn, and it was a long time in coming.

Glancing at his wristwatch, Jack realized, much to his embarrassment, that he'd been blabbering on about himself for nearly two hours. During that time, he'd managed to divulge his innermost thoughts about Allie. He wanted to win her heart. . .but how?

"I think you should send her roses," Jack heard his niece interject from the stairwell.

"Veronica, this is an adult conversation and you were not invited!" Nora scolded her oldest daughter.

"Yeah, well, I'm hardly a baby," she replied, rising from the carpeted step on which she'd been sitting. She strolled into the living room with a defiant lift of her chin. "You can't just send me out to ride my bike or play basketball like you did the other two."

Feeling irked by her eavesdropping, Jack narrowed his gaze at Veronica. However, a moment later, he had to chuckle. Her tenacity reminded him of himself. *Oh, Lord, it must run in the family,* he thought, his irritation retreating.

Settling back into the love seat, upholstered in a bright fabric with a geometric design, Jack patted the empty cushion beside him. "You've got some advice for me? Let's hear it."

After a wary glance at him, Veronica cautiously made her way over to Jack and sat down. She folded her slender arms tightly about her, and Jack sensed her sudden discomfort. Perhaps she'd been looking for an argument, a chance to exert her independence and thwart her parents' authority. Typical teenage tactic, but he'd called her bluff.

"Well?" he prompted with an amused grin.

Veronica looked up at him, uncertain at first, but then he spied a challenging spark in her blue-green eyes. Jack thought his pesky niece was blossoming into a very lovely young lady.

"You don't have a romantic bone in your body, do you?"

Steve cleared his throat. "Ronnie, change your tone. You're to respect your uncle."

"Stay out of this," Jack told his brother on a facetious note.

Steve raised his hands as if in surrender, and Jack looked back at his niece.

"I think romance is overplayed," he told her. "It's not real life."

"Define 'real life,' Uncle Jack."

He grinned. "Real as in not depicted in those silly romances you read."

Roni gave him a patronizing stare. "This has nothing to do with what I do or do not read."

"Good comeback," Jack said, looking over at Nora and giving her a wink. He sensed his sister-in-law was worried that her smart aleck daughter would offend him. But such wasn't the case at all. Jack rather enjoyed the sparring. "And, I'll be totally honest with you. You're right. I don't have a single romantic bone in my body."

"Well, that's gotta change if you want Mrs. Littenberg to marry you."

"Who says I want to get married?"

"Everyone wants to get married," the teenager replied. "I mean, who wants to be lonely and grow old?"

"You can take her over your knee anytime, Jack," Steve said. "I won't even call the cops."

Jack rolled his eyes at his brother's attempted pun. "What are you talking about? I rarely took Logan over my knee, and he deserved it more than Roni."

Jack stretched his arm out across the settee, and his niece began to relax.

"Do you have a boyfriend?" he asked.

"No. Dad won't allow me to date."

"Good for him."

Veronica made a *tsk* sound. "This isn't about me, Uncle Jack. It's about you."

"Oh, yeah. Right."

"If you want to be more than just friends, then you should send Mrs. Littenberg roses."

"Too expensive."

Roni rolled her teal-colored eyes. "You're investing in your future."

Jack chuckled, but thought over her suggestion. "Allie wouldn't be impressed by roses."

"I beg to differ," Nora said. "As much as I hate to admit it, my daughter is right. Women like to be. . ." She searched for the word. ". . .pursued."

"I don't know about that," Jack replied. "I answered plenty of calls from women who were being. . .*pursued*, and they didn't appreciate it."

"There's a difference between stalking and pursuing," Veronica said.

"How do you know?"

She turned and swatted his arm. "Stop being difficult! It's so annoying!"

Jack looked at Steve. "Maybe I'll take her over my knee after all."

"Be my guest."

Roni threw her hands in the air. "Oh, forget it. I give up!"

She stood, but Jack caught her wrist. "I'm sorry. I'll behave, and I'm a man of my word." He pulled her back into a sitting position. Maybe he'd send Allie roses just to please his niece. There was just something about Veronica that tugged at his heart— something about her or the impenetrable look on her face that Jack recognized, although he couldn't put a name to it. "So you think I should send her roses, huh? What color?"

Veronica shrugged, acting out her obvious discouragement.

"I think the traditional red would be nice," Nora said.

"Why don't you just pick some of those blue things growing in the lot next door and save a ton of money?" Steve suggested with a guffaw that made Jack chuckle.

"You two are hopeless," Veronica stated.

"Yes, they are," Nora replied. "And now we've agreed on something twice in the same day, Roni. What do you know?"

She bestowed on her mother a rare smile.

"You're lovely when you do that," Jack said honestly. "You

should smile more often."

Veronica swung her gaze at him with a measure of surprise splayed across her features. For a moment, she didn't know how to respond.

Finally, she said, "Thanks, Uncle Jack. That's the nicest thing anyone's ever said to me."

*　　*　　*

The sun began its descent in the western sky, and Allie watched it through the windows in Room 8. She glanced over her shoulder and saw that Cynthia rested comfortably now, since the clear plastic tubes containing a flow of oxygen had been placed in her nostrils. Before she'd drifted off, however, Cynthia, also once known as Roxi Callahan, managed to tell Allie more than she ever wanted to know about her marriage to Jack. But there was one aspect of the tragic tale that went ignored. Logan. Cynthia never mentioned the son whom she abandoned, and Allie found herself having little or no respect for a woman who would leave her baby.

Turning back to the sunset, Allie fought off self-righteousness. She knew she shouldn't judge Cynthia Matlock. They'd experienced similar situations. Hadn't the woman confessed to being afraid of Jack? Allie, herself, could relate on that account. She'd been terribly frightened of Erich at times. But where Cynthia had fled, Allie had stayed, and therein laid the difference between them.

"Angel?"

Allie cringed. She wished the woman would stop calling her that! "I'm still here," she murmured.

Cynthia glanced in her direction. "Did you and Jack ever get married?"

"Nope. We're just. . .friends." Allie hated the terse note in her voice. But she couldn't seem to help it. Part of her was angry with this woman, while the other part commiserated with her. "I married someone else, although my husband is dead now. I have one son named Nicholas."

Stepping toward the bedside, Allie continued, "I know you and Jack had a son. His name is Logan. I've met him. He's a fine man. A youth pastor. He's going to get married soon."

Huge tears spilled from Cynthia's eyes, and Allie felt a pinch of remorse for intentionally hurting someone who was so obviously already wounded. "My baby. . ."

"I'm sorry. Maybe I shouldn't have mentioned Logan."

"I've been thinking about him."

"Why did you leave him?" Allie whispered as tears filled her own eyes.

"I didn't mean to. I planned to get him, but Jack. . ." Cynthia sniffed. ". . .Jack threatened me."

Big deal, Allie thought. Erich had threatened her plenty of times, and Jack's temperament wasn't nearly as formidable.

"Did Jack ever hit you? Hurt you. . .physically?"

A long pause. "No, but I was young and fanciful. I thought he hired someone to kill me."

"Nonsense. Jack would never do something like that!"

"I know that now. But you probably don't believe me. You're his friend and he always loved you," she said, sounding weak. "Of course you'd take his side."

Allie shook her head. "I'm not taking sides. I'm merely trying to understand how you could have left your child."

"I wasn't thinking straight," Cynthia admitted, sounding as winded as if she'd just run a mile. "Looking back, I see Jack treated me better than the other jerks I married. Compared to them, Jack was a royal prince."

Pulling the padded armchair closer to the bed, Allie sat down. "Logan might like to meet you. Can I tell him that you're here? Can he visit you?"

"He must hate me," Cynthia wheezed.

"I doubt it. Logan isn't the type to hate anyone."

With rheumy eyes dulled by pain, she searched Allie's face. "What does he look like?"

"Dark hair, brown eyes. . .he looks very much like his dad."

"Yes, Jack's mother often made the same comparison. It used to grate on my nerves. I thought Logan looked more like my side of the family, like my father."

"Are your parents still living?"

"I have no idea. When I left home, I never looked back."

"Where are you from?"

"A little, nothing town in Iowa."

"Any brothers? Sisters?"

"One sister. Little Miss Perfect. My father adored her, but I was the one who was too fat, too ugly, too loud. I lost weight in high school, and he said I was too thin. When I got my first boyfriend, he called me a 'hussy,' but when my sister started dating, she was just 'popular.' "

Allie grimaced at the unjust treatment Cynthia had received as a girl. "Did your parents ever know you got married? Did Jack meet them? Did they know about Logan?"

"No." Cynthia rolled her head from side to side. "I told Jack my parents were dead because, in my mind, they were."

"What about your daughters?"

"Don't even mention them, those two. . .two gold-diggers!" Cynthia squeezed her eyes shut, but tears leaked from their corners anyway. "I'd call them something else, but you made me promise not to swear."

"I appreciate you keeping your end of the bargain," Allie replied. Tipping her head, she pressed the issue. "How are your daughters gold-diggers?"

"They said they'd take care of me," she cried in a broken voice, "but they went back on their word. They thought I had a life insurance policy. They found the papers. But it wasn't any good 'cause I'd quit paying on it years ago. When they found out, they stuck me in this place."

Allie felt her heart melt, and any residual anger she felt toward Cynthia Matlock vanished. How utterly sad it was that this poor lady's life had been marked by bad relationships.

With a shaky, bony hand, Cynthia dried her tears. Allie scooted her chair closer.

"You know what I think you've wanted all these years? You've wanted what every woman in the world wants. Love. We want to be wives who are cherished by their husbands and mothers who are adored by their children."

"No one has ever loved me," Cynthia wailed in her raspy voice. "Never."

"But that's not true. Jesus Christ loves you. He loves you so much, He went to the Cross for you."

"Where was He when I needed Him?"

"He was never far away. In fact, He's been waiting for you to call on Him. He's the Lover of your soul, and you'll never know true love until you know Him."

Cynthia gave her a helpless look, tears trickling from her eyes, so Allie sat on the bed and gathered her into her arms. With the dying woman's head resting on her shoulder, Allie rocked her like a little child.

*   *   *

"I've got to apologize for Roni's comment earlier this afternoon," Steve said as he walked Jack to his vehicle.

"What's to apologize for?" It was just past eight o'clock and night had fallen. The wind had shifted and now a cool wind blew out of the northwest, tickling a neighbor's wind chimes and rustling treetops. Fall had arrived and winter wasn't far off. Jack surreptitiously worried about how he would spend his days now that he'd retired. But he pushed that troublesome thought aside for the time being and looked at his brother.

Steve shrugged in answer to his question. "Roni made it sound like Nora and I never say anything nice to her. That's not true."

"I know it's not, but think about it. Sometimes compliments don't carry much weight when they come from parents."

"But coming from her uncle they mean more?" Pursing his

lips, Steve nodded. "I see your point."

"Well, to be honest, I don't think I've ever paid much attention to Veronica until today, and that's my fault. Maybe it's me who needs to do the apologizing."

"Naw, forget the past. What matters is you won her over, and now you're even more of a hero than Spiderman!"

"Yeah, right."

The two brothers shared a laugh. But Jack felt somewhat flattered that he'd made a positive impression on his niece. She certainly hadn't been thrilled with him on Labor Day.

"Hey, listen, thanks for everything," Jack said, unlocking his SUV.

"Let's do this again sometime."

Jack nodded and extended his right hand. Steve clasped it in an affectionate shake. "See ya later."

As he drove home, Jack had to admit that spending time with his family members had been a pleasant surprise. He might even be tempted to do it again next Sunday.

Arriving at his condominium, he reached up to the overhead visor and pressed the button on the remote control. Once the garage door had opened, he pulled his vehicle inside.

The telephone was ringing as he entered through the side door. Jack wasn't in any hurry to answer it. He sauntered into his bedroom and removed his jacket. The phone stopped. By the time he'd showered and changed into blue jeans and a sweatshirt, it started ringing again.

Portable phone in hand, he pressed the TALK button. "Hello?" he said gruffly, making his way to the kitchen.

"Jack?"

He halted in midstride. A bolt of concern shot through him. "Allie. What's up?"

"I've been trying to get a hold of you. . . ." Her tone of voice carried a tremulous note.

"Something wrong? You okay?"

"Yes, I'm okay. But I need to speak with you. It's important."

Jack glanced at the phone's caller ID. He didn't recognize the number. "Where are you?"

"I'm at a little coffee place on Central Avenue."

"I know the one. I'll be there in five minutes."

"No, wait. . ."

Jack paused.

"Under the circumstances, it might be best if I came to your place. I don't mean to intrude, but the matter I need to discuss with you is terribly personal."

"Is it about Friday night?" He hoped it was. He hoped Allie had changed her mind.

But his heart felt like a lead weight at her reply. "No."

"Well, just say what you have to say over the phone then," he said, his irritation concealing his hurt and disappointment.

When no answer was forthcoming, Jack wondered if she'd hung up on him. "Allie?"

"I'm here. I'm just a little upset right now."

He sighed and figured he should just face facts. He would always be a sap where Allie was concerned. "Yeah, okay, come on over. Need directions?"

"Yes."

Jack told her how to get to his condo; and not two minutes after he'd disconnected the call, Logan walked in, whistling some cheery melody.

"Hi ya," he said, pausing in the hallway. "Did you have a good afternoon?"

"It was all right," Jack replied as he entered the living room, where he began tidying up.

"I was glad to see you back at church tonight."

Jack nodded. "Listen, Allie's coming over, and—"

"I'd be happy to chaperone," Logan cut in. "No problem."

Jack grinned at the wisecrack. "That's not what I was going to suggest."

"I know," he said, making his way into the kitchen. "I'll make myself scarce. Don't worry. I'll just fix a PB and J and go read in my room."

"Thanks."

Minutes later, the doorbell sounded, and Jack answered it. He showed Allie into his home. When he saw her face beneath the foyer's beveled ceiling lamp, he immediately noticed the dark circles under her eyes. Had she been crying?

"Rough day?" he asked, taking hold of her elbow and escorting her upstairs into the living room.

"A troubling afternoon, that's for sure!"

"Have a seat."

Allie set down her purse and then lowered herself onto the plaid-upholstered couch. Jack sat in the matching armchair. He crossed his leg, ankle to knee, and considered Allie, sitting several feet away. She looked somewhat disheveled.

"Did you have another run-in with Brenda?"

Allie shook her head. "There's this lady at Arbor Springs. She's dying, and I befriended her. She's actually the one behind all the media hype because a CNA physically abused her. He's no longer employed by Lakeland Enterprises." She picked a stray thread from her shirtsleeve as she spoke.

"Anyway, I've continued to visit this woman because she's estranged from her family members. It's largely her own doing, I admit it, but I still feel sorry for her."

"What's this got to do with me?"

Allie held up her hand. "I'm getting there, Jack."

He nodded, tamping down his impatience.

"One of the things this woman has been doing is dwelling on her past. Sometimes when I walk into her room, she's muttering about some song she used to sing back in the sixties. She looks like a ninety-year-old bag of bones, but she's really only a few years older than I am. Now her liver is failing, so her skin is a sickly yellow. Her name is Cynthia Matlock."

Jack thought over the name, but it didn't register. He shrugged, and Allie continued.

"Cynthia has had four failed marriages, and apparently she's been thinking about her ex-husbands. Her first ex-husband in particular. . ."

Logan appeared at the doorway. "Hi, Mrs. Littenberg."

She glanced up, and Jack watched as she forced a little smile. Looking at his son, he said, "I thought you were going to make yourself scarce."

"I'm on my way to Scarceville right now." He held up a hand. "G'night."

"Actually, Logan, you should probably hear this, too," Allie said.

He pivoted and his questioning gaze met Jack's.

"If that's what the lady wants, come and join us."

"Okay, sure. . ."

Wearing a puzzled expression, Logan entered the living room. Jack moved next to Allie, leaving the armchair for his son.

Allie repeated everything she had just told Jack, catching Logan up on the preface.

"This afternoon when I walked in," Allie said, "Cynthia told me she knew who I was. That seemed obvious to me, since I've been visiting her for the past month. But then she said that she knew I was. . .I was 'the one Jack never could get over.'"

Frowning, he looked over at her, reran the story through his head. The name. . .

Then suddenly it struck. "Oh, Lord have mercy," he muttered, allowing his head to drop back so it rested on the top of the couch. "Cynthia Roxanne Scott."

"Matlock now."

Jack lifted his head and stared at Allie. "How in the—" His conscience pricked him, and he stopped before cursing. "You have a real knack for getting yourself all tangled up in people's lives, don't you?"

Allie didn't reply, but lowered her gaze.

"Dad, um, I don't think Mrs. Littenberg got herself tangled in anything on purpose."

"Oh, I know it," he groused. Feeling like a heel, he looked at Allie, but she kept her chin lowered. "I apologize," he said, softening his tone. "It's not your fault."

When she finally lifted her head, the anguished expression on her face crimped his heart.

"Trust me," she said, "I had no intention of walking into something like this."

"I believe you." He put his hand on top of hers, which were both folded over her knee.

Logan cleared his throat. "Pardon my ignorance, but is the woman you're talking about the same one that I think you're talking about?"

Jack removed his hand and stood. "No sense in my being in on the rest of this conversation. Allie, I care a great deal about you, but I couldn't give a hoot if that woman is dying." He stepped around the coffee table. "Logan," he said, glancing over his shoulder, "your search is over. Mrs. Littenberg has found your mother."

CHAPTER TWENTY-THREE

Logan sat forward and set his plate on the coffee table. "No way. You found my biological mother?"

Allie nodded.

"I've been scouring the Net for Roxi Scott, Roxanne Scott." He glanced off into the next room. "Dad could have told me her real name is Cynthia."

Jack appeared in the doorway. "Hey, can I help it that I blocked it out of my memory? Besides, you never asked." He turned and walked away, leaving Logan shaking his head in his wake.

Allie brushed an errant tear off her cheek. "Logan, your mother's dying and she doesn't know the Lord. I've told her about Him." Allie fetched a Kleenex from her purse. "She's so broken and sad. She's sorry for leaving you. She told me the whole story this afternoon."

Logan worked the corner of his lower lip between his teeth. His heart did a somersault at the mention of his mother's "leaving him;" and, as much as he hated to admit it, he felt a measure of insecurity well up in his being. It was true: He occasionally fretted over his impending marriage, wondering if Marilee would tire of him and leave him. In his soul, he knew she wouldn't; but his heart was, as the Bible described, "deceitful and desperately wicked." Satan would surely get a foothold if Logan ceased to fight those ungrounded fears. But if he got a chance to connect with his natural mother, he sensed the battle in that area would be won.

"She meant to come back and get you, but your father wouldn't allow it," Allie continued. "She had been arrested for prostitution, except she really didn't do anything wrong, other than dance at a nightclub behind your dad's back." Allie paused. "Oh, well, I guess that's 'wrong' enough, isn't it?"

Logan bobbed his head.

"The day she left you, she didn't think you would be alone for long because she worked herself up to believing your dad had people watching her and the house. But in lieu of the fact she left and had been arrested, your father got custody. Your mother left Illinois and changed her name back to Cynthia. And, Logan, I don't mean to sound callous or judgmental, but you can count your blessings that your mother didn't raise you. She's told me some of her past and about some of the people she's been involved with. . ." Allie shook her head. "There's no doubt in my mind that God protected you."

"I know He did," Logan replied. He had pretty much come to that same conclusion on his own. "I have no regrets. Just questions."

"Maybe she's the one who can answer them." Allie toyed with the tissue in her hand. "I asked Cynthia if I could tell you where she was and she said it would be all right. I told her that I planned to tell Jack, too. She wasn't thrilled about that, but she didn't forbid me to say anything."

"I want to meet her. I've already made up my mind. The fact that you're the one who located my natural mother just makes God's will all the more clear to me." Logan grinned. "See, I had prayed that the Lord would just drop all the information I needed in my lap. I didn't want to hurt my dad, even though he said he didn't care if I tried to find her."

"That makes me feel a little better. I would like to think that God has used me and that He'll use this circumstance for good."

"He will. No doubt about it."

Allie stood. "I need to warn you, though, you don't have a lot of time. Before entering Arbor Springs, your mother underwent extensive chemo treatments. They were hard on her body and ineffective. Now the cancer has spread. She's in a tremendous amount of pain and her major organs are shutting down."

"How soon can I show up? Tomorrow morning?"

Allie grinned at his enthusiasm. "Visiting hours start at eight A.M."

"I'll be there," Logan said, seeing her to the door.

"Oh, and you've got two half-sisters. They're here in the Chicago area. And you might have grandparents in Iowa."

"No kidding?" Logan grinned and let the idea sink in. . .siblings! Sisters!

"Good night, Logan."

He gave himself a mental shake. "Night, Mrs. Littenberg."

She paused and turned on her heel. "Please call me Allie." Her smile broadened. "All my friends do."

"Okay. . .Allie."

Logan watched her retreating form until she was safely in her car. Stepping back inside, he bolted the door. Awed by everything he'd just learned, he picked up his plate in the living room and made his way back into the kitchen where his father stood, leaning against the counter, drinking from a can of cola.

Logan grinned inwardly, noting it wasn't a beer in his hand. *Thank You, Jesus!*

"Allie sure knows how to drop a bomb. I'll give her that much," Jack said. "Every time I'm with her I feel like I get beat up."

Logan shook his head, grinning at his dad's comment.

"You know, after spending the afternoon with Steve and talking with Veronica, I've come to the conclusion that sarcasm runs in our family."

"I could have told you that long before this afternoon," Logan replied, chuckling.

"I think we get it from Dad. He was always making wise-cracks. Mom would laugh until her sides ached." Jack shook his head, remembering.

Several moments of silence passed between father and son. Logan took the opportunity to finish eating his peanut butter and jelly sandwich.

"So what are you going to do?" Jack finally asked.

"Visit my biological mother, of course."

He nodded. "I figured."

"Do you object?"

Jack expelled a heavy sigh. "No. . .and it's not my place to 'object' even if I did."

"Thanks," Logan said with a grin.

Pursing his lips, Jack gave the matter more thought. "You know, whether it's out of paranoia or prophesy, I predict that I'll wind up the hated enemy when this is all through."

"Not with me, you won't," Logan promised. "I appreciate everything you've done for me. The way I see it, you wanted the best for me and you went out of your way to see that I got it."

"I tried," Jack said with a shrug. "But Allie's such a pushover when it comes to needy people. She'll probably sympathize with Roxi and never want to speak to me again."

Pouring a glass of milk, Logan considered his dad while he took a drink. The idea dawned on him that perhaps he and his father shared more than their height, brown eyes, dark hair, and sarcastic wit—maybe they shared the fear of being left again— and left by the women they loved.

*   *   *

Speckles of Monday morning sunlight danced across the oak table in the conference room at Arbor Springs. Sitting adjacent to Evan Jacobs, Allie watched his expression darken.

"I'm sorry, Evan," she said sincerely. "As I mentioned earlier, I don't normally get myself so emotionally involved while I'm on an assignment."

He nodded, and Allie sensed he was weighing his options.

"I'll understand if you and the other board members want me to resign. In fact, I'll refund all your payments and you can even implement my suggestions thus far free of charge."

Evan grinned. "Pretty generous offer."

Allie shrugged. "Money is the last thing on my mind right now. However, you've got my word that, if I continue here in the capacity of consultant, you won't be sorry. I've got a lot of wonderful ideas that I want to share with you, but I felt I had to be honest about the situation here concerning Mrs. Matlock."

"I appreciate it, but I don't think I'll mention anything to the other board members. At least not right now. I just don't know what it'll accomplish."

Again, Allie shrugged. The decision was Evan's to make.

He glanced at his wristwatch. "Are you prepared for the meeting in fifteen minutes?"

"Absolutely," she replied with a smile. Pushing her chair back, she stood. "Allow me to set up my notebook computer, and I'll show the board members of Lakeland Enterprises a presentation they will not soon forget."

To her delight, Evan chuckled. "I'm going to get some coffee. Want a cup?"

"I'd love it," Allie replied as she plugged in her computer.

Once Evan left the room, Allie signed onto her computer

and launched the necessary program. Silently, she prayed for Logan and his first visit with Cynthia. He planned to arrive at eight o'clock—the same time as her meeting.

*   *   *

"Mrs. M, you've got a visitor."

Reclining in her bed after a female CNA had satisfactorily bathed her, Cynthia looked at the doorway. Nate sauntered into her room. She smiled, thinking that she was beginning to like this young man and his sassy disposition.

"Do you feel up to holding court, your highness?" he asked with a little bow.

"Oh, knock it off," Cynthia replied, unable to help a grin. However, she did feel better today than she had in weeks. "Who's here to see me?"

"Some guy about my age. . .maybe a little younger." Nate winked. "He's got flowers, so I think we should let him in."

Cynthia knew the identity of her visitor at once. Logan. "I. . .I don't know," she hedged, feeling suddenly nervous. What would she say to him?

"Let him in, Mrs. M. He says he's a family member."

Before she could utter a response, her unexpected visitor walked in and around Nate. Cynthia gasped at the resemblance he bore to his father. With trembling fingers, she touched her lips. "Logan," she whispered.

"I'll leave you two alone," Nate said. "If there's anything you need, Mrs. M, just holler."

Staring at her son, she didn't answer, but she watched as Logan thanked the nurse as he left the room. Then Logan looked back at her with those familiar brown eyes that had haunted her for nearly three decades.

"I take it you know who I am."

She nodded. "You're my son." Her voice failed her, so she cleared her throat. "You're Logan Michael Callahan."

"And you're my mother." He gave her a courteous smile before setting the flowers on the window ledge. Cynthia noted the lovely fall arrangement in a wicker basket.

"They're pretty," she murmured. "Thanks. I can't remember the last time someone brought me flowers."

"You're welcome."

An uncomfortable moment lapsed between them.

"I, um, have some pictures here," Logan said, pulling snapshots from his jacket pocket. He was meticulously dressed in a dark suit and coordinating tie. "I must say, you don't look anything like these photos."

"I'm dying. My angel must have told you that. What did you expect?"

Logan frowned. "Your angel?"

"That's my name for her. Her real name is Allie, but I call her my angel because, until I met her, this place was a living nightmare."

"Sorry to hear that. . .about this place, I mean." Logan glanced at the armchair beside her bed. "May I sit down?"

"I don't care." She saw him inch closer, regarding her all the while. Reaching the chair, he lowered himself into it.

"Lemme see those pictures."

Logan handed them over.

With shaky hands, she held them toward the small shaft of light coming through the draperies. The photographs felt like they weighed a pound apiece. "Our wedding day," she muttered, setting the first snapshot aside. "I don't remember when this one was taken," she said of the second, although she recognized her baby son in her arms. The last picture was taken at Christmastime, probably 1971 or '72.

Cynthia let her arms fall. The simple effort of holding three snapshots exhausted her, but she liked the way she looked in each of them. She wished she looked like that today. "I was pretty back then, wasn't I?" When she didn't hear a reply, she turned to look at her son. He gave her an uncomfortable little grin. "You sure do resemble your father."

The grin became a smile. "That's what everyone says."

"It's true."

Cynthia tore her gaze away from Logan's face. Remembering him as an infant was one thing; coming face-to-face with him as an adult was another. It was almost too painful. The baby she'd left sleeping in his crib was now a full-grown man. . .and a handsome one at that.

"What do you want?" she ground out, covering her vulnerability with terseness. "Do you want to tell me how much you hate me and how I've scarred your life forever? Do you want to find out if I have a will and life insurance and if you're listed as a beneficiary?"

"No, no, nothing like that."

She cursed before glancing his way again. "Then what? What do you want from me?"

"Answers."

"Answers," Cynthia replied. She wasn't sure she had any.

"I've actually been doing searches on the Internet in hopes of locating you," Logan continued. "But Mrs. Littenberg— Allie—found you here instead. I don't believe it was a mistake or a coincidence. It was answered prayer."

Cynthia sensed more Bible talk was on the way. "You're a minister. . .is that right?"

"A youth pastor, yes."

"Hm. . .did you come to preach at me?"

"If you'll listen."

Another obscenity escaped her lips; and when she looked at Logan, she didn't miss his expression of disappointment. Her heart ached. He looked so much like his dad.

"I loved your father," she confessed. "I honestly did. He was the first one who really cared about me. But he didn't love me. I wanted him to, and I tried every trick in the book to make that happen. Didn't work, though."

Logan didn't reply.

"Did he ever remarry?"

"No."

"So you. . .you never had a mother?"

"I had my grandmother and my aunt."

But not a mother. Cynthia's already-broken heart shattered even more. Her son never knew the love of a mother. But that was Jack's fault. "Why didn't your father remarry?"

Logan shrugged. "Guess the right one never came along."

"That's bull—" Cynthia stopped herself before swearing. No doubt, her son disliked profanity as much as her angel did; and for some reason, she didn't want to offend him. "That's ridiculous," she began again. "The 'right one' was in my room earlier this morning. She told me you might come to visit."

"Allie?"

"Bingo." Cynthia stared up at the ceiling while she replied. "Your father was hung up on her even after he married me." Slowly, she turned to Logan. "How could I compete with a memory?"

"I. . .I don't know what to say," Logan stammered.

"I guess there's nothing to say when it comes to your dad and me. That was so long ago, and our relationship was hopeless from the start. But if Allie is a widow and your dad isn't married, why don't the two of them finally get together?"

"I don't really know all the ins and outs."

"They should quit wasting time," Cynthia said, feeling suddenly drowsy. "Life's too short. Either one of them could end up like me in a year's time."

"That's true. Tomorrow isn't promised to any of us."

Another momentary pause of discomfort, then Logan spoke again. "Would you mind answering a few of my questions?"

Cynthia considered him while trying to keep her heavy eyelids from closing. "I owe you that much, don't I? Go ahead. What do you want to know?"

Logan glanced at his hands, folded over his knees. "I want to know why you never tried to contact me when I was a kid. You could have called me on my birthday or sent me a card at Christmas. Why didn't you?"

With a long sigh, Cynthia contemplated the question. "Fear," she finally answered. "I was afraid Jack would have me arrested if I tried to contact you."

"I can't see Dad doing something like that, but—"

"You were an infant," Cynthia cut in, "how could you know what your dad would or wouldn't do?"

Logan did a quick up and down of his dark eyebrows, a passive disagreement.

Cynthia looked away. "Besides, I figured you were better off with your father and his family. After the divorce, I started using my first name again and I headed to Las Vegas. I sang and danced in nightclubs there, and my career left no room for raising a kid." She chanced a peek at him. "Sounds selfish, doesn't it? Do you hate me now?"

He shook his head. "No, I don't hate you."

She closed her eyes, thinking he probably should.

"I don't completely understand your rationale behind leaving me and never contacting me. That part hurts. I'll admit it."

"What's not to understand?" Cynthia asked, opening her eyes and regarding her son.

"Your fear of my dad. He's a good man who devoted his life to helping others. He'd hurt himself before he'd hurt anyone else."

"Except he made it so I could never visit you, Logan. Can't you see? He threatened me. He played mind games with me until I ran away. Once I got my head together, I was afraid of going back for you because. . .because I was afraid of your father. It's his fault, Logan. It's all his fault!"

Standing, Logan placed a hand on her shoulder. The warmth of his touch penetrated her skin. "Shh," he said, "you're ill. Don't get yourself worked up." His voice was soothing.

"I can tell you're a good minister," Cynthia said. Tears pricked the backs of her eyes to think he'd turned out so well because she hadn't raised him. "Jack did a better job with you than I did with my daughters." She allowed her weighty eyelids to close. She wanted to sleep—sleep and never wake up.

"So I have sisters?" Logan prompted. "Half sisters? What are their names? I'd like to meet them."

"No, you wouldn't. Trust me," Cynthia groused. "They're a couple of hussies who only look out for themselves. They're the reason I'm in this place. They're the reason I'm dying. . .all alone." Her voice gave out on that last word.

"But you're not alone," she heard Logan say.

Through misty eyes, she stared up at him. He still had his hand on her shoulder and he gave it a gentle squeeze.

He smiled. "You've got me."

Cynthia closed her eyes and a sob wracked her emaciated body. Such undeserved kindness—and from a man who should hate her! It was more than she could bear.

"Go," she sniveled. "Go. . .please."

"All right. I'm sorry I upset you."

Shaking her head, she wanted to say it wasn't he who had upset her. It was herself. Her rotten, miserable self!

"I'll come back another time. When you're feeling better."

Cynthia managed a weak nod.

Then she reached for the CALL button. She needed more pain medication. However, she knew whatever Nate gave her wouldn't be strong enough to dull the deep-rooted ache in her soul.

CHAPTER TWENTY-FOUR

A llie walked down the corridor and rejoiced that her presentation had gone so well. Her ideas for restructuring Arbor Springs were well received by the board, and its members even agreed to allow her to hire the facility's new director as well as charge nurses for each shift on every floor. As for training security personnel, Allie was given the "green light" on that, too. Now if only the man she had in mind to do the training would take her up on the offer. . . .

Allie entered her office and had just set her computer on her desk when Logan appeared. He rapped his knuckles against her already opened door.

"Well, hello. How'd it go with Cynthia?"

Logan stepped inside. "Not sure. I think I upset her." He let go of a sigh. "But when I said I'd come back another time, she nodded. So I guess that's a good sign."

"Logan, I think she's carrying around a lifetime of guilt and remorse. I'm not trying to excuse anything she's done," Allie said, sitting on the corner of her desk. "But she's definitely a hurting individual."

"I agree." He pulled a few snapshots from the inside pocket of his suit jacket and handed them to Allie. "Ever see these?"

She took them, looked them over, and shook her head.

"Aunt Nora gave them to me. That's my biological mother in those photos."

Allie had guessed as much before Logan explained. However, it was hard to believe that the ghost of a woman upstairs was the same voluptuous creature in the pictures. Platinum-blond hair that was slightly teased for a fuller effect framed Cynthia's lovely oval face. In each picture, her clothes were snug, revealing the kind of figure Allie used to hope for in her youth. But seeing Cynthia with Jack on their wedding day caused Allie a pinch of jealousy.

She quickly handed back the photos. "She was beautiful," Allie admitted. "I think her youngest daughter resembles her."

"You met them?" Logan asked, tucking away the pictures. "My half-sisters?"

Allie nodded. "They were here fishing for information. They wondered if their mother had been victimized in that abuse scandal the media publicized. But neither of Cynthia's daughters wanted to check on her to make sure she was all right. They pretty much took my word for it."

"Can I have their phone numbers. . .addresses?"

"I don't have that information, but I could contact their lawyer. I have his business card. I'll leave a message with them and then the girls can decide if they want to call me back."

Logan took a moment to think it over. "Obviously my mother and half-sisters don't have a good relationship."

Allie widened her eyes for emphasis. "Obviously. What's worse is that Cynthia has pretty much destroyed every relationship she's ever had."

"Seems a shame. I'll bet those girls will regret not making peace with their mother before she dies."

"I'm sure you're right," Allie replied. "There are a lot of things I wish I would have said to my mother before she died."

Still looking thoughtful, Logan glanced down at the gray, speckled carpet before bringing his gaze back to Allie. "Well, I'll say this much: I've learned that a lot of lives are damaged by inane misunderstandings."

Regarding him askance, Allie asked, "How do you mean?"

"My biological mother, for instance. She said the reason she didn't try to contact me was because she was afraid of my father." Logan shook his head. "My dad wouldn't have harmed her. He might not have appreciated her phone calls or letters to me, but he wouldn't have tried to hurt her or throw her in jail just because she wanted to talk to me."

"I want to agree with you, Logan, but your father strikes me as the sort of man who would defend to the death what's his and those whom he loves. Did you know he was actually disappointed that he couldn't fight in Vietnam?"

Logan nodded. "I heard the story. The marines wouldn't take him because he had a heart murmur. It disappeared when he was in his mid-thirties."

"God healed him," Allie murmured. She hadn't known that. "In any case, I can see Jack being a regular papa bear when it comes to his cub. What's more, from what your mother has told me, she didn't exactly live a pristine life. Your dad probably knew it, and my guess is he purposely frightened Cynthia in order to keep her away. So, you see, it's not really an 'inane misunderstanding' that kept her from getting in touch with you."

Logan thought it over. "I see your point. And, yeah, that sounds like Dad. I can recall being intimidated by him as a kid on more than one occasion. Of course," he added with a chuckle, "I deserved every punishment I got. But, you know? He only spanked me two or three times in my entire life, and he never hauled off and cracked me upside the head or anything. Even after I mouthed off—which happened frequently when I was in high school."

Jack's refrain from "hauling off and cracking" Logan caused Allie a measure of comfort. . .and even hope. She had seen a similarity between Jack and Erich before, and it was good to know that, in this regard, the two men were very different.

"I want your dad to work for me," Allie said with a smile. "I want him to train our security personnel. Think he'll bite?"

"Maybe. . ." Logan grinned. "Can't hurt to ask, that's for sure." Glancing at his watch, he added, "Speaking of work, I'd better get going."

"I'll walk you out."

Allie escorted him into the lobby, where she wished him a good day and made him promise not to mention anything to Jack about the possible job opportunity. Logan made a motion like he was locking his lips with a key, and Allie laughed at his antics.

After he left, she headed back to her office, but the sight at the reception desk caused her to halt in her tracks. There behind the desk, the security guard reclined in his chair, his head resting against the wall, and his eyes closed.

"Hey, wake up," she said, smacking her hand on the desk a few times.

The guard, an older man with a large protruding belly, brought himself up quickly. "Oh, sorry," he mumbled with a snort. He finger-combed his gray hair. "Can I help you?"

"Yes, you can," Allie replied on a terse note. "You can refrain from sleeping on the job. We're paying you to keep an eye on things and watch the comings and goings so our patients are protected."

"Look," he shot back, "this is a part-time job for me and it pays minimum wage. It barely supplements my Medicare. If you want a cop sitting here, then hire a cop. But, if you do, you're gonna have to pay him like a cop."

"You know? You're right. In this world, you get what you

pay for. Thank you for illustrating that point."

The man muttered a vague obscenity, which Allie chose to ignore. She strode to her office taking quick, hard steps and biting her lip against the frustration she felt. When people entered Arbor Springs, they were greeted by one of the security personnel. What an impressive image!

Lord, I need Jack's help. . .and I think he needs this position. Will You work in his heart before I even ask him about it? And please, God, if You don't want me involved with Jack, please show me another way. If we work together, we're going to get romantically involved. It's inevitable—I feel it in my heart. But if that's not Your will, please give me other options.

Once inside her office, she took several deep breaths. She felt herself relax. She'd wait on the Lord to guide her—He hadn't let her down yet!

*   *   *

Jack set several bills on the counter while the florist wrapped his purchase in green tissue paper. "I can't believe I'm paying all this money for a dozen roses," he muttered to Veronica, who stood beside him. "What color did you say those were?"

"Pink Lipstick, Uncle Jack. . .and Mrs. Littenberg's going to love 'em."

"She'd better for this price!"

"Oh, Uncle Jack, stop being such a curmudgeon."

"A. . .who?"

"A crabby old man."

With raised eyebrow, he considered his sassy niece. Dressed in a multicolored striped sweater and a denim skirt, she carried a small purse over one shoulder. "I shouldn't have answered the phone when you called me this morning. And I really shouldn't have let you talk me into buying flowers."

Roni shrugged. "Too late now. Besides, I didn't feel like taking the bus this morning, so having you drop me off at school in time for second hour works great for my schedule."

Jack tried hard not to laugh, although a grin escaped him.

Moments passed and Roni got bored standing there. She began to wander, snooping around the shop. She paused by a large marble-top table and leaned forward to sniff an arrangement. Watching her, Jack's grin widened. "Hey," he called to the florist, "add one more of those Lipstick things to my bill."

The older man nodded and rang up his order, took the money, and handed him back his change. Jack gathered his purchase and called a "Let's go" to Roni, who followed him out the door.

When they arrived at his Explorer, Jack unlocked the passenger side and opened the door for Roni. Once she'd gotten in, he handed her the rose. "This is for you."

Taking the blossom, she smiled and put it to her nose, inhaling. "Thanks, Uncle Jack."

Setting the wrapped roses into the backseat, he smiled. "You know, women are a lot like roses. They're pretty and they smell nice, but they're prickly, too, so a guy's got to be really careful when he handles them."

He shut the back door and then moved to close Roni's, but he caught the awed expression on her face and stopped.

"Why are you looking at me like that?"

"You really do have a romantic side!" she declared. "I don't believe it!"

Jack felt embarrassed. "Just don't tell anybody, okay?" Closing the door, he walked around the SUV and climbed in behind the wheel.

"You should write a poem for Mrs. Littenberg."

"No, I shouldn't," Jack said, starting the engine. "I just said that rose thing because I pricked myself when the florist handed me your flower."

"But that was nice. . .not that you hurt yourself, but what you said. And it's true, too. We women need to be handled delicately."

Jack started feeling curious. "Don't you get treated delicately at home?"

"No! I get treated like a child." Roni held the rose against her cheek. "My dad still calls me 'baby.' "

"That's an endearment. He doesn't mean it literally."

"Yes, he does. He still thinks I'm twelve. It's like he's stuck in a time warp. And if I even mention a guy I'm sort of interested in, he goes ballistic."

Jack chuckled. "Well, I hate to be the one to break this to you, but you'll probably always be your daddy's little girl. After all, you were the one who changed his life forever. You made him a father, and my brother and I were taught to take that responsibility very seriously. Just ask Logan. I may not have been around a lot, but I always knew what my kid was up to."

"Except he's not a kid anymore."

"No, he's not. But I will admit that sometimes I treat him like one. . .and that's my fault, I know." Jack reached the public school and slowed at the side of the curb. He turned to Veronica. "Sometimes us parents can't help being parents—and someday you'll understand."

Tears pooled in Veronica's eyes. "I just want my mom and dad to accept me for who I am."

"Okay, but that works both ways. You have to accept them for who they are."

"I do, Uncle Jack."

"Hmm, well, I don't know what else to tell you, Kiddo."

She gave him a pointed stare and he laughed.

"See what I mean? We can't help it."

After a roll of her blue-green eyes, Roni's expression softened. She unlatched the door and swung it open. "Call me tonight and tell me what Mrs. Littenberg says about the roses."

"Yes, Ma'am." Jack grinned. "That better?"

"As a matter of fact, it was," she replied airily. With that, she picked up her backpack from between the seats and climbed out of the SUV.

Jack watched her walk to the front entrance of the high

school. It was like déjà vu. Ten years ago, he'd watched Logan walk up that same path to those same steps. Where did those ten years go?

Unable to answer that question without a sting of remorse and a pinch of regret, Jack shook himself. He had talked about acceptance with his young niece and maybe he ought to take a dose of his own medicine. After all, he had tried to raise Logan to the best of his ability, and he must have done something right because Logan turned out okay. Of course, the Lord had a lot to do with it. Jack couldn't deny it. But maybe it was time to accept himself for the man he was today. No more should-have-dones, could-have-dones. This was it. Here he was with all his failures and successes. Jesus accepted him as is, wasn't it time to accept himself?

Lord, help me forgive myself for my past mistakes and move on. Jack smiled and stepped on the accelerator, pulling away from the curb. *There's a certain lady I know of who needs a dozen Pink Lipstick roses.*

*   *   *

Cynthia relaxed as the medication Nate injected began to work its magic throughout her pain-riddled body. Unfortunately, it didn't dull her mind, and she found herself reliving the visit with her son. She kept hearing his voice say, "You're not alone. You've got me."

He doesn't really mean it. He was just being nice.

More thoughts flittered through her head—more thoughts and more memories. Cynthia soon realized that her son was like his dad in more ways than just appearance. Jack had been a nice man, too. . .when she'd first met him. The cops had raided the tavern from which her employer ran his escort service, and Cynthia had never been so frightened in her life. One officer got rough with her, but Jack had quickly stepped in. He spoke to her in a gentle voice and reassured her. He didn't manhandle her, but treated her with respect. Cynthia had fallen in love with him almost immediately. He was the first man ever to show her some kindness without wanting something in return, such as the use of her body. But all too soon, she wanted something from him—his heart. She never got it, however; and Cynthia was surprised to find that she still stung from that painful reality.

"Oh, God, why couldn't I ever find a man who loved me?" she wailed into the empty room. "Why wasn't I ever loved? Was that really too much to ask?"

She closed her eyes and allowed her tears to fall unchecked. Her misery increased until anguished sobs caused her body to convulse. She cried for that which she longed for, but never had. True love. If she died right now, the world would go on turning and her ex-husbands, son, and daughters would continue about their business. No one would even miss her. She felt like The Beatles' famed Eleanor Rigby, one of those lonely people who would die and never be remembered. Her life meant nothing. She should have never been born!

"Why, God? Why?" Cynthia lamented. "Why was I put on this planet? I'm worthless. I'm nothing!"

More cries from the depth of her soul until finally Cynthia lay exhausted on her hospital bed. At long last, she drifted off into a troubled sleep.

CHAPTER TWENTY-FIVE

Allie had no sooner turned on her computer than the surly security guard appeared in her doorway.

"Someone else is here asking for you," he barked.

"Who is it? Did you get a name?"

"Look, I'm not your personal secretary, okay?"

He lumbered away and Allie started fuming again. *The security people need to learn to use the phone system,* she thought, heading for the lobby. *They need to announce visitors and learn what to say to respective customers. They need to be trained to—*

She looked up. "Jack!"

He gave her a lopsided smile. "Hi, Allie. I didn't mean to bother you." He glanced at the security guard, then back at her. "I just wanted to give you these," he said, sweeping a package of green tissue paper off of the counter of the reception desk. He placed it in her arms.

Cradling the gift, Allie could tell they were flowers. "How thoughtful. Come on back to my office."

"I don't want to interrupt."

"You're no interruption." She inclined her head towards the hallway. "Come on."

As she walked with him to her office, Allie conversed with the Lord. *I'm taking this as a sign. You brought Jack right to me. I didn't have to phone him.*

Once inside, she offered Jack a seat while she dashed to the small kitchen area and borrowed one of the several pressed-glass vases. After filling it with water, she returned to her office. She found Jack studying the framed picture of Nick and Jennifer that she kept on her desk.

"This your son?" he asked.

"Yes. . .my son and daughter-in-law."

"He has your eyes. . .and your chin, I think."

"Nick is a veritable mix of his father and me." Allie gently tore the paper away and, seeing the roses, she smiled. "Oh, these are beautiful. Thank you, Jack."

He set down the picture. "You're welcome."

"So what do they mean?" she had to ask, thinking they were some sort of peace offering. "Why did you bring me roses?"

He shrugged. "My niece accused me of not having a romantic bone in my body and then she proceeded to talk me into buying you flowers."

"Oh." Allie frowned. "Well, I can't imagine why your niece would say such a thing. I mean, my goodness! Your poetic words just now make me want to swoon." She placed a hand across her forehead.

"Very funny." Jack sat back in the chair and crossed his leg. "I may not be a romantic, but you're a terrible actress."

"You're right. I am." Allie smiled and cupped a rose, inhaling its fragrant scent. "Mmm. Tell your niece she did a great job picking out the roses. They're my favorite."

"I'll tell her."

"Is the niece we're discussing Veronica?"

Jack nodded.

"I've met her a couple of times. She's a sweet girl."

"Yes, she is. . .even if she is seventeen."

Allie mulled over the remark. "That's how old I was when we met, Jack. Seventeen."

"Yeah, but you never seemed that young. Maybe because the world was a different place."

"Maybe." Allie thought it had more to do with the way she was raised. Her parents weren't Christians, nor were her stepfather and stepsisters.

With the roses in water now, Allie leaned back against her desk. She folded her arms and regarded her unexpected guest. Jack wore blue jeans and a thick green cotton sweater. His salt-and-pepper gray hair was cropped short, neatly combed, and parted to one side. To Allie, he was as handsome at fifty-five as he was in his mid-twenties.

"So," she said, pulling herself to the present, "what do you think of my office?"

Jack did a sweeping glance of his surroundings. "Nice," he replied. "Small, but nice."

"Cramped is the word I'd use to describe it. But it's temporary."

"It's better than anything I was assigned at the station."

"Guess I should count my blessings."

Jack sat forward. "Not to change the subject, Allie, but something's bugging me. It's that guy in the lobby. You might want to do something about him. He was snoozing when I walked in and he was rude when I woke him up."

"Funny you should mention the security guard. . ."

Jack raised his dark brows. "That's a security guard?"

Allie smiled. How good of the Lord to bring about this opportunity. Taking a sidestep, she gave her door a good push. It closed.

"Jack," she said, "you and I need to talk."

* * *

Sunshine spilled through the autumn-colored treetops as Marilee watched her third graders frolic on the playground. Tomorrow was October first and these perfect fall days would be fewer and far between. Then the snow would fly. Marilee, however, didn't mind the winter months. She loved the Christmas holidays shared with family and friends. She enjoyed ice-skating, sledding, skiing, and snowmobiling. She especially liked to cozy up in front of a glowing fireplace and read; however, she figured there wouldn't be much time for lounging since Logan would most likely keep the youth group kids and staff just as busy in winter as they were in the summer. Moreover, Marilee anticipated list after list of tasks to accomplish in preparation for their wedding. Before she'd know it, that special day would arrive.

As she sat on the park bench, one of four at this end of the playground, Marilee began to daydream. She imagined Logan looking handsome in his tux and saw herself as stunning in her white bridal gown with its pearls and lace bodice. The month of May couldn't get here fast enough, although Marilee cringed to think of everything she had to do before that time arrived.

Her reverie was suddenly interrupted when Katie Sanders and Lisa Dennison came running over to tattle on Bobby Ryan, who wouldn't let them play soccer. Marilee stood and walked over to the boy and heard his complaint about teams already being chosen. She explained that one team could take Katie and the other Lisa and the sides would still be fair. The pudgy, freckle-faced, red-haired boy, who had somehow endeared himself to Marilee already, acquiesced and the girls seemed satisfied with the outcome. Sitting back down on the bench, Marilee had no sooner gotten comfy, than a pair of hands covered her eyes.

"Guess who?" His warm breath tickled her neck.

She laughed and peeled away the strong fingers of her fiancé. "I don't have to guess, Silly. I'd know your voice anywhere."

In seconds, Logan was sitting beside her. She lost herself in his chocolate brown eyes, thinking how blessed she was that she'd get to stare at Logan Callahan for the rest of her life. "How'd it go this morning?" she asked. "I prayed for you while the kids were taking their Monday morning math quiz."

"Thanks," he said, turning his head and looking out over the playground. "Things went. . .pretty good, I guess. . .for a first meeting."

Marilee frowned. "You sound disappointed."

Pursing his lips, he mulled over the statement. "Maybe I am," he replied at last. "I had imagined something a little more dramatic. Tears and apologies. . ."

Marilee's heart went out to him. Tears and apologies were the least he deserved from his natural mother. "What happened instead?"

Logan exhaled audibly. "Instead, my mother spent a lot of time defending her reasons for leaving me as an infant. She blamed my father, making him reason number one why she left. But I figured that was coming since it's true. Dad told me as much."

"Were you able to discuss anything else?"

"No. When I questioned her further, I upset her. On the other hand," Logan said, bringing his gaze back to hers, "she said my dad did a better job raising me than she did with her daughters—she actually called them 'hussies' and tried to discourage me from getting in touch with them." He grinned. "But all I know is I have two sisters and I'm dying to meet them. Allie is going to try and contact them for me."

"Hussies?" Marilee hadn't gotten past that word. "That's a terrible thing for a mother to say about her daughters. Why would she call them that?"

"She's angry with them. They were the ones who admitted her to Arbor Springs. Regardless, my gut instinct tells me that my sisters, whoever they are, need to hear about the Lord and that I'm the one who's supposed to deliver the message."

A sense of foreboding crept over Marilee. "I hope you're not setting yourself up for more disappointment. You're such a friendly, loving person, but not everyone is like you. What if your sisters don't want anything to do with you? You just told me that your mother wasn't thrilled to see you this morning. What if your sisters react in the same way? What if they don't want to hear about the Lord?"

"Then I'll just have to accept it," he said with a cavalier shrug.

Marilee folded her arms in front of her. "I don't like the sound of this Logan." She thought it was precarious enough that he ventured into his natural mother's hospital room this morning. "I think you should reconsider."

He crossed his leg and stretched his arm out along the back of the bench. "Not this time, Sweetheart. The wedding date was one thing, but you're not talking me out of this. I've made up my mind to meet my half-sisters and that's that."

"Suit yourself," Marilee replied. His adamant tone hurt her feelings. "I was only thinking of you."

His hand came to rest on the back of her neck, and she had to fight the urge to snuggle in closer to him. "Are we going to have our first fight?" he asked, sounding amused.

Her agitation dissolved and she had to laugh. "I guess not."

"Whew! What a relief."

Still smiling, Marilee asked, "Want to come over for dinner tonight?"

"What are you making?"

"Whatever you want."

"Mm, okay. Let me decide what I'm hungry for."

"Oh, wait, Logan, that's not going to work." Marilee suddenly remembered her schedule. She had agreed to meet her mother after school, and they planned to drive into Chicago and check out a photographer for the wedding. "Tonight's not good. Mom and I have something to do. How 'bout tomorrow night?"

"Tomorrow's okay." He stood. "I'll just have to starve tonight."

Marilee laughed again. "Oh, sure. Make me feel guilty."

He chuckled as he took a few steps backwards. "I have to get going. Chapel starts in less than twenty minutes. I'll talk to you later."

"Bye, Logan." Since chapel services were held Mondays, Wednesdays, and Fridays for the high school students, Logan was obligated to sit in on them although he often did the preaching. "I'll call you later."

He gave her a wink before pivoting and walking toward the side doors of the building.

*   *   *

Allie explained the situation with the security personnel at Arbor Springs and then offered Jack the job. "You'd be terrific," she added. "Since you're a police officer, you've got the credibility—"

"Ex-police officer," Jack cut in.

"Same difference."

He grinned. "I don't know."

"Will you think about it? Pray about it?"

"Allie, I don't want to be your friend," he said, rising from the chair. "I don't want to be your coworker, and I definitely don't want to be your subordinate."

"In that case, I don't understand," she replied, feeling a bit wounded. "Why are you here? Why the roses?"

Jack took a step forward and, in one smooth gesture, pushed Allie's hair aside and placed the palm of his hand against her scarred cheek. "I still love you, Allie. I've always loved you." His hand moved to the back of her head and he pulled her close. Next, he lowered his mouth to hers and, as the kiss deepened, something of a thrill passed through Allie. But all too soon, reality gave her a forceful nudge.

She pushed Jack away. "Stop," she murmured, "we shouldn't be doing this."

"Why not?"

"It's not right. . . I'm at work, and—"

"Felt right as rain to me. Do you know that I've dreamed about kissing you like that?"

Allie felt her face growing warm. "That's about the most romantic thing anyone has ever said to me."

Jack grinned. "It's the truth."

Lowering her gaze, Allie was suddenly at a loss for words.

"Listen," he said, "if you want to take things one step at a time, then. . .well, it's fine by me. We ought to pray as we go. You were right. And maybe you were right about my 'unyielding demands,' too."

She stared at him intently, hopefully.

"Let's just say I don't want to make the same mistake twice, okay, Allie?"

"Okay," she said unable to keep from smiling.

They stood there, captive in each other's regard, for several lingering moments.

Then Allie's senses returned. "What do you think about training Arbor Springs's security personnel?"

Jack blew out a breath. "Let me think about it. I'll try to put some sort of outline together. That'll give me a better idea how much trouble I'm getting myself into."

Allie rolled her eyes and shook her head at him, smiling all the while.

"But right now," Jack continued, glancing at his wristwatch, "I've got to hit the road. This morning after my niece talked me into buying you flowers, my brother talked me into meeting him for lunch."

"Oh, Jack, you poor man. Your family members are absolutely heartless."

He smirked at her riposte.

Laughing, Allie opened her office door. They exited her small workspace and casually strode into the lobby.

"I'll call you later," he promised as he made the rest of his way to the double glass doors.

"Bye, Jack."

She watched him go, but as she turned, she met the gaze of the gruff security guard. He scowled at her, and Allie couldn't help thinking that with the proper instruction, the guy might be professionally daunting instead of just plain boorish.

CHAPTER TWENTY-SIX

A chilling wind blew off Lake Michigan on Friday evening as Logan and his cousin Rick set up the net for a volleyball game. It would be dark in an hour; so, while volunteers grilled hotdogs and prepared the rest of their picnic supper, the teens opted for a quick volleyball game. Logan went along with it, figuring it'd get their blood moving and keep them warm until the bonfire was lit.

His athletic shoes sunk into the sand as he sidestepped and tied the net onto the pole. With that done, he glanced up and down the beach but still didn't see Marilee. He couldn't imagine that she would forget about tonight. Logan and his staff had planned this event for months. They had recruited teens, and a good number had shown up. So where was she?

After a time of musing, Logan figured the reason he didn't know Marilee's whereabouts was probably as much his fault as hers. With their busy schedules, they hadn't said more than a few words to each other since Monday morning. He should have made time for her; however, his thoughts had been elsewhere and the week hadn't gone well. Not only were there issues at work to contend with, but for the past four nights after work he had driven the distance to Arbor Springs and visited his natural mother. Each night she grew more and more depressed, saying she wished she were dead. Logan talked to her about Jesus and read to her from the Bible, but his efforts had seemed in vain. He was at the point of giving up.

The volleyball net was now in place and secured. Logan put his thumb and forefinger into his mouth and blew out a shrill whistle. The teens stopped their chattering and gathered around him.

"We're going to form two teams," Logan told the kids. "It's Army versus Navy. Start counting off, every other one of you is Army, the other Navy."

The teenagers counted off. Army. Navy. Army. Navy. At last, the teams faced each other on opposite sides of the net.

"Which team are you going to be on, Pastor Callahan?" Sabina Lewis asked, her red hair blowing across her face. She quickly pushed it back. "I want to be on your team."

"I'm the coach. . .otherwise known as the drill sergeant," Logan replied diplomatically. "I won't play since the teams are even."

The girl pouted.

Oh, good grief, he thought. He was growing impatient with these schoolgirl crushes. He picked up the volleyball as a way to dismiss Sabina. She finally took the hint and walked away.

"Don't worry, Cuz," Veronica said, coming up behind him. "I'll protect you from all these insipid females since Marilee isn't here."

He gave her a hooded glance. "You wouldn't happen to know anything about that, would you?"

Roni shook her head. "Haven't seen her today, and I just got here."

"Glad you could make it."

She grabbed the ball out of Logan's hands. "Me, too. . .and look behind you."

He swung around to see a carful of kids heading their way. Logan turned back to his cousin with a questioning stare.

"I invited a bunch of people from school. . .people who aren't Christians. And they actually agreed to come!"

"That's great!" Logan smiled. "Roni, I'm proud of you."

She shrugged. "The Lord prompted me and I obeyed. . .but I was a little scared, I'll admit it." Veronica stepped closer so as not to be overheard. "Two of these girls have been picking on me since last year. You wouldn't believe the names they've called me and the lies they've told about me."

Logan winced. "Why didn't you say something?"

"Because I thought it would only make things worse."

His heart went out to her.

"But it doesn't matter anymore. Listen to this: A couple of days ago at lunch, it was, like, I just totally gave into the Holy Spirit and I walked right up to Lindsay and Pam. I felt like God did all the talking through me. But then, I almost fell over when they both said they'd come. I couldn't believe it." Veronica shook her head in amazement and her nut brown hair swung back and forth over her slender shoulders. "It was weird. I never experienced anything like it!"

"That's awesome," Logan replied, thinking he hadn't seen Roni so enthusiastic about anything in a long, long time. And that she was stirred by something spiritual encouraged him—so much so, he forgot about how miffed he was over Marilee's absence.

The other kids showed up, and Roni introduced them to Logan. He didn't miss the note of pride in her voice when she added, "We're cousins, but he's like my older brother."

The teens from Roni's high school said they wanted to play,

so Logan divided them up onto teams. This made room enough for him to participate, so he chose the Navy side to make things even. He got in line for the rotation and right in front of him stood a grinning Sabina Lewis.

"All right!" she said. "This is going to be a great night!" She bent her knees and lifted her arms as if she were a cheerleader. "Whoo-hoo!"

Logan burst out laughing. It was nice to know he'd made someone's day.

*   *   *

Allie sat in the restaurant waiting for Jack. He'd asked her out to dinner tonight and she had accepted, hoping to convince him to sign on with Lakeland Enterprises. Unfortunately, he was late, but not by much.

Adding a packet of honey to her cup, she stirred her hot tea with a spoon and thought about Cynthia Matlock. Allie had promised Logan she'd check on her before leaving for the weekend. Sadly, Cynthia's condition hadn't changed all week. She was still very depressed and in a lot of pain, which no amount of medication seemed to alleviate. Julie, the brand-new second-shift supervisor in that ward, said she'd phone Cynthia's doctor and see if he would prescribe a higher dose or a different brand of painkiller.

"Well, well, look who's here."

Allie glanced up from her steaming teacup to see Brenda standing in front of the table. She forced a smile at her stepsister. "Hi, how're you?"

"Just groovy."

Allie noticed the square-shaped Styrofoam container in Brenda's one hand and the glass of golden liquid in the other. On her face, she wore no cosmetics, only a mask of contention. Coupled with her bold stance and rough-and-tumble attire, Allie had a feeling that Brenda would like nothing better than to pick a fight.

"Mind if I join you?" Without waiting for an answer, Brenda sat down across from Allie.

"Is your husband with you?"

"Nope. I'm here with some girlfriends from work." She thumbed over her shoulder. The sleeves of her black T-shirt were rolled up, and she looked like she'd just stepped off the set of *Grease*. "They're next door—in the bar. I just came in here to get my carryout order. Great fish-fries at this place."

"Oh. . ."

"We stop over there every Friday night after work for a few beers. What about you? You waiting for somebody or are you alone?"

"Waiting for somebody."

"Lemme guess," Brenda said snidely, taking a gulp of beer. She reclined in the chair and crossed one jean-encased leg over the other. "You're waiting for Jack."

"Yes, that's right."

Brenda shook her head. "Some guys never learn, do they?"

Allie ignored the barb and sipped her tea.

"It would serve you right if Jack stood you up."

"Look, Brenda, you can join your friends in the bar any time. You're under no obligation to keep me company."

"What, are you ashamed to be seen with me—you in your expensive suit and me in my grubby factory clothes?"

"That's not it at all."

Brenda smirked. "Yes it is. You really think you're Miss High-and-Mighty, don't you? Well, I've got news for you. You're the same spoiled, selfish brat that you were when we were kids."

Allie closed her eyes against the tirade. *Lord, please shut this woman up. I'm tired and I don't feel very diplomatic at the moment.*

"You and your country-club religion." Brenda raised a brow. "You're on a first-name basis with God. Aren't you special?"

Allie didn't reply, but glanced in the direction of the doorway. She hoped to see Jack, but he wasn't anywhere to be found.

"Your husband should have slashed your other cheek. You probably deserved it."

The comment caused Allie to lose her patience. "Are you really that ignorant? No woman deserves to be abused. And you know what else? I think you are the spoiled and selfish brat. You've got a lot of growing up to do."

Detestation flashed across Brenda's hardened features as she threw the remainder of her beer in Allie's face. The cold liquid stung Allie's eyes, and she grappled for her linen napkin. Finding it, she dabbed her face before mopping her silk blouse, now stained and ruined. When she glanced across the table, Brenda smiled with satisfaction.

Allie set down the napkin and stood. "Little do you know that you just proved my point." Lifting her coat and purse off the adjacent chair, she mustered her dignity and made her way out of the restaurant.

"See ya, Sis," Brenda called on a malicious note. "And don't worry, I'll let Jack know you left."

Allie refused to answer. Continuing toward the red, neon EXIT sign, she paused at the cashier counter and instructed the hostess to charge her cup of tea to Brenda.

"She's the woman sitting right over there," Allie said pointing through the restaurant.

Brenda had the audacity to wave, and the hostess nodded.

Allie walked out the door. She turned left on the sidewalk and stepped off the curb, walking to her car. All the while, she fished in her purse for her cell phone, hoping to get hold of Jack.

"Allie!"

She paused and turned on her heel, hearing his voice. Although night had fallen, she could see his approaching form through the well-lit parking lot.

"Sorry I'm late," he said, catching up to her. "You weren't leaving, were you?"

"Yeah, I had a little run-in with Brenda."

Jack wrinkled his nose. "You smell like a brewery. What happened?"

"My darling sister tossed her beer in my face," Allie quipped, hoping to hide her anger, hurt, and humiliation.

"She did. . .what?" Jack threw his gaze at the restaurant before looking back at Allie. "No, she didn't!" he exclaimed on an incredulous note. "You're kidding, right?"

Allie shook her head as her heart swelled with remorse. "Oh, Jack, she hates me. . . ."

"I'll be right back."

"No!" As he took a step toward the restaurant, Allie caught the sleeve of his leather jacket. "You'll only make things worse if you go in there and confront her. Brenda's drunk and she's looking for a fight."

"Good. I'll give her the fight of her life."

"Forget it, Jack. She's not worth it."

Taking Allie by the shoulders, he bent slightly forward and peered into her face. She suddenly felt like a vulnerable little girl, and she bit her lower lip in an effort to forestall the threatening tears.

"I've been a cop for thirty-three years. Don't you think I know how to handle a drunk?"

"Yes, but—"

"Go home," he said in a gentle voice that only made Allie feel like crying all the more, "shower and change, and I'll meet you in the lobby of the hotel."

She didn't want to comply, but Jack was a responsible adult who knew his own mind. What's more, Allie was beginning to feel grimy under the beer's residue. A shower and a change of clothes was exactly what she wanted.

Getting into her car, she placed the key in the ignition and gave it a turn. Doing so, she watched Jack stride purposely for the restaurant; and in some small way, Allie felt sorry for her stepsister.

*   *   *

Marilee gripped the steering wheel as the volatile mix of impatience and frustration coursed through her veins with every heartbeat. Oh, why had she raced out of the house, forgetting her cell phone? She could have called Logan an hour ago. Instead, the interstate was a virtual parking lot, and she was caught up in the worse traffic jam she'd ever encountered. She couldn't even exit and use a pay phone. All four lanes were jammed. There seemed no way out!

Logan is going to kill me, she thought facetiously. When he found out that she had dashed off to meet her mother and purchase the bridesmaids' gifts, he'd likely lose his temper. Of course, she hadn't actually seen him lose his temper before—but that only made imagining his reaction to her missing the bonfire event all the more worrisome.

Marilee chided herself for allowing her mother to talk her into meeting her in Chicago this afternoon. However, last Monday they'd discovered a quaint little shop on Michigan Avenue, which just happened to offer fifty percent off some beautiful and unique sterling silver pendants that would make perfect gifts for the bridesmaids. The sale ran through today; and due to other appointments in the week, neither Marilee nor her mother could make the trip. . .until today. Unfortunately, Marilee's plans to make it back in time for the bonfire weren't panning out. She hadn't counted on getting stuck in traffic.

The vehicles in front of her began to move. They picked up speed, and Marilee felt like she was making some progress as she rounded a curve. But then brake lights up ahead signaled another standstill. She slowed and stopped, but just a little too close to the car ahead of her. She groaned aloud and, again, she wished she had her cell phone.

At that moment, Marilee glanced in her rearview mirror and saw a pickup truck rounding the same curve she'd just passed. As she watched its approach, she expected that it would slow down. But suddenly it became frighteningly apparent that the driver wasn't paying attention. Panicked, Marilee gave her steering wheel a sharp turn, intending to pull onto the shoulder and get out of harm's way; however, her bumper collided with the car in front of her, stalling her progress. In the next second, she heard the sickening sound of squealing tires, grinding, twisting metal, and shattering glass. The impact caused her car to career out of control and smash into the cement median like a wave against a rocky cliff.

CHAPTER TWENTY-SEVEN

Just as Logan stuffed the last of his hotdog into his mouth, his cell phone rang. He groaned with his mouth full, and the kids sitting around him at the picnic table laughed. In one quick move, he removed his phone from his pocket and handed it to Veronica, motioning her to answer it for him.

She rolled her eyes and pressed the appropriate button. "You have reached Pastor Logan Callahan," she said tartly. "He's unable to answer your call right now because he's got his mouth stuffed with food."

Everyone within earshot hooted, and Logan made fast work of swallowing his supper.

"Give me that!" Taking his phone, he figured it was Marilee. . .finally! And she had better have one terrific excuse!

"Hello?"

"Logan Callahan?"

"That's me." When he didn't recognize the female voice at the other end, he viewed the Caller ID. The phone number wasn't familiar, either. "Who's this?"

"I'm a nurse at Charity Medical Center and I'm calling on behalf of your fiancée, Marilee Domotor."

Logan perked up and rose from the picnic table. He walked several feet away from the noise so he could hear. "What's wrong with Marilee?"

"She was in a car accident this evening, and she's on her way to surgery as we speak. Her parents are on their way, but she asked that I call you, too."

Logan's gut dropped to his toes. "I'll be right there."

He snapped shut his phone and pocketed it. Hurrying back to the picnic table, he explained the situation to Veronica. Others overheard and the talking slowly ceased.

"I'm coming with you!" Veronica declared.

Logan didn't talk her out of it. He had a feeling he would need all the support he could get.

They ran to his car and jumped in. Just as quickly, they pulled away from the beach. Logan's pulse raced; and as it did, his foot pressed all the harder on the accelerator. He had to keep reminding himself to slow down and keep a level head.

"I'm praying, Logan," Roni said.

"That's good because all I can think about is getting to the hospital." He frowned. "Charity Medical Center? That's on the other side of Chicago. Why is Marilee at Charity?"

"Don't ask. Just drive."

Thirty-five minutes later, Logan pulled into the hospital's parking lot. He and Veronica entered via the emergency room, where they were greeted by two nurses, a male and a female, both wearing light blue scrubs. Logan rambled off the situation, and the male nurse directed him to a security officer, who, in turn, gave him a map and explained how to get around to the other side of the medical complex. Entering there, the guard said, they would find a waiting room designated for families of surgery patients.

Frustrated and worried, Logan jogged back to his car. Veronica followed.

"Did you see all those people in there?" she asked. "One dude had a bandage around his head and he was bleeding right through it. Another lady was in a wheelchair and she was throwing up. It was so nasty! I could never be a nurse!"

Logan barely heard Roni's discourse as he drove around the hospital. He parked for a second time, and they found their way to the waiting area. Stan and Eileen Domotor were already there, along with Noah Warren, the senior pastor at church.

"How is she?" Logan asked, somewhat breathless.

Eileen began to cry, and her husband put his sturdy arm around her shoulders.

"She's in surgery," Noah said.

Standing, Pastor Warren waved Logan and Veronica into the hallway. Outside the waiting area, they faced each other. The men were nearly the same height, but Noah had a good thirty-five years on Logan.

"Marilee's pretty banged up," Noah said in hushed tones. "She's got a fractured pelvis, a broken leg, and some internal injuries."

"But surgery should take care of that, right?" Logan's brain refused to register any diagnosis other than a full recovery.

"We hope so." With a sigh, Noah pulled a handkerchief from the back pocket of his tan trousers. He wiped the perspiration dotting his forehead and receding hairline. "It's the internal damage that's worrisome. But God's in control. Let's pray everything goes better than expected during surgery."

Still managing his shock, all Logan could do was nod.

*   *   *

Allie almost gave up waiting for Jack, but he finally entered the hotel's lobby just a few minutes before eight.

"I was wondering what happened to you," she said once he reached her. "What took so long?"

He took a seat beside her on the sofa. Several feet away, a cozy fire glowed in the fireplace and guests milled about; but for the most part, there wasn't a lot of activity. However, the neighboring tavern sounded lively tonight.

"As you probably guessed," Jack began, "Brenda and I had a few words, and then I called Dave and told him to come and pick her up. He showed up, but she insisted she could drive herself home. I warned her that I'd report her, but she didn't seem to care. So," he concluded with a shrug, "she drove off and I called the cops. Dave and I followed her, praying she wouldn't drive off the road and kill somebody. Fortunately, a squad spotted her and pulled her over. Seeing that this is her second DUI in six months, Brenda will probably stay in a jail a day or two."

Allie shook her head. "What a shame. She's so bent on self-destruction. She's so. . .angry, and not just at me, but at everyone and everything."

"In a way," Jack replied, "I can relate. But not to Brenda's extent. She's blaming everybody else for her troubles and I blamed myself. I still blame myself."

"Jack. . ."

Since he sat forward with his hands folded over his knees, Allie put a hand on his back. She gave him an encouraging pat.

"Oh, I'm getting over it," he said, sitting back and crossing his leg. "The Bible study I began attending is going to help, I think. We had our first meeting this afternoon."

Allie smiled. "I didn't know you were in a Bible study."

Jack nodded as he stared at the fire. "Logan gave my name to an older couple who holds Bible studies for prospective church members and/or new Christians. They normally meet with five or six people on Saturday mornings, but this weekend Jim and Betty are going out of town to see their grandkids, so they held their Bible study this afternoon." He looked at Allie.

"That's why I was late getting to the restaurant."

"Well, I guess I'll have to forgive you then, won't I?" she quipped.

"I got news for you, Allie," Jack shot right back. "You've got to forgive me regardless. It's your Christian duty." He chuckled at her feigned grimace. "Just so happens that's what today's lesson was all about. Bitterness versus forgiveness and how the two are on opposing sides. I thought it was going to be dull, but Jim Dabner's a good teacher. Turns out, he's a Vietnam vet—ex-fighter pilot. When he got discharged from the air force, he started doing a lot of drugs. Really screwed up his life—worse than me."

In her heart of hearts, Allie rejoiced that Jack had connected with another Christian man. And to hear Jack had gotten involved in a Bible study made her feel almost giddy.

He turned and stretched his arm across the top of the sofa. "So that should make your day, me attending a Bible study," he said as if reading her mind. "But now I suppose you're going to tell me you're hungry."

Allie laughed. "This mental-telepathy stuff is amazing. I just transmit my thoughts into your mind and—"

"Oh, brother, now I've heard it all."

After a roll of his eyes, Jack stood and offered his hand. Allie took it and he pulled her to her feet.

"I'm not hungry for Mexican food," she stated playfully. "I hope I transmit that idea to you."

"Got it loud and clear," Jack replied as they left the hotel.

Allie chuckled as they climbed into his Explorer. However, the easy banter brought back another host of memories, those of her two friends—or "troublemakers," as her stepfather used to call them. The three of them sure gave Jack a run for his money.

"Do you ever hear from Wendy or Blythe?"

He glanced at her as if to ask "Who?" but then the confused

frown on his face softened as he snapped his seatbelt into place. "Haven't talked to Wendy in at least thirty years. She disappeared sometime before you left for California. But I see Blythe occasionally. She lives in Chicago. In fact, she and I dated a few times. . .about ten years ago."

"You're kidding? You and Blythe?" Allie settled back in her seat, and a knowing little grin curved her mouth. "I knew all along that Blythe had a crush on you."

"You're wrong," Jack said, pulling his truck out of the parking lot. "Blythe was crazy about Wendy's brother, Rob. . .remember?"

"Oh, yeah. . ." It was coming back to her now. Rob Chadwyk. He was a professional draft-dodger and war protestor, and Jack couldn't stand the guy. But then tragedy struck, and Rob was killed in a riot during the '68 Democratic Convention. It happened just after Allie first met Jack. In fact, their second meeting occurred the night Rob died.

"Wendy was the one who had the crush on me." Jack chuckled, bringing Allie back to the present. She looked over at him and saw a flash of his grin beneath the quickly passing streetlights.

"That's right. It was Wendy." More snippets of the past flittered across her mind. "She and I had an awful argument over you one night. A real cat fight."

"Yeah, I remember hearing something about that. I think I was working the night it happened."

"I'm sure it wouldn't have occurred had you been around, Jack. You always kept the three of us in line."

Allie suddenly found herself wishing that she could find Wendy. Despite their single run-in, they had been good friends. Wendy was estranged from her parents and so was Allie. Their hurt and confusion had bonded them. But Blythe was another story. Her parents were "hip" and didn't care what she did, who she was with, or at what time of day or night she came home. This made Blythe's house the perfect hangout or runaway's destination.

When Allie left home after the big fight with her stepfamily, she stayed with Blythe, along with a half-dozen other teenagers. However, neighbors began phoning police about loud music and rowdy behavior, bringing Oakland Park's finest to the Seversons' front door. Jack happened to be one of the officers dispatched there; and when Allie met his brown-eyed gaze, she knew she'd met her match.

"What are you giggling about?" Jack wanted to know.

Allie felt embarrassed. She hadn't realized she laughed out loud. "I was thinking that we kids certainly did make you Oakland Park cops earn your money."

Jack chuckled, obviously remembering.

"So how did you and Blythe start dating?"

"She sends me a Christmas card every year; and since she never married, I called her up and asked her out. We went to dinner a few times, saw a movie, but things didn't gel between the two of us. I don't know what it was. . . ." Jack sent a smile Allie's way. "But Blythe still sends me a Christmas card. Faithful Blythe."

"What's she doing?"

"She owns an antique shop called *Precious Things.*"

"You mean it's not called *The Curbside Gallery?*" Allie laughed. "I remember Blythe had a knack for finding valuable stuff in garbage heaps along the road. She actually decorated her entire bedroom with junk, but it looked great. It was incredible."

"Blythe is an incredible lady. Even with all the specialty shops in downtown Chicago, her little store is holding its own."

After a moment's pondering, Allie turned to him. "Jack, I wonder. . ."

"I know what you're going to say. You want to see Blythe. Another reunion. Yeah, okay, I'll give you her phone number. And I'll try to find Wendy, but it'll take some doing. I have no idea where she is. . .although Blythe might have a clue."

"That would be great. I'd love to see both of them again."

Suddenly Jack's cell phone rang. He snatched it out from his inside jacket pocket and slowed to the side of the road, where he stopped. Checking the Caller ID, he pushed a button and placed the small phone to his ear. "What's up, Logan?"

Allie could hear chirps of the younger man's voice, but couldn't make out the words.

"Is she okay?" Jack asked to whatever Logan told him. He followed it by stating, "I'm with Allie. We'll get there as soon as we can."

Concern welled up in Allie. Something was wrong. "What happened, Jack?"

He pocketed his cell phone and glanced her way. "Marilee's been in a car accident."

"Oh, no! How bad?"

"She's in surgery," Jack replied, pulling away from the curb. "Naturally, Logan's upset. That's why I told him we'd meet him at the hospital. . .but if you don't feel up to it, I can drop you off first."

"No, Jack, I want to go with you."

"I hoped you'd say that."

A few minutes passed in silence, and then Jack slammed his palms against the steering wheel. Allie cringed and a shiver of fright shot through her. She knew from her past that an angry man behind the wheel of an automobile made for a dangerous ride.

"Jack, please. . ."

"Why, when things are going along nice and smooth, does stuff like this happen?"

Allie didn't have an answer.

"Why, God?" Jack cried, looking up through the windshield. "Why did You allow this to happen? Logan doesn't deserve this. He's a great kid! It's just not fair!"

"Jack, calm down," Allie pleaded, "or you'll be the next one in a car wreck."

He quieted and an awkward stillness ensued. Finally Allie felt as though she'd burst if she didn't say *something*. She could practically feel Jack's heart twisting with anguish as he worried over Logan and Marilee.

"Jack, in the course of my life, I've asked God why a lot of things have happened. But then I realized I was asking the wrong question. I started asking the Lord *what* He wanted me to learn through the situation I was dealing with and *how* I could minister to others through it."

Jack grunted out an inaudible reply.

"I know that's probably easy for me to say since Logan's not my son and Marilee isn't my future daughter-in-law. . .but Jack, don't you see? God loves us and wants the best for us, except we live in a sin-cursed earth and bad things really do happen to good people."

"You know, Allie, that's one of the things Brenda said really bugged her about you. She told me again tonight. It's your know-it-all, perfect answers."

She inhaled sharply as if she'd been struck. She'd only been trying to help, trying to put things into perspective for him.

"You've got it good, Allie," Jack continued, "but some of us face trial after trial, and your perfect answers really grate on our last nerves!"

She wanted to scream at him. He knew so little about her. Could he even imagine the lessons she'd learned from all the mistakes she'd made? Those "perfect answers" had come by way of a great price.

Allie didn't say another word and neither did Jack. But after he exited the interstate and braked for a stoplight, she moved on a rare impulse. Unfastening her seat belt, she opened the door and jumped out.

"Allie, what in the—"

She slammed the door on the incredulousness in his voice, turned, and ran across the street. It was a busy intersection, cars coming and going, and one screeched to a halt, nearly missing Allie. Its indignant driver laid on the horn.

But she survived the crossing and noticed a myriad of stores and strip malls around, so she knew it would take Jack some effort to drive around and catch up with her. Part of her couldn't believe she had braved such a maneuver as escaping from Jack's SUV; however, her heart lay in shards, and in that moment, Allie thought she might even hate Jack Callahan.

But, of course, she didn't. She loved him, and that's why his words had wounded her so.

Allie sprinted through the bustling parking lot of a K-Mart store and then climbed a cement knoll. She dashed onward through the parking lot of a mall containing four stores. Minutes later, she stopped in the shadows to catch her breath. Leaning against one of the buildings, she begged God to forgive her rash behavior. She was hardly following her own belief of sticking out the bad so God could use it for good. In fact, chances were the Lord had wanted her at the hospital to encourage and pray for Logan and Marilee's family. Instead, she'd jumped from Jack's SUV and out of God's will. And yet she couldn't seem to help it. For all intents and purposes, Jack had sided with Brenda tonight. He may as well have said Allie *deserved* the beer in the face—just like she *deserved* Erich's abuse and now Jack's displaced anger.

Oh! But she was tired of turning the other cheek.

I only have two, Lord, remember? And one of them isn't worth turning. . . .

Allie skimmed her surroundings and didn't see Jack's shiny, black vehicle, but she decided she'd better keep going unless she wanted him to catch up with her—and she didn't. Turning to her right, Allie walked up a flight of wooden stairs that led to another parking lot, this time that of a large garden center.

Her cell phone rang, and Allie had a hunch it was Jack. She had a mind to ignore the call; but her common sense returned, and she figured she should let him know that she was safe so he could get on with his trip to the hospital. Lifting the phone from her purse, she answered it.

"Allie, where are you?" His voice sounded calm, even apologetic.

"I'm okay," she replied, a bit breathless from her jaunt. "I'm about to call a cab and head back to the hotel. I'll be praying for Marilee and Logan."

"Look, whatever's bugging you can be discussed on the way to the hospital."

"Not tonight, Jack," she replied, feeling emotionally spent.

With that, Allie pushed the END button on her phone, disconnecting the call.

*   *   *

It was with a great measure of guilt that Jack entered Charity Medical Center. Guilt tinged with anger. If something happened to Allie, he'd never forgive himself; and yet he felt so furious with her that he hadn't even tried to find her in that maze of stores and parking lots, fearing he'd throttle her if he did.

I can't believe she did that! It still amazed Jack that she'd bolted from his vehicle with lightning speed. When she had nearly gotten herself hit by that oncoming car, his heart lurched upward into his throat from sheer panic. But once his shock wore off, he realized she had every right to run off the way she did. To his shame, Jack figured he'd behaved no better than her former husband had. *I probably blew it with Allie for good now. When am I ever going to learn?*

"Dad."

Hearing Logan's voice, Jack stopped short in the hallway of the hospital's large lobby. He spotted his son several feet away, but coming toward him.

"Marilee's out of surgery and ready to be moved from the recovery room. She's being transferred to a room upstairs. We can catch an elevator over here."

"How's she doing?" Jack asked, striding in his direction.

"As good as can be expected, I guess," Logan said in a discouraged tone, and Jack noted the worried frown marring his son's brow. "She, um, broke her leg and her pelvis, and there was some internal damage that had to be repaired." He swallowed hard. "Her uterine artery ruptured, so doctors had to perform an emergency hysterectomy. Marilee won't be able to have children."

Jack winced; and when he saw the tears pooling in Logan's eyes, his heart broke. "I'm so sorry," he said, putting an arm around him.

He waved his hand, dismissing the issue. "I've got to be strong, Dad. I've got to be strong for Marilee. She's got a long road to recovery ahead of her. The surgeon talked about extensive physical therapy. . . ."

Jack nodded and looked down at the polished tile floor. He knew that "road to recovery" only too well. He had spent months in physical therapy after the gunshot wound to his thigh.

"Where's Mrs. Littenberg. . .I mean Allie?"

Jack groaned. "Don't ask." He saw Logan's expression fall even further and decided he couldn't burden his son with more problems. He had to "stay strong," too. *Lord, if I ever could be a good father to Logan, let it be now.*

"Look," Jack began again. "Don't worry about your old man's love life. You've got bigger issues looming on the horizon, and I promise I'm going to be around to do whatever I can, okay?"

"Thanks. I appreciate it."

"How did the accident happen?" Jack wanted to know.

"Marilee got rear-ended while she was stopped in rush-hour traffic on the interstate. The pickup that hit her pushed her car into the median, and the sheriff said that to see the wreckage you'd never guess she made it out alive. God really had His hand on her."

The elevator's chrome doors opened and they stepped inside. Meanwhile, Jack played across his memory the several bad accidents he had been dispatched to over the years.

"I'm glad she's okay," he murmured. "I mean, it might not seem like she's 'okay,' but she's alive."

"Yeah. . ." Logan halted, before adding, "Marilee's mom is really upset. When she heard Marilee's prognosis, she actually became hysterical. Mr. Domotor had to take her home."

"Well, Marilee's her baby. . .her little girl."

"I suppose. I just hope Marilee won't react like her mom. Nothing like hysterics to make a guy feel really helpless."

Jack had to chuckle in spite of the grave situation.

The elevator doors opened. The two men stepped out of the car and walked in the direction of Marilee's hospital room.

CHAPTER TWENTY-EIGHT

Allie awoke on Saturday morning feeling stiff and sore. She realized just how out of shape she'd become. Jogging that short way through two parking lots had strained the muscles in the backs of her legs, and she could barely walk to the bathroom of her extended-stay hotel suite. But as she stood under a hot, steamy shower, she promised herself she'd start exercising more often.

After ten minutes, she shut off the water and dragged herself into the vanity area, where she spritzed on her favorite fragrance, slipped into her fuzzy pink bathrobe, and dried her hair. Watching herself in the mirror, she began to plan her day. When flashes of last night's argument with Jack crept into her thoughts, Allie found herself feeling ashamed for what she now deemed in the light of day as overreacting. She reminded herself that Jack's faith was fragile, and she chastened herself for preaching at him. She should have kept her mouth shut, but she wasn't very good at harboring her feelings.

Lord, forgive me.

With a deep breath, she let go of any remaining regret and focused on today's schedule. Grocery store, pharmacy, dry cleaners, order flowers for Marilee, finish up some work at Arbor Springs, visit Cynthia. . .

The phone rang, and Allie shut off the blow dryer. Setting it down on the counter, she walked into the bedroom area of her suite and lifted the receiver.

"Good morning," Jack said cordially. "I wanted to let you know that Marilee's going to be okay."

Allie felt elated and much relieved. "That's good news. I'm glad to hear it."

"Yeah, me, too. The bad news is there are going to be some residual effects, but she and Logan are just going to have to take things one step at a time."

"What sort of 'residual effects'?"

Jack paused. "Marilee had to have an emergency hysterectomy."

"Oh, no. . .how heartbreaking! She's so young and now. . ." Allie lowered herself onto the bed. ". . .now she can't bear children."

"Yeah, it's a crying shame, all right."

Allie wondered how Jack was handling things. It was hard to tell from the tone of his voice. Was he blaming God? However, she dared not ask—not after last night.

He changed the subject. "I thought as long as I had you on the line, I'd give you Blythe's address and phone number."

Allie set down the phone and scurried around to find a pen. Locating one in her attaché case on the kitchenette's counter, she returned to the nightstand and lifted the receiver. "I'm back." She wrote the information as Jack gave it.

"Thanks. I'll try to give her a call soon," she said.

Another awkward lull in the conversation ensued.

"About last night. . ."

"Jack, I'm sorry. I overreacted," Allie blurted. "But I was tired and, after my run-in with Brenda, I just couldn't handle any more. But I take total responsibility for my. . .stupidity."

"Well, that's good. . .I guess."

Allie raised her brows. "You guess?"

"What else?"

Allie frowned. "I don't know what you mean? What else?"

"Yeah, isn't now the part where you tell me what a jerk I was last night and that you never want to see me again?"

She couldn't help a little smile. "I'll go along with the jerk part, but. . ."

"But what?"

Letting her smile slip away, Allie realized his faith wasn't the only thing that was fragile. She had often viewed Jack as having a stubborn side and a resentful streak, but she always believed a sensitive heart beat in his chest. However, she'd never considered him vulnerable or insecure. Truth of the matter was, she could now see he possessed both those qualities.

"Well, I'm not about to say I never want to see you again, if that's what you're getting at. But, I'll admit, we've got a ways to go and some issues to work out before we can think along the lines of a serious relationship."

She heard him exhale at the other end of the line. It didn't sound like a sigh of relief, per se, but one of weariness.

"What were you thinking?" she queried.

"I guess I thought you'd want nothing more to do with me."

"Is that what you want?" She sensed he didn't, but felt she had to ask anyway.

"No!"

Allie grinned at his vehemence.

"Except how much better am I than your former husband? I could hardly sleep thinking about what I said. I knew I hurt your feelings, and I can't blame you for ditching me. I don't know, Allie. . .maybe I'm just not a nice guy."

"You're the only one who can change that." Allie sat back down on the edge of the bed. Pensive, she nibbled her lower lip. "Jack, may I suggest something?"

"Yeah, go ahead."

"Why don't you and I visit a Christian bookstore and purchase a couple of copies of a book that we can read together? Something that will help us delve into God's Word and something that will aid us in developing a healthy relationship."

Silence met her at the other end, but then Jack replied, "I guess we can do that."

Allie hesitated when the next suggestion entered her mind. But a moment later, she figured that as long as she was being candid, she might as well go all the way. "Getting biblical counseling is another option."

"I'm one up on you there. I'm planning to call Jim on Monday morning."

"Jim?" Allie brought her chin back, surprised on both accounts.

"Jim Dabner. The guy I told you about yesterday. The one whose Bible study I attended."

"Oh. . ." Allie wondered if Mr. Dabner had proper training, but Jack's next sentence put her mind at ease.

"Jim mentioned he's done a lot of counseling, particularly in the area of drug addiction. I know that's not my problem, but I've been through enough seminars as a cop to know that certain behavior patterns cross over into other areas of life. As for experience in 'healthy relationships,' as you put it, Jim's been married twenty-seven years. That says a lot for him. . .and it says even more for his wife."

Allie chuckled and heard him take a sip of something. She imagined Jack drinking his morning coffee as they conversed.

"Soul-searching isn't really something I want to do," he stated honestly. "Logan is famous for analyzing and internalizing situations. Drives me crazy. But I don't want to lose you, Allie. I really thought I had after last night."

"Lucky for you I don't scare that easily," she murmured.

"Thank God!" A moment passed before Jack spoke again. "Allie, I'm tired of being angry because I'm lonely. I've got no one to share my life with, and it even hurts to admit it. I've taken out my frustrations on everyone else. But I've finally concluded that it's time I stopped hurting the people I love."

His admission brought tears to her eyes, and she loved him all the more for it. Recognizing the problem was three-quarters of the solution!

*   *   *

Marilee blinked as she awakened in the strange room. She heard someone snoring and turned her head to see who it was. There she saw Logan sprawled out in a chair next to her bed and sleeping soundly. In the next moment, she realized that he held her hand through the guardrail. She smiled. It felt so nice to hold his hand.

But in the next moment, stark reality hit. Guardrails on the bed. This room. . .

In a flash, it all came back to her. The car accident. The deep, grinding pain. The ride in the ambulance to the hospital. The emergency room and the doctors hovering over her, asking a million questions. More pain. Needles poking, hands and fingers prodding. Her leg! Her hip! The pain grew in intensity. X-rays as she lay on the gurney. Talk of surgery and the jolt of fear that coursed through her upon hearing those words. Then a black mask covered her nose before she could ask questions, before she could pray. . . .

The next thing she knew she had awakened in this room.

Marilee tried to assess the damage to her body. She wiggled her toes, and white lightning-hot torment shot up her left leg. She bit back a cry and tried to take deep breaths. When the agony subsided, she realized her leg was encased in some sort of bandage or cast. Her hip and back. . .

She couldn't suppress the moan of anguish that rose up from the core of her being. The sound caused Logan to awaken. Sitting forward, he squeezed her hand. "It's okay. Just be still."

She closed her eyes and let out an anguished sigh. "I'm sorry I missed the bonfire."

"Me, too, but that's the least of my concerns."

She looked at him, feeling weak and afraid. "Am I going to die?"

Logan grinned. "Eventually. But I've been told you're going to live through this trial. Although, it might not feel like it at the moment."

He raised her hand to his lips and kissed her fingers. She smiled, but noticed Logan's strained expression.

"I've worried you, haven't I? I'm sorry."

"Stop apologizing," he said, although Marilee saw the tenderness in his brown eyes.

"Where are Mom and Dad?"

"They went home to get some sleep. They'll be back."

"What time is it?"

Logan glanced at his wristwatch. "Almost nine."

"Are my parents okay?"

"They're upset. . .your mom is really upset."

Marilee worked her lower lip between her teeth.

"Do you remember anything before you went into surgery?"

"Not much."

"Do you remember why you had surgery?"

"For my leg and my hip?"

"Your hip?" Logan shook his head. "Your hip is okay as far as I know, but you broke your leg and pelvis. Could be that's why your hip hurts."

"Yes. . ." Marilee suddenly became aware of the deep soreness inside her abdomen. With her left hand, she touched the top of her stomach and felt the bandages.

"There were some internal injuries, but the doctors are certain they patched them up."

She studied his face, sensing there was more. "But?"

He forced a smile. "You're going to be fine."

"What aren't you telling me?"

Pursing his lips, he brought Marilee's hand up and rested it against his unshaven cheek.

"What is it, Logan?"

He took several moments to weigh his words, and Marilee felt a swell of panic.

"Honey, you're going to be fine," he said as if sensing her growing fear. "It's just that your uterine artery ruptured in the accident so doctors had to. . .um. . .well, they had to do an emergency hysterectomy."

"No!" More than horrified, it took a second for Marilee to realize the shriek that had just filled the room came from her mouth. "No," she said more quietly but just as intense. Her ears tickled, and she realized that tears were slipping down her cheeks.

Logan had tears in his eyes, too. "Shh, it's okay. . . ."

"No, it's not okay," she cried, trying to pull her hand free. "I wanted to have children!"

"God can still give us children." Logan held onto her with his one hand, then wiped away her tears with the other.

"I wanted a baby. . .our baby!"

"I know. . .but there are a million babies in this world who need parents. We'll adopt one of them. Maybe two or three of them. They'll become ours."

"Oh, Logan, you don't know what you're saying!"

"And that's the truth. There are no words that'll console you right now, Marilee. I'm just sorry I had to be the one to tell you this news."

Choking on a sob, she tried to absorb the information. "I can't give you children, Logan," she said at last, feeling as though each word might strangle her. "A son or daughter is the most precious gift a woman can give her husband."

Marilee turned her face away and covered her mouth with her free hand. Another sob wracked her body, but the jerking movement brought more pain to her abdomen and leg. Oddly, the pain also brought back some semblance of reason. She willed herself to stop crying. Tears wouldn't give her back that which she'd lost.

Hearing Logan sniff, she returned her gaze to him and saw a tear trickle down his unshaven cheek. He wanted children, too. But now she couldn't give him any.

"Do you still love me? Do you still want to marry me?"

"Of course I do." He looked sincere.

"Maybe you should think it over."

"Maybe I don't have to."

"But—"

"Stop it, Marilee."

The warning glint in his eyes brought her up short. Logan had never spoken harshly to her before. . .ever! To hear it now was disconcerting; although given the subject matter, it was oddly reassuring, too.

She watched through misty eyes as his features softened. "If God showed me that you're the woman for me, a car accident isn't going to change things. I prayed about asking you to marry me for months. If it wasn't the Lord's will, I'm sure He would have shown me during that time. It's not as if I made a rash decision. In fact," he added with a charming grin, "as you recall, I was such a chicken, I dragged my feet a little."

"A little?"

"Okay, I dragged them a lot."

Marilee couldn't help a little smile.

"That's better," Logan said, smiling back at her. "God wants us to weather this storm together." Peering down at her hand that he held through the metal guardrail, he entwined his fingers with hers. "And we will." Looking back at her, he added,

"With His help, we will."

Doubt filled her soul, but Marilee prayed that Logan's words were true.

*   *   *

When Cynthia saw her angel enter the room, she felt a little less depressed, although she was fuzzyheaded from the medication. But at least it took the edge off her pain. Breathing had become increasingly difficult and now a clear plastic oxygen mask covered her nose and mouth. The nurse who administered it said it was not a life-sustaining device, but promised that it would make Cynthia more comfortable—and it had.

"How are you feeling this afternoon?" Angel wanted to know.

She shrugged, trying to save her words for a more important reply.

"I have some bad news," Angel said, sitting on the edge of the bed. "Logan's fiancée was in an awful car accident last night. As a result of her injuries, she's not going to be able to have children."

Cynthia tried to absorb the news into her hazy brain. No children. . .

"I stopped by the hospital earlier, and, naturally, Marilee's pretty upset. She's in a lot of pain and poor Logan's exhausted. He won't leave her, even to get some rest. I don't say all this to make you feel worse, Cynthia, but I wanted you to know why Logan hasn't come to see you."

Reaching up with one feeble hand, she pulled the mask off her face. "Why?" she rasped.

Her angel frowned. "Why, what?"

"Why. . .does. . .he. . .come. . .here?"

Angel replaced the mask. "I can't answer for Logan, but I would guess his purpose is twofold. First, you're his natural mother and he feels a sense of duty to visit you. He's wondered about you for most of his life. Second, he wants to share his faith with you."

Yes, he'd shared his faith. He read to her from the Bible.

He'd told her with tears rimming his brown eyes that he wanted to see her in heaven someday.

But Cynthia knew she didn't deserve heaven. Logan was proof of that—and he was only the tip of the iceberg. All the mistakes she'd made in her lifetime ran as deep as the Atlantic.

She pulled the oxygen mask down around her chin. "Why. . . was. . .I. . .even. . .born?"

Perched on the side of the bed and wearing a sweater as blue as her eyes, Angel shook her head. "What sort of a question is that?

Once again, she replaced the flow of oxygen, and Cynthia took another raspy breath.

"But I know what you mean," her angel stated. "I was once at a point in my own life where I wondered why I was ever born. But at my lowest point, I turned to God and cried out for Him to help me. I knew I was a Christian, but I had pushed God away. I think He allowed me to do things my way just to let me find out what sort of mess I could make on my own. And it was a fine mess, believe me."

Cynthia would have laughed if she were able. Hard to imagine this woman at a low point in her life. Indeed, she'd have to take her angel's word for it.

"But you know what God has shown me over the years? He's shown me that He has a plan for all of us. For instance, if it weren't for you, Logan wouldn't have been born."

Another blade in her heart. She shook her head. Cynthia had been prepared to have an abortion. She pulled on her mask. "No. . ."

Angel replaced it. "I know the story. You didn't want to have your baby. . .at first. But you changed your mind. Rejoice that you changed your mind, Cynthia. Logan was born and he's such a nice guy. He's not perfect, of course, but he tries to do right in every situation, and he's touched a lot of people's lives. Thank God his mother changed her mind and didn't terminate her pregnancy."

For the first time in a very, very long while, Cynthia felt a spark of hope. Yes, she had changed her mind. Jack persuaded her, but she had made the decision. Maybe she'd done something right after all.

"And as long as we're on the subject of children," her angel began, "your daughter Kelly returned the message I left last week. I called her back this afternoon and we talked a little bit. She had no idea about Logan, and I don't think she believed me when I told her that he was her half-brother. But she's curious, and I invited her and Patrice to church tomorrow—and lunch afterwards."

Cynthia hoped they'd go. If ever two girls needed church, it was Patty and Kelly.

CHAPTER TWENTY-NINE

L ogan, I don't know. . ."

Jack clenched his jaw, thinking his son asked far too much of him. On the other hand, he had promised Logan he would do anything he could to help.

Slipping four quarters into the soda machine, Jack made his selection and a plastic bottle bumped its way down. Once it exited the machine, he bent over and scooped it up. Standing, he faced Logan and twisted off the bottle's plastic cap.

"Dad, I haven't been able to see her since last Thursday, and I'm really burdened for her soul."

After taking a swig of his cola, he and Logan stepped out of the small vending area in the lower level of Charity Memorial. "That woman has heard God's plan of salvation from a lot of people. I told her about Jesus, my mother talked to her about eternity, Allie has, you have. . .what more can I do?"

"I'm not sure. I just think you're the one who might get through to her."

"Yeah, right." Jack chuckled. "I didn't behave like much of a Christian when Roxi and I were married. That woman had a knack for bringing out the devil in me."

"Dad. . ."

Jack lifted a hand to forestall the mini sermon he sensed was coming. "I know I can't blame your mother for my actions. But let's face it. There are people in this world who cause us to react in less than perfect ways. For me, your mother is one of those people."

Reaching the elevators, Logan pressed the UP button. "That was a long time ago. Things have changed. You've changed—and for the better now that you've come back to Christ."

"Maybe, but I've still got a long way to go."

"Well, okay. . .it's good you realize that. But wouldn't you say forgiveness is the key that set you free from years of pain and bitterness? Where you were before Allie came back to town is where my natural mother is right now."

Logan's words struck him like a slap upside the head. Allie had come back to set things right—and she had as far as he was concerned. Colleen, too; but Brenda was another story. Jack, on the other hand, didn't know if he possessed the courage to follow in Allie's footsteps.

The elevator doors opened, and after a group of people exited, he and Logan stepped inside. Logan selected the appropriate floor.

"Allie's a lot braver than I am," Jack confessed.

"We can do all things through Christ who strengthens us."

Jack wanted to groan at the reply because he recognized it as a paraphrase from the Bible, but he took another drink of his cola instead.

"For the past week, I've known that you must see my mother before she dies. I can't get through to her. Allie can't get through to her. But she said she really loved you once, and—"

"Logan, quit!" Jack growled. "Do you have any idea how hard I've tried to forget that part of my life?"

"But forgetting isn't the same as forgiving," his son pressed on, "and you said you'd do anything to help me out while Marilee's in the hospital."

"I know, I know, but I didn't think you'd ask me to see Roxi."

"Cynthia."

"Whatever."

The elevator arrived at the floor and its doors opened, revealing one of the many stark hallways of the hospital. Jack and Logan strode toward Marilee's room. The rubber soles of their shoes squeaked on the polished tile and seemed to echo down the walkway, announcing their approach. When they reached the north wing, they stepped onto blue-green carpeting and a less dismal atmosphere.

"Will you just think about what I asked, Dad?"

"Yeah, I'll think about it," Jack muttered; however, he was pretty certain of what his answer would be.

No!

Reaching Marilee's room, they were greeted by Eileen and Stan Domotor, who were just on their way out.

"She's finally sleeping," Eileen said.

"We're going to run out and get some supper," Stan informed them. "Would you two like to join us?"

Jack glanced at Logan, deciding he'd go along with whatever his son decided.

"No, thanks," came Logan's reply.

"Look, Son," Stan said gently, "you've been here since last night and you need a break. You're exhausted."

"I'll go home later and sleep. In the meantime, you two go get something to eat. . .you, too, Dad."

"No, I'm okay."

"We'll bring something back for you, Logan," Eileen declared;

and Jack noticed that, while she looked as regal as the day he'd first met her, the expression in her hazel eyes appeared weary. "A greasy cheeseburger and deep-fried onion rings. . .how's that sound?"

"Hey, now you're talking," Logan answered with a grin.

Standing beside him, Jack chuckled.

"Something for you, too?" Eileen asked him.

Jack shook his head. "No, thanks. I'm not hungry."

"All right. . .well, we'll see you later," she said.

Stan gave them a smile and a parting nod before the couple headed off in the direction of the elevators.

Jack stood in the doorway and drank more of his cola while Logan checked on Marilee. When he came back, they ambled into the lounge area, where cellular phones were allowed to be used. While Marilee slept, Logan checked his phone messages. Jack made himself comfortable on one of the tan vinyl sofas and began flipping through the television stations.

"Hey, Dad," Logan called across the lounge that only the two of them occupied for the moment, "Allie called about a half hour ago to say she's at Arbor Springs visiting my mother and that one of my half-sisters phoned. She invited both young ladies to church tomorrow."

Jack really could have cared less, but he nodded out a polite reply.

Logan turned off his phone and stuffed it into the breast pocket of his shirt. "Allie said she's going to finish up some work and then she'll come back over here to the hospital. We're supposed to call her if we want her to pick up anything on the way."

"Sounds good," Jack muttered, pretending to be engrossed in some college football game. However, on the inside he bristled, recalling Logan's request of just minutes ago. Visit Roxi? Man, he'd rather have a root canal! It irked him even more to think about how much attention Allie was giving to his repulsive ex-wife. Yes, at one time, he had been burdened for Roxi's soul—but that's what had gotten him into trouble in the first place. And once they were married, she hadn't wanted anything to do with Christianity. Of course, it didn't help that Jack was struggling in that area himself. But it almost seemed as though Roxi purposely did the opposite of what a believer would do in any given situation. She even made anything physical between them seem cheap. . .dirty. Jack grew to hate himself for reacting to her, and he began despising her all the more.

Lord, You can't really want me to see that woman again.

He closed his eyes and felt that old familiar nudge from above. A prompting, just like the one that told him he needed to attend church last Sunday and go to his brother's house for lunch afterwards. He remembered that prodding from days gone by; it was the same one that had caused him to be burdened for Allie's soul, and Blythe's and Wendy's. The same urge had caused him to volunteer at a shelter for alcoholics and drug addicts in downtown Chicago. He told those brokenhearted men and women about Jesus, read to them from the Bible, and they believed.

What happened to me, Lord? I used to be as enthusiastic about spiritual things as Logan is.

Jack drew in a deep breath. Well, one thing was certain—he had to see Roxi. He didn't want to. He loathed the thought of it. But something in the depth of his soul told him he needed to do this.

"Hey, Logan."

His son drew his gaze away from the game on TV. "Yeah?"

"You have Caller ID on your phone?"

He nodded.

"Great. Will you call Allie back and see if she's still at Arbor Springs."

"Sure. What for?"

Jack stood and grinned at Logan's perplexed expression. "If Allie's not there, ask her if she'll go back and meet me there."

Logan nodded, pressing buttons on his cell phone. Lifting

it to his ear, he gazed at Jack expectantly.

"I decided to go see your mother." He laughed. "Don't look so shocked. Just call Allie for me, and. . .I'll talk to you later."

With that, he left the waiting room, praying he wouldn't change his mind on the way.

*   *   *

Allie was four blocks away from Arbor Springs when she got Logan's message. She turned around and drove back to the facility, feeling a measure of shock at the news: Jack was on his way to see Cynthia!

Pulling into the lot, Allie parked her car; and as she walked the distance to the front doors, she noticed the sun was already sinking in the October sky and it was only six o'clock. Fall had officially arrived now, bringing with it the shorter days and a brisk northwest wind. The change in weather caused her to feel a tad homesick for sunny California.

She reentered Arbor Springs and let the security guard know she was expecting Jack and that she would wait for him in her office. The young man on duty this evening appeared quite competent, and Allie decided the department wasn't completely hopeless after all.

Unlocking her office door, she still couldn't believe Jack had agreed to see his ex-wife. On one hand, it was answered prayer. On the other, Allie found herself feeling protective toward Cynthia. What would Jack say to her? The poor woman was already wallowing in self-pity and couldn't see past it to God's forgiveness. One harsh word from Jack might seal her fate in a Christless eternity.

Allie putzed about her office, shuffling through some paperwork, praying as she inserted one folder after another into the metal filing cabinet. *Lord, please give Jack a tender heart. Please put Your words in his mouth.*

He arrived about half an hour later dressed in khaki slacks and a green and tan plaid Oxford button-down shirt.

"Thanks for sticking around," he said as, together, they walked to the elevators. "This sort of thing takes moral support."

Smiling, Allie pushed the UP button. "No problem."

"I really didn't want to come, but I felt God wanted me to see Roxi, although I haven't a clue as to what I should say. But I felt I needed to obey the Lord."

When the doors opened, they stepped into the car that would carry them to the fifth floor.

Jack ran his fingers through his salt-and-pepper gray hair. "For decades I disregarded the Lord's promptings—except I didn't realize that until recently. On the way over here, it occurred to me that Jesus had always been nearby. He was just waiting for me to want to come back to Him. I just never thought I deserved to."

"I think Cynthia's in a similar place. She's been depressed, thinking she doesn't deserve heaven. The fact is none of us deserves it."

"You got that right. Salvation is a precious gift. So is our walk of faith. I learned that lesson the hard way."

Allie felt her heart swell with affection. Like some kind of incredible metamorphosis, Jack was transforming into the man she remembered so long ago.

The doors opened once more, and they walked off the elevator. Allie paused in the small foyer, elevators on either side, and grabbed hold of his arm.

"Jack, wait, I need to warn you about something. Cynthia. . . well, she looks awful. Because of the cancer, she's nothing but skin and bones. Logan showed me pictures of her after you two were married, and she doesn't resemble that woman at all. You won't recognize her. I guarantee it."

Jack nodded, but Allie wondered if he really understood.

"She can also be rude. I. . .well, I usually ignore it."

"I'm expecting to see bad manners from my ex. My very presence will trigger it. Just watch."

Again, they headed for Room 8, and Allie felt apprehension clamor up her spine. Maybe this wasn't such a good idea; however, she quickly reminded herself that God had this matter under control.

They entered the room and found Cynthia asleep. The only sound came from the hissing oxygen tank. Allie walked to the foot of the hospital bed to allow Jack some space. Seeing his expression, Allie could tell she hadn't sufficiently prepared him.

"No way," he whispered, looking thunderstruck. "This can't be Roxi."

"It is."

"Can't be!"

Propped up slightly, Cynthia stirred. Her eyes fluttered open. They seemed to focus on him for an instant before closing again. She muttered something, and Allie came around to the other side of the bed and carefully pulled the mask off her hollowed face.

"Did you want to say something?"

The dying ghost of a woman in a baggy blue and white checked hospital gown looked at Allie, then at Jack. "I said. . ." She gasped for a breath. "Jack Callahan. . .I'd know you anywhere. . .you haven't changed. . .not one bit."

Allie caught his gaze and mouthed an "I told you so."

Jack appeared to give himself a mental shake. He placed his hands on the guardrails and peered down at the woman who once bore the title of his wife.

"Hi, Roxi." His tone was nondescript.

"What. . .what are you. . .doing here?"

Allie replaced the mask to ease Cynthia's intake of air while Jack replied.

"I'm here as a favor to—"

He cut himself off, and Allie watched as his features went from steely to sympathetic. "Actually," he began again, "I'm here because the Lord told me I needed to come."

Cynthia's eyelids flittered as though it were a great struggle to stay conscious. She said something, but her words were garbled. Allie pulled back the mask again.

"What did you say, Cynthia?" she asked. "We couldn't understand you."

"I said. . ." She sucked in a wheezy breath. ". . .so, you're a. . .a holy roller again, eh?"

"It's to my shame that you're so surprised." Jack leaned forward, his forearms resting on the rails now. "I sure wasn't much of a Christian when we were married, was I?"

Cynthia closed her eyes. Each breath seemed like an act of labor. Allie replaced the mask.

"But hindsight is twenty/twenty vision," Jack continued. "I owe you an apology, Roxi. I expected you to behave like a Christian wife, but you weren't a Christian. What I should have done is accepted you for who you were and where you were. I should have shown you Christ-like love. . .the way a husband should."

She pawed at the mask until Allie took it off. "Our marriage. . .was a sham. . .from the get-go," she panted.

"Not to me it wasn't," Jack said softly.

Allie felt herself growing misty at the exchange.

"I really thought it would work."

Incredulity widened Cynthia's eyes. "You. . .you hated me."

"Not at first. I wanted ours to be the kind of marriage my parents had." He glanced at Allie, and she saw his guilt-ridden expression. "But I guess I let a lot of things get in the way of making that happen."

"It doesn't. . .matter anymore."

"Maybe not. But I'd like to know that you've forgiven me."

A knowing look crossed her illness-battered features. "So that's why. . .why you came. . .so you could. . .show yourself. . .the big man. . .in front of. . .your precious Allie." A loud wheeze and a cough wracked Cynthia's body. When the spell ended, she laid against the pillows looking weak and exhausted; however, she found enough strength to add, "It's her you loved. . .from the start."

"I won't argue with you there," Jack said in a matter-of-fact tone, and Allie prayed his defenses weren't on the rise.

She set the mask over Cynthia's nose and mouth. With one hand, she stroked the dying woman's light brown hair back off her forehead.

"The three of us have made our share of mistakes, haven't we?" Allie said. "But now it's time to forgive. . .and to be forgiven."

For a time, Cynthia laid very still, her eyes closed, and Allie wondered if her words had been all but lost on the perishing soul. But then Cynthia turned her gaze on Jack and lifted her first two fingers in what was once a popular sign among young people.

Jack gave her a wry grin. He understood. "Peace, Roxi."

He reached for her bony hand and held it between the two of his, amazing Allie by the gesture. A tear trickled down Cynthia's cheek and Allie brushed it away.

Several long moments lapsed and Allie gazed at Jack. He winked at her, then looked back at his ex-wife.

"You still with us, Roxi?"

She answered, but the words were muffled by the oxygen mask.

"Logan's a great guy, isn't he?" Jack said.

She gave him a feeble nod.

"Well, he turned out despite my lousy parenting, so don't think I had anything to do with it."

To Allie's wonder, the woman laughed—a shoulder-shaking laugh of all things! But unfortunately, it sent her into a coughing fit.

When it was over, Jack grinned at her. With her free hand, Cynthia motioned for Allie to take off the mask again. She did.

"You. . .you were the best. . .the best husband. . .I had," she muttered, more winded now since laughing had taken the extra breath she didn't have to give.

"I'm sorry," Jack told her with a facetious smirk. "You must have married some real winners if I was your best husband."

"They were. . .terrible."

Jack looked sincere. "I am truly sorry, Roxi."

She looked up at him in almost a trancelike stare. "I. . .I believe you," she finally stated.

"Good." He gave her hand a pat. After a deep breath, he said, "Now, there's another order of business we need to get settled. It's the matter of your soul. . . ."

* * *

"Logan, do you want my pudding?" Marilee asked. "I think it's supposed to be banana."

"You don't want it?" he asked from the chair beside her bed.

"No."

"Sure, I'll eat it."

She handed him the spoon and the clear plastic bowl filled with a whipped yellow mixture. For herself, she wasn't very hungry. But her thirst seemed unquenchable.

"When you're done, will you get me another can of juice or a soda?"

"Absolutely." He took a bite and then another. "Hey, this stuff isn't bad. Wanna try just a little?"

She didn't, but he stood and put the spoon to her lips, so she forced herself to eat it. It tasted okay.

"How 'bout one more bite?"

"No, Logan." She turned her head away. He had already spoon-fed her a good dose of the blandest chicken and rice soup she'd ever eaten.

He took a seat on the edge of her bed. "When Roni was a baby, I'd feed her sometimes. I'd have to pretend the spoon was an airplane and it was coming in for a landing in order for her to open up." Logan tried those antics on her, complete with sound effects.

But Marilee wasn't amused. She pushed his hand away. "I'm not a child. Stop treating me like one."

Without a word, he stood and set the pudding back on the metal dinner tray. "I'll be right back with your juice."

He left the hospital room and Marilee's eyes filled with tears. She hurt all over. She felt like screaming. Her head ached, and she wished Logan would go home and leave her alone. She hated for him to see her like this—at her ultimate worst!

All too soon, he returned with a can of grape juice and Marilee grimaced. She couldn't stand grape juice.

"I'm going to hit the road, okay? I have some studying to do for tomorrow, and I should probably try to get a good night's sleep."

Marilee nodded. But suddenly she didn't want him to go. Up and down. She felt as though she'd been riding an emotional roller coaster all afternoon. Her mother had warned her that this might happen. Because of the surgery, her hormones were off balance.

"I'll stop by tomorrow after church," Logan said, collecting his jacket.

Marilee swatted at the tears on her cheeks.

"What's wrong?"

"Oh, Logan, I'm a mess," she said on a long, sad note.

He tossed his jacket into the chair and came to stand at her bedside. "I wish I had the perfect answer for you, but I haven't said anything right in the past two hours."

"I'm sorry. . ."

"Me, too. And I'm beyond tired right now. I need some sleep."

There was an edge to his voice that broke Marilee's heart. But she understood. She'd feel crabby, too, in his position.

She closed her eyes so he wouldn't catch sight of the fact that she was still crying.

"Your parents should be back from dinner any minute."

She didn't reply.

"I'll see you tomorrow."

Marilee listened to his footfalls as he left. Once she couldn't hear them anymore, she pulled the sheet up to her face and sobbed for all she was worth. She cried for the baby to whom she would never give birth. She cried for the fiancé who didn't understand. She cried and cried until she didn't think she had another tear left.

When it was all over, she didn't feel a single bit better.

Staring up at the ceiling, Marilee forced herself back into some semblance of sanity. Feeling sorry for herself wouldn't change her situation. She had to accept it.

The memory of a song she'd sung with her students only yesterday at music time came to mind.

When upon life's billows you are tempest tossed,
When you are discouraged thinking all is lost,
Count your many blessings name them one by one,
And it will surprise you what the Lord hath done.

Marilee sang the chorus out loud. "Count your blessings name them one by one." She cleared her throat. "Count your blessings—see what God hath done. Count your blessings—name them one by one; Count your many blessings—see what God hath done."

She began the second stanza. "Are you ever burdened with a load of care? Does the cross seem heavy you are called to bear?" More tears suddenly filled her eyes. "Count your many blessings every doubt will fly. . ." She couldn't go on. Her voice gave way.

At the doorway, she heard Logan finish. "And you will be singing as the days go by."

She felt thoroughly embarrassed. "I thought you went home to bed," she said with a sniff and wiping the moisture off her face.

He sauntered into the room, grinning like a little boy. "I had to come back and share the news."

"What news?"

He sat down on the edge of her bed. "My dad called. My mother became a Christian tonight!"

"That's. . .that's great, Logan." Marilee wished she felt more elated. She knew she should, but her own sadness loomed over her like a dark shadow.

"Dad was the one who led her to the Lord."

Now that was a miracle!

"Had you not been in that car accident last night, Marilee, my dad's heart would have never been moved to the extent it was. He would have never agreed to visit my mother. Not in a million years."

"God. . .God used my accident? Is that what you're saying?"

"It's my belief that He did. Another soul is born again, and the angels are rejoicing in heaven. And just think, Marilee," he added, leaning toward her, "this is only the beginning. Who knows how many other lives might be impacted by the trial we're facing." His eyes darkened with emotion. "God has a plan for our lives, and He's going to use us. You and me. The dynamic duo."

His vehemence and optimism were contagious. She especially liked his use of the words we, our, and us. For the past twelve hours, he'd promised, over and over again, that he would stick by her. Somehow, Marilee didn't believe him. Somehow, she thought Logan would want to reconsider their engagement since she could no longer have children. But suddenly she knew for certain that such was not the case. She could practically see the devotion shining in his brown eyes.

"Oh, Logan, I love you with all my heart."

"I love you with all my heart, too. And I'm so happy right now, I think I could stay up for another two days."

Smiling, Marilee reached for him and he took her hand. In that moment, her skewed world righted itself and somehow she knew that everything would be fine—just fine.

CHAPTER THIRTY

A llie walked into her hotel suite, feeling overjoyed from an incredible evening. Cynthia had asked Jesus into her heart; she had become a Christian! And if that weren't enough to thrill Allie—which it was—Jack had agreed to sign on with Lakeland Enterprises and develop a training program for its security personnel, beginning at Arbor Springs. He shared some of his ideas with her and they sounded fabulous.

Evan and the rest of the board are going to be pleased.

Kicking off her shoes, she entered the bathroom and turned on the hot water in the tub. She added some fragrant soap; and minutes later, while she soaked in a steaming bubble bath, she thought back on the pleasant dinner that she and Jack shared tonight after Cynthia had fallen asleep and they left Arbor Springs.

At the restaurant, with its peaceful ambiance, Jack said he felt like a man set free from years of bondage. He admitted the hatred he'd felt toward his ex-wife all these years had enslaved him. He'd never known just how much until tonight. But that same hatred had vanished when he'd seen Cynthia's withered form. How could he hate such a helpless creature? Jack said it was as if God's Holy Spirit took over from that point on.

What a miracle! Allie thought. *Oh, thank You, Lord, for allowing me to be a part of it!*

Feeling relaxed and drowsy now, Allie stepped out of the tub and put on her nightgown. No sooner had she crawled into bed and drifted off into a contented sleep when the telephone on the bedside table rang and startled her awake. She reached for the receiver, nearly knocking over her alarm clock in the process.

"Hello," she said, sounding groggy to her own ears.

"Angel!"

She perked up at the sound of the man's voice on the other end. She didn't recognize it. "Who is this?"

"It's Nate. . .you know, the RN at Arbor Springs."

Allie relaxed. "You gave me quite a fright there, Nate."

"Sorry. I got your number out of the computer. . .from when you had your lab work done."

Allie remembered. She'd given the hotel's address and phone number after she'd been stuck by Cynthia Matlock's flying IV needle.

"I figured I should call somebody, but I didn't know who. There're no family members listed in the chart."

"What are you talking about?"

A pause. "Mrs. M passed away a few minutes ago."

*   *   *

White puffy clouds inched their way across an azure sky. Allie watched them through the tall windows of Parkway Community Church. She sat in one of the floral armchairs in the lobby, Jack sat on a nearby loveseat, and Logan paced, his Bible tucked beneath one arm.

"You're going to wear out the carpet," Jack told him with a grin.

Logan stopped in midstride. "I'm just not sure how to handle this. Do I tell Patrice and Kelly before the service that our mother died, or do I wait until afterwards?"

"They might not even show up," Allie said, pulling her gaze from the window.

"Why don't you just play it by ear?" Jack suggested.

Allie glanced at him and decided he looked dashing in his charcoal gray suit.

"*If* they show up and there's time before the service," he continued, "tell them. If there isn't, wait until later."

"There's wisdom with age," Logan quipped with a spark of amusement in his eyes. He had dressed casually today, navy blue slacks and multicolored dress shirt, dark blue tie. But his brown eyes couldn't hide the weariness he obviously felt. Even so, Logan put up an enthusiastic front.

Jack chuckled at his son's quip.

At that moment, several teenage girls approached Logan, asking him about Marilee. He gave them a brief update and encouraged them to keep praying. They promised they would, and then they giggled and babbled on about everything Logan missed after supper at Friday night's bonfire event.

Allie couldn't suppress a laugh as the girls chattered like little magpies. She looked at Jack, who rolled his eyes and shook his head.

"See what we missed by not having daughters?"

"No comment," Jack replied.

Allie laughed again; but suddenly out of the corner of her eye, she spotted four people walking through the parking lot and heading for the front entrance. Two were males, one a brunette and one with light brown hair, and two females—the latter looked very much like Cynthia's daughters.

Standing, Allie interrupted Logan and pointed to where the couples had just stepped inside the church. He excused himself from the teens and walked over to the guests.

Allie and Jack followed.

"Welcome to Parkway. I'm Logan Callahan," he said, extending his right hand.

Both young ladies accepted the greeting, and Logan continued with the introductions. Patrice and Kelly remembered Allie, and they made Jack's acquaintance with polite smiles, commenting on how much Logan looked like his dad. Patrice and Kelly, in turn, introduced their boyfriends, Matt and Chris.

"So, you're a pastor at this church and. . .you're supposed to be our brother?" Kelly asked, studying his face. She had dressed in a knee-length black leather skirt and a silky red blouse, over which she wore a black leather jacket. Her dark brown hair was parted in the middle and hung in waves to her shoulders. "Ma never mentioned you." She looked at Jack. "Ma never mentioned you, either."

Allie watched as Jack sort of shrugged off the remark. This wasn't exactly the best place to discuss his less-than-blissful marriage.

Logan was the one to reply. "Yes, I'm both a pastor here and your half-brother."

"Hard to believe," Kelly, the younger of the two girls, said.

"Yeah, but for the life of us," Patrice added, her reddish brown hair pulled back into a clip, "we can't figure out why you'd lie. I mean it's not like we're the Judds or something."

Kelly laughed.

"Well, it's a long story," Logan answered with a patient smile, "one I'd like to tell you at lunch, assuming you'll accept my invitation."

The girls looked at their boyfriends, who both shrugged.

"Yeah, sure," Patrice replied, adjusting the collar of the white sweater she wore over a tea-length light blue skirt. "We can do lunch after church."

"Great. In the meantime. . ." Logan flipped open his Bible and pulled out the same photographs Allie had seen earlier in the week. "I've got some pictures you can look at. It's our mother. . .on her wedding day and with me as a baby."

After examining them, Patrice and Kelly looked at each other and then at Logan.

"So we really do have a brother," Kelly murmured, appearing surprised that it was true. "And Ma never told us, that witch!"

"I have a good mind to tell her what I think about her deceptive little ways," Patrice retorted. "I wonder what else she hasn't told us."

Allie bit her lip and glanced at Jack, who'd been quietly looking on.

"And I suppose you just found out about us, too, huh?" Patrice asked.

Logan gave her a solemn nod. "Listen, there's something I've got to tell you both. . . ."

"Ma's always been like this," Kelly went on. "She lied all the time. We could never trust her."

Jack stepped behind Allie and approached Matt and Chris, who were having their own private discussion. "Why don't you guys come with me and we'll find a soda or a cup of coffee."

At first, the young men didn't budge. But then Jack encouraged them with a friendly wave of his arm, and they trailed him across the lobby.

Allie stayed with Logan and his half-sisters.

"Ma told us there was insurance money if we took care of her," Kelly said. "We quit school and everything. Forfeited our scholarships. . ."

"But there wasn't any insurance money," Patrice added, "because she'd let the policy lapse just to be vindictive."

Kelly nodded. "All our lives she acted like we asked to be born or something."

"Ladies, you need to listen to what Logan has to say," Allie chimed in. "It's important."

He cleared his throat and began again. "The Bible makes it clear that we're to honor our parents, and God doesn't give us exceptions."

Patrice and Kelly appeared unimpressed, but they ceased their grumbling long enough to hear Logan out.

"Your mother—our mother—died early this morning," he said in a somber tone of voice. "I'm sorry to be the bearer of such bad news."

The young women's expressions remained impassive.

"We knew it was coming," Patrice said at last. "It's not like some big surprise."

"Yeah, she actually lasted longer than we expected."

"Well, there's good news in all of this, too," Logan said. "Our mother made a decision for Christ shortly before she died."

"Decision for Christ?" Kelly frowned. "What do you mean?"

Logan grinned. "I was hoping you'd ask."

Allie stepped back while Logan told them about Jesus. She prayed God would reach through their hardened exteriors and touch their hearts. Seeing Jack as he returned with Matt and Chris, she smiled. He smiled back, and Allie noted the small Styrofoam cups in each of the men's hands.

"Ah, success," she said. "You found the coffee."

"The office down the hall had a pot. I'm sorry, I should have asked, Allie. Did you want some? I'll go back. . . ."

She shook her head. "No, thanks, I'm fine."

A new topic of conversation ensued, and Allie kept a watchful eye on Cynthia's daughters. Neither, however, seemed remorseful. Quite the opposite, they laughed every so often at something that was said. Before long, Steve, Nora, Veronica, Rick, and Rachel joined them and more introductions were made.

Melodious strains from the piano and organ filled the lobby, signaling the beginning of the service. Jack collected cups and headed for the trash bin while Logan ushered his guests into the sanctuary. Allie walked behind Nora and Steve, finding a seat next to Patrice. Moments later, Jack claimed the aisle seat right beside her.

The service began in an ordinary fashion; the congregation joined in on a hymn, the choir sang, prayer requests were announced, and the congregation was informed of Marilee's car accident. Another hymn was sung, the lights in the sanctuary dimmed, and Pastor Warren strode to the pulpit with a welcoming smile and a determined sparkle in his eyes. But he didn't even get ten minutes into his message when Patrice began sniffling. Lifting her purse into her lap, Allie found a Kleenex and handed it over.

"Thanks," Patrice whispered. Her voice sounded constrained from emotion.

Allie slipped a comforting arm around the young lady's shoulders. While she empathized with Patrice's sense of loss, she also felt a measure of relief and gladness to know at least one of Cynthia Matlock's daughters felt enough remorse over her death to shed a few tears.

Forty-five minutes later, the service ended. Allie, Patrice, and a majority of the Callahan family regrouped in the lobby. Allie saw Nora exiting the sanctuary with her matronly arm around Kelly's shoulders. Upon closer scrutiny, Allie noticed the young lady's bleary eyes.

Thank You, Lord, for breaking these girls' hearts over their mother.

"Hey, everyone, I know the plan was to eat out this afternoon," Nora said, Kelly still at her side. "But I'd like to extend a lunch invitation to my place. We'll be more comfortable there than at an impersonal restaurant." She gazed at Allie, then at Jack. "What do you think?

"Is Steve cooking?" Jack asked with a smirk.

"Cooking? No, no, no. I'm grilling," Steve replied, lifting an indignant chin. "Chicken, hamburgers, Italian sausage, hotdogs. . .whatever Nora hands me, I'll slap it on the grill."

Jack rolled his eyes. "In that case, we'd better put the OPFD on alert."

Steve laughed and gave him a brotherly sock in the arm.

"You're all invited," Nora said, making sure to include Matt and Chris. She looked at Allie again. "It's a beautiful day. . .what do you think?"

"That's a generous offer, and I accept. . .as long as Patrice and Kelly don't mind the change in plans."

Both girls wagged their heads. With tissues in hand, they were still fending off their tears.

"What about Logan?" Nora asked, staring at Jack. "Do you think he'll care?"

"Naw, he's all about saving a few bucks."

"Great."

Nora smiled and glanced around the lobby. Allie thought the color of Nora's silk dress matched her teal eyes. "Where is Logan anyway?"

"Some well-intentioned church member probably waylaid him. . .as usual," Roni said. "But don't worry. I'll go find him. I'll tell him he has to give me a ride home and that way he won't get sidetracked again." She rolled her eyes, and as she walked away, she shook her nut brown head. "Marilee has her work cut out for her, that's for sure!"

"Who's Marilee?" Patrice wanted to know as they made their way to the front doors.

"That's Logan's fiancée," Nora said. "We'll tell you all about her this afternoon."

"I'm driving home with Uncle Jack!" Rachel declared, grabbing hold of his hand and skipping at his side.

"You're too young to drive," he teased.

She stopped and stared up at him, her blue-green eyes bright with a childish reprimand. "You know what I mean. . . ."

"Hey," Rick asked, "can I ride with you, too?"

"Sure," Jack replied on a tolerant note. "The more the merrier."

"They're all yours, Jack," Steve told him, putting an arm around his wife as they walked through the parking lot. "Maybe Nora and I'll take a romantic Sunday afternoon drive and let you man the grill and worry about the OPFD."

Jack ignored his younger brother's ribbing, but Allie couldn't suppress a laugh.

Reaching her rented Cavalier, she paused and pulled the keys from her purse.

Jack stopped beside her. "You know we're probably going to have to help these girls with funeral arrangements."

Allie met his steady brown-eyed gaze and nodded. "I figured as much. I've also been asking the Lord if I should offer to pay the expenses. I'm sure Patrice and Kelly can't afford the funeral home, casket, plot, and all the rest of the costs that go along with burying a loved one."

"Doesn't seem like Roxi was much loved," Jack remarked, his expression one of contrition. "Then, again, she was a hard woman to love."

"But we loved her enough to care for her soul," Allie maintained. "She's with Jesus right now because of it. We have nothing to regret."

"Guess you're right, Mrs. Littenberg," Jack said with a wry grin. "And about the funeral expenses. . .how about if we split them?"

Allie laughed. "You've got a deal there, Sarg."

His grin became a smile as he took her hand and gave it a gentle squeeze. "See you at Steve and Nora's." Turning on his heel, he walked the rest of the way to his SUV, where his niece and nephew were arguing about who got to sit in the front seat. Jack, ever the diplomat, told them they both had to sit in the back.

Still smiling, Allie climbed behind the steering wheel of her car, and in that moment, a portion of Pastor Warren's message flashed through her mind.

"Through His Son, Jesus Christ," he had said, "God has

done—and is doing—something about the needs in our world. He intervenes and saves broken lives by using us to proclaim the gospel. We're broken things apart from Christ, but God can use broken things. . . ."

He intervenes and saves broken lives by using us. . . .

Allie dwelled on the remark and applied it to her own life. God had taken her broken life and used it to reach Cynthia, Jack. . .and who knows how many more. Royce and Colleen, perhaps. Patrice and Kelly. . .maybe even Brenda.

As she drove the distance from the church to the Callahans' home in Oakland Park, she felt suddenly amazed at how large her world had become in such a short time. She had made lasting friendships—and she would likely find romance in her autumn years after all.

And to think it all started with an old faded photograph. . .

ABOUT THE AU

ANDREA BOESHAAR has been married for twenty-five yea
She and her husband, Daniel, have three adult sons. Andrea
attended college, first at the University of Wisconsin-Milwaukee,
where she majored in English, and then at Alverno College,
where she majored in Professional Communications and
Business Management.

Andrea has been writing stories and poems since she was a
little girl; however, it wasn't until 1984 that she started submit-
ting her work for publication. In 1991 she became a Christian
and realized her calling to write exclusively for the Christian
market. Since then Andrea has written articles, devotionals, and
over a dozen novels for Heartsong Presents as well as numerous
novellas for Barbour Publishing. In addition to her own writing, she works as an agent for Hartline Literary Agency.

When she's not at the computer, Andrea enjoys being active
in her local church and taking long walks with Daniel and their
"baby"—a golden Labrador-Retriever mix named Kasey.

HIDDEN THINGS

The Faded Photographs series—Book Two

Kylie had her life all planned out—with marriage to Matthew and a "happily-ever-after" in their sleepy Wisconsin hometown. But when she opens a wedding invitation and a decades-old faded photograph falls out, she uncovers a side of her mother Kylie never suspected. As she digs into the past, Kylie uncovers a whole world of hidden surprises—including grandparents she never knew existed. Suddenly, Kylie faces a choice between two worlds. . .and doesn't feel she fits into either. As the past changes, so does her whole foundation of security. Will Kylie learn who she really is and where she fits into God's plan?

ISBN 1-58660-970-X

Available wherever books are sold.

PRECIOUS THINGS

The Faded Photographs series—Book Three

It all started with a faded photograph and an invitation to restore relationships of decades ago. But Blythe has buried her past and moved ahead. . . that is until the daughter of the one man she loved and lost appears asking uncomfortable questions. Now this successful antique dealer is suddenly forced to undergo her own emotional and spiritual excavation. Amid the trauma, will she find precious treasures of love and faith?

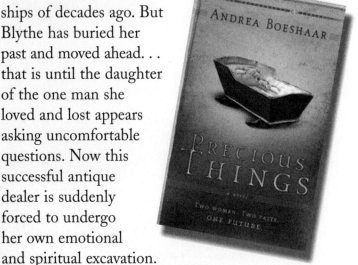

ISBN 1-59310-065-5

Available wherever books are sold.